bestse... 3 1135 01995 4285 ...ssen

Also available from Delores Fossen and HQN Books

A Wrangler's Creek Novel

Lone Star Cowboy (ebook novella)
Those Texas Nights
One Good Cowboy (ebook novella)
No Getting Over a Cowboy
Just Like a Cowboy (ebook novella)
Branded as Trouble
Cowboy Dreaming (ebook novella)
Texas-Sized Trouble

The McCord Brothers

What Happens on the Ranch (ebook novella)
Texas on My Mind
Cowboy Trouble (ebook novella)
Lone Star Nights
Cowboy Underneath It All (ebook novella)
Blame It on the Cowboy

To see the complete list of titles available from Delores Fossen, please visit www.deloresfossen.com.

DELORES FOSSEN

TEXAS-SIZED TROUBLE

HQN™

HQN™

ISBN-13: 978-1-335-63198-5

Recycling programs for this product may not exist in your area.

Texas-Sized Trouble

CONTENTS

TEXAS-SIZED TROUBLE

CHAPTER ONE

"YOU'VE GOT A curse on you, Lawson Granger," the woman said the moment that Lawson stepped from his pickup. "A curse the size of elephant balls."

That probably wasn't something most men heard in their entire lifetimes, but most men didn't live in Wrangler's Creek, Texas, where the occurrence was slightly higher. Lawson had lost count, but he figured this was his third or fourth curse in the past year.

It was the first for the elephant balls' part though.

"Good morning, Vita," Lawson greeted her, tipping his Stetson. His upbringing forced him to be polite to his elders even if this particular elder fell into the bat-shit crazy category.

Vita Banchini.

The town's resident fortune teller–weirdo who lived just up the road from the Granger Ranch, which Lawson helped run. Other towns had likely skipped the pleasure of having such a colorful character who sold love potions, chanted and foretold curses. Heck, most towns probably didn't have anyone who used the word *foretold*, but it was a staple in Vita's vocabulary.

"Did you put the curse on me, or was it somebody else's doing?" he asked. He didn't wait around for the answer though. Lawson hoisted his brand-spanking-new saddle from the truck seat and started for the barn.

"Not me. I don't do curses unless someone's wronged me or mine." Vita followed him, of course, and she was wearing enough beads and bangles that she sounded like she was hauling Jacob Marley's chains. "And by *somebody else*, are you talking about the woman whose heart you broke into a million little bitty pieces?"

There was no good answer to that since anything he said would give Vita unnecessary details about his ex, Darby Rester. So, Lawson just went with confirming it. "Yep, that's who I'm talking about."

"Hmmp," Vita snarled.

For something that wasn't even a real word, it had some stank attached to it. But then, the only person in town who'd thought it was a good idea for him to break up with Darby had been Lawson.

"Well, it wasn't Darby," Vita said. "It's the fates who did this one. I know I get the signs wrong sometimes—"

"The last time you said I was going to need stitches on my right butt cheek. Thankfully, that didn't happen."

"You're sure?"

He gave her a flat look. "I'm sure."

She plowed her fingers through her tangled mess of sugar-white hair and scratched her head. "Well, I must have misread the signs. But I didn't misread these. They were foretold to me in a dream."

Vita had jumped pretty quickly into "foretold" territory, so in her mind this must have been a serious matter. A lot of things in her mind were probably off-kilter.

Lawson kept walking, nodding a morning greeting to a couple of the ranch hands who worked for him and his cousin Garrett. It was a good fifty yards from the main house where Lawson had parked to the tack room in the barn where he was heading, but he doubted the little walk in the muggy ninety-five-degree heat would stop Vita from following him.

It didn't.

"The curse involves horns," Vita continued, keeping up with him.

Lawson couldn't even muster up a sound of surprise. They were on a large Texas cattle ranch where horns were plentiful. If that was the gist of the foretold stuff, then he'd been living under a curse since he'd started working here when he turned eighteen. But if so, it was good juju, too, because being a cowboy was the only thing he'd ever wanted to do.

"Lawson?" someone called out. Jake Walter, one of their top hands. He was on a corral fence and was about to get in with a new cutting horse they were training. "Garrett's looking for you. He said it's important."

"It might have something to do with the curse," Vita concluded.

Not in a million years. More likely it was about quarterly taxes or expenses. "Did Garrett tell you what it was about?" Lawson asked Jake.

The ranch hand shrugged. "Nope, but he said you should see him before you go to the guesthouse."

Lawson frowned. He had a master key to all the buildings on the ranch, including the guesthouse. But since he didn't normally have a reason to go in there, it was a strange comment. It went along with the strange woman who was still trailing along beside him.

"Anything else on this curse?" he asked Vita. Best to finish this conversation so she could leave.

"Concussion and babies," she readily answered.

Lawson stopped, turned to her and frowned. "Are

babies going to get concussions?" He reminded himself there was only a remote possibility of that, but it did trouble him because his cousin Sophie had twins who were toddling all over the place.

Vita huffed as if that was the dumbest question in the history of dumb questions. Lawson huffed as if her huff was the dumbest sound in the history of dumb sounds.

"They're separate things," she said. "Just like the horns. The final part of the curse is water."

He started walking again. Since the ranch was near the creek and it'd been raining on and off for two days, water was a given. Still, it gave him a split second of concern. He was having a house built close to that very creek, and it was possible the land could flood. Of course, if that happened, it'd have nothing to do with a curse, but Vita would likely take credit for the fates foretelling it.

"Horns, concussions, babies and water," Lawson repeated. "Sounds as if the fates had a little too much time on their hands when it came to me. Four things instead of just the butt stitches."

She wagged her bony finger at him. "Don't sass the fates, young man. And I only said concussion as in one, not multiple. But I am sorry to be the bearer of such bad news. If you need any soothing potions or such, just let me know."

Lawson made a grunt of agreement, knowing there was nothing that could make him turn to Vita for that, but he did manage a polite *goodbye* and *thank you* before she scurried away toward her bicycle. It was her standard mode of transportation, and she'd "parked" it in the side yard.

He dropped off the saddle in the tack room so he could head to the house to find Garrett. Then he could go over the schedule and take care of some paperwork. Not his favorite part of the day, but later he'd be able to work in a ride to see how the new herd was doing. And check on the progress of his house. The sooner the construction was done, the sooner he could get out of his place in town and move closer to the ranch.

There was plenty enough to do if he wanted to beat the next wave of rain that would hit in a couple of hours. But knowing it still didn't cause Lawson to keep walking when he reached the guesthouse. It wasn't as if he'd gone out of his way to get there. It was in the backyard between the main house and the barn.

Everything seemed normal—making him wonder why Garrett had issued the warning. Or rather it seemed normal until Lawson had a closer look. There was something brown on the welcome mat. At first Lawson thought it was an animal turd, but no.

It was a horn.

"What the hell?" He nudged it with the toe of his boot. Yeah, definitely a horn. Not from a cow though. His guess was maybe a goat, and there weren't any of them on the ranch.

It was impossible for him not to think of the curse. Impossible, too, for Lawson to see this as anything more than a coincidence. Heck, Vita could have put it there before he even arrived. After all, she'd been waiting for him when he'd first pulled up. And she was fond of leaving weird gifts and offerings.

Just in case Vita had left something inside, too, Lawson reached for the doorknob to have a look around the place. But reaching was as far as he got.

"Wait!" Garrett called out to him. His cousin was on the back porch of the sprawling main house, and Garrett barreled down the steps. "Don't go in there."

Lawson had worked on the ranch for seventeen years, and as best as he could recall, it was the first time any of his cousins had told him something was off-limits. It was one of the reasons this place had always felt like home. Ditto for Garrett seeming more like a brother to him than his own brothers did. But that wasn't exactly a brotherly look Garrett was giving him now.

"Uh, someone's staying there," Garrett added.

His cousin seemed to have a lot of urgency for something that wasn't that out of the ordinary. Plenty of people stayed in that guesthouse. Garrett's sister, Sophie, had a lot of college friends who came and went. So did her mother, Belle. However, Lawson was pretty sure that wasn't just an ordinary FYI that Garrett was giving him.

His cousin stopped directly in front of him and was a little out of breath from his sprint across the yard. He opened his mouth, no doubt to start explaining, but his attention landed on the horn.

"Shit. How'd that get there?" Garrett asked, but it seemed rhetorical since he just kept talking. "I tossed one just a half hour ago." He glanced around as if looking for the horn-dropper before his attention came back to Lawson. Garrett's eyebrow lifted.

"Hey, I didn't put it there. I think it was Vita's doing. She said my curse has something to do with horns."

Garrett kept looking around. "You're cursed again?"

"Appears so. It's becoming a quarterly thing now."

"Did Darby have Vita do this?" Garrett asked.

Lawson sighed. "No. This is all Vita and her fate friends. The horn could be her attempt to make sure at least some part of it comes true this time."

"No. I don't think it was Vita." Garrett paused, scrubbed his hand over his face. "I think we've got a trespasser who's leaving gifts for our guest."

For just a handful of words, they sure packed a punch. Everything inside Lawson went still. It would have been hard for a normal person to connect *guest*, *horn* and *trespasser*, but for him, there was only one logical conclusion.

"Eve," Lawson managed to say.

There was a frog in his throat. Heck, an entire pond of frogs and their lily pads, from the sound of it.

Garrett nodded, confirming what Lawson had just pieced together. His cousin didn't jump right into an explanation, though, of why Eve Cooper was here. Garrett seemed to know that Lawson would need a minute. Heck, he needed a week.

Lawson was long over the pain of having Eve crush his heart when she'd walked out on him when they'd been seventeen. He was long over the fact that she'd forgotten her down-home roots when she'd become an overnight teen TV star.

Well, maybe he wasn't completely over it, but it wasn't hurt he was feeling now. It was indifference. Maybe mixed with a smidge of being pissed off.

"That explains the horn," Lawson mumbled, and he, too, looked around for the culprit.

Eve had been the star of *Demon High*, where she'd played Ulyana Morningglory, a teenager who secretly fought demons in between pom-pom practice and dating her hunky half-demon boyfriend. The boyfriend,

Stavros, had horns—ones that looked like curled turds. To Lawson's way of thinking, anyway. Others clearly hadn't felt the same because Eve-Ulyana, Stavros and the horns had become a cult classic. The most rabid of fans had dubbed themselves the hornies.

Or so he'd heard.

Since the show had been off the air for more than a decade, Lawson would have thought the horn-lovers would have found something else to glom on to but apparently not.

Lawson had plenty of questions—for starters, why was Eve here after all this time? She no longer had family in Wrangler's Creek and hadn't been especially close friends with Sophie, Garrett or their brother, Roman. She no longer fell into the friend category with Lawson, either.

"I'm not sure how long she's staying," Garrett volunteered. "I haven't even seen her myself because she got here late last night. My mother's the one who gave her permission to stay."

Ah, Lawson had forgotten to factor in Garrett's mom, Belle, in this particular equation. Vita held the record for being the town's craziest resident, but Belle could often give the woman a run for her money.

Even though Belle no longer lived at the ranch, she seemed to like creating uncomfortable living arrangements. Two years ago, she had invited a group of widows to live in one of the houses on the grounds, and some of them were still there. Now she was rubbing salt in Lawson's old wound by putting Eve right underneath his nose.

"The person who left that horn trespassed because of Eve," Lawson commented. Not really a question, but Garrett answered it anyway.

"Yes. If you see him around, put the fear of God in him."

Lawson would kick his ass. That should do it. He'd found that worked better than divine fear on some people.

"Anyway, I thought you'd want to give Eve a wide berth," Garrett added. "According to my mom, Eve's, uh, going through a tough time right now, and she came back for some peace and quiet."

Lawson mumbled a "Yeah right."

He didn't want to speculate what would be a tough time for a rich celebrity who still had hordes of fans. Just the other day he'd seen a tabloid cover at the gas station with a headline about her on-again, off-again romance with her former costar, the turd-wearing Stavros.

"If she wants a wide berth, she's got it," Lawson assured his cousin. He tipped his head to the main house. "Want to get started on the schedule?"

"Sure." But the moment Garrett said that, his phone rang, and he glanced at the screen. "It's the seller for those new cutting horses. I need to get the file so I can go over the numbers with him." He headed to the house while he took the call.

Lawson was about to follow him when he heard a strange sound. A moan, as if someone was in pain, and it was coming from inside the guesthouse.

"Eve?" he said, tapping on the door.

No answer.

He got a bad thought though. Maybe the horn-delivering trespasser had broken in and was holding her hostage. Eve might have had demon-fighting skills on the TV set, but he doubted that translated to real life.

When he heard another of those sounds, Lawson

tested the doorknob. Locked. So, he used his key and threw open the door, ready to start that ass-whipping, but he didn't see an ass to whip. That's because it was dark in the cottage. All the blinds and curtains were drawn, and there wasn't a single light on in the entire place.

The next sound was considerably louder than the first and was more of a gasp than a moan. Lawson went in, groping for the light switch, but before he could reach it, his feet flew out from underneath him.

His butt hit first, then his elbows and hands before his head smacked into the wall. Hell, he saw stars. The pain radiated from his tailbone all the way to his eyeballs, and even though it'd knocked the breath out of him, he still managed to curse.

"For shit's sake. What happened?"

"I'm so sorry," she said.

Eve.

He didn't need to see her to recognize that voice. A real blast from the past to go with the pain that was blasting through him. It had reached his fingers now. And his balls. That was the worst, but he forced himself to a sitting position. Not easily because the floor was wet, and his hand kept slipping when he tried to get a grip.

Eve made another of those sounds. It seemed as if she was also in pain. "Did you slip, too?" he asked.

His vision was blurred, his ears were ringing, but he thought she said no. However, she was moving toward him. Or rather shuffling toward him.

"My water," she said.

There it was again. One of Vita's foretold words for the curse. Maybe he had the concussion to go along with it. If so, Vita would be batting three out of four for this latest whammy.

"My water," Eve repeated.

"Yeah, I got that." And he picked through the darkness to see her.

The main room was one big living–eating area, and Eve was by the kitchen counter. She was wearing a baggy white nightgown that made her look huge. She'd obviously put on a lot of weight.

Or…

Not.

Now that his eyes had adjusted to the darkness, Lawson could see that she was hunched over, her hand splayed on her belly.

Her *pregnant* belly.

"Please help me," she said, her voice cracking. "My water broke, and the baby's coming now."

CHAPTER TWO

SHE WAS DYING. Eve was sure of it.

The pain was knifing through her, and the contractions were so powerful that it felt as if King Kong were squeezing her belly with his hairy fist. Her breathing was too fast. Her heart, racing.

And now she was hallucinating.

Either that or Lawson Granger had indeed slipped in the puddle where her water had broken and was now dying from a head injury. Great. If it wasn't a hallucination, it meant she'd returned to Wrangler's Creek after all these years only to cause the death of her old flame.

Her old flame grunted, cursed, and he maneuvered himself onto all fours. So, not dead, just perhaps with critical internal injuries. Of course, anything she was thinking or considering right now could be blown out of proportion because of the god-awful pain that was vising her stomach.

"My water broke," she managed to say. "And my phone." She'd dropped it when one of the contractions had hit, and the phone was now scattered all over the stone entryway and hardwood floor.

Eve wouldn't mention that the reason her water had broken right by the door was because she'd been trying to hear who was talking outside the guesthouse.

She'd thought it was another of her *fans*. Apparently not though.

"This is too soon," she muttered. "I'm not due for three-and-a-half weeks. A baby shouldn't come this soon, should it?" Eve knew she sounded frantic, perhaps even crazy, but she couldn't make herself stop babbling. "Please tell me the baby will be all right."

Lawson lifted his head, making eye contact with her. Yes, he possibly did have a head injury because he looked dazed.

Oh, God. There was blood.

It was on his head and on the butt of his jeans. Eve saw it while he was still on all fours and trying to get to his feet.

"You're hurt," she said, but it was garbled because another contraction hit her. For this one, King Kong had brought one of his friends to help him squeeze her belly. Because Eve had no choice, she dropped to the floor.

She was sinking onto her knees just as Lawson was getting to his. He caught onto the wall, and, grunting and making sounds of pain, he got to his feet. He glanced around as if trying to get his bearings, and he growled out more of that profanity. Some of it had her name in the mix. It definitely wasn't the sweet tone he'd used when they'd been teenagers and he'd charmed her out of her underpants.

And speaking of underpants, hers were wet from where her water had broken. She was surprised she'd noticed something like that with the pain and with Lawson now looming over her. Since he seemed to have trouble figuring out what to do—possibly a result of his head injury—Eve spelled it out for him.

"Call a damn ambulance!" That was a lot louder and meaner than she'd planned, and she ended it with some of her own profanity. Eve also lay back on the floor.

Lawson shook his head as if to clear it, and he pulled out his phone. It took him a couple of tries to call 911. He poked at the numbers like a drunk man trying to hit a moving target, but he finally got through and requested an ambulance ASAP. When he'd finished that, he sank down next to her.

He did more cursing, followed by some wincing.

"I think you cut your butt," she told him. "And your head. You might have a concussion."

Considering that he'd seemed so dazed by everything else she'd said, it surprised Eve when that caused him to groan and mumble, "Vita."

She knew that name. Vita Banchini. Hard to forget someone like that, but Eve had no idea what Vita had to do with what was going on now. Maybe the woman had put a pain curse on her and an injury curse on Lawson.

"You're pregnant," Lawson stated. Even though it was stating the obvious to an absurd degree, it was a good start. He was actually sounding somewhat coherent now, and he'd managed that comment without profanity.

"The baby's coming, and he's three-and-a-half weeks early," she repeated. "How soon before the ambulance gets here?"

"Soon." Lawson placed his hand on her belly. "How far apart are your contractions?"

She would have answered him if the contraction from Hades hadn't hit her at the exact moment she opened her mouth. The sound that came out was nowhere recognizable as human speech.

"All right," Lawson mumbled. "All right. Stay steady. Try to relax. And breathe. Don't growl like a bear or it'll make your throat sore."

It was all stupid advice. She couldn't do any of those things. But she could latch on to his hand since it was right there on her whale-sized stomach. Eve latched on and squeezed.

It helped.

Well, it helped her, anyway, but Lawson yelped in pain and cursed again. He worked his hand out of her grip—which she wanted to point out was mild compared to the contraction—and he shot her a look that could have frozen central Texas in August. That wasn't his charming look, either, but it coordinated well with his noncharming tone and useless advice.

Over the past eighteen years, she'd fantasized about what it would be like to come home and see Lawson again, but never once had she thought it would be like this. Of course, she hadn't expected him to welcome her back with open arms, either. Good thing, too, since he wouldn't be able to get his arms around her right now.

How the heck had it come to this?

Here she was thirty-five, almost thirty-six, and was about to give birth to a baby she certainly hadn't planned. A baby she loved and desperately wanted though. She just hadn't wanted him to decide to come this early.

Added to that, she was without any medical help other than the man whose heart she'd crushed. Maybe this was some kind of karma playing out. If so, she wanted karma to know that she was really suffering. Maybe even dying.

Oh, mercy.

Was she dying?

No, she couldn't be. Not with so much unsettled in her life. But maybe that's how most people felt. There hadn't been nearly enough time for her to get her ducks in a row. Heck, she wasn't even sure she had a row yet, and her main duck was missing.

"Tessie," she sobbed.

That came through loud and clear, and it caused Lawson to stare at her. "Your daughter."

Since it wasn't a question, that meant Lawson knew some of what had gone on in her life since she'd left Wrangler's Creek. Of course he did. Most of her adult life had been tabloid news even after she'd stopped acting. *Entertainment*. Well, it didn't feel so blasted entertaining right now.

"If I don't make it," Eve said, "please call Tessie for me and tell her I love her."

Again, she didn't hear Lawson's answer because the next contraction roared through her. Eve hadn't timed them, but she was betting they were less than a nanosecond apart.

"What about the baby's father?" Lawson asked. "You want me to call him, too?"

Her heartbeat was drumming in her ears, King Kong and his posse were squeezing, and she was about to explode. Yet she heard that. Heard the edge in his voice, as well. She'd managed to keep the baby daddy's identity out of the press, but Lawson probably figured that it was no one he would approve of.

Well, neither did she.

But she couldn't do anything about that right now

other than give birth to this precious child and start putting the pieces of her life back together.

"How long before the ambulance gets here?" she asked again, this time through the grunts and groans.

Lawson might have given her the answer, but Eve didn't hear it because another contraction came. She hadn't thought the pain could get worse, but she'd been wrong about that. She nearly reached for Lawson's hand again, but everything inside her was screaming to do something else.

"Help me get out of my panties," she gritted through clenched teeth.

The words were very familiar. Probably because she'd said them, or something similar, to Lawson moments before he'd rid her of her virginity. There'd been pain that night, too, but it was a drop in the bucket compared to this. Medieval torture was nothing compared to this.

Lawson's forehead bunched up. "Uh, maybe the medics can take them off. Or I could call Garrett. He's in the house."

"No. Not Garrett." She didn't want anyone other than the medics or a doctor seeing her like this. It was bad enough that Lawson was having to witness it. Plus, she didn't want Garrett slipping in the puddle. "Just help me with the panties."

Lawson was clearly uncomfortable getting her partially naked, but that screaming inside her was still going on. Along with another loud message for her to push. But she couldn't do that, not until the medics came because it would make the baby come before they got there.

She pushed.

Eve couldn't stop herself. She bore down, making that bear growl that Lawson had already warned her about, and since he wasn't ridding her of her panties, she fought to get them off.

"Please don't let me die," she told him. "Please let my baby be all right."

Lawson looked up at the ceiling as if searching for some kind of divine assistance. "You're not dying. Both you and your baby will be fine."

Oh, she wanted to latch on to that poorly attempted reassurance, but the craziness was building and building. "How do you know we'll be fine? Have you ever delivered a baby before?"

"No. Just calves." He shimmied the panties off her. "But I suspect it's about the same."

The horrified look on his face said otherwise.

"Is something wrong?" Eve asked.

"No, nothing's wrong. But I see the top of a head." The color drained from his face.

Eve was certain the color drained from her face, too, but it didn't last because she had to push again. That no doubt put some color back in her cheeks since she was straining and grunting.

"Here." Lawson thrust his left hand at her again, an invitation for her to squeeze the crap out of it.

So, that's what Eve did. She squeezed, pushed, cursed and grunted. Lawson was doing some of those things, too, in addition to putting his right hand between her legs.

"You're almost there," he said. "One more push should do it."

She honed in on the sound of his voice and pushed. Then, just like that, the pain vanished. Not just a little bit of it, either. It completely went away. She looked down to see if Lawson had worked some kind of magic. No magic though.

Lawson was holding her son in his lap.

There was a split second of stunned silence from all three of them, but it didn't last. The baby started to cry, and Eve could tell from the loud wail that there was absolutely nothing wrong with his lungs. That nothing wrong applied to the rest of him, either.

He was perfect.

Yes, *perfect*. Even with that squalling red face, balled-up fists and spindly legs. And huge feet. He was like a really pissed-off Hobbit. But he was her precious little Hobbit.

Lawson reached up on the kitchen counter, grabbed the roll of paper towels, and he coiled them around the baby like a hooded blanket. They certainly made a picture with him tending the baby like that. The boy she'd once loved holding the newborn boy she already loved with all her heart.

"No horns," Lawson said.

She froze, blinked, but Eve quickly stopped the horrified look that was forming on her face when she realized he was joking. The corner of his mouth lifted into a smile, and he eased the baby into her arms.

Suddenly, her life didn't seem like so much of a mess. All things seemed possible. But it didn't last. It was gone in a flash—as was Lawson's smile when his gaze connected with hers. Eve saw it then. The hurt she'd caused because of the choices she'd made.

No, not all things were possible.

"I'll see what's keeping the ambulance," Lawson said, getting to his feet.

He was still bleeding, and limping, but Eve had never seen a man move so fast. At least until he reached the puddle, and his feet flew out from under him again. He dropped like a stone, his backside and head smacking the floor a second time.

Knocked out cold.

And that's how the medics found Lawson when they came rushing through the door.

CHAPTER THREE

"You know, most people don't scowl when they look at newborns," Lawson heard Garrett say.

His cousin was coming up the hall of the hospital toward him, and Garrett stopped shoulder to shoulder with Lawson outside the nursery viewing room. Lawson figured he was indeed scowling, and he was doing that while looking at the baby in the incubator on the other side of the glass.

Eve's baby.

The scowl wasn't for the newborn though. Nope. It wasn't the kid's fault that he'd been born three-and-a-half weeks early and that his mom was someplace she shouldn't have been—the Granger Ranch.

"Most people don't have a concussion and stitches on their ass," Lawson grumbled. Or a wrecked image.

There was nothing left of his tough cowboy reputation. Lawson was certain of it. He knew both of the medics who'd come to the ranch, and they were blabbermouths. Blabbermouths who would embellish what they'd seen on the floor of the guesthouse, and pretty soon the gossip all over town would be about his ass stitches.

"I heard about the stitches," Garrett confirmed. "Did a rhinestone from Eve's phone really get embedded into your butt cheek?"

And that comment confirmed Lawson's theory about the blabbermouths. Lawson certainly hadn't called his cousin and told him what had gone on with him in the ER after the ambulance had brought Eve and the baby to the hospital.

"It wasn't a rhinestone," Lawson corrected him, and he was pretty sure it would be a correction he'd have to make a lot. "It was a jagged piece of her rhinestone phone case that broke when Eve dropped it."

But yeah, the doctor had had to pluck out a rhinestone, too, that had been like a sparkly BB in his butt cheek.

Damn Vita, and damn her stupid foretellings.

"Are you okay?" Garrett asked.

"I'll live." With somewhat reduced dignity, but somehow he'd muster through.

Garrett tipped his head to the baby. "How about him? Is he okay, too?"

"Yeah," Lawson said. "According to one of the docs, he's in the incubator because he was a little premature, but he's fine. I didn't screw up anything when I delivered him."

Garrett made a sound of approval. "And how about Eve? How is she?"

"Don't know. I've been busy for the past hour, remember." Lawson hiked his thumb to his right butt cheek, then his forehead. He could have kept "hiking" what with all his cuts and bruises, but Garrett had no doubt gotten the point.

Garrett smiled, though other than the healthy baby, Lawson couldn't see much to smile about. "Not busy enough to find out about the newborn. But I guess you feel…*vested* in him since you're the one who brought him into the world."

Lawson scowled again. "No vestment. I just looked in on him while I was waiting for you."

That was the partial truth. Garrett had followed the ambulance from the ranch to the hospital, but once Lawson realized he was going to need stitches and an X-ray, he'd sent Garrett home to deal with that horse seller. Lawson hadn't called Garrett for a ride home until about ten minutes ago when he'd found out that the baby was okay. So yeah, he had a slight vested interest. But that interest only applied to the kid.

"Why didn't your mom tell me that Eve was coming back to Wrangler's Creek?" Lawson asked.

It was a question born out of frustration, and it only caused Garrett to give him a *how the hell should I know?* grunt. And Garrett truly wouldn't have known what was going on in Belle's often loony head. Belle was one of those oddball mysteries of life.

As was Eve.

Not once had there been a hint that she might want to come back. For that matter, Lawson hadn't read anything about her being pregnant. Not that he'd looked for that kind of gossip about her, but as often enough as she still appeared on tawdry tabloid covers, it made him wonder why there hadn't been a story about it—tawdry or otherwise.

Garrett moved closer to the glass, his attention on the baby. The kid was cocooned in a blue blanket and was sacked out. Occasionally, he would open his eyes, but the light must have bothered him because he would make a face and go back to sleep.

"It doesn't seem right for him to be in there all

alone," Lawson muttered, and he immediately wished that he'd kept the thought in his head because it caused Garrett to look at him. Not just any old look, either. It was the slightly amused one that made Lawson want to punch him.

"I'm sure the nurses are watching him on a monitor," Garrett said, tipping his head to a camera just over the incubator. "Look, there's a nurse in that room." A room that was right next to the nursery. "And we're here, too."

True, but they'd be leaving any minute now. Not that Lawson wanted to stay. He didn't.

"Plus, they'll probably take him to Eve soon," Garrett went on. "She might plan to nurse him."

Maybe. But Lawson didn't like thinking of Eve's breasts. Way too many memories of those since they'd been the first breasts he'd ever touched. Of course, he had the freshest memories of her nether regions when he'd been delivering the kid.

"I'm sure Eve will be getting visitors, too," Garrett added. "And they'll see the baby."

Obviously, Garrett was still pleading his case about the baby not really being alone. But that only reminded Lawson of something else. "When Eve was in labor, she mentioned her adopted daughter, Tessie. You think Belle might know of a way to get in touch with the girl?"

"Possibly. Or you could just ask Eve." But Garrett waved that off. "I'll ask her if Belle doesn't know. Are you about ready to go home now?" Garrett tacked on a moment later. But he didn't budge. He just kept staring at the baby.

At first Lawson thought that was because this was

bringing back bad memories for him. Four years ago, Garrett and his now ex-wife had had a stillborn daughter. It had crushed him, but lately there'd been some much better memories of this place. A year ago, Garrett's sister had delivered her twins here, and just six months ago, Garrett's wife, Nicky, had given birth to a healthy baby boy. Sometimes, though, the good stuff couldn't outweigh the bad.

Lawson knew that firsthand.

And he got a jolt of his own memories. Oh, hell. Not now.

His best friend, Brett, had died in this hospital. Since at the moment he couldn't deal with that, Lawson shoved it back in the little box he'd built in his head.

"There are reporters outside," Garrett told him. "The security guard's insisting he won't let them in, but I figure they'll sneak in first chance they get. Plus, there are a couple of people out there carrying horns."

Lawson didn't think that was horns of the musical variety. He didn't want to face either the reporters or the lunatics. He added yet another person to that mental list.

Darby. His ex-girlfriend.

But he was apparently going to have to face her because she was headed their way. It wasn't a shocker to see her, not the way it'd been for him at the guesthouse with Eve. After all, Darby was a nurse and worked here at the hospital. In fact, Lawson was surprised he hadn't seen her sooner, but he'd just figured she was avoiding him.

The way he'd been avoiding her.

No chance of avoiding her right now though, because she stopped directly in front of him. She was wearing purple scrubs today, her favorite color, and she had some magazines clutched to her chest.

"I came on shift about an hour ago, just as the ambulance arrived with Eve and you," Darby said. "I heard you needed stitches."

She said it with concern, too. Of course, Garrett had been concerned as well, but his cousin had found the butt injury funny.

Lawson settled for saying, "I'm fine."

Darby scrounged up a smile, and her gaze lingered on him a moment. As if she was waiting for him to return the smile.

He didn't. Lawson had learned that Darby could interpret something as small as a smile as a sign of their reunion. She was a smart woman, but she hadn't figured out yet that it was never going to work between them.

And that she was too good for him.

Darby gave a soft, frustrated sigh and turned to the baby. "Eve's son," she muttered. "I think he looks exactly like her."

But again, she seemed to be waiting for something. Maybe she wanted confirmation of the gossip she'd no doubt already heard? Lawson kept watch of her from the corner of his eye, and he saw the slight tightening of her mouth and her bunched-up forehead.

"He's not my kid," Lawson growled. "Before today, I hadn't seen Eve since she left town our senior year of high school."

The next sigh Darby made seemed to be one of relief, and it caused Lawson to silently curse.

Crap.

Had people really thought he'd knocked up Eve? Apparently so. And the fact that he hadn't seemed to put

a sparkle of hope in Darby's eyes since he'd just confirmed to her that he hadn't been with Eve. The sparkle
dimmed considerably when she looked at him again.

"I was just in Eve's room," Darby said. "I wasn't
snooping or anything. This is my floor, and it's my
job to check on patients, but a couple of the staff also
wanted me to get her to sign these." She shifted the
magazines so he could see them. Well, he could see
the one on top, anyway.

Damn. It was those tabloids and not a recent one,
either. According to the date, it had come out about six
months after Eve had left. It was also about the time
Demon High had become a hit.

And there were the hit-makers on the cover.

Eve, aka Ulyana. She was wearing her body-hugging,
red leather fighting costume complete with a sickle knife.
Kellan Carver, aka Stavros, was in his body-hugging,
black leather demon garb, and yeah, he had the horns.
He also had Eve. His black leather garb wasn't the only
thing doing some hugging because Stavros was standing behind Eve, his arms coiled possessively around her.

The headline said it all: Stavros Is Demon Hot.

Lawson had the same reaction now as he had
seventeen-and-a-half years ago. He threw up a little
in his mouth. The only reason he didn't throw up a lot
was because Eve had indeed signed the cover—and her
signature was right over Kellan–Stavros's smug face.

"I know," Darby went on. "I really didn't want to
bother Eve with these, but she said she didn't mind."
Darby made eye contact with Lawson again. "Anyway,
she wants to see you."

"Why?" Lawson practically snapped.

Heck, that snap seemed to bring back the sparkle

to Darby, too. "She mentioned something about wanting to thank you. You wouldn't even have to go to her room because she's insisting she'll come down here to the nursery and stay until her baby is out of the incubator. She'll probably be here any minute."

"No thanks needed. I'm surprised she's not here already," he added without even pausing.

"Oh, she was until about thirty minutes ago, but the doctor made her get back in bed so he could examine her."

Lawson had just missed her since that was about the time he'd arrived at the nursery window. Of course, if he'd seen Eve, he would have slipped out and not interrupted her time with her baby.

"Are you ready to go?" Lawson asked Garrett.

"Uh, sure, but if you want to pop in for a second and see Eve—"

"I don't." He wanted to get out of there—now. It was like being a contestant on a bad game show. Behind door number one was Eve—old memories and fresh butt-stitch humiliation. Behind door number two was Darby and her needy eyes.

"Tell Eve I'll be by to see her later," Garrett added to Darby, and he hurried to catch up with Lawson. "I guess it really is over between you two."

Lawson glanced at him, trying to decide if his cousin was talking about Eve or Darby now. It didn't matter. The answer to both was yes.

"I think I'll leave early for that cattle auction in Amarillo," Lawson said, throwing it out there. "I could be on the road in just a couple of hours."

"The auction's next week." There was a reason for the skepticism in Garrett's voice. Lawson didn't like buying trips or hotels, and leaving today would mean a week and a half in a hotel.

"It'll give my stitches time to heal," Lawson reasoned.

It was stupid reasoning. His stitches would heal at the ranch, too. Plus, he probably shouldn't be gone that long since his house was close to being finished. The contractor might have things to show him, questions to ask. But that could wait. He had to get out of there.

"We should go out the back," Garrett said when they reached the main waiting room. "Remember, there are reporters out front."

Lawson hadn't forgotten about them, but the numbing meds were wearing off, and he didn't want to take the long way around to get to the parking lot.

"They know you delivered the baby," Garrett added.

Lawson groaned. That said it all. They'd want pictures. They'd have questions about what Eve was doing in town. They might even know that Eve and he used to date way back when and try to connect unconnectable dots as Darby had done when she'd considered the baby might be his.

Garrett and he headed for the back exit. However, it wasn't obstacle-free, either, because just as they reached the door, Belle came rushing in. She was wearing a black raincoat, dark sunglasses and a neon yellow straw hat that was the size of a truck tire.

"I didn't want anyone to see me," Belle said as if that explained her getup. "There are reporters out there, and someone left a bunch of these on the porch at the ranch." She reached in both her pockets and pulled out the turd-shaped horns.

Garrett cursed. "We might need to hire some security."

No. Lawson just needed to kick some asses. That had a twofold purpose. It'd get rid of the trespassers along with burning off some of this restless energy inside him. But he rethought that. Best not to pop any stitches, or he'd end up back here.

"I'll have Sophie send down some of the security guards who work at the company," Garrett added.

That was a good idea. Sophie ran the family business, Granger Western—or Cowboy Mart, as most folks called it since it sold discount Western supplies. It was a huge operation with no doubt plenty of security at the warehouses. It wouldn't hurt to have a few of them on the ranch...unless Eve wouldn't be returning there. Lawson was about to bring up that possibility/hope, but Garrett spoke before he could.

"Lawson wanted to know if you knew how to get in touch with Eve's daughter, Tessie," Garrett said to his mom. "Eve broke her phone when she went into labor, so she might not know the number right off the top of her head."

"Oh, I already called her and told her about Eve having the baby. Eve had left her number with me. You know, in case there was some kind of emergency. But Tessie didn't answer. I think she must have been in class or something, so I left her a message. I'm sure she'll be calling back soon when she hears she's got a baby brother."

Good. Somehow, Tessie's photo hadn't landed in the tabloids, but Lawson remembered the news when Eve had adopted her. Eve had been in her early twenties, which meant Tessie was either a teenager or close to being one. It did make Lawson wonder, though, why Tessie hadn't made the move with Eve, but maybe the girl was at boarding school.

"How long will Eve be staying?" Lawson asked.

"Until her house is ready. She's having some remodeling done before she moves in. She runs a charity foundation, and she needed an office for that. Plus, she had to redo rooms for the nursery and the baby's nanny."

Lawson was certain he'd missed something—and no, it wasn't the room-usage part. "What house? Is it here in Wrangler's Creek?"

Belle didn't seem to notice his surprise because she dropped some more of the horns, and they clattered onto the tile floor. "Your brother Lucian sold her one of the houses on your family's land."

Well, hell in a shit-lined handbasket. Yeah, he had definitely missed something, and apparently he had another ass to kick because Lucian should have told him something that monumental.

"Which house and why did Lucian sell it to Eve?" Lawson snapped. Because last he heard, there were at least four houses on the property, and none of them were occupied full-time. None of them had been for sale, either.

Belle looked up from her horn retrieval and shook her head. She tsk-tsked him. "I know you don't get on with your brothers, but you really should make more of an effort."

No, because he wanted to stay sane. That's why he worked for Garrett. He didn't intend to go back into the viper pit owned by his immediate gene pool, and Garrett and Roman felt the same way about Lawson's kin.

It was enough of a compromise that Lawson was building his new place on land that would get him marginally closer to his brothers. Or more specifically, Lucian. But it'd been his land, and Lawson had decided he could live with *marginally closer* to have the home he'd always wanted.

"Eve bought your mom's house," Belle continued. "It was the place your great-grandpa built and where she moved after she divorced your dad. She hasn't lived there in donkey's years though, so I guess Lucian figured it'd make a good home for Eve."

That particular house was only about a quarter of a mile from the one Lawson was building. Eve and he would practically be neighbors. If he couldn't stop the sale, that is.

He would stop it.

No way did he want daily reminders of Eve, and he was certain she wouldn't want that, either. Lucian must not have told her that she'd be so close to him and the main house on the Granger Ranch.

On second thought…

Lucian wouldn't have brought that up. His family and Garrett's had been feuding over some acreage for over sixty years now. Acres that lay directly between the Granger Ranch and Lawson's family's land. Lucian was always threatening a lawsuit, and if it happened, that would put Eve's house right smack in the middle. Once Eve learned that, no way would she want the house.

And Lawson was going to be the one to clue her in.

He turned, ready to head to her room—and maybe have one last look at the baby—but the commotion stopped him. There were footsteps, loud voices and the flashes from cameras.

"The reporters got in," Garrett mumbled.

Yes, and Lawson was about to send them right back out, but then he saw who was in the middle of that commotion.

Kellan Carver, aka Stavros.

No black leather today, but he was dressed like a rock star. Sorta looked like one, too, and he was talking and posing for pictures at the same time. There were two nurses trailing along behind him. A patient, too, on crutches and another in a wheelchair. They all looked giddy and starstruck.

"There you are," Kellan said, aiming a smile that was more blinding than the camera flashes, and he was aiming it at Lawson.

Lawson hated him on sight.

Kellan went to him, automatically taking Lawson's hand for the side-by-side posed handshake photos that quickly followed. The flashes were like being swarmed by giant lightning bugs.

"This is the hero of the hour," Kellan announced, lifting Lawson's arm the way a ref would lift a prizewinning fighter. "Lawson Granger. Thanks, man," Kellan added to him in a whisper that was still plenty loud enough for everyone to hear.

Lawson pulled back his hand. "Thanks for what?" he asked once he got his teeth unclenched.

Kellan's plastic smile never wavered. "For being there when Eve and me needed you." He slapped Lawson on the back, his hand landing right on a giant bruise. "Man, you delivered my son."

CHAPTER FOUR

"IN MY MAMA'S DAY, women gave birth and then went out and tended the herd," the nurse said to Eve. "After they hung out the wash and cooked supper, that is."

Eve felt as if she'd done all of those things. She was bone-tired, but it was covered with a layer of giddiness.

She had a son.

A perfectly healthy one, from what the doctors had told her, and now she wanted nothing more than to hold him again. She had a sudden urge to check every inch of his little body and make sure everything was there and where it should be. She hadn't gotten a chance to do that in the ambulance ride to the hospital, and after they'd arrived, the doctors had insisted on putting him in an incubator while they examined her.

"Women didn't get overnight hospital stays for birthing in my mama's day," the nurse went on. "Now we got all these rules."

The nurse was Mildred Wheeler, who, according to her introduction, had worked at the hospital since it was first built in the late fifties. Eve didn't know exactly how old the woman was, but her stories had a distinctive "I walked twenty miles to school in the snow, up-hill both ways" slant to them.

"You said something about getting me a wheelchair so I could go to the nursery," Eve reminded the woman.

That'd been five minutes ago when Mildred had come in to check on her. "Now that the doctor finished examining me, I really want to see my baby."

"Just hold your horses. The wheelchair won't be much longer. One of the orderlies is bringing it here. Uh-uh," she scolded and shook her finger when Eve started to get out of the bed. "That's a lawsuit waiting to happen if you was to fall or something. Like Lawson did." Mildred helped herself to one of the melon chunks that was on Eve's breakfast tray. "Of course, Lawson can't sue you because he was on the Granger Ranch when his butt got cut bad enough to need stitches."

So, everyone obviously knew about that. That wouldn't please Lawson. It didn't please Eve, either, because she didn't need any other reason for Lawson to be upset with her.

"Lawson's fall coulda been bad fortune on account of him breaking up with Darby. You know his girlfriend, Darby?" Mildred asked. "Or rather his *ex*-girlfriend?"

Mildred was still chewing on the honeydew when she put that question to Eve, but Eve detected a little snarkiness in it. Since Mildred had already told her that Darby was a nurse at this hospital, it was reasonable that the staff would take Darby's side in a breakup. But that had nothing to do with Eve.

Though Mildred's sour-milk expression indicated otherwise.

Good gravy. The woman thought she was why Lawson had ended the relationship. Blaming Eve could be the reason that there was a delay in the wheelchair arrival. Maybe everyone in the hospital wanted to give her a dose of their own version of payback.

Too bad Eve didn't have her phone or she could

have called someone to get that chair here ASAP. Of course, if she had her phone, she could also call Tessie and check on her.

Well, if Tessie would answer, that is.

Eve figured her chances of Tessie accepting her call were about the same as Mildred limiting herself to a single piece of honeydew.

Mildred chomped down on another piece, leaving little globs of green melon on the thick coating of neon pink lipstick. "Darby said you used to be some big-time television actress in Hollywood. Why'd you come back after all this time?"

Good question, and the answer probably wasn't something Mildred would understand. But Eve had wanted "normal" again, and the last time she'd felt anything close to that had been here in Wrangler's Creek. Ditto for this being the only place that had ever felt like home. Plus, she would be much closer to Tessie. That was a huge bonus.

Normal and *home* came with consequences, though, because this was Lawson's home, too, but Eve had thought it was time to confront that part of her past. Not so she could fix things with Lawson.

There was little or no chance of that happening.

Maybe though she could figure out a way to be in the same general vicinity with him while trying to piece together all those other things that she needed to piece together to stay sane.

Mildred glanced at her, her raised eyebrow questioning Eve's decision to return to Wrangler's Creek. Then the nurse shrugged as if it didn't matter anyway. "Never watched TV myself. Mama's doing. She always said there was no place in her house for such hooey phooey or poppycock."

Well, *Demon High* hadn't exactly been brainy viewing, but Eve wasn't sure it fell into the hooey phooey or poppycock category. She decided to take that as a cue for her to do something to end this annoying chat.

"Lawsuits aside," Eve said, getting out of the bed, "I'm seeing my baby."

Eve wasn't in any shape to fight off even a senior citizen–honeydew-stealing nurse, but she would somehow manage it. She'd already spent too much time away from her little boy.

"I'm telling the doctor," Mildred declared, and she scurried out—taking another melon chunk with her. The woman no longer sounded like a relic from the past but rather like a tattling schoolgirl.

Eve figured this was going to earn her a good chewing out from assorted medical personnel, but it would be so worth it. Using the wall for support, she groped her way across the room while she tried to pinch the back of her open gown together so her butt would be covered. The adult diaper they'd given her to wear was completely sheer except for the strip down the middle, and she didn't want to flash anyone on her way to the nursery.

She'd worked up a sweat by the time she got to the door. Eve opened it, stepped into the hall.

And came face-to-face with a circus.

There were balloons, someone dancing in a bear suit and people. Lots of people. Some of them snapped pictures of her while calling out her name to look their way. They pushed forward toward her, causing her to stagger back. The shock and temporary blindness al-

most caused her to miss the man in the center of this
unholy hoopla.

Kellan.

She didn't quite manage to contain the glare before
it made it to her face. A glare that would almost certainly be on a tabloid cover come tomorrow.

"Baby-Cakes," Kellan purred.

Eve hated the nickname and hated the kiss that Kellan dropped on her mouth. It was possible the kiss
bruised him a little since her lips were pinched and
tight.

"Sorry that we caught you without your makeup,"
Kellan added, giving her a quick once-over. The once-
over ended with him frowning at her hair. "Don't they
give out combs in this place?"

Eve hadn't thought her mouth could get any tighter,
but she'd been wrong. She was about to muster up
something polite about everyone needing to leave so
Kellan and she could have some *privacy*, but she didn't
get the chance.

"Y'all gotta leave," someone called out. Nurse Mil-
dred. "Right now." The tattling schoolgirl was gone.
This was a mean middle-school teacher's voice, and
Eve was thankful for it.

Mildred wagged her index finger at the paparazzi
and then used that same finger to point to the near-
est exit. Even her pointing gestures were mean. There
were some protests, more pictures flashed, but Mildred
managed to start them moving.

"You get out of here, too," Mildred added to the
dancing bear. "And take those stupid balloons with you.
Latex allergy is a real thing, people." She grumbled
something else under her breath that Eve didn't catch.

"In my mama's day, she would have busted a tushy or two for causing a commotion like this."

Mildred turned her chilly gaze on Kellan next. Normally, most women softened or even melted when they got an up-close look at Kellan's pretty face and bedroom blue eyes, but his looks had no effect whatsoever on the woman. She kept up the chilliness and the scowl.

"Are your ears plugged up from all those earrings you're wearing?" Mildred snapped. "Because I'm pretty sure I said you had to leave."

Kellan didn't seem fazed by that. He upped his usually charming smile a notch. "But I'm the father of Eve's baby. I want to see her and my son."

Mildred gave him the squinty eye as if trying to figure out if that was true. She was still squinting when Eve sighed and nodded. "Yes, he's the father."

Eve hadn't intended for "father" to have the same tone as "yeast infection," but Kellan was not on her happy list. The only thing on that list right now was the baby and Tessie, and Tessie's name had an asterisk next to it since at the moment she was causing Eve more worry than happiness.

Mildred finally gave a nod of her own, which was her okay for Kellan to stay. "But no more bears, photographers or balloons."

"The bear and balloons were for the baby," Kellan said to Eve.

Not exactly normal offerings for a newborn, but no one had ever accused Kellan of being normal. "And the paparazzi?" she questioned.

He smiled. "Free publicity, Baby-Cakes. You know how it is."

Yes, she did, and it caused Eve to sigh again. She

was too old for publicity. Too old to be having one-night stands with Kellan. And too old not to have used multiple means of birth control instead of relying solely on a condom. But she'd been in a really bad place that night, and besides, she didn't regret having her baby.

"I'll see about getting you that wheelchair," Mildred grumbled, and she marched off as if that might actually happen.

Eve wouldn't wait for her though. Catching onto the wall again, she started for the nursery.

"Uh, shouldn't you be in bed or something?" Kellan asked, trotting after her. "Or maybe looking for a hairbrush?"

"I'm seeing my son."

"*Our* son," he corrected her. He smiled again. "Remember, I was there for his creation. That was one hot night, Baby-Cakes."

Hot? Not really. She hadn't even had an orgasm. And Kellan hadn't noticed.

"Say, are you down or something?" Kellan blathered on. "Is this about Tessie, because you're still on the outs with her?"

In part, but it was also because she was having to put up with Kellan while slogging her way up the hall.

"Well, if that's all it is," Kellan continued, "then you've got nothing to be down about. Tessie's just being a teenager. You remember what it was like."

Not really. Well, except for the memories that involved Lawson. Those had stayed with her despite the plastic veneer that had been smeared over the real memories that she'd had after she left him and Wrangler's Creek.

"Hey, I recognize that ass," someone called out from behind them.

Eve didn't have to look back to know who'd said that. Cassidy Vale, her friend and human BS meter. Eve adjusted the grip she had on the back of her gown to make sure she was covered up.

"Not that ass," Cassidy said. She tipped her head to Kellan. "That one."

"Hardy-har-har," Kellan said sarcastically. "What are you doing here, Acidy?"

"Helping a friend." Cassidy ignored the nickname dig and hurried to Eve.

Despite her Hollywood roots, Cassidy was definitely no fashionista. She was wearing her usual yoga pants, flip-flops and T-shirt, and she'd scooped up her auburn hair in a sloppy ponytail. Cassidy looped her arm around Eve's waist and even helped her hold her gown together.

"Thanks." Eve leaned against her. "How'd you get here so fast?"

"She put a booster jet on her broomstick," Kellan grumbled.

Cassidy didn't miss a step. She just glanced at Kellan's hair and made a face. "That wind really got to you, didn't it? Hope there's no photographer around to see you this messed up. Is that some hair-gel flecks I see, or is it dandruff? Maybe it's head lice. I've heard nits are easy to pick up around hospitals."

Kellan made a face, too, as if he knew she was just giving him flak, but when he spotted the men's room ahead, he hurried and ducked inside it.

"Thought he'd never leave," Cassidy said. She hugged Eve closer to her. "I was already on my way here when

I heard about the baby. Is it true? Did *Hot Cowboy* really deliver him?"

Eve nodded. No clarification was needed on Hot Cowboy's identity. Cassidy knew all about Lawson. In fact, Cassidy knew everything about Eve.

Everything.

That's because Cassidy and she had been friends since the day Eve had arrived in Hollywood eighteen years ago. She'd started out as Eve's rival on *Demon High* but had been killed off at the end of the first season. When Cassidy hadn't been able to land any other acting jobs, Eve had hired her as a personal assistant. Then later on she'd become Tessie's nanny. These days, Cassidy was also an artist who did illustrations for children's books.

They finally made it to the glass window of the nursery, and Eve peered in. There he was. Alone in the incubator. For some strange reason, she'd thought that Lawson might be here to look in on him, and she hated the disappointment she felt that he wasn't. Lawson probably didn't want to get anywhere near her, and that meant not being near the baby, either.

With Cassidy's help, Eve made it into the area just off the nursery, and she spotted the nurse there. Not Darby or Mildred, but according to her name tag, she was Wanda Kay Busby.

"The doctor said it was okay if I held my baby," Eve told her. "It's not dangerous for him to be out of the incubator, is it?"

The nurse shook her head. "He's not having trouble breathing or anything. The incubator's just a precaution."

That caused Eve to feel some relief, but she wouldn't get a full dose of that until she had him in her arms.

"I'm surprised your OB let you fly when you were in your eighth month," Wanda Kay commented. "Usually they warn against it."

There went the relief. "My doctor thought it would be okay. And the flight wasn't that long because I flew direct to San Antonio on a friend's private jet. Could the trip have caused me to go into early labor?"

"Probably not, but most OBs would rather their patients deliver in a hospital, not on an airplane. Or a guesthouse." Wanda Kay shrugged. "Still, it all worked out just fine."

Eve hoped that was true. But now she had some more guilt to add to her guilt-riddled life.

Wanda Kay had Cassidy and Eve wash their hands and put on green paper robes before letting them into the actual nursery. The nurse then had Eve sit in a rocking chair. No easy feat with her sore bottom, but she would have sat on fire ants to have this chance.

"Don't nurse him yet though," Wanda Kay added. "I'll need to check with the doctor first and make sure it's okay."

Eve doubted the baby would be hungry since she'd nursed him in the ambulance. In hindsight, that had probably given Lawson an uncomfortable moment or two, but she'd gotten so caught up in feeding her son that she hadn't noticed.

The nurse lifted him from the incubator and eased him into Eve's waiting arms. And Eve could have sworn that her heart doubled in size. She didn't care that he wasn't planned or that he shared DNA with Kellan, Eve

loved him from the top of his curly-haired head down
to his feet, which she checked.

All ten fingers. All ten toes.

The tears came, and they were bittersweet.

"Brings back memories of Tessie, huh?" Cassidy
said after Wanda Kay went back into the office. Since
the nurse hadn't given her a chair, Cassidy sat on the
arm of the rocker.

Yes, this did remind Eve of Tessie, and that was the
reason for the next tears that fell.

"So, what did you decide to name him?" Cassidy
asked. "And please don't say Kellan, Jr."

Not a chance. And Cassidy knew that. "Aiden James
Cooper."

"After your grandfather. Good choice."

Cassidy knew about Eve's grandpa James, too. Knew
that he'd basically raised Eve after her mom and dad
had divorced. Her dad had disappeared shortly thereafter, and in between her mom's job and her constant
dating, there hadn't been much time for Eve. Grandpa
James had always made time. Too bad he wasn't here to
see his namesake, but he'd died of a heart attack seven
years ago. Her folks wouldn't be around, either, since
they hadn't spoken since she'd left Wrangler's Creek.

"I considered naming him Brett," Eve added, "but I
wasn't sure that'd be a good idea. I mean, Brett's family
might not like that. Lawson probably wouldn't, either."

There was also no need for Eve to explain Brett to
Cassidy. There'd been too many times when Eve had
broken down over the memories of the teenager who'd
once been Lawson's and her best friend.

A friend they'd let die.

Sometimes, like now, the memories still crushed

her heart, and she figured it did the same to Lawson. Or rather what memories Lawson had of that horrible night. Unlike Eve, Lawson hadn't been able to recall a lot of details. Of course, that might have changed over the years. Though Eve hoped it hadn't. She had enough of those memories for both of them.

"Are the tears of the happy variety or are they because of Brett or Tessie?" Cassidy asked.

"All three." Eve looked up at her friend. "Is there any chance you can convince Tessie to take my calls?"

"You know I've already tried. And I'll keep trying." She patted Eve's arm. "Just give it time, and Tessie will come around."

Maybe, but it certainly didn't feel like it at the moment.

"I talked to her briefly on the way here," Cassidy went on. "She's busy with her summer classes. And yes, she's fitting in."

Since that was about to be Eve's question, she just waited for Cassidy to continue, but she didn't because Darby came in. Eve tried to smile. Tried not to look as uncomfortable as her bottom felt. It was bad enough that Eve had to see Lawson's ex, but the nurse also had yet more of those fan magazines.

"Oh, good. You're up," Darby said. She seemed a lot perkier than she had earlier when she'd stopped by Eve's room. Of course, Eve didn't really know the woman since Darby and her family had moved to Wrangler's Creek after she'd already left.

"I just saw Kellan in the hall," Darby went on. "He's giving an interview to some reporters, and you can tell he's bursting with pride over his son." She ran her hand over the baby's toes.

So, Eve had been right about Darby's perkiness. And Eve didn't have to guess why the woman was in this giddy mood. She knew that Kellan was the baby's father and not Lawson. Eve didn't like that Kellan was using their son to milk some publicity, but at least now folks might not blame her for causing Lawson and Darby's breakup.

"Kellan told the reporter that you'd be splitting time between LA and here," Darby remarked. "He said that way you'd be ready if the studio goes through with the *Demon High* reunion."

Those were obviously fishing-expedition comments. And they weren't true. Eve had no plans to live anywhere but the place she'd bought from Lucian. Kellan knew that. The studio knew that. But yet it kept coming up—from Kellan.

Eve didn't mind if that was one particular bridge that got burned, but anything she said to Darby could end up as some twisted version of a story in a tabloid. Once a reporter had heard Eve belch after downing a few swigs of a Diet Coke and then had reported that she had a rare intestinal disorder that could be life-threatening. It had resulted in her "hornies" fans sending her hundreds of cards, flowers, herbal remedies and baskets of horns.

When Eve's silence dragged on, Darby gave a nervous smile and turned to Cassidy. "I don't believe we've met. I'm Darby Rester."

"You're Lawson's ex. I heard about you. One of the other nurses mentioned you when I asked about Eve. I'm Cassidy Vale."

Eve frowned at Cassidy. There was no need to rub that *ex* part in or make it seem as if she'd heard something unsavory about Darby, but Eve suspected it was

Cassidy's way of reminding Darby that she didn't have a right to play the "I'm the wronged woman here" with Eve. After all, Lawson had been Eve's ex long before Darby had come into the picture.

"Yes, Lawson," Darby repeated. "I nearly forgot. He wanted me to tell you that he's leaving on a long business trip and didn't have time to stop by."

There it was again. The little pang of disappointment because she wouldn't be seeing Lawson anytime soon. Eve reminded herself that Lawson wasn't hers to *pang* about, and this absence might be a good thing.

"Is Lawson, uh, all right?" Eve asked.

Darby blinked as if that was a trick question, but then the aha light went on in her eyes. "You mean because of the stitches. And the other cuts, concussion and the bruises. Yes, he'll be fine."

That was good. Except for the laundry list of injuries, of course.

"I know I've already bothered you with autographs," Darby said a moment later. "But more of the staff had magazines and they were wondering if you'd sign them. No pressure. I can just leave them, and if you're feeling up to it, that's great. If not, I'm sure they'll understand."

Darby handed the magazines to Cassidy, and she looked at Eve as if waiting for her to say something about the covers or how she was feeling. Eve didn't give her anything because of that whole fear-of-backfiring thing. Darby didn't have any experience dealing with entertainment reporters who had sneaky ways of getting dirt. Of course, with whatever bull Kellan was doling out, it was possible the reporters had enough dirt to last them awhile.

Cassidy glanced at the magazine covers when Darby

left, and she plucked one from the stack to show to Eve. "Remember this one?"

It was the one of Stavros and Ulyana in full costume, back to back, with stern looks on their made-up faces. Both of them were armed to the hilt with the prop weapons that managed to look real. Actually, the picture looked real, too.

Amazing, since it was heavily Photoshopped.

Eve measured out her life by specific events, and that cover was one of them. So were the events that had led up to it.

Eighteen years and two months ago, her drama class at the high school had been chosen to participate in an online audition for extras in a yet-to-be-named TV series. Eve had been going through a comic-book phase then, and since she really hadn't planned on being an actress, she'd sent in a goofball rendition of an air fight scene that she'd "choreographed" to "Welcome to the Jungle" while wearing an old Halloween costume.

Apparently, the studio thought it was good enough for a real audition over Christmas break, but she hadn't gotten her hopes up. She'd been so certain they'd choose a real actress. Certain, too, that she wouldn't leave Lawson—even for a chance of fame in Hollywood. But she'd been young and naive enough to believe that if by some miracle she did get offered the part, she could have convinced Lawson to go with her.

The next "life measurement" had been Brett's death. That'd been in January. Shortly afterward, things had changed between Lawson and her.

The double whammy of painful life measurements.

She'd still loved Lawson, but Eve had seen the resentment in his eyes and had known it would only grow. He might have never said it in words, but he blamed her for what'd happened. Just as she blamed herself.

That was the main reason she'd accepted the role when the studio had called, and she'd moved almost immediately. After she had made a clean break with Lawson, that is. Well, as clean of a break as she could make over something that was ripping her heart out.

Shortly thereafter, she'd started rehearsing for the filming of the first episode of *Demon High*. Another life measurement. The cover had been shot in July that year, and it and all the covers that followed for the next few months were done with a body double. As had been all of Eve's action scenes on the set.

Because she'd been pregnant with Tessie.

Cassidy had known that, so had the rest of the cast, but it'd stayed a secret for years. Until Tessie had found out.

Tessie certainly hadn't taken it well, either, when she'd learned that she wasn't adopted after all, that she was indeed Eve's biological daughter. Definitely another painful life measurement.

But Tessie's anger was a drop in the bucket compared to what Lawson's would be. He already hated her, but he would hate her a whole lot more if he ever found out the truth.

That he was Tessie's father.

CHAPTER FIVE

LAWSON WAS NOT daddy material. He'd always believed that when he was a teenager, but he'd thought he might change his mind when he became an adult.

Nope.

He was 100 percent certain of his particular stance in life after delivering Eve's baby.

It had been like some kind of revelation—a foretelling from the fates, maybe—but holding that kid had reminded him of just how hard it would be to love a child and then have to let that kid loose in this crapshoot of a world.

A world where people died too young. Where hearts got crushed. And shit happened at an alarming rate. If he wanted that kind of pain in his life, he could just hit himself on the head with a big rock.

Or visit his brother Lucian, which he was about to do.

A rock to the head or seeing his oldest brother were on par, but the difference was, he could beat the crap out of Lucian should it become necessary. With a baby, there was no skill set to help with the fear of loving someone so much that it could break you for good. Lawson had been broken, several times, and he didn't want another dose of that.

The best way to avoid a heart shit-kicking was to stay

out of the "heart" business altogether. That meshed well with the no-fatherhood-for-him revelation. Commitments—those engagements, marriages and, yeah, kids—led to failure. And that wasn't a theory, either. He'd seen it with his own two eyes. His folks' nasty divorce. Belle's bad marriage to Roman and Garrett's dad. And his soured relationship with Eve.

All commitments gone wrong.

He took the final turn to his family's place, and he pressed in the code on the security panel to open the arched gate with the name Heavenly Pastures scrolled out in wrought iron. It was pure irony, like when a hooker was named Chastity. Because there was no heavenly vibe, nor had there ever been any on these grounds. But yet his great-grandfather Jeremiah, who'd built the place, had chosen the name, maybe believing that it would rub off on the occupants.

So far, it hadn't.

Lawson had higher hopes for the place he was building, but that hope was there only because it was a good half mile from the main house that Lucian called home. For a few months out of the year, anyway.

Since the townsfolk had dubbed him Lucifer, the joke was that his local residence was Hell Sweet Hell instead of Heavenly Pastures. But Lawson knew that his big brother preferred the sprawling ranch he'd built for himself two counties over. Or the equally sprawling house he'd bought near his office in San Antonio.

Apparently, this county hadn't been suitable for his big brother because Heavenly Pastures hadn't been running a full ranch operation since Lawson had left to work for Garrett.

It was more of a battleground these days.

When Lawson's and Garrett's grandfathers had had a falling-out decades ago, it had started a Texas-sized feud. They'd divided the land they co-owned except for about a hundred acres that at the time had been leased to another rancher. The lease had long since expired, and that meant the ownership of the land was in question. It was a prized chunk of acreage to own because the creek coiled through it. Garrett needed the creek water to keep the ranch growing. Lucian wanted to hang on to it because he was, well, Lucian, and he liked to own stuff even when he didn't have a use for it.

Lawson passed by the road that led to his house, and he could see it in the distance. It was on the creek.

Yep, the very one in question.

But he was having the house built on Heavenly Pastures' land that wasn't in dispute. It was his. A twenty-first birthday gift from his dad as a way to lure Lawson back to the ranch so he could work for Lucian instead of Garrett. That ploy hadn't worked, but the gift made a pretty spot for his future home.

A home that was no longer just a shell. Lawson could see the progress from the road, and it was really coming together with walls and a roof. He'd drop by and check on it once he'd had it out with Lucian. And the reason Lucian was on his shit list was because of the next house that came into view.

His mother's.

Except now Eve believed she was the owner.

It was a white-and-yellow Victorian that looked out of place on a Texas ranch, and it was identical—in floor plan, anyway—to the one on the Granger Ranch where Lawson worked. Garrett's great-granddaddy Z. T. Granger had built that place over a hundred years ago, and Lawson's great-granddaddy had built a nearly identical one on Heavenly Pastures.

When Lawson reached the main house, he pulled to a stop in the circular drive—and cursed. Because Lucian's truck wasn't there. It was a sign that his brother wasn't, either, since Lucian always parked in front or on the side of the house and not in the garage. Lawson figured the parking preference had to do with Lucian's quick exits.

Like this one, for example.

Lawson had called the house just an hour earlier, and when he'd spoken to Lucian's assistant, she'd said he wasn't taking any calls but that he was there. And maybe he was. Lawson held out hope that his brother's car was being serviced or something.

He parked in Lucian's usual spot and got out as best he could. Each movement and step caused him to wince and grunt in pain, a reminder that a butt-kicking might be physically impossible. Still, he'd try.

Lawson threw open the door to the house and made a beeline to Lucian's office. Well, as much of a beeline as he could make considering the place was massive. A woman he didn't recognize peered down at him from the staircase and then scurried away. She was probably a housekeeper, and the reason he didn't recognize her was that Lucian went through employees as frequently as he did cars.

He glanced in the sunroom since it was where Lucian often sat to read reports and such. No Lucian. However, the cook, Abe Wiser, was there. His feet were propped up on an ottoman, his body stretched out, and the guy was snoring. Abe was a lousy cook, an equally lousy worker, but unlike the revolving door of housekeepers, Lucian had kept Abe—for reasons that were unclear to anyone but Lucian.

"He's not here," someone mumbled.

Now, that was a voice he did recognize despite the mumbling. It was his brother Dylan. It wasn't a surprise that he was there since unlike Lucian, Heavenly Pastures really was Dylan's home. And the fact that he hadn't smothered Lucian in his sleep was a testament to Dylan's "I really don't give a shit" attitude.

Dylan was coming from the direction of the kitchen, a beer in one hand, some papers tucked under his arm and the remainder of a pizza slice clamped between his teeth. He removed the pizza and gave Lawson that "Dylan Granger" smile that melted women into puddles of, well, whatever women melted into when they saw that pretty face and the endless supply of rodeo buckles. Dylan wasn't just a cowboy. He was a rich bronc-riding champion.

Unlike Lucian, Dylan had definitely inherited all the charm in the family, and he was the reason Lawson had such a small dating pool. Dylan had slept with at least half the eligible women of Wrangler's Creek. A good portion of the ineligible women, too. Since Lawson had a rule about dating any of his brother's exes, that had limited him to only a handful of prospects.

"Karlee said Lucian was here," Lawson pointed out. And since Karlee was the most efficient assistant in the state of Texas, Lawson had believed her. That's why he'd driven out right after he packed for his trip.

"He was, but he left about fifteen minutes ago. You must have just missed him." Dylan tipped his head to Lawson's midsection. "Do you really have stitches on your ass?"

"Yeah, and you might need some when I'm finished with you. Why the hell would you let Lucian or Mom sell the house to Eve?"

"So, that's why you're here." Dylan munched another bite of his pizza and got to walking, heading in the direction of his office. Which was on the other end of the house from Lucian's. Apparently, the most charming cowboy in Texas wanted to keep his distance from the least charming one.

Dylan went in his office, setting the papers, beer and remainder of the pizza slice on his desk before he put his hands on his hips and faced Lawson. "I didn't get a chance to talk anyone out of anything because it was a done deal before I even heard about it. Mom gave Lucian her power of attorney to sell it, and he did." Dylan shrugged. "Lucian always did have a soft spot for Eve."

"Lucian's never had a soft spot for anyone," he grumbled.

Lawson took out his phone to call his mother, Regina. She didn't answer, of course, and Lawson had no idea where she was. Regina wasn't exactly motherly in the normal sense of the word and rarely returned his calls. Still, he left her a message.

"It won't do any good, you know," Dylan commented. "The papers have been signed."

"Since when? Because the gossips in this town are too good for me not to have heard about this."

Dylan shrugged. "My guess is Lucian kept it quiet by using his San Antonio lawyer. He probably didn't want you putting up a fuss before the deal was finalized."

"Putting up a fuss" made him sound like a toddler

who didn't want a nap. Shit. This was serious. "Eve will practically be my neighbor."

Dylan showed no sympathy whatsoever about that. "It's a quarter of a mile from yours, and pardon me if I don't boo-hoo about you having a hot actress to gawk at every now and then."

Lawson wouldn't be gawking because if he couldn't figure out a way to nix this deal…well, he didn't know what he was going to do, but it might involve building a very high fence. And yeah, he did sound like a cranky toddler.

"Eve doesn't know the house she bought could be right on the edge of the land that might eventually be part of a lawsuit," Lawson pointed out. And that was something he could enlighten her about.

But Dylan quickly burst that bubble. "I told her all about it."

Lawson frowned. "What about her knowing that I'll be her neighbor?"

"I mentioned that part, too, and she still wanted the place. I have no idea why."

Hell. Lawson did. But it couldn't be that. Eve had lost her virginity to him in that house on her seventeenth birthday. It was definitely memorable, but after the way she'd left town and broken off things with him, she couldn't be sentimental about the location of her de-virging.

Could she?

He thought about that a second and decided the answer was no.

"So, I heard Eve named the baby Aiden," Dylan continued while he sipped his beer. "I guess she decided against Brett."

That pulled Lawson right out of his de-virging thought. "Brett?"

"Yeah. I talked to her last night when she got in, and she mentioned it was one of the names on her list."

Lawson was glad she'd nixed it. He didn't need anything to remind him of the friend he'd lost, not when he was working so hard to forget it. Of course, Eve would likely think it was easier for him to forget since he couldn't remember much. Only bits and pieces. In a way that made it worse because Lawson had filled in those gaps with some god-awful stuff.

"Why'd you talk to Eve?" Lawson asked, getting his mind back on the conversation with his brother. "Better yet, why didn't you tell me you'd talked to her? And is there any reason you didn't mention to me that she was coming here or that she was pregnant?"

Dylan scratched his chin. "That's a lot of questions. Angry-sounding questions. Are you jealous?"

"Hell, no." And he gave Dylan "the big brother" look that often had preceded a butt-whipping when they were kids.

Dylan smiled, made a *yeah whatever* sound. That sound had often preceded a butt-whipping, too. "Eve called me right before she bought the house. She asked me how I thought you'd take her moving back. She was worried that you'd be upset—"

"Damn straight I'm upset—"

"But I told her you were a grown man," Dylan said, talking right over him, "and that the stuff that happened between you two was water under the bridge."

"I'm a grown man *with a memory*," Lawson fired back, which, of course, sounded toddler-ish again. He huffed. Since he wasn't gaining any ground here, it was best he headed out, and he was about to do that until Dylan spoke again.

"If you talk to Eve," his brother went on, "let her know that I did try to call Tessie for her. She'd given me the girl's number and address in case of an emergency."

She'd given the number to Belle, too, and Eve had also asked him to call Tessie if something went wrong with the delivery. "Did you talk to Tessie?"

Dylan shook his head. "I tried, but the call went straight to voice mail." He paused. "Eve and Tessie are on the outs, and Eve's all torn up about it. That's why you need to cut her some slack about this house business. She's going through a rough time right now."

Well, Lawson wasn't going through a picnic what with the breakup with Darby, the flashbacks about Brett and the butt stitches, but this sounded like more than just a mother-daughter spat. "What happened?"

"Eve didn't say, but considering the timing, maybe Tessie didn't approve of her mom having a baby. Or her mom having sex with Kellan Carver."

Hell, Lawson didn't approve of her having sex with the turd, and he didn't have a say in this.

"Have you met Tessie?" Lawson pressed.

"No, but she moved to Texas earlier this year. She's going to school in Austin."

So, not far. And it was sort of on his way to and from the cattle auction. *Sort of.* "Could you text me Tessie's phone number and address?"

That wasn't a charming look Dylan gave him. It was a suspicious one. "What are you planning on doing?"

"I'm planning on leaving for a cattle-buying trip," Lawson snapped. He checked his watch, but it was all for show. It was a seven-hour drive, and he had a week to get there and would be gone for well over a month. A calendar would have been better use to him than his watch. "But I was thinking on the way back that I could stop by and see Tessie. You know, just to make sure she's okay."

Dylan squinted one eye. "Why?"

For such a simple one-word question, it was plenty hard to answer. Because it was going to make him sound like a toddler again. That's why he kept it to himself. But if things were patched up between Tessie and Eve, then Eve might not want to live at the ranch. Maybe she'd leave and go back to LA or even to Austin with Tessie.

And maybe, just maybe, she'd take the trail of memories, broken and otherwise, with her.

CHAPTER SIX

WHEN EVE DROVE up in front of her house, the first thing she noticed was a hot cowboy on the porch. Not *the* hot cowboy, Lawson, but rather his cousin, *a* hot cowboy from the same sizzling Granger gene pool.

Roman.

The second thing she noticed was the disturbing stuffed horse next to him. It was at least five feet tall, had urine-yellow spots, large black owl eyes and a neck crooked at such an angle that it looked as if someone had strangled it. There was a large purple-wrapped box next to it.

"Wow," Cassidy murmured. She was in the passenger seat, and with her mouth open, she stared up at the porch.

Eve figured Cassidy's reaction wasn't for the horse, and she got confirmation of that when Cassidy made a sound as if she'd just taken a lick of something sinfully delicious.

That was most women's reaction to Roman.

Since she wasn't blind, Eve could appreciate Roman's good looks, but he'd always been too much of a bad boy for her. Plus, in her younger days, she'd never been able to see past Lawson. That hadn't stopped Roman and her from becoming friends though.

"Please tell me he's not an actor," Cassidy said. "Or a mirage brought on by this heat."

Well, it was hot. August in Texas always was, and the temp was close to triple digits. It was probably hotter, though, around Roman. She suspected the Granger men lit little thermal fires wherever they went.

"And please tell me he's not married," Cassidy added. "And that he didn't bring that god-awful spotted horse."

The last one was easy. The horse had to be from Kellan. He hadn't called her or visited Aiden in the past six weeks, but for some reason he kept sending large stuffed animals that were scary enough to provoke nightmares. Eve had been shoving them into one of the guest rooms where they'd be out of sight. And that's where this latest one would go.

As for the other question, Eve hated to burst the bubble of a naughty fantasy that Cassidy was obviously weaving, but she had to know that Roman was off-limits. "No, he's not an actor or a mirage, and I doubt he's clueless about appropriate gifts to send an infant. But yes, he's married. He's Roman Granger, Lawson's cousin. He's a big-time rodeo promoter, and he's married to Mila, who owns the bookstore on Main Street."

Cassidy's next sound was one of disappointment. "Well, Mila is one lucky woman."

Yes, she was. But Eve suspected that Roman thought he was the lucky one. According to the gossip—and there was plenty of it—Roman had gone through a string of women before he'd finally fallen hard for his childhood friend.

"Sorry that I didn't call first, but I was in the area and decided to check on you," Roman said when she got out of the car. He scooped up the package and started toward them.

"No worries. It's good to see you." She kissed Roman's cheek, made introductions, and when Roman tipped his Stetson in greeting to Cassidy, Eve could have sworn that her friend sighed. A swoony sigh that made Eve smile. Then frown. Too bad there wasn't a way to make women immune to the Granger charm.

"I hope you haven't been waiting long," Eve added. She scooped up Aiden from his car seat. "I was in town."

"I've only been here a couple of minutes." He shifted the gift under his arm and helped her with the diaper bag. "Yeah, and I knew you were in town. For the baby's six-week checkup. I heard. You and this little man make news wherever you go."

It was the truth. The reporters and paparazzi had left her alone for the most part. So had the hornies. But the townsfolk still paid attention to her every move. Of course, they did that to plenty of other people, including Lawson.

On her weekly trips into Wrangler's Creek for groceries and such, nearly everyone who crossed her path had the urge to tell her that Lawson was still on a business trip, one that had no end in sight since he'd been gone for six weeks and had no projected return date.

Beneath the gossip, there was the underlying tone that she was responsible for that, and Eve had no doubts that she was. Lawson didn't want her here, which meant when he finally did return, they were going to talk. Maybe she could convince him this town was big enough for both of them. Maybe while she was at it, she could convince herself that the old memories in this house were nothing but memories.

"I was out checking on Lawson's place for him and figured you'd be back soon," Roman explained. "Wanted to see how you and the baby were doing." As they went up the steps, he touched his finger to Aiden's nose, causing the baby to give him a sleepy smile.

"You didn't have to bring a gift." Eve tipped her head to the purple box he was holding.

"Oh, it's not from me. It's from Dylan. He dropped by, too. Said it was a housewarming present." Roman paused. "Someone also left a horn by the gate, but he tossed that."

Good grief. Not another one. At least the person hadn't gotten onto the grounds, but then, one of the reasons she wanted this house was because of its remote location and the security that the gate offered.

"That's not from me, either." Roman motioned toward the horse. "Dylan was at the post office earlier, and the clerk begged him to bring it out to you since it was taking up the whole sorting room and giving folks the willies. He brought it over with the gift. Is it an old prop from *Demon High*?"

"No, it's from a dimwit ass," Cassidy grumbled.

Eve gave Cassidy a scolding glance. Yes, it was true that Kellan was clueless and was frequently ass-like, but he was Aiden's father, and Eve didn't want her son to grow up hearing things like that. Not from his nanny and mother, anyway. She was certain Aiden would figure it all out soon enough.

Probably by age two.

Then one day Eve would have to explain that on a troublesome night in her life she, too, had gotten clueless and stupid and slept with someone who was, well, a dimwit ass.

"Come in and I'll fix you some iced tea or something," Eve offered Roman when Cassidy unlocked the door, and they went inside.

Roman hauled in the horse and stood it in the foyer. Cassidy also took the baby from Eve so that she in turn could take the gift from Roman.

"Thanks," Roman said, "but I can't stay. I need to go to Lawson's place and chew out the contractor. Apparently, there was some miscommunication that resulted in a green quartz countertop instead of a white one. Lawson didn't feel he was getting his point across over the phone, so he asked me to go."

Eve was certain Roman would indeed get the point across. He hadn't lost that bad-boy edge.

"Plus, I don't really like hanging around at Heavenly Pastures," Roman added in a grumble.

"But you came to see Dylan," she pointed out.

"Lucian's threatening the lawsuit again, says he's thinking about bringing in livestock and making this place a full-scale working ranch again. I came out here to attempt a bud-nipping."

Oh. That. The lawsuit generated a lot of gossip, but from what Eve could tell, it was something Lucian had been threatening for years.

"Did you succeed?" she asked.

"No. If Lucian wins, you could have cattle or horses right in your backyard."

"Better than horns or paparazzi."

He smiled at her. "Are you okay?"

She considered a lie or a smidge of BS but went with the truth. "Most days. I stay busy," she amended.

"Yep, a baby can do that." He knew that firsthand, too, because Roman had become a father when he was a teenager. "And I've heard your charity foundation keeps you working hard."

It did, but thankfully no one in town had made the connection that the foundation helped pregnant teens. Nor were they aware it was something she knew about firsthand.

Of course, unlike a lot of teens, she'd had plenty of money when she had been carrying Tessie. Plenty afterward, too, from her residuals off the reruns of *Demon High* and the investments she'd made from her salary during the show's run. And she'd had some support.

Sort of.

Cassidy had been there for her, and the studio had worked hard to keep the pregnancy a secret so she could continue doing *Demon High*. The studio's motives, though, had been driven not by her well-being but by profit. Sponsors would have dropped the show if they'd learned the costar was a pregnant teenager.

"You've been busy, too," Eve commented.

Roman nodded, pointed to his wedding ring. "I heard hell froze over that day."

"And I heard the sound of hundreds of broken hearts."

"Hearts mend. Those women who'd once been interested in me have already moved on to Dylan. And Lawson."

She hoped she didn't look too shocked by Lawson's name being mentioned in the same sentence with Dylan, the reigning king of heartbreakers. "I thought most women in town wanted Lawson to get back together with Darby."

"They do," he readily admitted. "Those are the women going after Dylan. Lawson's getting attention from the rest, those not on Team Darby. In case you're wondering, there's a Team Eve, too."

She'd missed that particular tidbit of gossip. "Who's on that team?"

Roman smiled. "Me."

"I'm not sure you count," she said under her breath. Since Roman was already heading out the door, Eve followed him out onto the porch. "Any idea when Lawson will be back?"

"I figure another week, maybe less. He's had time to look at every bull, steer, heifer and calf in the whole state."

It sure seemed like it.

Since she couldn't figure out a subtle way to put this, she just put it out there. "Mary Ellen Betterton, the nurse at the pediatrician's office, said she thought Lawson and Darby were getting back together. He apparently called her last week on her birthday, and Mary Ellen thought that was a good sign."

Roman blew out a long breath. "You know how confused and frustrated you're feeling about Lawson?" He didn't wait for her to answer. "Well, he feels the same way about you. Of course, he'd rather eat that rabid stuffed horse than admit it. That's my way of saying, don't read anything into what Lawson's doing right now. He's just trying to sort it all out."

Those were very wise words, and Eve brushed another kiss on his cheek to let him know that. "Thanks."

He shrugged in that lazy way that only he or a Greek

god could have managed. "It's good to have you home, Eve."

It was good to be home, but the jury was still out on whether or not anyone other than Roman and she felt that way.

By the time Eve made it back inside, Cassidy had already taken Aiden to the nursery, and she was carrying the pair of baby monitors—one of which she handed to Eve. It had seemed like overkill for both of them to have monitors, but Cassidy had a suite upstairs where she did her paintings for the illustrations for kids' books. That way, if Cassidy was on a roll with the artwork, she could signal Eve to get the baby.

Not that Eve was far from him anyway.

Her bedroom and office were right next to Aiden's bedroom, and the baby napped in her arms almost as often as he did in his crib.

"Your housewarming gift," Cassidy reminded her, and she handed her the box.

Eve opened it and saw the binoculars. Not the cheap kids' kind. These looked more like something the military would use on recon missions. There was a note attached.

"'Go to your family room bay window and look out,'" she read aloud.

With Cassidy following her, Eve did indeed go to the window, and she set aside the box so she could adjust the focus on the binoculars. After she'd done that, she had a zoomed-in view of Lawson's house.

Eve rolled her eyes and handed the binoculars to Cassidy so she could have a look, as well. "Good choice of gifts. Well, it will be if and when Hot Cowboy comes back." She shifted the binoculars toward the road. "In the meantime, I'll be content with memories of Roman."

"You don't have to settle for *memories*," Eve reminded her. "I know you won't date actors, but there's none around here. Plenty of cowboys though."

"Hmm. Maybe the elusive Lucian, then? I've yet to see him, but if he's as hot as Roman, Lawson and Dylan, then it might be fun to have a late-summer fling with him."

Eve couldn't shake her head fast enough. Cassidy had been burned more than a couple of times by falling for the wrong man, and Lucian was almost certainly in that *wrong man* category.

"Lucian isn't the summer-flinging type," Eve told her.

Cassidy gave her a flat look. "I keep hearing what a badass ass he is, but are you saying he doesn't have sex?"

"I'm sure he does, but it'd be like playing with fire while running with scissors and skating on thin ice."

The flat look turned to a sly smile. "Or it could be like taking the bull by the horns while taking time to smell the roses and sowing some oats." She paused. "Unless there's another Granger I don't know about yet."

"Reed," Eve said quickly. "But he's out of the picture. He left Wrangler's Creek years ago."

"All that testosterone in one house," Cassidy commented.

Yes, and Eve had often felt sorry for their kid sister, Lily Rose. She'd had an abundance of big-brother interference in her life, but all was well now. Lily

Rose was married and ran her own horse-training business.

Eve checked the monitor. Aiden was still sacked out, so she should probably catch up on some paperwork for the foundation. She was about to head to her office, but her phone rang. When she took it from her pocket and saw the name on the screen, her heart went to her knees.

Tessie.

Eve's hands were suddenly shaking so hard that she bobbled her phone and nearly dropped it. She finally managed to hit the answer button.

"Tessie, it's good to hear from you." Eve tried to tamp down the emotion in her voice but was certain she failed.

"Yesterday, you left six messages for me to call you," Tessie greeted her. "Five the day before. You're going in the wrong direction, Mom. I told you I wasn't ready to talk to you."

"I know." And as harsh as Tessie's tone was, it still gave Eve a warm feeling to hear her say *Mom*. "I'm sorry. I just miss you, that's all."

"No, that's not all. You want me to forgive you. Well, I can't. You lied to me. You made me believe I was adopted."

"I know," Eve repeated. And she couldn't even defend or excuse herself. The studio had created the lie, and Eve had taken that lie and run with it. A way of having her cake and eating it, too. "But I'm sorry that I hurt you."

Tessie made a *yeah right* sound that was identical to one Lawson had made. "I saw a magazine in the grocery store, and it had an interview with Kellan. He was bragging about his son." Tessie paused. "Is Kellan my father, too?"

"No." She didn't add more, though she was pretty sure Tessie was waiting for her to do that. But what could she say? Nothing that would make this better, that's for sure. "Just please let me come and see you in Austin."

"Don't you dare come." Tessie didn't wait on that response. She blurted it out. "There's a whole *Demon High* cult club here, and they don't know we're related. I want to keep it that way."

Because Tessie was embarrassed about it. Always had been. It was one of the reasons she'd been so co-operative about keeping a low profile. It was probably also why she'd wanted to attend an out-of-state college. She wanted to get far away from anyone who knew her.

Little did Tessie know how close she was to her blood kin.

"I gotta go. I have a class that's about to start." Tessie ended the call before Eve could get in another word.

The first tear spilled down Eve's cheek before she could even put away her phone, and Cassidy was right there to pull Eve into her arms. Cassidy just held her and let her cry it out, but the tears wouldn't help. This was an ache that Eve felt all the way to her soul. Her daughter might never forgive her, might never love her again.

"So, let me play devil's advocate," Cassidy said. She led Eve into the powder room just off the foyer and grabbed her a handful of tissues.

"That's the role you played on *Demon High*," Eve muttered as she blew her nose.

Cassidy shrugged. "Well, now I want to reprise it to give you a glimpse of the double poop-storm that could be brewing."

Poop-storm was one of Cassidy's go-to curse words. Once, Cassidy had had a serious cursing problem, but after she'd become Tessie's nanny, she'd toned it down—other than calling Kellan an ass. Eve only wished her toning down didn't sound so, well, toned down when she was talking with adults.

"Tessie doesn't know that Lawson's her father," Cassidy went on, "but one day she'll find out. Heck, one look at him, and she'll know."

She would. Because Tessie looked very much like Lawson's cousin Sophie. "I plan to tell her…eventually."

"If *eventually* doesn't happen before she finds out from someone else, then Tessie will get mad again that you didn't come completely clean with her. She'll go to Lawson since she'll be curious what he's like, and he'll see her and will almost certainly suspect she's his daughter. Then they'll both be mad at you. Hence, the poop-storm times two."

It wasn't exactly a revelation, but it did stir a new urgency in Eve. Cassidy was right. This secret had already blown up in her face once, but there could be a secondary explosion.

One that might cause her to lose Tessie forever.

"Deep down, I think you had another reason for moving back here to Wrangler's Creek," Cassidy went on. "Yes, you wanted to get away from Hollywood and start a new life, but you also knew Tessie was just an hour away. She'd been talking about going to the college in Texas for years. And I believe you realized then that the time had come for her to know the truth."

It had. God, it had.

"Help me get the baby ready," Eve said. "I need to go to Austin right now."

CHAPTER SEVEN

LAWSON HAD DONE some pretty stupid things in his life, but this might make his top ten. Top five if he didn't figure out something better to say other than *Uh, Tessie, I'm just here in Austin to check on you because my ditzy aunt Belle and your mom are worried about you.*

This was definitely an example of sticking his nose where it didn't belong. And even though he'd told Dylan he might visit Tessie, Lawson had also dismissed it shortly after the dumb-assed notion had first entered his head. So, why had he let Belle talk him into it with her repeated pestering calls and garbled texts?

Because he'd obviously wanted to be talked into it, that's why.

Despite his dismissing this visit, he was still running with the self-serving theory that if he could smooth things over between Eve and Tessie, Eve would leave Wrangler's Creek. Then he wouldn't have to risk seeing her every day in a house and place that would eventually make her miserable because it would bring back old memories of why she'd left in the first place.

Every time that theory played out in his head, he felt lower than squished shit beneath a horse's hoof. But a happy resolution between mother and daughter with Tessie would benefit Eve, too, since Belle had assured him that Eve was sick with worry about the rift with Tessie. So, even if this didn't make Eve leave Wrangler's Creek, at least she wouldn't be miserable if she could reconnect with her daughter.

Following the directions of his GPS, Lawson took the final turn onto a narrow street lined on both sides with parked cars. He didn't have the name of the building, only the address that he'd gotten from Dylan, but there'd probably be a sign for the boarding school or whatever it was called. But no school sign. It was just rows of apartments.

"Arriving at destination on left," the GPS told him.

Yep, definitely an apartment building, but maybe the middle or high school that Tessie was attending was using some of the units as dorm rooms. Top-of-the-line dorm rooms, since this was a pricey area of Austin. Lawson knew that because his cousins' business headquarters, Granger Western, wasn't too far from here, and it certainly fell into the pricey category. Eve was loaded though, so she probably didn't mind shelling out the money if this was a good place for her daughter.

There were no parking spots nearby, so Lawson kept driving until he found one at the end of the street. The August heat slammed into him the moment he stepped from his truck, and he hated to admit it, but it almost felt like some bad omen. Maybe like one of Vita's foretellings that he dismissed but still gave him an uneasy feeling. He shook that off, went up the steps to the building, but the door flew open before he could even reach for it.

And the smell of booze came rushing out at him.

Lawson quickly saw the source of the smell. Three teenagers, two girls and a guy, who were trying to come out the door despite the fact that he was directly in front of them. They were giggling and wobbling but tried to straighten and look sober when they spotted him.

"Shh," the guy said to the others. "Just keep walkin'." His attempt at a whisper could have probably been heard as far away as Kansas.

The guy, who had stringy long blond hair, was on one side of one of the girls—a brunette with her head down—and he had his arm hooked around her waist, obviously supporting her weight. The other girl, a blonde, was doing the same thing on the other side of the middle girl.

Even though the trio was trying to get by, Lawson didn't move. "Are y'all all right?" he asked.

It didn't matter what they said because he already knew the answer. They were drunk. And clearly underage. A bad combination. But that wasn't even the worst of it. The worst was the flashbacks that hit Lawson like a mean kick from a rodeo bull.

Brett.

It all came back—the handful of parts that he could remember, anyway. The party. The drinking. And yeah, Eve, Brett and he had been underage, too. They'd been so sure they weren't doing anything wrong, that it was something plenty of kids did. Kids like these. But it had been wrong, and Brett had died.

"We're doin' just fine, man," the guy said, or at least attempted to. He missed a couple of syllables and slurred the ones he did manage to say. Even the smile he tried was off the mark and looked as if someone had yanked up the right side of his mouth with an invisible fish hook. "'Kay?"

No, it wasn't okay, and Lawson felt the anger slide

through him. It wasn't anger directed at the kids but rather himself. Yeah, and Eve, too. The trifecta of Eve, Brett and him usually led to his piss-poor attempt to completely shut out what he'd failed to shut out for the past eighteen years.

And he failed today, too.

The anger was there all right, but Lawson tried to keep his touch gentle when he put his fingers beneath the middle girl's chin to lift it. His heart felt as if it stopped until he saw her eyelids flutter open.

Alive.

Thank God. But she wouldn't stay that way if she got any more booze in her or if her blood alcohol was already too high.

Most people wouldn't have thought the worst-case scenario in a situation like this, but since Lawson had been there, done that in the worst-case department, he knew how fast things could turn ugly.

"All of you live here in this building?" Lawson asked.

That got the attention of the girl on the end. "You a cop?"

"Yeah," he lied.

Her eyes widened to the size of hubcaps, and she suddenly looked as if she might puke. Good. That would get the booze out of her stomach. The guy did puke, and when he turned his head to do that, he let go of the brunette in the middle. If Lawson hadn't caught her, she would have probably splatted on the floor. He hooked his arm around her, moving her away from the puking—which was only getting worse because the blonde girl started barfing her guts out, too.

There was nothing worse than the smell of booze-vomit, so he took the semiconscious girl several yards away to the massive stairs in the center of the foyer and he had her sit down. At least she stayed upright. Mostly, anyway. She drifted into a slow lean until her arm was against the banister.

While he took out his phone to call an ambulance and the real cops, Lawson turned back to the two pukers. They obviously didn't have the mobility issues of the nonpuker, though, because they ran out the front door. He didn't go after them but was about to go through with the ambulance call when he heard the footsteps on the stairs. Lawson soon spotted a young woman making her way toward them. She didn't look much older than the brunette, but at least she wasn't drunk.

"What's going on?" she asked. But she got her own answer because she groaned, then made a face when she got a whiff of the brunette and the puke. "Idiot," she muttered to the girl. She caught hold of her, pulling her to her feet before she looked at Lawson. "Are you a cop?"

He frowned because he was reasonably sure he looked nothing like a cop. Hell, he still had some cow dung on his boots from the stockyard he'd visited earlier, and he was wearing one of his prize rodeo buckles.

"You know this girl?" he asked. Yeah, it was a cop maneuver, answering a question with a question, but he wanted to know what was going on.

The newcomer nodded. "She's a sorority sister." She rattled off some Greek letters. "And she's my roommate."

"Sorority?" His frown deepened. "As in college?"

She was no longer giving him an *are you a cop?* look. She was staring at him now as if he was an idiot. "Uh, yes. We're staying here temporarily until our sorority house is ready."

All right. So, maybe the brunette wasn't underage after all if she was in college. But that immediately led Lawson to something that didn't fit.

What was Tessie doing here if this was for college students?

Maybe there was still a boarding school along with the sorority sisters? Or it could be that Tessie was indeed college age. Since he'd never seen a picture of her, it was possible that Eve had adopted her when she was four or five instead of an infant.

"I'll take her back to the room, and I'll call the janitor about the throw-up," the young woman said. "I'll make sure she's okay. Just please don't arrest her. Wellsmore College has a no-drinking policy, and she could get in big trouble."

Lawson wasn't letting her off the hook just yet. "There were two other people with her, and they were also drunk. A guy and a girl, both blond."

"Idiots," she repeated. "I know them, too. They're the ones who threw up?"

He nodded. "Someone will need to check on them."

"I'll make some calls," she jumped to answer. "Just please—no arrests. If my mom hears about stuff like this going on, she'll make me move back home."

Lawson really didn't want to let this slide, but the young woman did seem to be on top of this, and that "idiot" label hopefully meant she was going to give all three of them some grief over this screwup.

He finally put his hands on his hips. "When she

sobers up, tell her I'll be keeping an eye on her, and I will put her butt in jail if she does this again."

She gave a shaky nod, and even the brunette attempted some kind of an agreement to that. It came out as a groan-belch-nod, but Lawson thought he'd gotten his point across. That's why he didn't stop the other woman from taking the brunette up the stairs.

However, it was only after he'd allowed them to leave that he remembered he hadn't accomplished what he'd come here to do.

Find Tessie. Attempt a rift-mending. Go home.

He was about to call out to the sober girl to ask her if she knew Tessie, but the front door inched open. The pukers hadn't returned though. This was a redhead in her thirties. She was wearing yoga pants and was carrying a baby in her arms. She was in midsmile— aimed at the baby, whose cheek she was touching— but she "ewww'ed" when she noticed the puke. She sidestepped it on her tiptoes and froze when her attention landed on him.

"Holy shit," she spit out. Then her mouth twisted up. "Sorry," she added to the baby. "Holy crackers."

Despite the toned-down version of the profanity, her expression was pretty much still in the "holy shit" mode. Her gaze slashed around. At every corner of the foyer. Then at the stairs. The sorority sisters were already around the bend of the stairs and out of sight, but the redhead kept looking as if she expected someone to materialize out of the putrid air.

"It wasn't me who got sick," Lawson said when she glanced at the puke again. Then the door. But at the same moment he spoke, she said, "What are you doing here?"

He didn't think that was a general kind of question. As in what was a grown man doing in an apartment building for a sorority? She seemed to want some specific information. "Do I know you?"

"Oh." Her forehead bunched up. "Oh. No. We've never met, but I'm Cassidy Vale. What are you doing here?" she repeated.

It took Lawson a moment to realize that this was the actress who used to be on *Demon High*. Maybe Eve and she were still friends, and Eve had sent her to check on Tessie.

He tipped his cowboy hat and was about to introduce himself, but she spoke before he could. "I know who you are. You're Hot Cowboy." She frowned as if sorry she'd admitted that. "That's what Eve used to call you. She kept your picture in her purse when she first moved to LA." Another frown. "Now, why are you here?" She made one more of those nervous looks up the staircase.

Hot Cowboy? Well, it was better than cop. Actually, a lot better. But why had Eve talked about him like that? And carried his picture? She'd been finished with him when she left Wrangler's Creek.

Or so he'd thought.

At the exact second he was thinking that, the baby made a fussing sound and squirmed, drawing Lawson's attention to it. Or rather to *him*. It was a baby boy wearing denim shorts and a shirt that said Number One Son. The kid smiled at him. And Lawson instantly knew who he was.

"Eve's baby," he muttered.

"Yes. Aiden," Cassidy confirmed.

Well, the kid had changed a lot in the six weeks

since Lawson had delivered him. For one thing, he was bigger, and his eyes were open. He didn't look pissed off and ready to kick the world in the balls. Nope. He looked, well, like a cute kid. One who was smiling at him, and Lawson found himself smiling right back.

"Eve's parking the car," Cassidy went on. "Now, why exactly are you here?"

Lawson heard the repeated question, but his brain latched on to the first part of what Cassidy had said. Eve was parking the car, which meant she'd soon be there. He didn't especially want to avoid her.

Okay, he did.

But the important thing was there was no reason for him to be there if Eve had personally come to check on Tessie. It was best for him to leave. Immediately.

This time he tipped his hat in farewell and had even managed a couple of steps when the door opened and Eve came in. Like Cassidy, she made an *ewww* sound when she spotted the vomit. Lawson wasn't *ewww*ing though. He was cursing. Because, hell, there it was again.

Lust.

Apparently, old lust was just as potent as the fresh stuff because one look at her, and it heated up every inch of him. Which only caused him to mentally curse himself even more. Thankfully, he didn't have to deal with the lust for very long because the inevitable second reaction came.

Grief.

Yeah, this was the Brett-effect again because all of that came back, too. Since he'd just had to fight off the flashbacks minutes earlier after seeing the drunk teenager, he didn't have them tamped down enough. They came much too fast to the surface. At least it was a cure for the lust, but Lawson knew it was a temporary one.

Eve shifted her attention from the floor. To Cassidy. And then she spotted him.

"Shit," Eve snapped. "I mean, shoot. What are you doing here?"

Lawson had heard that question more today than he had in years. "I was on my way back from a buying trip, and Belle asked me to come by and check on Tessie."

Judging from the way the color vanished from Eve's face, that wasn't an answer she'd expected. Or one that she wanted to hear.

"Belle?" Eve repeated. She looked at Cassidy as if she expected her to have some enlightening thing to say, but Cassidy only shook her head.

"Uh, you saw Tessie?" Eve asked. She scooped up the baby from Cassidy's arms, but for some reason, the kid kept looking at Lawson. Kept smiling, too.

Lawson shook his head and hitched his thumb toward the stairs. "According to the address Dylan gave me, Tessie's on the second floor. I was about to head up there, but I had some…interruptions. Not the puke," he added when Eve glanced at it again. "The people who did that were the distractions."

Along with Cassidy, the baby and Eve.

Like her son, Eve looked a whole lot different from the last time he'd seen her. Her face wasn't screwed up in pain, and of course, she didn't have a pregnant belly. She was back to looking like her old self. Plus,

eighteen years. Those eighteen years had settled nicely
on her though.

And he had to curse another hit from that old lust.

"How are you?" Eve asked. But she wasn't looking at his face. No, her attention was flickering in the
general area of his crotch, which meant she was probably talking about his butt injury.

"I'm fine. A doc in Abilene took the stitches out
while I was up there. I'm as right as rain." He couldn't
believe that had just come out of his mouth and didn't
know what the hell it meant. What the heck was right
about rain, anyway? "Since you're here, there's no
need for me to check on Tessie," he added in a grumble.

Cassidy and Eve both blew out large enough breaths
to fan a small forest fire. Lawson figured he should
wonder what that relief exhaling was all about. Maybe
even question it, but to do that, he'd have to hang
around. Right now though, there was something he
wanted more than answers.

A whole lot more.

And that was distancing himself from Eve, the puke
and this tangled mess of memories leaking from their
old baggage.

"Tessie?" He heard Eve call out at exactly the same
moment that Lawson headed for the door. The sound
of his own footsteps blended with those coming down
the stairs. Tessie's, no doubt.

Good. Eve was going to get to see her daughter and
maybe accomplish the very thing that he should have
never come here to try to do.

Maybe.

Tessie certainly didn't respond with a welcome

greeting to her mom, but Lawson didn't wait around to see how this would play out. Nope. He headed home, knowing he'd filled his "stupid things to do" quota for the day.

CHAPTER EIGHT

TANGLED MEMORIES DIDN'T go away just because you were sick and tired of trying to untangle them. Lawson already knew that, of course, but coming home to Wrangler's Creek made it much harder to shove those memories to the back of his mind.

To get to the Granger Ranch, he had to drive through town and right down Main Street. That meant going past the high school that Eve and he had attended.

Brett, too.

There'd been football games, pop quizzes and more goofing off than studying. Things that all three of them had done together. The only times Brett had been excluded had been when lust played its hot little hand with Lawson and Eve. Lawson had made out with her too many times to count beneath the bleachers of the football field. And the baseball dugout. Oh, and in the gym where the basketball team played.

Apparently, sports venues had been libido triggers for Eve and him.

Once he'd driven past the high school, he got another blast from the past. He had to go right by Eve's grandfather's old house. Of course, her grandfather was long gone, and the place had changed hands several times over the past decade and a half. But Lawson had spent enough time in that house with Eve that even after all this time, it was approximately twenty-two thousand square feet of memories. Specifically, memories of him making out with Eve there in her bedroom.

In fact, the whole damn town, surrounding area and much of the county had become their make-out zones, which meant there were few places he could go that wouldn't trigger the past.

His new house was an exception.

Even though she lived only a short distance away, there were no traces of Eve inside his place. The trick would be to keep it that way. Lawson knew he was tough, but he wasn't sure his heart could stand another stomping. Darby had been safe. No chance of her hurting him because he would have never let things get deep with her. But Eve, well, she could still do some more damage after all these years. Seeing her in Austin had only confirmed that.

Lawson drove to the Granger Ranch. More memories. The barn, this time where Eve and he had had a romp or two. He made a mental note to limit his future sexual escapades to places he didn't have to see on a daily basis.

Thankfully, there was work to do when he got to the ranch. A long buying trip like his came with paperwork, invoices and adjusting work schedules so there'd be enough hands around to deal with the shipments of the new cattle as they came in. No Garrett though. His cousin had apparently taken a rare day off to spend time with his wife and kids. Sophie was doing the same with her husband and twins.

Lawson still didn't want a spouse or kids, but now that Eve had likely managed a reunion with Tessie, he was feeling a little like the odd man out. Yeah, he was stuck in a rut, but it was a rut that suited him.

Or rather it had until Eve had come back with that crapload of memories in tow.

Now he'd just have to work harder to make that rut the way it had been six weeks earlier.

Once he finished his work, he drove to his new house. *Home*, he mentally corrected himself, and he wondered just how long it would take for *home* to be his go-to word for the life he was trying to build for himself. Maybe a while—especially since there was an unwelcome sight waiting for him by the Heavenly Pastures' gate.

Vita.

Her bicycle was leaning against the fence, and she had a chicken tucked under her arm. A live, ugly one. Emphasis on *ugly*. Of course, he'd never actually seen what he'd call a pretty chicken, but this one was dingy mouse gray with sprigs of black feathers poking out in random spots—including on its head.

Lawson stopped and lowered his window. "Yeah, I know. There's a curse on me the size of elephant balls."

Vita stared at him as if he'd just said the most ridiculous thing possible. Since those were the very words she'd *foretold* six weeks ago, he just stared back at her.

"There's no more curse—for the time being, anyway," Vita finally said after the staring match went on for several seconds. She tried to hand him the chicken, but when he didn't take it, she frowned again. "You want more stitches in your heinie, do you?"

Lawson wasn't sure if that was a threat or if it was chicken related. "Not especially."

"Then take the hen." She practically tossed it onto

his seat. "Her name is Prissy Pants, and she'll make things play out the way they should."

There were so many things wrong with that explanation. "Play out?" he repeated. "You mean, it'll go the way you say it'll go?"

She huffed. "Not me. The fates, of course." She mumbled something, but the only word he caught was *stupid*. "Keep Prissy Pants with you for a month, and your life will be back on its right course. All your bad karma over breaking up with Darby will be fixed."

Lawson had been about to hand the chicken back to Vita, but that stopped him. Vita had indeed been right about the horns-baby-concussion-stitches curse. And while he really didn't want to believe in anything Vita said, he didn't want another butt injury, either.

"Uh, does Prissy Pants need a cage or anything?" he asked. Yeah, he was apparently buying into this. With a chicken whose name he didn't want to say aloud.

"No. Just let her roam around your yard. You got some low trees, and she can roost in one of them. She'll eat bugs until you get a chance to buy her some chicken feed."

Great. Now he would have to buy feed to keep this hope alive of righted fates and karma.

"I'll be back for Prissy Pants in a month," Vita called out to him as she went to her bike.

Feeling duped and oh-so skeptical, Lawson looked at the chicken, but he could have sworn that Prissy Pants was exhibiting some skepticism of her own.

"It's just for a month," he muttered. Then he cursed himself for talking to poultry before he pressed in the security numbers on the panel to open the gate.

The chicken squawked when Lawson released the

brake and the truck lurched forward. And she just kept on squawking and flapping her wings around. The rest of her didn't stay still, either, and Lawson damn near ran off the road when she flew right in his face.

This wasn't a good start to karma-fixing.

Thankfully, his house wasn't far from the gate, and the moment he pulled into his driveway, he threw open the passenger's door so the chicken could jump out. She stayed put, and this time when she looked at Lawson, there appeared to be a smidge of stink eye. A sort of *if you want me out of here, then move me yourself.*

He'd already compromised enough of his dignity for one day, so he merely left the truck doors open, got out and hoped the hen would be able to find her own way into the yard.

As he always did when he went in the new place, he held his breath. There'd been so many hitches with the idiotic construction crew that he was never quite sure what he was going to face. And that's why he was pleasantly surprised that nothing looked wrong. Just the opposite. It looked like, well, home.

Lawson dropped his keys on the foyer table, smiling at the fact there was not only a table but also a completed foyer. With flooring and painted walls. The flooring and paint carried through the rest of the house where he saw his furniture. Obviously, the hands had moved the things from his house in town, and even though there were still plenty of boxes that needed to be unpacked, he made a mental note to give them all big fat bonuses.

The smiling, however, stopped when he made it to the kitchen. The green countertop that he'd nixed several times was still in place, but it seemed to be the only screwup. Maybe he could learn to live with stone that looked like pond scum with dabs of yellow fungus in it. Someone had even stocked his fridge with beer and put a few groceries in his pantry. Hell, there were flowers on the breakfast table, and next to it was a big purple box.

He opened the card on the package and read the note. *A housewarming gift. Go to your living room window and look out. Dylan.*

The gift was a pair of binoculars, and Lawson didn't intend to thank his brother for it. Because before he even took the binoculars to the specified location—his living room—he knew what he would see.

Eve's house.

What Lawson hadn't expected to see was Eve herself. But there she was. She was in the garden on the side of her house and appeared to be tending to the roses. Obviously, she hadn't stayed in Austin very long if she was already back. Maybe that meant the reconciliation with Tessie had flopped.

He zoomed in to try to get a better look at Eve's face and expression. Just to see if she was upset or something.

Hell.

The binoculars were good enough that he could see her crying. He doubted this was allergy related. No. He was betting this had to do with the problems she was having with Tessie. Issues that had nothing to do with him, he reminded himself, and that's why he put the binoculars on the foyer table and turned away.

Not easily.

But he managed it.

Since he knew he should put some distance between

the front window and him, Lawson grabbed a beer and headed out back and had a look around. No fence nor was there any landscaping as there was at Eve's—his mom's old house, and he intended to keep it that way.

He wanted the view of the creek even though it coiled around the very land that could ultimately fuel a feud. Lawson was hoping since he was smack-dab in the middle of that contentious land that both sides of the Grangers would eventually agree to sell him those acres.

By then, Eve would have probably moved on and gone back to California.

The idea of that didn't settle as well in his gut as he'd thought it would. It especially didn't settle well in a specific part of him. That brainless wonder behind the zipper of his jeans.

Well, crap.

Now his dick had apparently decided that he was going to be damned if Eve stayed or even more damned if she left.

He was still cursing himself and his idiotic body part when he heard the sound of a car engine, so Lawson made his way back through the house to the front door. He threw it open, definitely not expecting to see the person who was now on his front porch.

Darby.

She had her index finger positioned over the doorbell that she was obviously about to ring, and she shrieked when she saw him. Lawson made his own sound of surprise, but his was mixed with a little confusion. He had no idea why his ex was there. Or better yet, why she was in red stiletto heels and a raincoat. There wasn't a cloud in the sky.

"Oh," she said, studying his face. "You didn't get my message." Before he could answer that, though, she motioned toward the driveway. "What's Prissy Pants doing here?"

Since the chicken was now pecking at the grass in the front yard, she'd obviously figured out how to get out of his truck. "How'd you know that was her name?"

Darby's eyes widened. Her mouth opened. And she suddenly looked about as comfortable as a steer's rump on a hot branding iron.

"I saw her at Vita's," Darby stated.

Lawson could fill in the blanks. There was only one reason people went to see Vita. For fortune telling, curses or potions. Great. Maybe Vita had put together a curse for Darby.

"And you really didn't get my message?" Darby continued, again before he could speak. "I came by earlier to bring over some beer and food, and I left it with one of the workers."

So, Darby had done that. The cold beer suddenly didn't taste that good, so he set it aside. "Thanks. That was nice of you." Well, it would have been if Lawson had wanted her to do that. He didn't. "What'd the note say?"

She got another of those uncomfortable "branding" looks. "That I'd heard you were back from your trip and that I was coming over. I added if that didn't work for you, then you could call me."

He tried not to sigh too loud but failed. "It's not a good time."

Darby's uncomfortable look morphed into one of desperation. Lawson might have added an explanation to go with that bad-timing remark if Darby hadn't thrown open her raincoat. She didn't have on a stitch of clothes underneath.

And she'd obviously opted for a Brazilian wax and gold navel ring. Body glitter, too.

Normally, those were things he would have noticed and perhaps even appreciated. Of course, a naturally adorned naked woman would have gotten his attention just the same. But in this case, the attention didn't result in a hard-on. Heck, he didn't intend to admit this to anyone, but he didn't even get any twinges in that area.

"Lawson," Darby said, and she launched herself at him.

He caught her, whirling her around so that her naked body didn't smack against his, and in the same motion, he maneuvered her inside. It was best not to have any ranch hands or visitors witness this. Because this was going to lead to Darby feeling embarrassed. Something he was already feeling.

Lawson didn't say anything, but Darby must have realized that he wasn't exactly taking her up on this not-so-subtle offer. In fact, while keeping her at arm's length, he pulled the sides of the raincoat back together.

She stared at him, her bottom lip trembling a little. "I thought…well, I thought…" But Darby waved that off. "Vita said if I had any chance of winning you back that it would be today."

Lawson just lifted an eyebrow. No need for him to spell out that Vita just wasn't a reliable source for relationship advice. Of course, he did have a chicken prancing around in his yard, and that was proof that Vita could be convincing.

"I know it was stupid to believe her, and now I feel stupid, too." Tears welled up in Darby's eyes.

Lawson hated the tears. Hated even more that he was responsible for them. But what he hated most was that he had no idea what to say to Darby that could fix this. That's why he settled for an "I'm sorry."

She nodded, blinked back the tears and then tipped her head to his beer. "Can I have one of those, and then I'll be on my way?"

It was a simple request, but Lawson wondered if this was some kind of ploy. Maybe Darby thought if she got drunk, or if she got him drunk, they'd land in bed.

"It's just a beer," she added because she probably saw his hesitation.

Lawson continued with the hesitation a couple more seconds before he sighed and headed to the fridge.

"I saw the for-sale sign on your house in town," she called out. Apparently, she'd moved on from a seduction attempt to small talk. "Any offers yet?"

"No." But sometimes houses in Wrangler's Creek stayed on the market for months. This wasn't exactly a hotbed of Realtor activity. That was okay though. There was no mortgage on either of his places, so he wasn't strapped for cash. That was one of the few advantages of being a Granger.

When Lawson came back into the living room, he was pleased that Darby had kept her raincoat closed. He wasn't pleased, though, that she had picked up the binoculars and was using them to look out the front window.

"Oh," she said.

For just one syllable, it had a lot of emotion in it. Hurt, yes. Some anger, too. And her eyes were narrowed a little when she looked back at him.

"Eve," she added.

"Dylan," he explained. "That's his idea of a house-warming gift." He so wished, though, that he hadn't explained that because it put a new spark of hope in Darby's eyes.

"Oh," Darby repeated. This time a sliver of a smile tugged at her mouth. She looked out the binoculars again and no doubt had Eve in her sights. "Oh."

This time, though, the *oh* was different. There seemed to be some alarm in it. Lawson got confirmation of the alarm when Darby added, "Oh, God. You have to do something to help her."

That sent Lawson scurrying to the window. He practically shoved the beer into Darby's hand so he could take the binoculars and have a look for himself. It was Eve all right, and she was still in the garden.

But she was no longer alone.

Eve appeared to be having a showdown with none other than the Grim Reaper.

CHAPTER NINE

ALL THE CRYING had made her congested and plugged up her ears, and that's probably why Eve hadn't heard the footsteps behind her a lot sooner.

Especially these footsteps.

When she finally heard them and whirled around, she immediately spotted the intruder. It would have been impossible to miss him. He was wearing a shiny black cape that puddled on the ground and thigh-high leather boots with platform heels that added a good four inches to his already six-foot height. He was also carrying a black metal shield and a scythe blade.

Clearly, this was one of the hornies but one who preferred to dress the part rather than just deposit horns here or there. He had on the garb of a Swaron warrior, the characters who routinely kidnapped and tortured Ulyana so they could in turn use her to get to Stavros.

In the scripts, Eve had the same reaction every time a Swaron appeared. A sharp gasp, followed by a look of terror in her eyes. She did that now out of habit. And also out of habit, she reached for one of her prop knives. Which wasn't there, of course.

The bottle of environmentally friendly aphid spray didn't seem nearly as menacing as a poison-laced switchblade.

"Ulyana?" the intruder said. "Uh, is that you?"

Obviously, he didn't follow script because he didn't have a gravelly, threatening voice. What he did have was a Texas-sized amount of surprise in his tone. Probably because he hadn't expected the teen demon hunter to be a thirtysomething-year-old woman in cutoff sweatpants and with a slightly pudgy baby belly. Well, they were even. She hadn't expected a "fan" to be here.

"How'd you get on this ranch?" she asked.

He lifted his shoulder, causing his body armor to clang and ping. "The woman in the raincoat didn't shut the gate after she drove through. I was parked on the side of the road and followed her in. If the gate's open, it's not trespassing."

She huffed. Eve had no idea who the woman in the raincoat was, but this warrior wannabe had a warped notion of what constituted trespassing.

"She didn't have on any clothes underneath the coat," he added a moment later. "When she opened her car door to press in the code for the gate, she put her foot on the ground so she could lean in better. The side of her raincoat came open, and I saw her hoo-hoo and ta-tas."

"Too much information," Eve muttered. "And this is private property. You need to leave right now."

Normally, she didn't feel threatened by the hornies. Only frustrated that they seemingly had too much time on their hands. But this guy was big, and her baby was just inside the house. So was Cassidy. And Eve considered calling out to her, but she wasn't ready to sound the alarm just yet.

He came even closer, and even though most of his head was covered with the bulky hood, she could see his face. He was probably about Tessie's age, maybe younger, and she saw the disillusionment when he studied her.

"You don't look like Ulyana," he said. "She's beautiful, and you're, well, just okay. You're kinda old, and your body's a little...squishy."

Gee, this wasn't doing much for her ego, but it would make it easier for her to be rude and send this Swaron running. But before she could do that, she heard someone who was already running. With her head clearing, she had no trouble making out the footsteps this time.

And she saw the blur of motion as it went past her.

The blur was Lawson, and he cut right in between her and the Swaron. "What the hell are you doing here?" Lawson snarled to the intruder, and he had the menacing tone down pat.

"Uh" was all the teenager managed before he volleyed some nervous glances between Lawson and her. In the middle of those glances, he turned and took off.

Lawson looked ready to chase him down, but Eve caught his arm. "It's okay. Let him go."

"Did he hurt you?" Lawson snapped.

And that's when she noticed Lawson's body language. For one thing, he was out of breath, and since his truck wasn't there, it likely meant he'd run—in cowboy boots—from his place to hers. The muscles in his neck were corded, his right hand was in a fist and his eyes were narrowed to slits.

And that's when she noticed her own body language.

She had the bottle of aphid spray poised in the air, the way someone would wield a weapon. She probably looked a little on the defensive, too. That meant Lawson had thought she was in danger and had come to her rescue.

Wow.

That gave her a nice, warm feeling that chased away the bruised ego from the Swaron. She tried not to read too much into it though. After all, Lawson obviously hadn't wanted to be near her in Austin, and that's why he'd taken off the way he had.

Lawson clearly wasn't feeling nice or warm though. He whipped out his phone and made a call to police chief Clay McKinnon to tell him that he wanted the "asshole in the Grim Reaper cape" arrested. Even though Lawson didn't put the call on speaker, Eve was close enough that she heard Clay tell him that he'd send someone out right away.

When Lawson finished the call, Eve was about to assure him that she was okay, but he hooked his arm around her waist and got her moving toward the porch. "Wait inside, and I'll go looking for that idiot. How'd he get onto the ranch, anyway?"

"He said some half-naked woman in a raincoat left the gate open. I figure it was someone coming to see Dylan."

Lawson turned toward her so fast that his neck popped, and he did some more cursing. She didn't know what to make of that, but when they went into the house, his cursing stopped. For a couple of seconds, anyway. Then he uttered some more after he did a double take. Eve didn't approve of cussing near the baby, but in this case, it was warranted.

"Shit," Lawson spit out. "What the heck is that?"

Good question, and Eve had another look at the massive stuffed animal to see if she could figure it out. She didn't have any better luck identifying it now than she had when it'd been delivered about an hour earlier. If

Jabba the Hutt and a mutant koala had had a baby to-gether, it might resemble this creature. Of course, it also looked like a thirty-pound blob of hairy mucus.

"It's from Kellan," she said. She set down the bottle of aphid spray and checked the baby monitor to make sure Aiden was still asleep. He was. "It's a *gift* for Aiden."

Lawson made a face. Maybe because he, too, was hav-ing trouble understanding why anyone would consider that ugly thing gift material for anyone. "So, Kellan's seeing the baby," he commented.

"No. He just keeps sending creatures like that. Actu-ally, I'd rather see the creatures than him, so it's a good trade-off."

Lawson made another face.

She'd probably already said too much, but that didn't stop her from adding, "That should tell you just how much I don't want to see Kellan."

Yes, it was too much, and Lawson no longer seemed interested in running after the Swaron intruder. "You two had a falling-out?"

Anything she said at this point would only lead to more TMI and possible questions from Lawson, but he had more or less rescued her, so the least she could do was answer him. "Kellan and I were never actually together to have a falling-out. I had a one-night stand with him after Tessie and I got into a big argument."

That made her sound impulsive and stupid. Which she had been. No one could tag her with labels any worse than those she'd already given herself.

"Tessie," Lawson repeated. But he seemed to be speaking to himself rather than her.

Lawson muttered their daughter's name again, didn't make another face, though, or even look at her. He went into the adjacent family room and peered out the bay window. Maybe keeping watch for the Swaron in case he returned. He also glanced at the three stacks of boxes that were next to the coffee table.

"That's some stuff that arrived from my house in California," she said, though he didn't ask for an explanation. "I haven't had a chance to go through it."

The boxes were all labeled with things like baby clothes, photos and such, but one in particular seemed to flash at her like a neon light. It was the box with *Lawson, etc.* written on it in black marker. No way did she want to go through it with Lawson right there, so she stepped in front of it. But Lawson's attention definitely wasn't on the boxes. He was still looking out the window.

"The intruder won't be back," Eve insisted. "He came here looking for Ulyana and was disappointed when he found me instead. He said I was old and that my body was squishy."

That caused Lawson to glance back at her. Except it didn't stay a glance with those scorcher eyes. He slid a slow look over her from head to toe, and he didn't linger on the squishy parts. However, he did linger a bit on her mouth. His gaze shifted from one side of her lips to the other before settling right in the middle. In the exact spot that would get the brunt of a kiss. If he kissed her, that is, and it certainly felt as if he had.

Mercy. It felt like foreplay, too.

And sex.

She was warm and tingly in a place that hadn't been tingled in a very long time. That part of her was sending her a rather strong reminder of that.

Lawson finally looked away from her, his attention

leaving her mouth, and he turned as if to go out the door. It reminded her of how fast he'd moved in Austin.

"Why don't you wait here with us until Clay arrives?" she asked.

Having him here was playing with fire, and Eve blamed the tingling. She wasn't ready for him to go just yet even if his going would probably be a good thing.

She saw the debate in his eyes, but in the end, he stayed put, probably because he was indeed concerned about her and the baby's safety. He came back into the family room, but his attention landed on the binoculars on the table by the window.

"Dylan," he grumbled. "He gave me a pair, too."

Because Eve's mind was still in the sex mode, it took her a moment to follow through on what Lawson was no doubt thinking. "I swear, I don't use them to look at you. Well, I did once, but that was only because Dylan left a note saying I should use them to look, and I didn't know exactly what I'd be seeing. And that's the only time."

Now she was babbling, and apparently confessing, too, because Eve added even more.

"But Cassidy has used them a time or two to try to get a glimpse of Lucian. She has a mini-fixation on him," Eve added when Lawson glanced back at her. His raised eyebrow caused her to add even more. "Cassidy has a thing for bad boys."

A muscle flickered in his jaw. "Lucian's not a bad boy. He's a son of a bitch. Big difference."

Yes, it was a big difference, and yes, it was true about Lucian.

"Steer Cassidy away from him if you can," Lawson added, and again, he turned back to the window.

"I'll try, but Cassidy can be stubborn about that sort of thing. She's in her room," Eve explained when Lawson glanced at the stairs as if looking for her. "She's working on illustrations for a kids' book."

Possibly spying, too. Eve wouldn't mention that Cassidy had ordered her own binoculars and that her room upstairs faced the direction of the Granger house where Lucian stayed when he wasn't at one of his other two homes.

"Were you able to patch things up with Tessie?" Lawson asked several moments later.

His question got the discussion off the privacy-invading housewarming gift from Dylan, but that didn't mean this conversation was going to be any more comfortable. "No. I saw her, but only briefly."

Eve cursed the tears that threatened again. Lawson cursed, too, when he noticed them.

"I saw you crying earlier," he said. "While you were in the garden. Don't worry. I won't be using the binoculars again to spy on you."

It hadn't occurred to her how Lawson had known about the Swaron intruder, but he'd obviously been following Dylan's instructions as she had done. That gave her a different twist in her stomach. She'd been sweaty, blubbering and not looking her best, and Lawson had seen her like that. Heck, he was still seeing her that way minus a little less sweat now that she was in the A/C.

"I need to run to the bathroom," she grumbled and had started in that direction when there was some crying. Not her this time. It was Aiden, and the sound was coming from the baby monitor in her pocket.

Freshening herself up would have to wait, and instead she headed for the nursery. "I'll get him," she called out to Cassidy.

Because she thought both Lawson and she could use it—Aiden, too—she took her time changing the baby's diaper and washing up again. She gave Aiden some extra kisses before she made her way back to the family room. Lawson was still there, still keeping watch at the window.

Aiden grinned a big gummy grin at Lawson. He was a happy baby—most of the time, anyway—but he rarely smiled at strangers, making her wonder if he sensed that Lawson had been the one to bring him into the world. Or maybe the baby just felt her heartbeat rev up whenever Lawson was around.

Lawson gave Aiden a small grin back and brushed his fingers over the baby's toes. "He's getting big."

Yes, he was growing fast. And getting hungry. Aiden turned his head, brushing his mouth against her nipple. She wouldn't put him off too long, but Eve wanted to wait a few more minutes for Clay to arrive. Then Lawson would almost certainly leave. To stave off Aiden a little while, she put him against her shoulder and gently rocked him.

"You redecorated," Lawson said, turning back to the window. "The place looks better."

It did, but the bar had been set pretty low when it came to the previous decor. "Your mother seemed to have been aiming for a Vegas showgirls theme. Lots of red, feathers and sequins."

Come to think of it, that's how Regina Granger dressed, too. Like the hornies and their time management, she had not used her champagne budget wisely.

"Are you still upset that your mom sold me the

house?" Eve asked. When Aiden kept squirming, she moved him back to the crook of her arm.

"Yes." He huffed, looked back at her again. "Why exactly do you think she did that? I mean, she got this house as part of her divorce settlement twenty years ago, and before you bought it, it'd been empty for nearly a decade. So, why sell it?"

"She said it was because the house needed some attention and love."

His next huff was louder. "She's up to something. Possibly matchmaking."

Eve had to shake her head. "Matchmaking for us?"

"No. I suspect she's looking at you as a wife for Dylan."

The laugh just burst out of her and was so loud that it startled Aiden. He jumped, his little arms and legs flying out, and he started to fuss, so Eve rocked him again. "Dylan's like a brother to me."

She winced, though, because the reason she felt that way was because as a teenager, she'd spun so many fantasies about Lawson and her getting married—that was despite Lawson repeatedly telling her that marriage for him was never going to happen. Regina had helped fuel them by making it known that she wanted all of her children to give her grandkids. Eve had given up on the fantasy of marrying Lawson, but that didn't stop her from filling in the blanks on what he was telling her.

She tossed out there, "Your mother wants me with Dylan and you with Darby."

Lawson certainly didn't toss that theory right back at her. Which meant he believed it was true.

Well, Regina was obviously in the Team Darby camp. And Eve had to admit that it made sense. If Regina wanted Lawson to settle down and have a family, then she'd prefer someone like Darby to have her first grandchild. Little did Regina know, though, that she already had a granddaughter.

A granddaughter who Eve would tell both Lawson and her about as soon as Tessie knew the truth about the identity of her father.

Eve had attempted to do just that on the visit to Austin, but she'd failed. When Eve had spotted Tessie on the stairs in the sorority building, her daughter had hurried off, refusing to say anything to Eve other than that she didn't want to talk to her.

Aiden, however, wasn't refusing to *speak*. His fussing got even louder, and he rooted around on the front of her shirt until he located her nipple. Her son apparently didn't want to wait any longer for his dinner.

"I need to nurse him." That was all Eve had to say to get Lawson's forehead to bunch up, and he started toward the front door.

"Lock up after I go out," he said. "I'll have a look around the place while I'm waiting for Clay."

Even though she doubted there was a need for it, she did indeed lock the door behind him, and she lifted her top so she could unhook the cup of her nursing bra. Aiden wasted no time latching on.

While she nursed him, she went back to the window to have her own look around, but she stayed back from the glass so that if Lawson happened to stroll by, he wouldn't see her with her boob hanging out. As expected, there was no sign of the Swaron warrior.

Since the binoculars were right there on the table, Eve used them to have a better look. Lawson was making his way to the road where he no doubt intended to meet up with Clay once he arrived.

A glint of sunlight on metal caught her eye, and for a moment she thought it might be Clay's cruiser. But this was coming from Lawson's house. She groaned, hoping the Swaron hadn't gone there.

He hadn't.

When Eve shifted the binoculars in that direction, she saw the woman in Lawson's doorway. A woman wearing a raincoat.

Darby.

Like Eve, she had a pair of binoculars pressed to her eyes. And Darby seemed to have her attention aimed at Eve.

The wind shifted the side of Darby's raincoat, and even though Eve didn't need further proof that this was the very woman who had left the gate open, she got confirmation anyway. Because with that shift of the raincoat, Eve got a glimpse of something.

A hoo-hoo that was no doubt waiting for Lawson to return.

CHAPTER TEN

LAWSON DROPPED DOWN on his bed, wondering if there was anyone else in the entire state of Texas who'd had such a shitty day as his. Running off a dickhead Swaron who had decent escape skills, his own personal lusting after Eve and then turning away a half-naked woman—Darby—who'd been waiting for him after he'd finally made it back home.

He wasn't sure which of those three things bothered him the most. He hadn't wanted to hurt Darby, had wanted the Swaron caught and locked up, but the one that would likely give him the most trouble was Eve. And that was the thought running through his mind when he finally fell asleep.

Ironic that with all the lusting, it wasn't Eve who first came to him in the dream. It was Brett.

Lawson knew he was dreaming, but he couldn't make it stop. Couldn't force himself to wake up. So, he had no choice but to relive the bits and pieces he remembered. Things that should have never happened in the first place.

But they had.

And the nightmares reminded him of that way too often.

Just as it had that night, the dream started with laughter and fun at Brett's house. Brett's folks were out of town visiting relatives, and Lawson and Brett hadn't wasted any time putting together a party. Complete with plenty of beer that they'd sweet-talked the convenience-store clerk into selling them.

Lawson had been good at sweet talk in those days.

Eve was there at the party, of course, and he'd seen that look burning in her eyes. He hadn't hesitated even for a second when she'd kissed him, and he'd felt that kick of pleasure that he always got whenever she was around him.

Brett had laughed when he'd spotted them in the corner and had yelled out *get a room*. Unlike Eve's eyes, Brett's were already glazed over from the "sweet-talked" beer he'd been drinking most of the night. Lawson and Eve had indeed gotten a room. They'd gone to Brett's bedroom upstairs, where they'd had sex.

While their friend was dying.

Of course, Lawson didn't remember any of the dying part. He'd crashed shortly after having sex with Eve and didn't recall anything until he heard the frantic shouts for someone to call an ambulance.

Later, Lawson would learn that Brett's blood alcohol level was .30 percent. That would have been way too high even if he hadn't been underage. And it had apparently been high enough for Brett to slip into a coma.

Lawson hadn't checked on his friend. Because he'd gone to sleep. But Eve had gone downstairs to get a glass of water, and she'd seen Brett passed out on the sofa. Even in the dream, Lawson knew that hindsight was 20/20, that there had been no logical reason for a seventeen-year-old girl to make sure her friend wasn't so drunk that it was going to kill him.

However, hindsight didn't give Lawson any peace.

The nightmares still came. The guilt stayed like a meaty fist clamped around his heart. And it wouldn't go away, no matter how many years he grieved. Because that night, he'd lost a part of himself. And he'd ultimately lost Eve since that was the last time they were together.

Those were the thoughts that were right at the front of his mind when Lawson finally managed to force himself awake. Even after his eyes opened though, he could still see the images. Still hear the sounds the medics made that night as they tried, and failed, to save Brett's life. But even that hadn't been the end of it. Brett had lingered for several days before his family had been forced to accept he was brain-dead and pull the plug on his life support.

No way did he want to go back to sleep with those images still so fresh in his mind. The nightmare would just come again.

In that moment, he hated whiskey, hated himself for needing it. It was a familiar feeling, and Lawson knew the outcome.

He didn't pour himself a shot.

Because he had a trick to counter the need. He imagined the drink in Brett's hand. Imagined the kid who was more of a brother than a friend dying because Brett had not only poured the shot but had also drunk it. And the other shots he'd poured, too.

There was no trick, though, to deal with the pain and emotion. Well, no trick that Lawson had found yet, anyway. So, he did what he couldn't seem to stop himself from doing.

He remembered every detail he could remember. Letting it repeat in his head. Letting the pain that he deserved eat away at him.

"THE MAILMAN JUST delivered two more gifts," Cassidy called out.

Eve knew that hearing something like that didn't usually cause people to groan, but most people didn't have to deal with Kellan's steady stream of creepy stuffed toys. The stream had tapered off, however, and since it'd been a month since the green snot blob had arrived, Eve had thought maybe Kellan had forgotten about Aiden. Apparently not though.

She hit the save button on her computer for the spreadsheet that she'd been working on, and while trying to brace herself for whatever levels of depravity she might face, Eve went into the foyer. No visible depravity though. There was a bouquet of flowers and a wrapped gift box on the table. It was much too small to contain the behemoth-sized gifts that Kellan had been sending, but Cassidy was still eyeing it with concern.

The person who wasn't concerned was Aiden. Cassidy had him on her hip, and the moment he spotted Eve, he grinned and clapped his hands. But it was no longer just a gummy grin. The little speck of white was a tooth that had appeared a couple of days earlier.

All of the parenting books had said that three months old was early for teething, but Aiden had proved the books wrong. He'd also used that tiny tooth to bite the devil out of her when he nursed. And that was the reason Cassidy now had a bottle in her hand. Eve missed nursing him, but she didn't miss the pain. Besides, she could still hold him close when she gave him the bottle.

Eve went to the flowers first. A dozen red roses. When she pulled out the card, the relief came. Not from Kellan trying to make some attempt to romance her.

"It's from Mrs. Hattersfield. She was my high school drama teacher."

Cassidy looked over her shoulder and read the card. "'Here's hoping you'll come by the new drama center soon at Wrangler's Creek High. Welcome home, Eve.' Ah, that's nice."

Yes, it was, but Eve imagined how this would play out. The high school students were about the same age as that ego-bruising Swaron and probably wouldn't think much of an aging Ulyana.

Eve put aside the card from the flowers and tackled the box next.

"Kellan?" Cassidy asked when Eve opened it.

No, but when she took the contents out of the box, it still caused her to groan. Because it was another pair of binoculars almost identical to the ones Dylan had given her. The very ones that Eve had used when she'd seen a nearly naked Darby in Lawson's house. After that, Eve had shut the binoculars in a storage closet and vowed never to use them again. No way did she want to see Darby making booty-call trips to see Lawson.

Eve took out the card to see who would be so misguided as to send her another pair. "'Regina,'" she read aloud.

"Lawson's mom?" Cassidy asked, leaning in to read the card, as well.

Eve nodded. "'A little gift to spice up your life,'" Regina had written. "'Take them to your kitchen window and have a peek.'"

That caused Eve to groan again because she knew what she'd see out that particular window. The Granger house. And she just might get a glimpse of Dylan.

While she liked Dylan, she wouldn't get much of a thrill spying on him.

"Matchmaking," Cassidy concluded. She gave both the note and the binoculars some stink eye.

Eve had filled Cassidy in on what Lawson had said about his mother, and what had happened with the raincoat episode. Cassidy, being the good friend that she was, had assured her that maybe nothing had happened between Darby and Lawson, that maybe Lawson had sent a nearly naked attractive woman away once he made it back to his house.

Part of Eve had wanted to latch on to that because she was pathetic and delusional. She was still clinging just a little bit to those old fantasies of her being with Lawson. And she was still clinging a lot to the lust she still felt for him. What had helped cool her down some was the fact she hadn't seen hide nor hair of Lawson in the month since that'd happened. Of course, he'd done a great job of avoiding her since she'd moved back to Wrangler's Creek, so maybe this latest avoidance had nothing to do with Darby.

"Say, when are you going to finish going through the rest of the boxes in the family room?" Cassidy asked, and she headed back in that direction. "Especially the one marked *Lawson, etc.*"

Eve followed her though it wasn't necessary for her to see which boxes Cassidy meant. She certainly hadn't forgotten about them, and while the neat freak in her wanted them cleared up, she hadn't quite brought herself to go through the last two. Because in addition to *Lawson, etc.*, the other was labeled *high school crap*. Eve had packed them away years ago—eighteen, to be exact—and while she couldn't remember everything that was in them, she was certain some of the things were going to trigger a trip down misery lane.

"I can open them for you if you like," Cassidy volunteered. Then she mumbled some G-rated profanity under her breath. "Okay, I've already peeked. I know what's in them."

Eve huffed though she wasn't really surprised or upset. Cassidy was nosy, but she might have been looking for anything that she felt would be too much for Eve to handle.

"Well?" Eve prompted. "What's the verdict?"

"You'll be okay with the high school junk." Cassidy obviously knew exactly what Eve was talking about. "Yearbooks, drama-club stuff and a plaque for chess-club champion. I didn't even know you knew how to play chess."

"I have layers," Eve grumbled. The studio had known about her being a chess champion, but it hadn't gone with Ulyana's kick-ass image, so they'd told her not to mention it. Ditto for her love of gardening. "What about the Lawson box?"

"Possible land mines throughout it. Pictures of you two. You obviously couldn't keep your hands off him. And vice versa. There's a junior rodeo buckle. More layers?" Cassidy asked.

"No, it was Lawson's. He won it after he let a bull sling him around like a rag doll for eight seconds, and then he gave the buckle to me. Possibly while he was mildly concussed and had a dislocated shoulder."

"Awww, romantic in a cowboy, heavy testosterone kind of way." Cassidy paused. "There's also a dress in a plastic bag. Crud," she quietly added several moments later. "Judging from the look on your face, it's a land mine, not a layer."

Yes, to the land mine, but now that Eve knew it was there, she figured she had to face it. She set the binoculars aside, ripped the tape off the box, and the moment she opened it, she saw the dress on top. It was rose pink, strapless, and even though Eve couldn't actually see it because of the way it was folded, it had a corset back. And she'd intended to use those ties to make sure it gloved her figure—which was more flat than curvy in those days.

Cassidy stared at it when Eve held it up in front of her. No way would it fit now. "Was it for the prom?"

Eve shook her head, but it was a good guess because Cassidy knew that she'd moved from Wrangler's Creek before the senior prom, so she hadn't gone to it. "It was for the Sadie Hawkins dance. And yes, we still had them back then."

"You mean a dance where the girl asked the guy to go with her?"

"That's the one. I asked Lawson, of course." In fact, she'd asked him that December, two months prior to the dance. Not that either of them would have gone with anyone else—not at that point in their relationship, anyway.

"I spent every penny of my babysitting savings on this," Eve added. She ran her thumb over the beading in the bodice. "And for weeks, I dreamed about Lawson dancing with me in that dress."

"Dancing?" Cassidy questioned. "Lawson had a dancing layer?"

"No. He'd never danced with me before, but it was one of my fantasies. That night, that dress, Lawson, and me telling him that I wanted to spend the rest of my life with him."

"How sweet. Or not," Cassidy amended when she looked at her again. The "or not" was probably because Eve's expression wasn't that of a gushing sweet teenager who'd been in love.

"I'd never said anything like that," Eve explained. "Lawson had a problem with the c-word. Not that c-word," she quickly added. "Commitment. He made sure he worked it into conversations at least once a week that he was never getting married. Or having kids," Eve added.

Cassidy stared at her. "Shit."

She didn't even scold her for cursing because Eve was silently saying the same thing. "Lawson didn't have a happy childhood, and he thought he'd end up being as lousy of a parent as his own dad." Eve looked at the dress again. "But that night I was going for it. Heck, I remember thinking that once he knew I wanted to be with him forever, he might tell me he loved me and ask me to marry him."

Cassidy stared at her. "You were both seventeen and hadn't even finished high school yet."

Eve shrugged. "Obviously, I was thinking like a seventeen-year-old."

But that had changed a few weeks later with Brett's death, and then she'd left town. There'd been no Sadie Hawkins dance for her. No prom. No graduation. Instead, Eve had gotten her GED and never looked back.

Not until now, anyway.

Since looking back was putting her in a blue mood, Eve stuffed the dress back in the box and nearly told Cassidy to donate it to the town's resale charity shop.

But for now, out of sight, out of mind would work, and she would put the boxes in the attic.

"I'm sorry." Cassidy gave her arm a pat. Aiden reached out as if he might try to pat her, too, but then he rubbed his eyes and whined a little. "It's time for his nap," Cassidy said, glancing at her watch.

Eve was about to volunteer to put him to bed so she could get in some snuggling time with her little guy, but her phone rang before she could reach out for him. When she saw the name on the screen, she knew she needed to answer right away.

"Tessie," she answered, her breath already racing.

Cassidy smiled, made a toodle-do wave and headed upstairs with the baby, no doubt so that Eve would have some privacy. She might need it, too. The last time Tessie had called her, it hadn't gone well.

"Thanks for the care package," Tessie greeted her. Except it wasn't much of a greeting. Her voice was stiff as if talking to a stranger. But maybe Tessie did feel as if she didn't really know her own mother. After all, Eve had lied to her for years.

"You're welcome. I thought you might want some of your favorite snacks for your room now that the new semester's started." In fact, Eve had another box ready to go. "How are your classes? Are they hard? And how are you?" Eve clamped her teeth over her bottom lip to stop herself from adding even more questions.

"Everything's fine."

It wasn't, and it crushed Eve's heart to feel this distance from her daughter. "I was hoping I could bring Aiden to see you."

"No." Eve would have felt a little better if Tessie had hesitated at least a second or two. "I'm not ready for that yet." Now she hesitated. "But keep sending me pictures of him. He's my brother no matter what happened between us."

Yes, he was, and Eve supposed she was going to have to be satisfied with that. For now. But it couldn't stay that way. "Tessie, we eventually need to talk. There are some things I have to tell you."

"Right. Okay. Right," she repeated. Now Tessie sounded flustered and annoyed. "Maybe during fall break."

Since Eve had memorized the school calendar, she knew that was still over a month away, but she latched on to it as a glimmer of hope. And dread. Because she was going to have to tell Tessie about Lawson. That wouldn't necessarily cause the rift to deepen between Tessie and her, but once Tessie knew, Eve would tell Lawson. A *rift* might be the least of his reactions.

"Your birthday is before fall break," Eve reminded her. "There must be something on your wish list that I can send to you."

"Not really. Just keep a running total of tuition and my expenses so I know how much to pay you back."

That caused Eve to sigh. She didn't want her daughter paying her back for college, but Tessie had insisted on it. Plus, it really wasn't that much since Tessie had a great scholarship that covered a good chunk of it.

"I wanted you to know that I had my stuff shipped from the house in LA to a storage unit here in Austin," Tessie added a moment later. "I won't be going back there, so if you want to sell the place, that's fine with me."

Eve had been so busy with the baby that she hadn't thought much about selling the LA house. But she certainly thought about it now. Even though it'd never felt like home, it was where she'd raised Tessie. It was also where Tessie and she had had their falling-out. She had no immediate plans to move back there, either, but she'd considered keeping it just in case.

"Does that mean you'll be staying in Austin?" Eve asked.

"Probably. I can finish my undergrad here and then go to A&M for Veterinary Medicine."

So, Tessie was sticking to her plan. Well, her revised plan, anyway. Before the rift between them, Tessie had been considering other schools, but her major had always stayed the same. She'd wanted to be a veterinarian since first grade, when Eve had taken her for riding lessons.

"Who was the cowboy cop who came to the sorority house last month?" Tessie asked.

Eve's muscles went stiff because she doubted that Clay had gone there. "Do you mean Lawson Granger? If so, he's not a cop. He's a rancher. I went to high school with him."

Because she was talking about him, Eve picked up the new binoculars and went to the window to have a look. Lawson was there all right. With Vita. They were in the yard and appeared to be trying to catch a chicken.

If she hadn't been chatting with Tessie, that would have definitely held her attention and caused her to break her no-spying rule, but Eve also thought of something else. Something that sent her stomach to her kneecaps.

"Uh, I didn't realize you'd seen Lawson that day," Eve commented, and she tried not to sound panicked.

Silence. For a very long time. Oh, no. Had Tessie seen him and then noticed the resemblance between them?

"Why'd he come to Austin?" Tessie finally asked. What she hadn't done was respond to Eve's statement.

"He was traveling through on business, and his aunt asked him to check on you. She knew I was worried about you, and Lawson didn't know I'd be there." But Eve had certainly known about his visit, and that's why she'd rushed there.

"So, you didn't ask him to come?"

God, no. But Eve tamped down her emotions enough to give a hopefully calm answer. "I didn't."

"And he didn't say anything about me?" Tessie quickly added.

Eve had to tamp down even more emotions. Mainly fear. This was what happened when you lived a lie. You were always afraid of being outed, which meant Lawson and Tessie needed to know the truth.

"Lawson was just worried about you," Eve settled for saying. She took a deep breath, ready to insist that Tessie and she meet so they could talk. However, Tessie spoke before Eve had even finished her breath.

"Mom, I have to go. 'Bye."

"Wait!" But she was talking to the air because Tessie had already ended the call.

Eve sighed. She really did need to practice exactly how she was going to tell Tessie the news. Also, since it was highly likely that Tessie wouldn't see her anytime soon, Eve also needed to practice saying it very quickly to get it all out before another hang-up.

Frustrated, she scrubbed her hand over her face and peeked out through the binoculars again. The chicken-chase was still going on and had escalated. Lawson had taken off his shirt and appeared to be using it to try to grab the running chicken.

The chicken was winning.

It was like an old Keystone Cops scene playing out in front of her. Except that the cop had never looked that good. It was a reminder of why they'd become lovers in the first place. Lawson was still Hot Cowboy.

She watched as he lunged forward, causing all those muscles to respond to the movement. Eve responded, too, and she suddenly wished she were the chicken when Lawson scooped it up in his shirt and held it against his chest. Once, he'd held her that way. Well, not with her head wrapped in his shirt, but Eve remembered in complete detail what it was like to be in his arms.

Vita went to Lawson, extracted the chicken from the shirt and took it from him. That brought an end to the chase. And the peep show, because he put his shirt back on. With the chicken now tucked under her arm, Vita headed to her bicycle, which was leaning against Lawson's truck.

He said something to the old woman, probably an offer to give her a ride, but Vita waved him off and peddled away, somehow managing to keep hold of both the chicken and the handlebars. Lawson watched her for a few seconds before he went to his porch. He stopped though, and with his back to Eve, he stayed there a few seconds before he glanced over his shoulder.

At her.

Or rather in her direction.

That sent Eve scurrying back in case he could see

her. She doubted that he actually could, but her heart was sprinting as if she'd just gotten caught doing something she shouldn't have been doing. Which she was.

Lawson didn't make the glance a lingering one. Instead, he went inside. There was nothing particularly life-changing about the moment, but it hit Eve like a slam from a rodeo bull. She needed to amend her plan about telling Tessie and give the news to Lawson first. That way, maybe they could tell Tessie together. And there was no time better than the present to fill in Lawson, so before she could talk herself out of it, she pulled her phone from her pocket and called him.

She hadn't thought it possible, but her heart rate went up a notch with the first ring. It went up even more with the second. By the fourth ring, Eve thought she might be about to go into cardiac arrest.

And then the call went to voice mail.

His recorded greeting was short and sweet. "This is Lawson Granger. Leave me a message."

Eve didn't do that. She would just call him back later. After the chicken-chase, he'd probably headed straight to the shower.

Or not.

She peered through the binoculars again and saw him at the back of his house. He was drinking a beer and looking out at the creek. Maybe he'd forgotten to take his phone outside with him.

At the exact moment she had that thought, he took his phone from his jeans pocket and glanced at it. Then he glanced in her direction again. A missed call with her name on it was likely on his screen. Eve kept watching, waiting to see what he was going to do, and she tried to steel herself for him to call her back. The steeling took a nosedive though when her phone rang, the sound causing her to shriek like a schoolgirl.

But it wasn't Lawson. It was his cousin Sophie.

Since Sophie hadn't called her in weeks, Eve answered as fast as she could get her fingers working. She hoped nothing had gone wrong.

"How many baby throw-up stains do you have on the shirt you're wearing right now?" Sophie immediately asked.

It certainly wasn't a question Eve got every day, but she knew where this was going since Sophie was the mom of toddler twins. "Only one. But you caught me on a good day." Eve smiled. "How about you?"

"I've graduated from throw-up to food stains. My son can squish a pea between his index finger and thumb and then flick it in the same motion. My daughter pretends her mouth is the blowhole of a whale and spews out apple juice."

Eve laughed. Sophie wasn't making motherhood sound fun or sanitary, but she'd seen Sophie with the twins and knew that motherhood suited her.

"And that brings me to why I'm calling," Sophie went on. "Want a girls' night out, one where we can wear unstained clothes, speak in complete sentences and not have to change a diaper?"

"Does such a night exist?" Eve joked. "After three months, I can't remember."

"Oh, yes. It exists all right. How about a week from this Saturday at the Longhorn Bar? That'll give you some time to get a sitter because I also want you to bring your friend Cassidy. I'll bring Mila and Nicky."

Mila was Roman's wife and Nicky was married to Sophie's other brother, Garrett. Eve knew them both and had even seen them around town, but she hadn't had time to catch up with what was going on in their lives.

"A sitter?" Eve repeated.

Now Sophie chuckled. "Yeah, I know. You probably haven't left him with a sitter other than Cassidy, but there are several good ones in town. I'll text you a list, and if none of them are available, you can try Karlee's cousin."

Eve knew Karlee O'Malley, as well. She was Lucian's assistant, but Eve didn't remember the woman having a cousin, only Karlee's brothers. There were three, maybe four of them.

"So, we're on?" Sophie pressed.

"Sure." But Eve thought there was a good chance she'd cancel. Aiden was almost certainly ready to stay with a sitter, but she wasn't sure she was.

"How's Lawson, by the way?" Sophie asked.

Eve didn't think that was a casual question, and she certainly didn't want to confess that it'd only been minutes since her last Lawson sighting. She glanced through the binoculars again to update the timing of that sighting, but Lawson was no longer in the yard.

"Uh, why do you ask?" Eve countered.

"Just wondering since you're practically neighbors now. And I haven't seen him in a while. He seems to be taking a lot of business trips lately. I think he's trying to avoid Darby."

"More likely he's trying to avoid me." Eve muttered that a little louder than planned. She hadn't intended for Sophie to hear.

"No, definitely Darby," Sophie argued. "A couple of weeks ago, I walked into his office at the ranch, and Lawson was holding a copy of one of those old tabloids with you on the cover. He was staring at it but put it away when I saw him."

Lawson was more likely glaring at it rather than staring.

"And he was touching it," Sophie added.

Eve did a mental double take. "He was doing what?"

"Touching it," Sophie repeated. "It was hard to tell from the angle where I was standing, but it looked as if he was running his fingers over the picture of your face."

Eve didn't intend to read anything into that. He could have been brushing off crumbs he'd dropped there from his lunch. "Why'd he have a copy of a magazine like that, anyway?"

"Tate's girlfriend, Arwen. Have you met Tate yet?"

"Yes. He's Roman's son. I saw them together in town the other day."

"Well, Arwen is a fan of *Demon High* and has watched all the episodes. She got some magazines from eBay and left them there with him so he could ask you about signing them. Lawson didn't mention anything about doing that?"

"It probably slipped his mind." And she hoped he hadn't tossed the girl's magazines just so he wouldn't have to see her to get the autographs. Just in case he'd done that, Eve would make sure to send her some signed copies.

Sophie huffed. "Not to worry. I'll get them from Lawson and bring them to the Longhorn for our girls' night out. See you then."

Sophie obviously didn't catch the "maybe" that Eve tossed out there before Sophie ended the call. It was a slim maybe, too, but she would at least look into getting a sitter in case there was some kind of emergency in the future.

She put her phone back in her pocket and had one final peek through the binoculars. Still no sign of Lawson, so Eve shifted them to the other side of his house where there was a grove of pecan trees.

And that's when she saw the monster.

A hairy blob with giant eyeballs.

She let out a garbled scream and scurried back, bashing into the sofa. The collision off-balanced her, and she fell onto the cushions. She got up as fast as she could, taking out her phone again to call 911. But when she looked out the window, there was no monster.

Just Lawson.

His face was only a few inches from the glass. Without the magnification of the binocular lens, he no longer looked monstrous. Though he did look confused.

"Is everything okay?" Cassidy called out.

"Fine," Eve managed to say, but there was no way she sounded fine. Her heart was somewhere in the vicinity of her toenails, and she was certain she was beet red from blushing.

Because Lawson had caught her spying.

Dreading what he might say about that, she went to the door and opened it. She didn't have to wait long to see him since he was already on the porch.

"I didn't want to knock or ring the bell in case the baby was sleeping, so when I spotted you in the window, I thought I'd get your attention," he said. "Uh, are you all right?"

Eve repeated that lie of a response. "Fine." And he had gotten her attention.

She definitely wasn't *fine* though, but Lawson sure

seemed to be. His face was a little misted with sweat. Not the kind that made you beet red from embarrassment, either. This was the sort of stuff added to underwear models' chiseled faces for a photo shoot.

And speaking of underwear, she could see the top of his boxer shorts. That's because he'd missed some of the bottom buttons on his shirt, and he hadn't tucked it in. Since his jeans were low on his hips, she could see his stomach and belly button. Usually she didn't consider navels to have any sexual appeal, but they apparently did on Lawson. Ditto for those boxers.

There'd been times when she had run her hand right down into his jeans to touch him. Times when her mouth had been in that general vicinity, too. She'd never managed to give him a successful blow job, mainly because she hadn't known how, but she'd gotten pretty darn close back when they'd been seventeen.

"Are you sure you're okay?" she heard him repeat.

That's when Eve realized she was staring at the front of his jeans. And it was when she realized, too, that Lawson had noticed where she was staring. Great. Now she'd embarrassed herself twice in under a minute.

"Uh, did you want something?" Eve asked.

Lawson tipped his head to his pocket where she could see his phone. "I'd put my phone on silent when I was…well, trying to catch a chicken. Don't ask," he quickly added. "But when I finally looked at the screen, I saw that you'd called me."

Yes, that. At the time, it'd seemed like the right thing to do, but that was before she'd gotten all hot from her *hand-in-his-pants* memories. Eve wasn't sure what she was going to say to him, and she soon realized not speaking wasn't a big deal.

"Damn you," he snarled.

Even though that didn't sound like it was the start of something good, it was. Lawson slung his hand around the back of her neck, yanked her to him. And he did the last thing on earth that Eve expected.

He kissed her.

LAWSON DIDN'T HAVE to think about this. Plain and simple, it was a mistake. One that he seemed hell-bent on making, so he just decided to go with it so it'd be a mistake worth making.

Eve obviously hadn't been toying with dirty thoughts as he had thought because she made a sound of surprise when he kissed her. That sound sort of got trapped there in between their lips, and it mingled well with the next sound she made.

A little purr of pleasure.

He knew that purr. Knew the feel of her body against his when she slipped right into his arms. It was like coming home, a birthday, losing his virginity and Christmas all rolled into one. Except this particular celebration was going to give him a raging hard-on. And regrets.

Best not to forget that part.

There'd definitely be regrets, and it wouldn't be long before they arrived. Did that stop him? No. The hard-on in the making was in control here, and it convinced the rest of his body that if he didn't kiss Eve, he was going to explode. And that was the justification Lawson used to keep on kissing her.

Thankfully, Eve kissed him right back, too. In fact, she was the one who deepened the kiss, and the purr turned to a hot, hungry, needy sound. As a general rule, it was what he preferred to hear after he'd gotten naked with a woman and not while he was making out with her on her porch. Still, it upped the speed of his full-blown hard-on.

Lawson couldn't make himself stop kissing Eve, but he could do something about the porch issue. Without breaking the lip-lock or the grip he had with his arm around her waist, he maneuvered her into the foyer, and he kicked the door shut. Of course, being inside wasn't necessarily obstacle-free, and he opened his eyes long enough to make sure Cassidy, the baby and no one else wasn't around.

They weren't.

Eve and he had the foyer to themselves.

Now that they had some possible privacy, Lawson went for a whole new level of stupid. He pushed her back against the wall and made the contact body-to-body with his chest against her breasts. Even after all these years, they still fit in all the right places. At least they did with their clothes on. Lawson figured it'd be the same if they were in their birthday suits.

Of course, that couldn't happen.

It was one thing to kiss each other silly, but sex would complicate the hell out of things. His erection begged him to take on that complication, but there was still a glimmer of sanity left in his brain. And that's why Lawson finally pulled back from her.

With her breath gusting, Eve stared at him and blinked. "Oh," she said.

He had no clue what that meant or how to respond, so Lawson just stayed quiet while he tried to level his own breathing. It would have been better if he could put some distance between them, but he couldn't walk just yet.

Eve didn't move, either, but her attention did drift lower. At first, he thought she was going to look at the front of his jeans again—the very thing that had started the kissing. But she looked at the front of her own shirt.

It was wet.

Not an ordinary kind of wet. There were two circles of moisture right over her breasts.

"My milk," she mumbled. She scooted away from him and folded her arms over her chest. "I've weaned Aiden to the bottle, but my milk still sometimes lets down. It's a reflex action."

Lawson wasn't sure how that worked, but Eve suddenly seemed very uncomfortable. Maybe even in pain because her face was screwed up a little.

"I'm sorry," he said.

That encompassed not just the possible pain but the kiss itself. Yeah, the regrets had set in. And when he heard the knock on the door, Lawson figured the regrets were going to skyrocket. Because now someone was going to see Eve and him like this. Of course, whoever it was might not know how to interpret the wet spots on her shirt or their heavy breathing, but unless they were blind, the erection straining against his jeans would be a no-brainer.

"Yoo-hoo?" someone called out.

From that single-word greeting, Lawson knew who was on the other side of the door. Hell. What was she doing here?

"Uh, is that your mother?" Eve asked, and she sounded just as shocked, and alarmed, by that as he was.

Because, yes, it was indeed his mom.

"Yoo-hoo?" Regina repeated, and this time the knock on the door was much louder.

CHAPTER ELEVEN

ᴇᴠᴇ ʜᴀᴅ ʜᴀᴅ no trouble turning down Dylan's date request. Especially after she'd suspected that Regina had
put him up to it. Dylan had actually seemed relieved
at her nixing the idiotic idea, and Lawson might have
been relieved, too, but he had hurried off before Eve
had even given Dylan her answer.

If Lawson had hung around, he would have also
heard how adamant Eve had been about declining.
That was despite Regina's insistence that Dylan and
she were perfect for each other. Even if they had been,
which they weren't, there was no way she could have
gone out with Dylan, especially after the kissing match
that'd gone on between Lawson and her.

And there was no way she should have followed
through on Sophie's girls' night offer, either.

Yet, here she was, thanks to Cassidy's weeklong
wedding. At the Longhorn Bar, in a dark corner booth,
sipping a bitter glass of merlot while she pretended to
have fun. What Eve was actually doing though was
wondering how Aiden was dealing with both Cassidy and her not being there with him, and that's why
she'd checked her phone again to make sure she hadn't
missed a call from Adaline O'Malley, the sitter.

She wouldn't admit it to anyone, not even Cassidy,
that she'd actually hired a private detective to check

Footsteps followed, and several moments later, his
mom was at the window, peering into the family room.
It didn't stretch her gaze much to continue that peering into the foyer. She smiled and waved at Eve. She
quit smiling and waving though when her attention
landed on Lawson.

Judging from the sound Eve made this time, she
was trying to choke back a groan at the sight of her
visitor. Lawson didn't bother choking back his, but he
did move behind Eve when she opened the door. His
erection was going fast, but he didn't want his mom to
see the remnants of it.

The moment Eve had the door open, Regina pulled
her into a hug. "It's so good to see you. I'm back for a
visit and just had to stop by."

It had been nearly six months since he'd last seen
his mother, and there'd been some changes. For her
last visit, she'd been a brunette, but today her hair was
flame red thanks to the wig she was wearing. So were
her skinny jeans, top, heels and earrings. And her nail
polish and lipstick. Apparently, Regina didn't believe
in mixing it up when it came to color schemes.

As his mom had done at the window, she was all
smiles for Eve until she looked at him. "Why are you
here?"

Lawson didn't have a good answer for that, but no
way was he going to admit he'd been there to kiss
Eve's lights out. Mission accomplished, which meant
he should get the heck out and go back home. He slid
his hat over the front of his jeans so he could walk past
Regina, but that only seemed to make her notice what
he was trying to hide.

Regina hugged him but then put her mouth right against his ear. "What's going on?" she asked.

"Nothing," Lawson whispered, and it wasn't a lie because nothing indeed was going on. *Now.*

She pulled back, and one of Regina's needle-thin eyebrows lifted. "You really think it's wise to get involved with Eve again?" she whispered to him. Of course, Eve heard it because she was standing right there.

No, it wasn't wise, far from it, but that's what happened when you thought with your dick.

Thankfully, his mom didn't press him for an answer on that because she began to look around at the foyer and the family room. There were two boxes on the floor, and Lawson saw his name on one of them.

What the heck was that about?

Lawson wanted to know but not at the expense of staying there and having his mom also catch sight of the bulge around his zipper.

"Oh, you've redecorated," Regina told Eve. "And you've gone with neutrals."

Lawson moved past her toward the door but immediately encountered another obstacle, and this one was smiling at him.

Dylan.

"Why are you here?" Lawson snapped.

Dylan chuckled in a way that made Lawson want to bust in his face. That said, pretty much anything Dylan did at this point would make him feel that way. That's because his brother was smirking. It probably wasn't obvious to Eve and his mother that his brother was doing it, but Lawson knew him and that smirk. Dylan was enjoying watching him squirm.

"Oh, I asked Dylan to come here with said, as if that explained everything. It di diddly-squat because Lawson still wasn't s mother was there.

"Eve," Dylan greeted her as he walked pa

This would have been a good time for leave, but his feet stayed planted to the flo Stetson stayed in front of his hard-on. Yeah, there and would likely stay until he was no lor ing at, or thinking about, Eve.

Dylan went to Eve, and as if it was the most thing in the world, his brother kissed her. It wa cheek, but it was still a kiss.

"Dylan's here to ask you something," Regina prompting him with an elbow nudge.

Judging from the way Dylan and his mom were acting, Lawson was about 1000 percent sure he wasn't going to like anything that came out of hi mouth.

And he was right.

"Eve," Dylan drawled, "I'm here to asl a date."

out Adaline before she'd called her and asked her to babysit. Adaline was a premed student and came with stellar references. Added to that, Eve had left her pages of instructions and multiple phone numbers in case of an emergency. It had taken Eve five hours just to prepare to leave for what she hoped would be less than a two-hour event.

"So, are you going to tell us all about the hot Hollywood hunks you dated?" Sophie prompted Eve. "I especially want to know about Kellan Carver. I had such a big crush on him when I was in middle school. There were posters of him all over my room."

Cassidy and Eve exchanged glances. "Should I be the one to tell her that Kellan is a shallow, narcissistic dickwad?" Cassidy asked.

"I think you just did," Eve answered.

Obviously, Sophie, Mila and Nicky hadn't been expecting, well, the truth, so Eve added, "Kellan and I never dated. I mean, he's Aiden's father, but we were never a couple."

Obviously disillusioned, Sophie's chest fell. "Did he at least look good naked underneath that leather demon suit?"

Eve didn't want to see any more fallen chests or disappointed looks, so she lied. "Of course."

That was possibly true. Eve hadn't actually seen him naked since they'd kept on most of their clothes for their one-nighter.

"So, who did you date in Hollywood?" Mila asked. "I kept seeing gossip about you with one hottie after another."

All of it was manufactured by the studio or her publicist, but Eve didn't want them to think she'd spent the past eighteen years pining away for Lawson.

"I went out with Jason Winters a time or two." Since they gave her a blank stare, Eve figured they didn't know who that was. "He's the actor who played Elba, the Swaron warrior who used to help Cassidy's character."

The women gave variations of "oh" and some head nods though they clearly weren't impressed.

Eve hadn't been, either.

That's because Eve had spent her free time being a mom to Tessie, and she didn't regret any of it. All right, she did regret not telling Tessie sooner the truth about the nonadoption. If she'd done that, then she might not be in this position.

Eve checked her phone again, just to make sure Adaline hadn't sent her a message. Nothing. So, Eve texted the sitter just to make sure everything was all right. Adaline answered back right away with a thumbs-up and a smiley face.

"You're missing out on the conversation about Lawson and you having sex," Cassidy leaned in and whispered to her.

That got Eve's head whipping up from the phone screen only to discover that all eyes were on her. Sophie's, Nicky's, Mila's and Cassidy's. There was a moment of silence before they all burst out laughing.

"Told you," Sophie said, giving Mila's arm a nudge. "I knew sex with my cousin would get your attention."

Eve shook her head. "I'm not sleeping with Lawson."

"Sophie knows that," Nicky assured her. She reached across the booth and patted Eve's hand. "She's just trying to get your worries off the baby. He'll be fine with Adaline. She's babysat for my two kids plenty of times, and they love her."

Yes, Nicky had mentioned that when Eve had called her to check out Adaline's references, and since Nicky had two children, Eve was hoping Adaline wouldn't have trouble handling just one.

"But we should talk about Lawson." Nicky smiled as she sipped her beer. "And that means the conversation will, of course, lead to the subject of sex—both past, present and future."

Cassidy made a loud sound of agreement that might have been fueled by the tequila cocktail she was drinking. "The Granger men do make you think of sex, don't they?"

Mila and Nicky made their own sounds of agreement. Of course they felt that way since they were married to two of them. Past, present and future sex were a given for them.

Eve stayed quiet on the subject. But yes, Lawson did cause a flurry of sexual desire in her. And confusion. Yes, she wanted him, bad, but sex came with big price tags. No way did she want to get involved with Lawson when her own life was such a mess. Regina had been right when she'd warned Lawson about it not being wise to get involved with her again.

"What about Lucian?" Cassidy asked, looking at Mila and Nicky. "Did either of you ever—"

"God, no," Mila jumped to answer. Nicky echoed the same. "But I did have a coffee date with Dylan once," Mila added as she turned to Eve. "I understand you turned him down."

Mercy, was that all over town? "How'd you hear that?"

"Regina told Belle, and Belle called me to see if I would try to change your mind. I said no as fast as I could."

"She called me, too," Nicky volunteered. "I told her I'd leave the matchmaking to Vita and her."

"Vita?" Eve groaned. "How is she involved in this?"

"My mom is usually involved in stuff that isn't any of her business," Mila piped in. "I don't think she's actually matchmaking this time, but she's got it in her head that Lawson and you have some bad karma or something together."

Many people probably thought that, Eve included. Because of Brett. And just like that, her mood was even lower than it had been when she'd been focused on Aiden and the sitter.

"Don't worry," Mila went on. "I've told my mom to stay out of it, that you don't think of Dylan as lover material, that he's more like a brother to you."

Sophie, Cassidy and Nicky all made sounds of agreement.

That was absolutely true about Eve's feelings for Dylan. And it seemed they were all on the same page there.

There was probably nothing Eve could say about the Granger men that would be news to this bunch. Well, other than the fact that Lawson and she had done all that kissing just a week and a half ago. That would be a shocker since everyone at the table believed Lawson and she were succeeding in keeping their hands off each other.

Eve heard the chatter and laughter by the main entrance of the bar, and when she glanced in that direction, she saw someone else who would be surprised and no doubt upset about the Lawson kiss fest.

Darby.

No raincoat tonight. She was wearing her green nursing scrubs and was with two other women dressed the same way. Maybe they were also having a girls' night out after work. Darby shot her a cool glance as did the other women. Eve turned her attention back to her wine, but Cassidy gave the trio a big smile and waved before they disappeared into the bar.

"Remember, Lawson dumped her," Cassidy reminded Eve in a whisper. "And he did that before you were even in the picture."

Darby would argue that Eve had never been out of the picture. Her, and her heart-crushing memories. Darby's opinion of her wasn't going to improve once everyone learned the truth about what she'd done. Not just the kissing, either, but also about Lawson being Tessie's father.

"So, has Eve told you all about her steamy romance with Lawson?" Sophie asked Cassidy. "All that kissing!"

Eve hoped her eyes hadn't widened too much because Sophie quickly added, "When they were in high school." Eve unwidened her eyes, but she was certain that Sophie hadn't missed her reaction.

"Yeah, I know about Hot Cowboy." Cassidy smiled. "Eve always had a picture of him. In fact, if you ever watch episode nine of *Demon High*, you'll get a glimpse of Lawson's picture." Eve groaned softly, but Cassidy didn't pick up on the cue to stop. "Eve was moping around, looking at it while she was waiting for the scene to start, and she left it on the table on the set. It made it into the shot."

Mila and Nicky muttered something about having to rewatch that episode. Great. Eve didn't want them focusing too much on that one because her stomach had just started to show. She hadn't been using a body double just yet, but the camera crew had been careful about catching her at a side angle. It hadn't always worked, and she'd gotten some "fan mail" about her getting fat.

"Moping around, huh?" Sophie questioned. "I remember Lawson doing plenty of that after you left."

Eve figured there'd been gobs of anger to go along with that moping. Lawson hadn't taken her calls after she'd broken things off, but the last conversation they'd had back then had not been a pleasant one.

Sophie smiled, leaned in closer to Eve. "So, does Lawson know your secret?"

Eve got choked on the sip of wine she'd just taken. "Uh, what secret?"

"That you still think he's Hot Cowboy and—" Sophie stopped, and her smile changed when she looked at who was making their way toward their booth.

Roman, Garrett, Clay and Lawson.

Roman, Garrett and Clay were smiling, too, their attention on their spouses. But Lawson looked as if he were being led directly into a brushfire while his protruding body parts were coated with accelerant.

"Ladies," Garrett greeted them. "We stopped by for a beer before heading to poker." He tipped his Stetson. But he saved the best greeting for Nicky. He leaned down and kissed her.

Clay didn't do the hat-tipping, but he also kissed Sophie.

"Hell, I can do better than that," Roman grumbled. He hauled Mila to her feet and did indeed *do better* with the kiss that he delivered. It went on so long and was so scalding that it caused Cassidy, Clay, Sophie, Garrett and Nicky to laugh.

"Keep that up, and I'll have to arrest you," Clay joked.

Lawson wasn't laughing though. Neither was Eve. That was mainly because the kiss was a reminder of how it felt to have Lawson's mouth on hers. It didn't help that she could see him now. He was a hot visual aid. One who was looking at her.

"Can we talk?" Lawson asked her. "In private," he added one skipped heartbeat later.

Eve wasn't sure who was more shocked at the table, but she thought maybe she was the front-runner. Lawson's request certainly got everyone's attention though, and they turned toward her, waiting for her to answer.

She tried to sound casual when she smiled and answered, "Sure," but she wasn't fooling anyone.

Especially herself.

Her hand was trembling a little when she set her glass on the table and followed Lawson away from the booth. He didn't take her to another part of the bar but rather out the side exit that was usually reserved for those on the prowl for a make-out spot or for avoiding someone you didn't want to see.

Eve hadn't realized it was drizzling until they stepped outside. Lawson immediately took hold of her arm and moved her away from the steps and beneath the awning. That let her know just how important this had to be for him to take her out in the rain. This was probably about that kiss at her house. He was no doubt going to tell her that it could never happen again and that he was moving to Alaska or someplace else to put some distance between them.

"Tessie called me about an hour ago," Lawson said after he put his hands on his hips.

Of all the things she thought he might say, that sure wasn't one of them, and her heart skipped another beat. Oh, mercy. That couldn't be good. "Uh, what did Tessie want?" Eve managed to ask.

His short hesitation didn't help her rattled nerves one bit. "For me to tell you to give her some space, that she didn't want you to keep asking to see her."

That stung because Eve had already given Tessie so much space that she didn't have any more to give. A year of it, as a matter of fact. But she knew Tessie could have said something much worse to Lawson.

If Tessie suspected that Lawson was her dad, that is. Eve had told her that Kellan wasn't her father, so Tessie might have found out about Lawson and her being high school sweethearts and could have pieced the truth together.

Eve glanced around, considering if this was a good time for her to spill all to Lawson. It wasn't. There was a couple kissing and groping each other at the back of the building. Plus, someone else could come walking out at any second.

Maybe they could talk in her car?

But Eve nixed that, too, because it was best if Lawson didn't have his inevitable meltdown in a public place with his cousins and his ex-girlfriend inside.

"Tessie thinks you and I are together…or something," Lawson added a moment later.

Not together, but the *or something* was true. The air was zinging again, and Eve didn't think it was because there was any lightning nearby. Nope. These sparks were all caused by Lawson.

"She came out and said that?" Eve asked. "Or was that just a feeling you got?" Because if it was a feeling, she could dismiss it.

"She came out and said it," Lawson stated.

So, no dismissal, but it did make her wonder why Tessie would be concerned about who she was or wasn't seeing. "Did she say anything else?" Maybe ask about their shared past?

"She wanted to know why I went to Austin to see her."

Oh, that. Eve certainly hadn't forgotten about the visit. "How did she know you'd been there? And for that matter, how'd she get your number?"

"She didn't say, but she probably got it from Belle. She mentioned that Belle had called her a time or two. I didn't tell anyone I'd gone to her sorority house in Austin, but Belle might have heard about it somehow."

"Small-town gossip," Eve muttered.

Lawson nodded. "More efficient than tabloids or paparazzi. Faster, too." He looked up at the awning and at the alley that led to the back. "We made out here once after a school dance."

Eve didn't need a glance to confirm it, but they had indeed done that. It was one of the rare times when the Longhorn had closed the bar so the teenagers could have a dance. Lawson and she had been barely seventeen, and just like the couple at the back of the bar, there'd been groping and kissing involved. Perhaps even one of those hand slides down into his jeans since that was around the time they'd become full-blown lovers.

"Yes. That happened in a lot of different places," she admitted. "I can't drive by the high school bleachers without blushing."

He smiled, just a little, but she didn't think it was from humor, and she thought he was about to let her know that this chat was over and that it was time for him to go. But that didn't happen.

"This staying away from each other isn't working for me," he said, his voice a low easy drawl. If foreplay had a voice, that's how it would sound. "How about you?"

The drawl, the question and the look he gave her would have caused chrome to melt. "No."

It was the truth, but she winced. She shouldn't be admitting stuff like that. She shouldn't be giving him the look, either. The look that was almost certainly begging him to launch her on the path to a much-needed orgasm.

"No," he repeated.

He drawled that, too, and she didn't think he was changing his mind about what he'd said. The alley didn't have the best lighting, just a yellowish bulb above the door, but it was more than enough for her to see his attention lower to her mouth. Then to her breasts.

Then lower.

The look he was giving her seemed very familiar. "Are you playing the game we used to play?" she asked.

He didn't ask *what game?* Which meant they were

likely playing it. It was one they'd started about the same time they'd made out in this alley. Long, lingering looks at places on each other's bodies that they wanted to touch or kiss. Followed by the question—touch, lick or kiss?

It was their sexed-up version of "Truth or Dare?"

The game had gotten her into trouble once when she'd glanced down at Lawson's man parts just as he'd blurted out "lick." Until then "lick" had usually been reserved for necks, earlobes and nipples. They'd been in his truck at the time and parked on the back of his family's property so they had some privacy. But, alas, her seventeen-year-old skill set had failed her, and he'd gotten one short lick instead of what he'd been expecting. A few minutes after that, they'd had sex, so it probably wasn't a huge disappointment.

"It was a fun game," she said. There was too much breath in her voice, and the pulse on her throat was starting to throb. Actually, several parts of her were throbbing. "But this isn't the best place to play it."

She sounded hesitant, and her brain was, but the rest of her was nudging her to go for anything, including but not limited to sex against the wall.

"Probably not." His words agreed with her, but the look he gave her didn't. He dropped his gaze to that runaway pulse on her throat.

"Kiss," she blurted out, and she might have waved it off if Lawson hadn't moved in and put his mouth there.

Oh, my. That was like flipping on a switch. A hot, needy one. It always had been, and Lawson had been the one who'd discovered that ultrasensitive spot on her. Of course, he'd discovered most of her *spots*.

"You're right," he whispered, his warm breath hitting against her neck in the very area he'd just kissed. "Wrong place, wrong time."

Yes, that was the only thing wrong about it. Everything else was so right. She leaned back to tell him something that she hoped would sound sensible, but she glanced at his mouth first.

"Touch," he said. Obviously, they were still playing the game, so maybe sensibility could wait for a few more seconds. Interesting, though, that he hadn't gone for the obvious—kiss.

She wet her index finger with her tongue and gave him her own version of touching. Eve slid her finger over his top lip. Then his bottom. And while it was fun, it soon wasn't nearly enough. She upped the touching by grabbing on to a fistful of his shirt, snapping him to her and kissing him.

It was as if the floodgates opened. Hot, mind-blowing floodgates that made her want to touch, kiss and lick at the same time. And she might have done all three, too, if Lawson hadn't jerked away from her.

That's when she saw the person coming up the alley from the Main Street sidewalk. Because her heartbeat was drumming in her ears, Eve hadn't heard their visitor approaching, but she had no trouble hearing what she said.

"Mom?" Tessie called out. "Is that you?"

And her daughter came walking straight toward her.

CHAPTER TWELVE

FOR JUST A split second, Tessie thought that maybe she'd stepped onto a set where Eve Cooper and another actor were playing out a scene. But nope. There were no cameras, no lighting. No crew. Only the strange thing she'd just witnessed.

Her mom kissing a cowboy in a dark alley outside a bar.

It was a first. Even when guys had taken her mother to studio parties and such, there hadn't been any kissing in front of her. And neither the paparazzi nor the hornies had managed to snap any lip-lock photos like that. Of course, there must have been some kind of kissing going on the night her mom had gotten pregnant with Aiden, but again, Tessie hadn't been around to see that—thank God.

"Tessie," her mother said.

It wasn't exactly a squeal of delight, but one quickly followed, and she ran to Tessie and dragged her into her arms. She didn't hug her long though. Probably because her mom felt her go stiff.

Tessie hadn't meant to react like that, but all the hurt came. Feelings that her mother probably understood—from her own way of seeing things, that is. Her mom almost certainly knew that the lie she'd told her for so long had cut at her in a way that would never heal. At least that's how Tessie felt about it.

Somehow, though, despite Tessie's stiffness, her mom was still smiling when she pulled back and looked at her. "You came," she said, but then she shook her head. "How'd you know I'd be here?"

"Your sitter. I went by your new house at the Heavenly Pastures Ranch, and she said Cassidy and you were here at the Longhorn. She gave me the address and directions. I was about to go in and ask for you, but then I saw you. With him." Tessie tipped her head to him. "Who is he?"

But it wasn't necessary for her mother to answer. That's because at that exact moment, the cowboy stepped from the shadows, and Tessie got a good look at his face.

Oh, shit.

It was Lawson Granger.

He came closer, and for a second it seemed as if he was going to shake her hand or introduce himself. No intro, though, when he looked at her. His mouth dropped open for a couple of seconds, but like her mom's hug, it didn't last. His breathing became a little noisy, and his eyes narrowed.

Tessie mentally repeated her *oh, shit* and added some more curse words.

She hadn't exactly looked her best when he'd come to the sorority house in Austin because she'd been falling-down drunk and slumped in the middle of two puking classmates. Lawson hadn't known who she was that day, but he certainly knew who she was now since Eve had blurted out her name.

Tessie had avoided Eve discovering the drunk-thing that day because once she'd heard her mom in the foyer of the building, she'd stayed at the top of the stairs to talk to her. No chance of Eve sniffing her breath that way. Then Tessie had lied through her teeth by saying she had the stomach flu. Even with that, her mom had wanted to come up and see her, but Tessie had put down her foot and said no.

Good thing Tessie hadn't actually had to put down her foot, or she might have toppled down the stairs. During the entire forty-five-second conversation, she'd had to steady herself by gripping the railing.

Lawson's mouth moved a little, and while he didn't actually say any words, his body language let Tessie know what he was thinking.

He was so going to rat her out.

That would add a nasty layer of crap to her already crap-coated relationship with her mother. She hadn't come to Wrangler's Creek to bury the hatchet with her mom—not exactly, anyway—but after prodding from Cassidy, Tessie had thought it was a good time to start trying to work things out. Obviously, her timing for that sucked though, and her mom might be thinking the same thing since she'd seemed pretty wrapped up in that kiss.

A kiss from the very man who could make this much worse than it already was.

"Oh," her mom said, volleying glances at both Lawson and her. Uneasy glances. Great. Eve was probably picking up on the tension. "I haven't introduced you. Tessie, this is Lawson Granger. Lawson, this is my daughter."

Tessie certainly wasn't going to be the first to say anything and step in something she was trying to step around. But Lawson didn't exactly jump to chat, either.

"Tessie and I spoke on the phone earlier," he growled.

"Yes, he just told me that you'd called him." Her mom sounded relieved and on edge at the same time.

Tessie knew exactly how she felt. The cowboy wasn't blurting out anything. That was the good news. The bad news was that he probably didn't have amnesia, so he might just be keeping his mouth shut to try to figure out a way to break the news to her mother.

"It's nice to meet you," Tessie said to Lawson. It wasn't, but she had no idea what else to say to him. However, she did know what to tell her mother. "I need to be going. I just wanted to stop by and say hello."

"Going?" Eve repeated, making it sound as if Tessie had just told her she was about to elope to Vegas. "You just got here. And it's dark. You don't want to drive back to Austin in the dark. You can stay the night at my house—*our* house," she corrected herself. "I have a room fixed up for you."

Tessie could have predicted all of that word for word, but as she'd done on the stairs that day in Austin, she shook her head. This time, it didn't cause a severe dizzy spell because she hadn't had a drop to drink.

"Let's just take this in baby steps," Tessie told her.

"It was good to meet you," she repeated to Lawson, and she headed out of the alley.

Of course, her mother came after her, and she fell in step alongside Tessie as she walked to her car. "Maybe before you go, we can just pop by the diner and have a cup of coffee," Eve suggested.

"I really do need to get back." That was partly true. She didn't need to stand around there even though it seemed as if the cowboy was going to keep his mouth shut. That was a surprise. He really did have cop's eyes.

Her mom tried again. "Please, let's just go somewhere and talk." She glanced back at the cowboy who was making his way toward them. "There's something important I need to tell you," she added in a whisper.

Tessie knew where this was going. Her mom wanted to apologize, again. But she wasn't in the mood to hear it. It'd been a huge mistake coming here, and now she needed to cut her losses and get going.

She threw open her car door as soon as she reached it and got inside. Thankfully, her mom didn't try to get in with her. With the cowboy behind her staring holes in Tessie, Eve stayed put on the sidewalk and looked ready to launch into some more moping and crying. After what her mom had done with the lying, Tessie didn't want to feel bad about that.

But she did.

Tessie felt like crap.

Despite what'd happened, Eve was her mom, and Tessie loved her. Still, it was going to take a little more time for her to get to a point where her stomach didn't twist into a knot at the thought of that lie. A lie that hadn't been for Tessie's benefit, either, but for her own. Eve hadn't wanted her hornies fans to know that she'd gotten knocked up because it would have ruined her kick-ass, perfect image.

Tessie started the car and looked at the front doorway of the bar. There was another guy in jeans and a cowboy hat, and he was watching them. She hadn't wanted to start any gossip for her mom, but this would probably do it. The effed-up daughter had returned to eff-up things even more.

The glaring cowboy behind her mom would see it that way.

She shifted her attention back to Eve. She'd seen her

a couple of times since learning the truth that she was her real mother. And just like those other times, Tessie tried to pick through the features of her face to see if she could see any part of herself there.

She couldn't.

Her mom with her blond hair and green eyes, and there she was with brown hair and blue eyes. That was why Tessie had never once suspected that they shared any DNA.

But…

The cowboy was a different story. Dark brown hair. Like hers. But then, lots of people had hair that color.

He came closer, and the streetlights caught his eyes just right so she could see the color. Blue. Again, like hers. But again, lots of people had blue eyes.

How many of those blue-eyed, brown-haired men, though, had she ever seen kissing her mother?

Just this one.

Tessie got that knot in her stomach again and was ready to hit the accelerator and get out of there. However, when she went to shut the car door, the cowboy caught onto it as if to help her.

"If you don't tell your mom, I will," he whispered just loud enough so that only Tessie would hear it.

She didn't have to guess what he meant. He was talking about her getting drunk. And while Tessie was indeed concerned about that, she had a new concern. A new knot in her stomach. Because she glanced at both her mom and him.

And that's when Tessie knew her mother had yet one more truth she needed to come clean about.

WHEN LAWSON CAME out of the barn, he saw Cassidy and his mom on the back porch of the Granger house.

Cassidy had the baby in one of those front-facing pouch carriers, and with Aiden's little arms and legs flailing around, it made it look as if she had a turtle strapped to her.

Seeing them was a surprise since the porch had been empty about fifteen minutes earlier. That's when Lawson had left the office inside the house to go to the barn to have a chat with one of the horse trainers.

What was especially bad was that Cassidy and his mom appeared to be waiting for him.

When he first spotted them, both were looking down at the baby and grinning, but that stopped when their eyes landed on him.

"Is there a fire inside?" he asked, only half joking. "Is that why you're out here?"

"No fire," his mother jumped to answer. "I was on my way to the barn to find you. I didn't know Cassidy was coming, too, but we're here to talk to you."

Lawson sighed. "Is this about Eve, Darby or that stain you found on your red silk dress when I was seven?"

Regina had already opened her mouth to answer until he threw in that last one. She did indeed want to know about the stain that he had denied many times over the years, but obviously, she wasn't going to let that distract her.

"Eve," his mom said.

Cassidy made a sound of agreement. Aiden just belched and then giggled about it. Lawson thought maybe the kid had the right reaction. There was nothing he could do to stop whatever lecture he was about to get, so maybe belching was the answer. He tried it and got a laugh from Aiden. His mom and Cassidy weren't as easily amused though.

Since it was hot and he didn't want the baby outside for too long, Lawson walked past them and into the sunroom so they would follow him.

They did.

Lawson turned to meet head-on whatever his mother's beef was. "Okay, hit me with what you got, but do it one at a time and do it fast because I've got a mountain of paperwork on my desk."

Regina apparently thought she had first dibs because she started. "It's all over town about you kissing Eve outside the Longhorn last night."

He was about to ask how the heck that had gotten around. To the best of his knowledge, no one other than Tessie had seen them kissing, and he doubted that she'd blabbed. The other couple making out likely hadn't looked away from each other long enough to draw breath, much less see what had gone on. But in Wrangler's Creek, the gossips seemed to have mind-reading skills to assist them.

"You know I hate to interfere with your life," Regina went on, "but I feel I have to say something."

It was true for the most part. Regina didn't interfere because she was rarely around. But when she did show up, yes, interference for at least one of her kids was on the agenda.

"Are you telling me not to get involved with Eve again?" Lawson came out and asked.

Regina nodded. "But not for the reason you think. I've given up on Darby and you. I can see that it's just not going to work. But Eve's in a vulnerable place right now. She just had that precious baby, and she's upset about her breakup with Kellan Carver. It's all over the tabloids that she's falling apart over losing him."

Cassidy rolled her eyes, verifying what Lawson already knew from personal knowledge. Eve was indeed upset, but it had nothing to do with the horn-boy. It was all because of Tessie. And maybe because the kissing that Lawson and she had been doing was confusing her some. It was certainly confusing him.

"Anyway, I'm here to ask you to give Eve some time to work out her feelings. You'd be just a Band-Aid now to her broken heart, which means you could end up getting hurt again, too."

Part of that was true. He could end up getting hurt. But he could have argued about Eve's broken heart since she'd been the one to leave him. If he did that though, it would only lengthen the lecture, and that was the last thing he wanted to do since it appeared his mom was winding down.

She smiled, kissed Aiden on the top of his head and turned to Cassidy. "Make sure you come by so I can introduce you to Lucian." Regina winked at Cassidy.

Lawson hoped that unholy intro didn't happen, but Cassidy was a grown woman, and he didn't want to interfere—as his mom had just done. And as Cassidy was likely about to do.

"And you come by the house, too," Regina added to Lawson. He also got a kiss on the cheek before his mom headed out back.

One down, one to go. He took a deep breath to steel himself for the next round, which might have more bite to it than motherly concern.

Cassidy put her hands over Aiden's ears. "Don't dick around with Eve's feelings. Got that?" And with the shortest lecture in recent history, she would have just walked out if Lawson hadn't stepped in front of Cassidy to stop her.

"Did Eve say something to you about me?" he asked.

She looked at him as if he'd sprouted an extra nose. "For nearly every minute of the eighteen years that I've known Eve, she's talked about you. Or Tessie. Or Brett. She has nightmares about Brett, you know? She cries about Tessie. But you're the one who can send her into a tailspin. She's my best friend, and I'd like to avoid future tailspinning."

Yeah, so would he, but it almost seemed inevitable when it came to Eve.

He kept vowing to keep his distance from her, kept vowing to not kiss her, and then that plan would go to hell in a handbasket the moment he laid eyes on her. He had to do better. Because Cassidy was right. Eve wasn't in a good place to have her feelings dicked with.

"Eve kept that dress, you know," Cassidy went on a moment later. "The one she bought with all her baby-sitting money."

Lawson had been following this conversation just fine. Until now. "What dress?"

"The pink strapless one she was going to wear to the Sadie Hawkins dance your senior year. She was going to wear it and tell you…something important."

Well, hell. Now he was really interested. "Tell me what?"

But Cassidy immediately waved that off. "I'm not sure, but I know that dress meant a lot to her. When she took it out of the *Lawson, etc.* box, she got misty-eyed."

At least he wasn't clueless about the box because he'd seen it at her house, but cluelessness was plentiful on the rest of this. "Why would a dress make her misty-eyed? Especially a dress she never even wor—"

He stopped. Because he got it then. She'd bought the dress when they were still together, and it was probably a reminder that she'd broken off things with him and moved before she could wear it.

Lawson was still a little confused, though, on the misty-eyed part.

"Are you saying that Eve regrets breaking up with me?" Lawson asked, but then he decided it was best not to hear the answer. He gave his own take on it. "I didn't end that relationship. She did."

Cassidy acknowledged that with a nod. "But that doesn't mean she can't be all sad about something she'd planned and fantasized about for months. She kept that dress, so that means it was very important to her."

"Fantasized?" he questioned.

"Not that kind of fantasy," Cassidy scolded. "She wanted you to dance with her while she was wearing that dress. It's a metaphor for lost youth, innocence and all that shit." She covered Aiden's ears for the last word.

Now they were talking metaphors. Well, Lawson knew some things about lost innocence and other shit. And that dance was going to be an important night for him, too.

Not the dancing part though.

No way had he ever intended to do that.

But Lawson had planned on going and giving Eve the gift he'd bought her over Christmas break. He hadn't given it to her at Christmas because the timing hadn't felt right. But instead he'd saved it for the night of Sadie Hawkins. A night that had never come because Eve had already moved to California by then.

"Why are you telling me all of this?" he asked.

Cassidy got in his face, which meant Aiden was right there, too. The kid smiled and kicked his feet, his toes landing against Lawson's stomach. "I'm telling you because Eve is still hanging on to a lot more than just that dress and the *Lawson, etc.* box. Remember what I said about not dicking around with her feelings." She didn't cover Aiden's ears that time, but she only mouthed the word *dicking*.

Lawson had already gotten the point without the dress story. That didn't mean though that he wouldn't screw up again. Especially since there was a big reason he might get pulled right back in. A reason that didn't have anything to do with lust, dresses or dances that he would have never danced.

"Did Eve tell you that Tessie came to the Longhorn last night?" Lawson asked.

Cassidy nodded, sighed and moved back out of his face. "Tears were involved. Lots of them. Despite Eve's crying, I see it as a good start that Tessie came here. Any idea why Tessie left so suddenly after driving all this way to see Eve?"

Lawson knew all right. It was because Tessie had probably been scared that he was going to tell on her. And he would if the girl hadn't come clean with Eve. But he didn't intend to get into that with Cassidy.

"Tessie saw Eve and me kissing," Lawson admitted. "That might have upset her."

"Maybe," Cassidy said as if giving that some thought. But dismissed whatever she was thinking with a head shake. "When all of us were still in California, Tessie was always trying to get Eve to go out on dates, so I doubt that would have bothered her."

Cassidy looked him straight in the eyes as if waiting for him to tell her the truth, but Lawson didn't spill anything. He gave Aiden's toes another jiggle and changed the subject. "How's this little man doing?"

Cassidy's long stare continued a moment longer before she dragged in a long breath. "He's a crappy sleeper, is frequently gassy, as you heard, and he will pinch any part of your body that he can reach when you're feeding him a bottle. Not soft pinching, either. He gets a good grip." She kissed Aiden and grinned at him. "But he owns every bit of my heart, and the little shit knows it." She covered Aiden's ears for the *shit* word.

Aiden laughed.

Lawson could see how this kid could manage some heart-claiming. Of course, maybe he felt that way because he'd been the one to bring him into the world.

"It won't be long before he'll be ready to go out riding." Lawson hadn't intended to say that out loud. It made him seem too, well, involved. And that's when he knew it was time to skedaddle.

"I'll watch my step with Eve," he added.

Lawson said goodbye and headed toward his office. He nearly made it, too, but then he saw Nicky coming out of the kitchen. Like Cassidy, she was also carrying a baby. Her six-month-old son, Ben. The kid was sacked out with his head dropped down on Nicky's shoulder.

Since Nicky and Garrett lived here now, it wasn't a surprise to see her there, but then he saw the serious look on her face. Not a frown exactly but close. Which meant Lawson was probably about to get another round of lecturing. If Cassidy and his mom had heard about the kissing going on between Eve and him, then Nicky almost certainly had heard, as well.

First, he put his hands over Ben's ears even though there was little chance the sleeping kid could hear it. "Don't worry. I'm not going to dick around with Eve," Lawson volunteered.

Nicky blinked, clearly surprised by that confession. "Oh. Okay." She tipped her head toward the hall just off the kitchen. "Might be a good thing since she just arrived and is waiting for you in your office."

Lawson blinked, too. "Eve's here?"

Nicky used her free hand to pat his arm. "Maybe it's a good time for you to clear up that no dicking around. First, though, you should probably try to convince yourself that it isn't going to happen again."

And with that wise but smart-ass advice, Nicky smiled and strolled away.

Lawson didn't stroll. He made a beeline to his office, walking faster than he usually would, but he stopped in the hall when he caught sight of Eve. She was standing and looking at something on his desk.

It wasn't something he'd planned to do, but he took a moment to admire the view.

She was wearing a blue dress that hit a couple of inches above her knees. It was just short enough for him to see plenty of her legs. Her butt, too, when she leaned farther across his desk. The motion caused the dress to slide and cling in all the best places.

Speaking of the best *places*, she turned to the side, giving him a nice view of her breasts. Again, the fabric cooperated, and it was almost as if he could see her without her clothes. And he suddenly wished he could do just that.

Of course, this wasn't helping him convince himself about that no-dicking-around promise.

Thankfully, she didn't notice him ogling her. She kept her attention on his desk, but she was moving back and forth the way a person would if they were trying to look at something from a different angle or in a different light. Since he had payroll reports, orders for worming meds and a memo to the hands about the lousy job they'd done mucking horseshit from the west barn, he couldn't imagine what she found so riveting.

Maybe she sensed he was there because she whirled around. Her eyes widened as if she'd been caught doing something wrong. Lawson felt that way, too. Except he was betting his "something wrong" upped hers. He'd been undressing her with his eyes while she'd just been reading paperwork.

"I hope this isn't a bad time for a visit," she said. "As I was pulling into the driveway, I saw Cassidy leaving out on the side road and figured she'd come here to talk to you." Her breath was unsteady, and it was causing her chest to heave a little. Just what he didn't need if he wanted to keep his attention off her breasts.

He went in but didn't close the door. Best not to add the temptation of privacy to this mix. "Cassidy's worried about you, that's all. Are you okay? I mean because of Tessie," he added when she just stared at him.

"Yes." She stuttered on that word. "I mean, I was upset when she drove off like that last night, and that's why I had to leave, too, and go home."

Yeah, Lawson had gotten that. He hadn't been in much of a mood to stick around, either. He was about to ask her if she'd talked to Tessie since then, but when he went closer, he saw what she'd been looking at on his desk. Not mucking memos or deworming orders. But rather those damn tabloid magazines with Eve's picture on the cover.

"Tate's girlfriend brought them over," Lawson said as fast as he could manage.

She nodded. "Sophie mentioned it. I'll sign them for her before I leave."

Good. Then he could get them off his desk and not have daily visual reminders of one of the worst times of his life. Of course, he had no good explanation for why they were on his desk and not tucked away in a drawer where he couldn't see them. He had tried to do that, but it hadn't lasted more than a couple of minutes.

"Was something wrong with them?" he asked. "You were looking at them pretty hard when I came in."

There was the traditional deer-in-the-headlights look, and then there was a deer-in-the-headlights look on steroids. Eve had the second one.

"I, uh, just thought I saw fingerprints or something on the covers," she muttered.

On the surface that seemed a dumb thing to say. The magazines were old, had glossy finishes and had been handled by plenty of people. But then he remembered Sophie had seen him looking at, and touching, one of the covers.

Hell.

Had Sophie actually spilled the beans about it? Judging from Eve's expression, Sophie had indeed done that, and he was going to take it up with Miss Tattletale the next time he saw her.

Since Lawson wasn't about to confess to picture fondling, he moved on to an even more uncomfortable topic. "Did Tessie call you after she saw us last night?"

She shook her head. "You mean to talk about us kissing." Eve didn't wait for him to say no, that his question wasn't about that. "Honestly, I was surprised, but she must have been upset to run off like that."

Lawson took a deep breath because he knew he was going to need it. He didn't like applying the tattletale label here because this wasn't something that should stay a secret. Still, it was going to feel pretty crappy to do this.

He took Eve by the hand and led her to the sofa across from his desk. That alone let her know that something bad was up, but Lawson suspected he had a grim look on his face, too.

"Remember when I went to Austin to try to talk to Tessie?" That was all he managed to say before the color drained from her face.

"Oh, God." And she repeated that a couple of times. "You saw her. And she saw you." There went another round of the repeated *Oh, God*, and Lawson didn't think it was part of some prayer, either.

Lawson hated that she was having this kind of reaction when he hadn't even gotten to the bad stuff yet, but there was no easy way to soften the blow.

"Tessie was drunk when I got there. I stopped her two puking friends from taking her out of the building and then handed her off to her roommate when she came down the stairs. Her *sober* roommate," he said, clarifying his last statement.

Eve's mouth dropped open, and while he was expecting it, Eve quit *Oh, God*-ing. In fact, she seemed a little relieved. For a few seconds, anyway.

"Tessie was drunk?" she asked.

"Yeah. Staggering, falling-down-on-her-ass drunk." And he gave her a moment to absorb that.

Eve didn't absorb it well.

Her mouth stayed open, tears sprang to her eyes, and she made a sound that only a really pissed-off mother could make. He knew about that sound because he'd heard his own mom make it a time or two.

"What the heck was she thinking?" Eve blurted out. "Why would she do something that stupid?"

That was just the start of Eve's questions that he couldn't answer, and he was feeling pissed off and emotional about it, too. Because it had indeed been a stupid thing for Tessie to do. Along with being downright dangerous, it had brought back the memories of Brett. Hell, it was still bringing them back.

Eve continued asking a few more angry questions before she got to the one he'd been expecting. "Why didn't you tell me this sooner?"

He didn't have to answer because he saw the light bulb go on in her eyes. "You didn't know it was Tessie until last night." And she filled in the rest of the blanks. "That's why she drove off like that, because she was afraid you were going to tell me what happened."

The tears filled her eyes again, and this time they spilled down her cheeks. Lawson couldn't do much to soothe this, but he pulled her into his arms and let her cry it out.

"She knows how I feel about someone her age drinking," Eve went on.

Yes, and that might have been the reason Tessie had done it. Maybe this had been her way of getting back at her mom, or he could be just overthinking it. She could just have the wrong friends.

"God, what am I going to do?" Eve sobbed. "She's barely talking to me." She lifted her head off his shoulder, and Lawson saw she'd moved past the shock and gone back to being pissed off. "Well, she'll talk to me because I'm going up to Austin to have it out with her."

While Lawson thought that talking could be a good thing, he had to stop Eve from bolting for the door. "Best to think this through, and then if you still want to go, I'll take you. We can even talk to her together if you want."

That put a new emotion in her eyes. Not so much anger but something else. Regret, maybe. Yeah, he had plenty of that, too.

"Just take a deep breath," he instructed. And he waited until she'd taken a couple of them. "If you go up there this mad, it's only going to drive you two further apart. Plus, she's in college, not exactly a kid."

In fact, now that he thought about it, Tessie might not even be underage. Still, she had done something stupid. Getting drunk and then leaving to go God knew where with God knew who. She could have gotten in a car accident or been a victim of date rape.

Lawson put a stop to those thoughts because he was getting riled again. And he was thinking too much like a parent and not a "friend" of someone who was one—Eve. He took some deep breaths of his own before he continued.

"Because of what happened to Brett, we automatically think the worst in situations like this," he went on. He tried to keep his voice level. "We've got that holding us back from drinking too much. At least it's held me back."

She nodded. "Yes, I just cry it out when things start to get to me. It's hard to be drunk when you're a mom."

True. And Eve had adopted Tessie around the time she'd been of actual legal drinking age, so there probably hadn't been a lot of opportunities for that sort of thing.

"Tessie was sort of your anchor," he said.

She looked up at him, opened her mouth again and then closed it as if she'd changed her mind about what she had been about to say. "You didn't have an anchor."

That was true, as well. By the time Brett died, Lawson's folks had long been divorced, and with both of them more in than out of Wrangler's Creek, the housekeepers and Lucian had ended up raising him.

Which meant there wasn't much raising going on.

It was the same for his brothers, Dylan and Reed. At least Lawson had had Garrett. Not exactly an anchor since they were close to the same age, but Garrett had kicked his butt when it needed kicking. Something he'd needed quite often.

"What am I going to do?" Eve repeated, still looking up at him.

"You'll talk to Tessie once you've finished your cry."

But she seemed to have already finished that. And he wasn't entirely sure she was just talking about Tessie here. Judging from the look in her eyes, he was part of that million-dollar question, too.

Lawson knew it was a mistake for the long look she was giving him to continue. Especially since he was in the long-looking mode, too. However, he gathered up every ounce of willpower he had to make sure he didn't kiss her. Apparently though, Eve hadn't done any such gathering because she leaned in and kissed him.

It was a struggle, but he didn't take hold of her and pull her to him. Didn't deepen the kiss, either. He just sat there while she pressed her lips to his and while he felt that willpower burning to ash.

She lingered a little while with the kiss. Long enough for him to pick up her taste and scent. And plenty long enough for him to want a whole lot more.

"What are we doing?" she whispered when she eased back and met his gaze.

"To hell if I know." He tipped his head to his desk. "See those reports and memo? They follow a thread of logic. Shit needs to be removed, so I assign the task and it gets done. All this kissing we're doing isn't logical."

It did make sense though. Well, it did if he accepted lust as a sensible reason. Since they were no longer teenagers, that probably wasn't an acceptable excuse.

That didn't stop him.

Without any willpower to help him out, Lawson slid his hand around the back of her head and kissed her. And this time, there was indeed some deepening involved.

It was as if he snapped. As if Eve snapped, too. All the lust and hunger hit them both like a scorcher heat wave that raced right through them. Not good. Because deep kisses led to jockeying for position so they could get closer to each other.

Lawson fixed that problem by hauling Eve onto his lap.

Since this was their third set of kissing as adults, Lawson couldn't fix the problem of dismissing it. Nope. It seemed stupid not to admit that this attraction just wasn't going away, and since it wasn't, Lawson made the most of the kissing. And of his favorite part, the touching. Even though he knew this was going to lead to something much more that they'd likely end up regretting.

Regrets aside for now, his hand ended up between them, which, all in all, was a good place for it to be, and she slid his hand around her back. Then to her butt. It not only gave him some premium touching, but it allowed him to align their lower bodies just right.

Again, he was thankful for that blue dress because it just slid right up on her thighs, making room for the front of her panties to land against the front of his zipper.

Definitely some premium touching now.

And it would have continued if he hadn't heard the sound of someone saying, "Am I interrupting anything, Baby-Cakes?"

At this point, Lawson wouldn't have wanted to hear anything other than Eve's continuing purr, but this voice was one that was especially unwelcome.

Because it was Kellan Carver's. And the asshole was standing in the doorway, grinning at them.

CHAPTER THIRTEEN

KELLAN FIGURED SOME men would have cared much seeing their baby mama on the verge of having sex with another man, but truth was, he just didn't feel that way about Eve. Yeah, they'd been onetime lovers, but it wasn't as if he was especially eager to get back in her pants.

Unlike Lawson. The cowboy was clearly trying to do that.

Clearly furious, too, at the interruption because he was scowling at Kellan the whole time that Eve was crawling off his lap.

"What are you doing here?" Eve asked at the exact moment Lawson barked, "What the hell do you want?"

"I'm here to talk to you," he said to Lawson. "About a business proposition."

All right, that obviously didn't go over well because Eve and Lawson gave him a blank look. Kellan tried again. "I have a movie-producer friend who wants to use some real cowboys as extras—"

"No," Lawson interrupted. He got to his feet, put his hands on his hips and generally looked as if he wanted to punch Kellan in the face.

Kellan had seen that look on him before. That day Aiden was born, when he'd shown up at the hospital with the camera crew. Kellan had just smiled his way through that as he was doing right now.

Actually, he'd found smiling helped him get through plenty of things.

"This isn't a business proposition for you but for some of your ranch hands," Kellan went on. "It could earn them some extra money. The producer wants to use the Longhorn Bar, too, to film some scenes. Let me just go over the details with you."

Still no sign that Lawson was letting up on his desire to rearrange Kellan's body parts. But Eve's expression changed.

"I should be going," she said to Lawson after she sighed. She took a pen off his desk and signed a bunch of magazines. "Cassidy wanted to try to get some work done this afternoon, and I should be there in case Aiden gets fussy." She headed for the door but then stopped when her eyes met Kellan's. "Uh, will you be stopping by to see him?"

"Of course." Kellan intended to make this a "kill three birds with one stone" kind of trip. He could see his kid, talk to the owner of the Longhorn and have a heart-to-heart with Lawson. In reverse order since he had to deal with the still-scowling cowboy first.

Eve's mouth went in a straight line, maybe because she wasn't enthusiastic about the visit to see Aiden, but Kellan would keep it short. He liked the kid well enough, but visiting him was more out of obligation. His publicist had said he'd been getting requests for pictures of him with his son, and he could get a few of those while he was there.

That, of course, made him a shithead.

Kellan was well aware of his shithead way of thinking, but he just didn't feel the same connection to the kid as Eve obviously did. Still, he'd pay child support and stuff. He'd be there for anything that Eve asked him to be there for, but so far, she wasn't putting out the welcome mat for him. Which was probably the best possible arrangement for both of them.

Eve started out of the room, then stopped, and she looked at Lawson as if she should say or do something. Maybe kiss him goodbye. Kellan noticed that she dropped her gaze to the vicinity of his mouth. Yes, the same mouth that went in a straight line again when she glanced at Kellan.

"I'll call you later," she said to Lawson. "We need to talk."

That didn't please the cowboy, either, and his scowl stayed in place as she went out the door. A door that Kellan quickly closed. Best not to have anyone walking in on them for this part of the conversation.

Lawson looked at him as if sizing him up. "Are you here to tell me not to dick around with Eve's feelings?"

Kellan pulled back his shoulders. It hadn't even occurred to him to interfere in Eve's private life. "No. She can dick around with whatever guy or cowboy she wants." Obviously, he needed to get some things straight. "Look, it was a one-nighter between Eve and me. Nothing more."

"Nothing more except for the baby you created with her," Lawson quickly pointed out.

Great. This was going to be one of those lectures. He already got enough of them from some of his friends who had kids of their own. Apparently because they were into the whole daddy thing, they thought he should be, too. But he just wasn't wired that way.

"Yes, we created a kid together, but that doesn't mean Eve and I have to be joined at the hip or anything." And then he asked the question that usually got his friends to back off. "Do you really believe it would help Aiden or Eve if I were around them more often?"

That at least untightened Lawson's scowl a bit. "No. Because you're an asshole."

No argument from Kellan on that. He was. And until someone gave him a good reason to change, he was keeping things as they were. It had worked well for him so far, and if it wasn't broken, he wasn't going to fix it.

"For what it's worth, Eve didn't even want to be with me that night," Kellan explained. "She was going on about you, mumbling stuff that didn't make sense. She was upset, and that's the only reason we had sex."

Lawson's forehead bunched up. "She was going on about me?"

The cowboy didn't have much range in his tone. He barked or snarled everything. But maybe he only did that to Kellan.

Kellan nodded. "She was talking about the past, and your name kept coming up. Other stuff, too, but remember I was a little drunk, too, so I don't recall it all." He snapped his fingers. "Oh, and she also mentioned Tessie a lot. And speaking of Tessie, she's another of the reasons that I'm here," Kellan said. Best to move this along so he could make it back to the airport in time. "Tessie called me late last night and gave me this sad spiel about her getting drunk and you seeing her and her not wanting her mom to know."

Lawson stayed frozen a moment as if absorbing that, and then he cursed. This time, though, his profanity didn't seem to be aimed at Kellan. "I already told Eve, right before you showed up."

Well, obviously Eve hadn't taken it too hard if her go-to reaction was to kiss a cowboy. Kellan shrugged. "I'll call Tessie and let her know."

"No." Lawson squeezed his eyes shut a moment. "I'll phone Tessie and tell her."

That sounded as if it was the last thing Lawson wanted to do, but Kellan was glad he'd volunteered. This seemed like a sticky situation he wanted to avoid.

"What'd you say to Tessie when she told you she'd gotten drunk?" Lawson asked him.

"At first, I said I couldn't come see you, but that I'd call you instead. She insisted I had to come in person because I could convince you." He smiled. "She has a lot of faith in my skills of persuasion."

Some of Lawson's scowl returned. "What'd you say to her about the drinking? I hope you told her that it'd been a stupid thing for her to do since she's underage or close to it."

"Oh, she's underage all right. Her eighteenth birthday isn't until next month. I hadn't actually remembered that on my own, but Tessie brought it up when she called last night. She said something about once she turned eighteen in three weeks, then maybe her mom would stop trying to coddle her. I told her good luck with that. Eve'll still coddle her when she's forty."

"Tessie's seventeen?" This was less of a bark and more of a howl. "Hell's fucking bells. I should have had her butt arrested. And how is she in college already if she's so young?"

"She's smart, I guess, because she graduated from

high school a year early and took some online college courses even before she moved to Texas."

"Well, she's not very smart if she got drunk." Lawson turned his glare back on Kellan. "And when you talked to her, you should have told her that drinking at her age was reckless and stupid."

"Uh, I don't think so. Tessie treats me like a friend, and I want to keep it that way. Eve can bust her chops for shit like that."

Lawson's index finger poked against his chest. "You should have busted her chops for it, too."

Kellan took the risk of pushing the poking finger away. "Hey, I'm not her father. And be thankful she has me for a sounding board after what Eve did to her."

Lawson's shoulder went back. "What the hell are you talking about?"

"Duh. The rift between them. It's all Eve's fault. I'd be pissed, too, if my mom had lied to me like that, and I'm an adult. Imagine, having to hear something like that when you're just a teenager. That rift happened a year ago, when Tessie was only sixteen."

Oops. He probably shouldn't have mentioned that since Eve had sworn him to secrecy. But he'd been trying to make a point. Which Kellan thought he'd more or less succeeded in doing.

"What the hell are you talking about?" Lawson repeated. Finally, there was a different tone that wasn't barkish, snarlish or growlish. This one had a subdued edge to it.

Since the cat was out of the bag, there was no use trying to put the kitty back in. "Tessie isn't adopted. Eve gave birth while she was still filming *Demon High*.

Last year, Tessie found her original birth certificate with Eve's name on it."

Kellan was surprised at the relief he felt in getting that off his chest. But Lawson obviously wasn't feeling any such relief at all. However, he was counting something on his fingers. The months. And he was going backward from October. When he made it to the ninth month, January, the growl was back. Again, with a different edge.

A dangerous-sounding one.

Lawson spit out a single word of profanity coupled with Eve's name before he stormed out the door.

LAWSON CURSED THE whole way out of the house. Kept cursing when he reached the sunroom. And continued onto the porch. He could have kept it up, easily, all the way to his truck, but he ran into an obstacle—literally.

Roman.

Lawson smacked right into him as he was barreling down the steps. He cursed and apologized at the same time but kept moving. He had one goal now. To get in his truck, drive to Eve's and demand to know why she'd done this. Of course, there was no explanation she could give him that would smooth this over, but damn it all to hell, she'd better have some kind of answer.

"Wait up," Roman called out to him.

Lawson didn't, but he'd forgotten just how dang fast Roman could run. He caught up with him and moved in front of his truck door. Maybe some attempt so that Lawson couldn't get it open, but if necessary he'd kick Roman's ass to do what needed to get done.

"Is this about Eve?" Roman asked.

"Yeah, and get the fuck out of my way."

Turns out that whipping Roman's ass wasn't easy. When Lawson went to shove him aside, Roman held his ground, and because he was bigger and stronger than Lawson, he managed that just fine.

"What happened?" Roman pressed, and he sounded awfully calm for someone who had pinned a very pissed-off cousin against the side of his truck.

"This is between Eve and me." He rammed his elbow into Roman's stomach, but that part of his cousin was obviously as hard as his head because Roman still didn't budge.

"Stop and think about this for a moment. You really believe you'll accomplish anything with Eve when you're seeing red like this? The veins are bulging in your neck, and your nostrils are puffed out so wide you look like a mutant cobra. Eve doesn't need this shit from you."

"My shit?" Lawson yelled. "This is Eve's shit!" His voice was a lot louder than he wanted it to be, but it was impossible to rein in anything right now. His voice, his temper and that fiery ball that was boiling up from his gut.

By now, they'd gotten the attention of some ranch hands who were gathering outside the barn. None of them were rushing to interfere or help though, probably because they didn't want to incur the wrath of either Roman or Lawson. But there'd be talk and speculation about what had caused one of their bosses to act like this.

"Use your inside voice and tell me what she did," Roman insisted. "Does it have anything to do with the horn-boy actor who showed up?"

It took Lawson a couple of seconds just to get

enough control of his vocal cords so he could speak. "Sort of. He's the one who spilled Eve's shit." And even with the rage he was feeling, he had to wince at the way he'd said that. Anger didn't make him very articulate.

Roman relaxed the grip he had on Lawson, and he stepped back enough that Lawson could have tried to punch him again. But the look that came over Roman's face had him holding back on the punch. For now, anyway. But Roman was going to pay for this.

Eve was *really* going to pay for it.

"Is this about Tessie being your daughter?" Roman asked.

That stopped any punching thoughts and had Lawson whipping up his head so he could look Roman in the eye. Lawson so didn't like what he saw there. Of course, Roman's question itself wasn't high on Lawson's likability scale.

"You knew?" Lawson said.

Roman lifted his shoulder. "I was in the doorway of the Longhorn last night when she was going to her car. I thought there was a family resemblance. She looks a lot like Sophie did at that age."

"Well, fuck me." Lawson groaned, put his hands on the side of his head and groaned some more. Since someone had just pulled the ground out from beneath his feet, he leaned against his truck for support. When that didn't help, he sank on his butt to the ground.

"I take it you had no idea," Roman added.

That was the most understated statement Lawson had ever heard. "None. Because Eve would have told me something like that. Or at least I thought she would." And then Lawson thought of something. "Those magazine covers—"

"Probably Photoshopped." Roman caught onto him and hauled him to his feet. "Are you feeling less pissed off now so we can talk with cooler heads?"

"Hell, no."

With as much anger as he was feeling, it might take light-years for him to stop feeling...well, whatever the hell he was feeling. The only emotion Lawson could latch on to was the anger, but he was certain there were other things lurking around. Feelings that would soon come to bite him in the ass.

"Why wouldn't Eve have told me?" Lawson grumbled.

Roman blew out a long breath. "That's something you're going to need to ask her. But I can go with you to do that. You need something to drink before I drive you over there to see her?"

It was tempting, both the liquor and Roman's offer to go with him. The whiskey would smooth down some of the edges of this raw anger, but Lawson wasn't sure smoothing was the way to go here. Eve needed to see his face. Needed to know that what she'd done was wrong in every way possible.

"Thanks," Lawson said, "but I'm doing this on my own." He tried to sound as calm as he could manage. Which probably wasn't very calm. But he didn't need his cousin for support. "This is between Eve and me."

Roman stared at him, clearly debating if he was going to let a solo visit happen, but Lawson didn't give him any more input on that. He was thankful that Roman had moved him from the stunned rage to the stunned anger stage, but Lawson didn't want Roman there when he confronted Eve.

Lawson got in his truck, and as soon as he got it started, he slammed his foot on the accelerator, leaving Roman scowling at him in his rearview mirror.

CHAPTER FOURTEEN

EVE NORMALLY ENJOYED feeding Aiden his bottle, but her son was drinking at a snail's pace. He was far more interested in playing with his toes and pinching her than he was finishing up so that Eve could make arrangements to go to Austin.

Where she had to confront Tessie.

Eve still wasn't sure what she was going to say to her daughter about getting drunk, but Tessie clearly needed help. Counseling, for starters. She doubted Tessie would just agree to that, but Eve was going to have to put her foot down. Tessie was still a minor—for a few more weeks, anyway—and if necessary Eve would force her to talk to a therapist about what had made her do such a dangerous, irresponsible thing.

God, it crushed her heart to think of Tessie drunk like that. It crushed her even more to think of what Tessie must have been feeling to try to drown her troubles with booze. Even if Tessie had done this as some kind of thrill or because of peer pressure and not because of all the anger, it still wasn't acceptable. And Eve had to do something about that.

Sometimes being a parent sucked.

"You want me to finish up feeding Aiden?" Cassidy called down from the top of the stairs. Since Eve was in the family room, she couldn't actually see her, but she had no trouble hearing her. "That way, you can get ready for Kellan's visit and the drive to Austin."

Cassidy knew about both because Eve had blurted out everything to her the moment she'd gotten back from the Granger Ranch. But Eve had no intention of doing anything to get ready for Kellan. In fact, she'd like to avoid him altogether. She hated to put that visit on Cassidy, but she couldn't sit there any longer while worrying about Tessie.

"Yes, please," Eve answered. "And when and if Kellan gets here, maybe you can try to find out if he lied about coming to Wrangler's Creek to check out using the ranch hands as extras."

There was possibly something fishy about that, but then again, this was Kellan. He came up with a lot of dumb ideas, and he didn't mind spreading those ideas to others.

Whatever plan it turned out to be, Lawson wouldn't take the bait, she was certain of that, but Kellan might be able to convince someone else in the area to go along with a scheme that might not be totally aboveboard.

Once, Kellan had invested in a coffee farm in South America that had turned out to be a brothel. Another time he'd talked his friends into putting up funds so a screenwriter-girlfriend could get her play into production. The girlfriend–con artist had left as soon as she had the money.

Cassidy came in the family room, scooping up Aiden and kissing him at the same time. Aiden giggled, pinched and played with his toes some more, which meant Eve had been right to hand him off. The feeding could have gone on way too long, and she wanted to get to Austin so she could catch Tessie as soon as she finished her classes.

"Wish me luck," Eve said, getting her purse and keys from the foyer table.

"You might need more than luck," Cassidy grumbled. "Any idea what you're going to say to Tessie?"

"You mean other than 'you're grounded for the rest of your life'?" Eve groaned. "This was so much easier when she was a kid."

"Yeah. You probably can't manage this with a gold-sticker chart."

No. And even though Eve didn't want to consider it, she might lose Tessie for good. With that dismal fear running like wildfire through her head, she threw open the door and immediately spotted Lawson's truck barreling up her driveway. He was going way too fast, as was the truck behind him.

Roman's.

Her first thought was there'd been some kind of emergency. One that might involve Kellan. Maybe Lawson had punched him or something, but that probably wouldn't have brought Roman here, chasing after him, and that's clearly what Roman was doing.

Her heart went straight to her throat.

When Lawson stopped and got out of his truck, he was still in the "barreling" mode, but so was Roman. He braked to a noisy stop behind Lawson, and while calling out Lawson's name, he tried to catch up with him before he made it to the door. Roman didn't quite succeed at that. He was still a good five yards behind when Lawson stepped onto her porch.

"What happened?" she asked.

Though it was obvious Lawson had been in a hurry to get there, he had some trouble speaking. Probably because his jaw was clamped tight from the equally tight muscles in his face.

"Tessie," he growled, managing to get the word out.

That didn't help her heart in her throat, and Eve was about to ask him if something bad had happened to Tessie.

And then she saw it in his eyes.

Lawson *knew*.

"Don't do this," Roman warned him when he bolted up the steps to the porch. He was out of breath and clearly very concerned. "Let's just sit down and *calmly* talk this out."

"Fuck off," Lawson snarled to him, and Eve suspected this was a continuation of a profanity-riddled conversation that had started at the Granger Ranch.

"Kellan told you?" she asked Lawson.

He didn't confirm it with words, but she thought maybe his grunt-growl was of agreement. Eve would settle up with Kellan later, but for now, she obviously had a more pressing problem. Lawson looked ready to implode.

Since she didn't want Aiden to hear any of this, she stepped out onto the porch, shutting the door behind her. She went to the far end of the porch in case this turned to shouting. Judging from Lawson's expression, she could expect it. That's why she gathered her breath and just put it all out there.

"Yes, Tessie's your daughter, and yes, I was wrong to keep her from you. Yes, I have no excuse that's going to help this situation, so if you want to yell at me, go ahead. I certainly deserve it." Maybe all those yeses would help soothe that rage in his eyes.

Eve had intended to stop talking, to give Lawson a

chance to start the shouting, but the wave of emotion just swept right over her. Not just the secret of keeping his daughter from him but also the rift with Tessie.

"I've made such a mess of things," she went on. The blasted tears came, and even though she tried to blink them back, it didn't help. "And now I've screwed up Tessie. That's why she was drinking. Because of me. Because I suck at being a good mom and a good person."

Lawson still looked primed for a good yell, but he just stood there, glaring at her and cursing under his breath.

"I didn't tell you because I didn't think you'd want to know," she went on. "You always made it clear that you never wanted kids. And things were so bad between us when I left. We were both grieving Brett's death, blaming ourselves, and I just kept hearing the last words we said to each other." Eve looked up at him. "You remember those words?"

The muscles in his face didn't exactly relax, but his shoulders dropped a little. "I wish to hell I'd never met you."

That was it verbatim, which meant it'd stuck with him over the years, too.

"I know you said that in anger," she continued. "I also know you had a right to say it because of Brett and because I was leaving. But those are the words I heard when I picked up the phone to call you and tell you I was pregnant. Needless to say, I didn't make that call."

"You should have," he snapped.

Roman was poised on the steps as if waiting to see if he should intervene. Lawson's snap caused him to go up a step, but Eve didn't want him to come to her aid.

She was feeling so low that she didn't deserve anyone on her side right now.

"Yes, I should have," she agreed. "And plenty of times I wanted to do just that despite the words in my head. But the years went by, and I convinced myself that I had done the right thing. If you didn't want to be a father as a teenager, then you probably wouldn't have wanted to be one as an adult."

Eve sent an apologetic look Roman's way because he'd gotten his high school girlfriend pregnant, and when she'd skipped out on him shortly after giving birth, Roman had ended up raising the boy on his own.

"How the hell could you have managed to keep something like this a secret?" Lawson demanded.

"Lies and secrets. Something I'm good at. The studio used body doubles and Photoshop to help cover it up. And the other actors and crew signed nondisclosure statements. Even with all that, though, no one was more surprised than I was when it stayed under wraps."

Lawson's eyes narrowed. "I'm pretty sure I've got you beat in the surprised department. Does Tessie know?"

Eve shook her head. "Well, she knows she's not adopted, but she doesn't know you're her father."

And she braced herself for Lawson to say that was soon going to change, that he was going to drive to Austin right now and tell Tessie everything. Of course, Lawson could take a different direction. He could repeat those words that had served him so well nearly eighteen years ago.

I wish to hell I'd never met you.

This time though, he wouldn't be just saying them out of anger. But because they were true.

She could see the hate in his eyes. At least she thought it was hate. Hard to tell because the tears were making her vision blurry. However, even blurry vision couldn't stop her from seeing the limo driving toward the house.

"Kellan," she muttered. She definitely didn't need this now.

"Sorry, I left the gate open," Roman explained. "I was in kind of a hurry to stop an impending apocalypse. Are you two going to play nice now, or do I need to stay awhile longer?"

Eve could promise him that playing nice wasn't something Lawson had in mind, but there was no need for Roman to put in any more time here. If Lawson got violent, it wouldn't be with her. Kellan might be fair game though, but she had too much else on her mind to worry if his often smart-mouth was going to put him in the path of Lawson's fist. Besides, she wasn't exactly pleased that Kellan had been the one to spill her secret, not when it should have come from her.

Oblivious to the shit-storm that was happening on the porch, Kellan was talking on the phone when he stepped from the limo.

"I'll get rid of him," Roman volunteered.

Eve was considering that when she heard him say something to the person on the other end of the phone line. "Don't worry, Baby-Cakes, Jr. I'll talk to her. That sort of thing is my specialty."

To the best of Eve's knowledge, Kellan only called one person by that ridiculous name of Baby-Cakes, Jr.

Tessie.

Now it was Eve who did some barreling. She ran

off the porch, going past Roman. "Why are you on the phone with Tessie?" she snapped.

Kellan lifted his eyebrow as if the answer was obvious and that she was stupid for even asking, and he put the call on mute. "Tessie knows the cowboy told you about the drinking, and I'm here to try to smooth things over. Or at least I think that's what she wants me to do. It's hard to tell with all the crying. The girl knows how to turn on the waterworks."

Nothing in the world could have stopped Eve from snatching the phone from Kellan. "Tessie?" she said the moment she unmuted it. But that was the only thing she managed to say before Tessie interrupted her.

"Mom, don't overreact." There was no chance of her not doing that, either. And yes, Tessie was crying. "I'm taking care of things. I don't need or want you here."

That wasn't something the mother of a teenager wanted to hear. "I'm coming to see you right now."

"No. Don't. They won't let you in."

Again, not something a mom wanted to hear. "What do you mean? Where are you?" This time, Tessie didn't answer though Eve could hear some muffled chatter. "Where are you?" Eve practically shouted it into the phone.

"Miss Cooper?" someone finally said. Definitely not Tessie.

"Put my daughter back on the line," Eve demanded.

"I'm sorry, but I can't. Tessie's not allowed any phone calls until she's had her assessment."

"Assessment?" Lawson repeated, and that's when Eve realized he was right behind her, listening to every word.

"Yes," the person verified. "Tessie's just checked herself into rehab."

EVE WAS CERTAIN that if she sat down, she was going to fly apart. No way could she keep seated, so she just paced across the floor of the waiting room of the Hope Sanctuary, the private rehab facility where Tessie was apparently now a patient.

And Eve wasn't pacing alone, either.

Lawson was right there with her in the small twelve-by-twelve-foot area. Considering there were chairs and a reception desk behind security glass, that didn't give them a lot of room to maneuver, and they kept running into each other.

Literally.

But the two times that had happened, Lawson had moved away from her as if she'd scalded him. An extreme reaction, considering he got routinely kicked, butted and stepped on by broncos and assorted cattle. Still, Eve couldn't blame him. At the moment she wanted to get away from herself.

Mercy, things were falling apart. Tessie was in here. In rehab! Lawson hated her, and the worst part about all of it was that it would likely get worse before there was any chance of things getting better. Both Tessie and Lawson had to heal, and God knew how long of a process that would be.

Lawson's phone buzzed, the sound cutting through the shuffling of their footsteps. "Dylan," he muttered when he glanced at the screen, and he let the call go to voice mail. He probably wasn't ready to try to explain any of this to members of his family.

She checked the time. Lawson and she had been there nearly an hour. Way too long with no news. Of course, the drive there had been too long as well, especially since Lawson had insisted on making the trip with her. Eve hadn't even bothered to try to dissuade him. Now that he knew he was Tessie's father, he probably thought he had as much right to be here as she did.

"Welcome to fatherhood," Eve grumbled. She hadn't meant to say that loud enough for Lawson to hear. It'd just slipped out, but it was a good sarcastic assessment of what was going on. And he heard it all right.

He slowed his pacing enough to look at her. It was a glare, but like the other stink eye he'd been giving her, she deserved it.

But she also deserved answers as to what was happening with her child.

There was a sign on the counter next to the opaque glass surrounding the reception desk. A sign that warned Do Not Tap on the Glass. There were other warnings below that about not using a cell phone, no weapons and no loud conversations. Lawson and she had the last one down pat since they hadn't spoken directly to each other, but Eve had already violated the cell-phone rule when she'd called Cassidy to check on Aiden.

And she'd broken the glass-tap rule when they'd first arrived.

That had earned her more stink eye, this time from the sour-faced receptionist-nurse who'd first had them fill out a contact info form and then had told them to wait, that the doctor or someone on their medical staff would be out shortly to talk to her. Since *shortly* had now turned into an hour, Eve tapped on the glass again. She'd barely managed to move her fingers away when the glass slid open, and the grouch puss stared at her. According to her name tag, she was Loralee McCarthy, but Eve had halfway expected it to be Nurse Ratched.

"The doctor or someone on our medical staff will be out shortly to talk to you," the woman said, repeating the exact words she'd used before.

Nurse Ratched came through loud and clear in that tone, and the woman would have shut the glass right in Eve's face if Lawson hadn't caught onto it.

"Get the doctor or someone who can answer our questions out here now," he ordered.

The woman opened her mouth as if to howl out a protest.

"Now!" Lawson insisted, and he had bested Nurse Ratched with enough badass that the woman picked up her phone.

"Can you see if Dr. Patel is done with the patient?" She paused. "Yes, that's the one. Her *actress* mother keeps tapping on the glass." She said *actress* as if it were navel lint.

Eve couldn't hear the response from the person on the other end of the line, but several seconds later, Loralee ended the call. "She'll be right out."

"Tessie will be?" Eve asked.

That got her an eye roll. "Dr. Patel. She'll talk to you about your daughter." Her gaze cut to Lawson. "Is he her father?"

"No," Lawson said as Eve fumbled around to get out a yes. "I don't think this is a good time for Tessie to find out," he added in a whisper to Eve.

It wasn't a good time, but Eve wasn't certain when that "good time" would magically appear. Still, she was appreciative that Lawson had put Tessie first in this.

"It's complicated," Eve told Loralee, who was still waiting for an answer.

The woman's next eye roll let Eve know that she

didn't care. "Dr. Patel can only discuss things with the patient's parents or legal guardian."

Lawson and Eve exchanged glances. "We're the parents," Eve said. And maybe that wouldn't get back to Tessie before she'd had a chance to tell her in person.

The door next to the reception area opened, and a tall, slim woman in a white coat greeted them with a thin smile. The kind of smile that was probably an attempt to reassure them that life as they knew it wasn't about to end, but it was hard for Eve not to feel that way. Because it had.

"Ms. Cooper," she said and looked at Lawson.

"Lawson Granger, Tessie's father." Lawson didn't stutter on the last word, but Eve heard the hesitation. Eve didn't resent it. She'd had nearly eighteen years to come to terms with being a parent. Lawson had had two hours.

The woman made another of those attempted smiles. "I'm Dr. Patel. Come with me, please."

She motioned for them to follow her, and they went down a short hall to an office. Neither the hall nor the office looked especially big. For that matter, neither did the building. It wasn't much larger than a two-story house.

Lawson's phone buzzed again with another call. Eve saw Dylan's name on the screen again, but like the other one, Lawson let this one go to voice mail, too.

"What happened to Tessie?" Eve asked the moment they were seated.

Dr. Patel took her time answering. "Your daughter said I could share some things with you," she said, emphasizing the *some*. "Since Tessie is still a minor, you can insist that I show you her medical records, which has a summary of her intake exam, but she's asked that you not do that."

Mercy. What a decision. If she didn't ask, she might not learn something important, but if she did ask, Tessie would have even more fodder not to trust her. She looked at Lawson to see if he had a take on this. It wasn't fair to place any of this on his shoulders, but Eve was walking on eggshells with him, too.

"Tell us what Tessie said it was okay to share," Eve finally answered, and she prayed that was the right thing to do.

The doctor nodded. "Several hours ago, Tessie came here saying that she needed help, and she voluntarily checked herself in. This is a privately funded free rehab facility, so there was no need to get her medical insurance information from you." She paused. "Were you aware that she's been drinking?"

"I just learned about it." Eve tried not to blame Lawson for not telling her sooner, but she wished that was something he'd done. That way, she could have forced Tessie to talk to her about the night Tessie and he had met face-to-face.

Maybe.

Tessie hadn't exactly been a font of two-way communication since this adoption-reveal had happened.

"Had Tessie been drinking when she got here?" Lawson asked.

"She didn't appear to have been, but I don't have the results of her blood test yet."

Eve thought there was a good chance that Tessie hadn't had a drop of alcohol today. "I think Tessie came here because she found out that I'd learned about her drinking. This could be her way of avoiding me."

The doctor made such a quick sound of agreement that it meant she'd already given that some thought and had come to the same conclusion. "Tessie's angry at something that happened between you and her, but she accepted responsibility for her drinking."

Eve still wasn't convinced. "If she's here just to avoid me, then being here won't help her. I'm thinking we should have family therapy sessions."

"I agree about the family sessions. I'm hoping Tessie will let me set up something like that in the near future. For now though, being here might indeed help her. She needs to sort through her feelings and get her life back on track, and here at Hope Sanctuary, we can assist her in making that happen."

Eve couldn't argue with anything Dr. Patel was saying. Tessie did need to get her life back on track. But eventually Tessie was going to have to face her.

"How long will she be here?" Lawson asked.

The doctor lifted her hands, palms up. "That depends on Tessie and how fast she works through the steps in the program. It could be days or weeks." She took out some brochures and handed a copy to each of them. "Read through those, and I'll be contacting you about when you can visit Tessie. Remember though, she's free to decline seeing you. And also free to check herself out of here at any time."

Lawson's phone buzzed again just as he opened the brochure. It wasn't a call but rather a text from Dylan. Eve wasn't about to see what it said, but it caused Lawson to get to his feet.

"Excuse me for a second," he said. "I need to make a call." He stepped out into the hall.

That got Eve's attention because she doubted Lawson would hit the pause button on the meeting unless there was some kind of emergency. It was true that he didn't really know Tessie, but the fact that he was here with her told Eve that he intended to be part of Tessie's life. Or rather as much of a part as Tessie would let either of them be.

Eve had questions for the doctor. She wanted to know if she could press Tessie to see her. One minute she wanted to coddle her baby girl, and the next minute she wanted to ground her and demand that she move back home. But Eve decided to postpone the questions a few seconds and find out what was going on with Lawson.

"I'll be right back," she told the doctor, and Eve went into the hall with him.

One look at Lawson's face, and she knew something was indeed wrong. This time, she didn't think it was anger that had caused his forehead to bunch up like that.

"It's my mother," he told her after several snail-crawling moments. "She's in the hospital, and Dylan said I should come right away."

CHAPTER FIFTEEN

ONCE AGAIN LAWSON found himself pacing in yet another room. This time, though, it was at the Wrangler's Creek Hospital, where he'd had the taxi drop him off.

Lawson hadn't had his truck in Austin because he'd ridden up there with Eve, and he hadn't wanted to wait for someone from the ranch to send a vehicle. Since he couldn't teleport, the taxi had been his best option to meet Dylan's come right now request. Judging from the bits and pieces he'd learned, Dylan's urgency was spot-on since his mom was still being worked on by the doctors.

Exactly what she was being worked on for, Lawson didn't know. But there'd better be some answers soon.

At least Lawson wasn't alone. His sister, Lily Rose, was pacing right along with him and nibbling her bottom lip. Dylan had apparently paced himself out because he was seated, his legs stretched out in front of him, his head resting on the back of the chair. To a casual observer, it might look as if Dylan was about to nod off, but Lawson knew his brother was just as concerned as Lily Rose and he were.

None of them were especially close to Regina. Hard to be close to someone who was never around. But blood was blood.

That thought stopped him for a couple of steps. Yes,

blood was indeed blood, and that's why he was torn between being here and being with Tessie. The difference was that Regina would want him to be there. And she knew that Lawson was her son. To Tessie, he was practically a stranger. One who had tattled on her for drinking. He was betting that was going to cause a rift between them for a long time to come.

A rift on Tessie's part, anyway.

No way was Lawson going to let her shut him out of her life. Especially since Eve had shut him out all these years.

"Why aren't they telling us anything?" his sister snapped. "And where the heck is Lucian? He should be here by now."

Lawson didn't have an answer for either question, but yeah, Lucian should have made it from his office in San Antonio by now. They'd let their other brother, Reed, know, as well. Or rather they'd tried, but Reed was a cop on an undercover assignment. His handler, boss or whatever the heck his job title was had told Dylan that he would try to get a message to Reed.

His phone buzzed again, something it'd been doing for the past half hour since he'd arrived at the hospital. His cousins and some of the hands had texted to find out if there was anything they could do. And Eve had sent a text, too, to give him an update about Tessie and ask about his mom. Neither Lawson nor she had had good news. Eve hadn't been able to see Tessie and was on her way back home, and Lawson still had no word on why his mom had collapsed while Dylan and she were at the diner having coffee.

"I knew something was wrong," Lily Rose went on.

"When I saw Mom yesterday, she looked pale. Didn't you notice that?" she asked Lawson.

He had to shrug. He hadn't really noticed because that'd been the day Regina had interrupted Eve and him kissing. Lawson probably wouldn't have noticed if Regina had walked in with a chicken on her head. And that made him only curse himself more. His head was a tangled mess right now at a time when he needed to focus.

"Should one of us try to get in touch with Dad?" Lily Rose asked.

Lawson's first reaction was to say no. Truth was, his folks had never gotten along, and his dad had remarried. Multiple times. Lawson thought he was on wife number four now. His dad had clearly moved on. And on. And on. But there was a slim chance that he would want to know that the mother of his children was in the hospital.

"I'll call him later," Lawson answered. Once they knew what the heck was going on.

Since the pacing was wearing thin, Lawson went to the chairs and sank down in the one next to Dylan. His brother was texting, and before Dylan put his phone away, Lawson saw Eve's name on the screen.

"She's just worried about you," Dylan said when Lawson tried to get a better look at the message, and he put his phone away. "Really, that's all," his brother added when he continued to stare at him. Actually, Lawson had to admit that he was probably glaring. "Sheesh. Jealous much?"

"I'm not jealous," Lawson snapped. The rest of him nearly snapped, too, and that's when he realized he needed to rein in everything that was bubbling up inside him.

"Any idea what you'll do about Tessie?" Dylan asked.

That put a stop to the reining in, and the question caused Lawson to stare at him again. "Eve told you what was going on with Tessie?"

"No. But I've got eyes. When I saw Tessie the other night at the Longhorn, I figured she was yours."

"Shit," Lawson spit out. That was almost identical to what Roman had said. "Am I the only one who didn't know?"

"Appears that way. You never were very bright about that sort of thing."

Under normal circumstances, those would have been fighting words between brothers, but Lawson was beginning to think Dylan might have a point. He hadn't noticed the resemblance between him and Tessie, and he hadn't a clue that his mom had looked weak.

"Things with Tessie are screwed up," Lawson told him. "Things with Eve and me, too."

Lawson figured that would prompt Dylan to give another of those brotherly jabs. Something like *You're just spreading sunshine wherever you go.* But Dylan didn't head in that direction.

"Anything I can do to help?" Dylan asked. "I've talked to Tessie a couple of times on the phone, and I don't think things are screwed up between me and her. I can try to have another chat with her."

"You talked to Tessie? When?"

Dylan shrugged. "I called her a time or two after Eve moved back. Mom asked me to try to smooth things over between Eve and her."

"And Tessie actually took your calls?"

"Yeah. I guess I'm sort of like Switzerland for her. Neutral ground." Dylan paused. "What's going on with Tessie, anyway? And don't lie and say that nothing's wrong because if someone painted a picture of a giant pulsing nerve, it'd have the expression you have right now."

Yeah, he was right, and Lawson took a deep breath, ready to tell Dylan, but then he saw Darby making her way toward him.

Hell.

He hoped this wasn't personal, and thankfully, it wasn't.

"Your mom wants to see you. All of you," Darby added to Lily Rose and Dylan. "But the doctor left orders for her to have only one visitor at a time. She asked to see you first."

The *you* in this case was Lawson. A shocker. Lily Rose was her baby, and Dylan was the one who got along with everybody. Lucian was the one in charge, the boss, and Reed was the semiprodigal son who she would have welcomed back with open arms. If Reed were to ever come back, that is.

And then there was Lawson.

Smack in the middle of the five kids. A hell-raising teenager who cut school, drank and was so wrapped up in Eve that he hadn't noticed his family for three or four years.

The last thing he'd expected to be was first in the visiting pecking order, but Lawson didn't hesitate. When Darby motioned for him to follow her, he got right to his feet.

"What happened to my mother? Why did she collapse?" Lawson asked.

She opened her mouth, maybe some kind of rote reaction left over from when they'd been lovers. In those days, she wouldn't have hidden anything from him.

Unlike what seemingly the rest of the world had done.

But Darby shook her head when she no doubt remembered that ex-lover status wouldn't get you squat.

"I'm sure Regina will tell you everything she wants you to know," Darby finally said. She stopped outside the ICU. "Just don't upset her, and keep your visit short. I'll be back in five minutes to bring in Lily Rose."

Lawson nodded, stepped into the room and didn't like anything he saw. His mom was hooked up to monitors and had an IV. And she was practically bald. He knew she wore wigs, of course, but he hadn't known that beneath them were just sprigs and tufts of cottony white hair.

Speaking of white, now he saw the paleness that Lily Rose had mentioned. There was no color in his mom's face, but she managed a smile when she saw him, and she waggled her fingers for him to come closer. He tried to steel himself for whatever she might say, and he prayed she hadn't brought him there to say goodbye.

"You're grounded," she said, her voice surprisingly strong since she didn't look as if she could have fought off a wet piece of paper.

"For what?" he snapped, and then he remembered he was no longer thirteen and acting out.

Since he was pretty sure it was a joke, he managed to lighten up his expression some, and he maneuvered around the machines so he could brush a kiss on her cheek.

"What's wrong with you, Mom?" he asked.

Her breath was a little ragged. "I had an allergic reaction to my cancer meds. You know, the pharmacists read out all those possible scary symptoms, but apparently they weren't kidding about the chance of sudden death. My heart stopped, but it's nothing to worry about because I'm stable now."

Lawson wanted to look around and make sure a Mack truck hadn't just slammed into him. Considering he'd already been hit with stunner news, he wondered for a moment if his own heart might give out.

"Cancer," he repeated. "Sudden death. What the heck are you talking about?" He thankfully remembered to omit any of the curse words that nearly got mixed into that.

"Breast cancer." She patted his hand, which told him just how bad he must look right now for her to be comforting him. "I had the surgery about two months ago and went through chemo, but the latest meds they put me on really didn't agree with my system."

Obviously not, if a phrase like *sudden death* was getting bandied around. "You should have told me. You shouldn't have kept something like that to yourself."

Her right eyebrow winged up. "I'm not the only one keeping a secret. You didn't tell me about Tessie."

Lawson felt another slam of his heart but wondered why he was even surprised that she knew. Everyone else did.

"How long have you known?" he asked.

"For about four months. I was in California and ran into Eve." She stopped a moment and dragged in a shallow breath. "I could see she was pregnant and having a hard time. We had coffee so we could catch up, and that's when she showed me a picture of Tessie that she had on her phone. One look at her, and I knew she was my granddaughter."

The events of the last three months suddenly became very clear. "And you talked Eve into moving here."

"I didn't have to do much talking. She was looking to make a change, and by then Tessie had already moved to Austin to go to school. Eve wanted to be close to her without being right on her doorstep." She patted his hand again. "Don't be cross with Eve about all of this. She was young and made a mistake."

No, it was more than just a mistake, but he wasn't going to upset his mom by verbally blasting Eve. He could do that later. But he could get something clarified right now.

"If you knew Tessie was my daughter, then why did you try to set Eve up with Dylan?" he asked. "And why'd you tell me that it wasn't wise to get involved with Eve again?"

Darby came to the door and tapped her watch, indicating his time was up, but Lawson held up his finger in a "wait a sec" gesture.

"I didn't try to set them up," Regina insisted. "Not really. I mean, I knew Eve wouldn't go for Dylan, not when she only has eyes for you. I was just hoping it would spur you into action."

Lawson had already been spurred by kissing Eve, and his mom and Dylan had interrupted what might have turned into sex against the family room wall. Best not to mention that to his mom, either.

"I said all that about it not being wise," she went on, "because you like to disagree with me."

He nearly said *I do not*, which would have only proved her point. "Reverse psychology," he muttered. He wasn't a fan of it, but it had indeed gotten him to consider if he should try to make another go of it with Eve.

Or at least have sex with her.

But then Eve's secret had come to light and blown that idea to smithereens. He still wanted to have sex with her, but at this point, it would be angry sex.

Darby motioned to him again, so Lawson brushed another kiss on his mom's cheek. "Get some rest. And get better."

Regina caught onto his hand as he was leaving. "Will you bring Tessie to see me?" she whispered. "Please."

Until she added that *please*, Lawson had been about to say that it might not be possible. But somehow, he would make it happen.

"You're my favorite child, you know that?" his mom added in a weak whisper.

He looked at her with what he was sure was plenty of skepticism. "You're going to tell all the others that, too, aren't you?"

She smiled. And while the smile was just as weak as she looked, it was probably about the best send-off he was going to get, considering the condition she was in.

"Are you okay?" Darby asked when he came out of the room. She walked back with him toward the waiting room, probably so she could escort another one of his siblings in for a visit.

Lawson wasn't sure if he was fine or not, but he did think it was civil of Darby to ask. "How about you?

Are you all right?" No need for him to clarify what he meant. The last time they'd spoken was the day of the raincoat incident. When he'd turned her down flat, Darby had probably been hurt and humiliated.

"I'll live." There wasn't any sarcasm in her voice. "Why does Regina want to see Eve's daughter?"

He groaned. He definitely hadn't known that Darby had heard that. "She just wants to meet her."

If there was an award for half-assed reasons, Lawson would have just won it. Until he said that, there hadn't been any real suspicion in Darby's eyes, but it was sure as hellfire there now. Obviously though, Darby hadn't seen Tessie. If she had, she would have used the invisible gene-pool goggles that everybody but Lawson seemed to have to determine that Tessie was a Granger.

With the suspicion still there, Darby traded off escort duties, taking Lily Rose toward the ICU. Lawson made a beeline to Dylan so he could find out if he knew anything about their mom's cancer.

However, Lawson didn't even get to ask the question because his phone buzzed. He didn't recognize the number on the screen, but when he realized it was an Austin area code, he answered it fast. Good thing, too, because while he hadn't known the number, he recognized the voice.

"Mr. Granger, this is Dr. Patel," the caller said. "I just contacted Ms. Cooper, but I thought you should know, too."

And with just that handful of words, his stomach went to the floor. "Is something wrong with Tessie?"

It didn't help when the doctor didn't jump right in to answer. "Maybe. I thought you should know that

Tessie just checked herself out of rehab. I strongly advised her against it, but she left anyway. She said I was to tell you and her mother that she was okay, that she just needed some time to be alone. That might be, Mr. Granger, but I think you and Ms. Cooper need to find her right away."

CHAPTER SIXTEEN

EVE HELD HER BREATH, knocked on Tessie's door at the sorority house and prayed that this time there'd be an answer.

There wasn't.

So, Eve went through the routine she'd been following for the past two days since Tessie had checked herself out of rehab and had seemingly disappeared off the face of the earth except for a text message to repeat what she'd told Dr. Patel—that she was okay and needed some space. Well, two days was enough space, as far as Eve was concerned, and she needed to see Tessie.

She knocked again. And again. And again. She kept knocking until someone from the room next door yelled out, "Shut up!"

The shouted *shut up*, which was often accompanied by profanity, was part of the routine now, too, since someone usually started yelling at her when the knocking went on for more than five minutes. On the first day, someone had called the cops. After Eve had explained to the officers why she was there, they'd managed to get a key so they could get inside to have a look around.

No Tessie.

Many of her things were still there, but her laptop

and her phone were gone—things that she could have already had with her when she'd gone to rehab. Tessie's roommate had shown up around the same time that the cops were there, but she was clueless as to where Tessie was. However, she had assured Eve she would call her if Tessie returned.

There'd been no call either from Tessie or the roommate, so Eve had continued to go to the room with the hopes of running into either Tessie or someone who had answers. She'd also left sticky notes outside the door with messages for Tessie to call her ASAP.

Eve added another sticky-note message now, bringing the total to eleven.

Seeing each one of them caused the fear to wash over her again. Her daughter was officially a runaway since she'd had to file a missing person's report. Eve wasn't about to sink into a deep enough pit of despair to start looking in ditches and running up and down the street calling out for her. But she had hired two PIs to try to track Tessie down.

Well, actually she'd hired one, and Lawson had hired one, as well. They hadn't known about the double hiring until they'd been a couple of hours into the search.

She'd also contacted the Austin cops so they could do an Amber Alert. That would mean dealing with the fallout from the publicity, but at this point that seemed minor.

Eve pressed down the sticky note again to make sure it didn't give way and flutter to the floor, where it might get swept away, and she went back down the stairs. Slowly. Just in case this could be the exact time that Tessie might come running in. And someone came in all right. But it wasn't Tessie.

It was Lawson.

Their gazes connected, and Eve nearly missed the step that could have sent her sprawling. She righted herself by grabbing on to the railing.

"Anything?" he said. Over the past two days, he'd asked her that a lot. She shook her head.

"I just found out that Tessie texted Clay." He took out his phone to show her a copy of the message.

"'I'm okay,'" Eve read. "'Call off the search. I don't want to be found because I don't want to see my mother.'"

That gave Eve both some relief and crushed her heart. "I don't want the search called off," she insisted.

"It won't be. In fact, I hired another PI."

Good. They were of a like mind about that.

"I left her another note," Eve added. No need to clarify what note because Lawson had obviously seen them. He'd also made several trips here, too. "I don't suppose you've heard anything else?"

He lifted his shoulder. "The first PI I hired said she hasn't used her credit card or accessed her bank account in the last forty-eight hours."

Her PI had told her the same thing. "I don't even know how much cash she would have had," Eve admitted. "Her last cash withdrawal was a week ago for two hundred dollars, but if she's having to pay for a place to stay and meals, that money would have probably already run out."

Lawson looked depressed enough to get on her worry-train, but then he shook his head. "Maybe she's staying with a friend. A friend we haven't managed to talk to yet. Once she's good and ready, she'll turn up," he assured her.

"What if she doesn't?" The darn tears started again. "What if Tessie learned the truth about you being her father, and she's so upset that she won't face us?"

He didn't answer her, but he did slide his arm around her waist to give her a pseudo hug. A very short one. Because he stepped back almost right away. Despite its brevity, Eve knew it was a big concession on his part because he still had to be angry with her. But she certainly wasn't feeling anger, and being in his arms helped. A lot. It made her feel as if she wasn't alone in this.

It also made her feel guilty. Because Tessie wasn't the only thing that Lawson had on his plate.

"How's Regina?" she asked.

"Better. Dylan said she should be released from the hospital tomorrow. She's insisting on coming up here to help us look for Tessie."

Good grief. That definitely wasn't a good idea, and Lawson no doubt agreed.

"Tessie is her grandchild," Lawson added. "And she's complaining that at the rate her kids are going, she might end up being the only one she ever gets. Dylan joked that he could knock up a woman or two, but she wasn't amused."

No. And Regina probably wasn't *amused* when she'd first found out that Lawson had a child. Eve certainly hadn't been thrilled when she'd first learned she was pregnant, but then, the love of a child, or a grandchild, could smooth over all sorts of things like doubt, disappointment and even a broken heart.

"Maybe we'll find Tessie before Regina gets out of the hospital," Eve said.

That might keep the woman from making a trip up here. *Might*. But Regina could be just as insistent on coming so that she could meet Tessie. Eve would try to dissuade that since it definitely wasn't a good time for making extended-family introductions. Not with so many things uncertain.

"The cops and the PI are still questioning Tessie's friends and sorority sisters," Eve continued a moment later. "And I've talked to every one of them who'll talk to me."

He nodded. "Same here. I spent my day at the campus. She didn't have any classes scheduled for today, but she missed the ones yesterday."

Eve already knew that. In fact, she suspected there wasn't much they could say about their search results that they each didn't already know. Since there was nothing new they could do, they both just kept tracing and retracing their steps. Eve had even considered that Tessie might try to go to Wrangler's Creek, so she'd alerted folks there, too, in case that happened.

"I talked to Dr. Patel again," Lawson went on. So had Eve. And she'd gotten nothing from her or the crotchety woman at reception. "But Clay's calling Austin PD to try to get surveillance-camera access for us. There's a bank up the street from the rehab clinic, and the camera might show which direction Tessie went when she left."

That got her attention. It was a lead that Eve hadn't chased yet. "Maybe it'll help if I call Austin PD, too? They might work faster to get the footage."

He stared at her with a disapproving look, and she

knew why. There was a fine line between pushing and pestering, and it was probably best to leave this to Clay. Maybe it wouldn't take him too long to get it.

"Are you heading back home tonight?" she asked. It wasn't late, barely 8:00 p.m., but it was an hour's drive back for both of them.

"No." He tipped his head toward the street. "Granger Western owns an apartment a couple of blocks from here, and no one ever uses it now that Sophie's moved her office to Wrangler's Creek. I'm staying there tonight."

That told her just how worried he was to be away from work at the ranch. Plus, Lawson wasn't exactly a city kind of guy.

"You're welcome to stay there, too," he added, though he didn't look completely comfortable with that invitation. Not at first, anyway. Then he huffed. "It's probably not safe for you to keep driving back and forth while you're so worried. I figure you've been running around town all day, trying to find any lead you can latch on to."

She had been, and Eve almost certainly wouldn't have felt the fatigue as much if she'd actually found a lead. Or Tessie. But she'd found neither.

"If Austin PD gets us the camera footage," he went on, "I want to be here to see it. That's why I'm staying. That, and I have to believe that eventually Tessie will come back here if for no other reason than to get the rest of her things from the sorority house."

Yet another reason for her to be nearby. Still…

"The apartment has two bedrooms," he added a moment later.

Until he'd said the last part, she had been about to

decline. In her state of mind, it definitely wouldn't be a good idea to share quarters with Lawson. But she was exhausted and was dreading the drive home. Partially dreading it, anyway. If she went home, she'd get to see Aiden, so that was a huge plus.

"It's the first time you've left Aiden overnight with Cassidy," Lawson remarked. He didn't need ESP to know where her thoughts were going. "But you know he'll be just fine with her."

Yes, Aiden would be, and Cassidy would definitely agree with a plan like this. But Lawson was still in this particular equation, which made Eve skeptical about doing it.

"Maybe we're both too tired and out of our minds with worry to even think about kissing," she grumbled. "Or anything else we lapse into whenever we're around each other."

Despite everything, a corner of his mouth lifted for just a second. It was enough of a smile to remind her that maybe there was no fatigue level too high to keep sex off her mind whenever she was around Lawson. She didn't put on the brakes, though, when Lawson led her outside to his truck that was parked just up the street.

As he drove, she texted Cassidy to make sure it was okay for her to be away for the night. Eve got an almost immediate answer.

You betcha. Aiden and I are doing just fine. I'm guessing Lawson will be with you?

It was a simple enough question, but Eve wasn't sure how to answer. If she said yes, Cassidy would assume this was a stayover with a side of sex. Cassidy knew that Eve's first priority would be finding Tessie, but Lawson had a way of working himself between the lines of priorities.

Maybe, Eve texted back. Then she cursed herself for lying. Yes, he'll be there, she added. Nothing's going to happen.

Cassidy texted back several rows of laughing emojis.

Eve texted back some frowny-face emojis.

Cassidy countered with what appeared to be a dancing penis.

"A problem?" Lawson asked her. He glanced at her phone screen, but she quickly turned it off.

"No. Everything's fine." She had no intention of admitting that she'd just had a high school encounter with her best friend. "What's the address of this place so I can let Cassidy know in case of an emergency?"

It was overkill because if there truly was an emergency, Cassidy would just call her, but Eve always liked to provide all information when it came to the baby. As soon as Lawson rattled off the address, she sent the info in what she hoped would be a final text to Cassidy tonight.

Eve also messaged Tessie the address, too, though if she actually read the text, that might prompt Tessie to go anywhere but there. It was pretty clear that her daughter was trying to avoid her.

Lawson had been right about the apartment being only a few blocks away. Not enough time for them to launch into a discussion about just how angry he was at her right now. With her energy level near zero, Eve considered that a good thing, but she knew that eventually they were going to have to talk this out.

Work this out, too.

Considering how much time Lawson was putting into finding Tessie, she seriously doubted that he was just going to disappear from their daughter's life. However, Tessie might not want him anywhere near her. That also applied to Eve. Still, they were going to have to come up with some solution, one that couldn't even get started until they found Tessie.

After Lawson had parked his truck in the building's garage, they made their way to the apartment on the top floor. Eve hadn't needed any reminders that the Grangers were rich, but she got one anyway. The place was huge, with incredible views of the city. But those views were only a reminder of just how big Austin was and that Tessie was like a needle in this urban haystack.

"Sophie used to live here before Clay and she got married," Lawson explained. "Garrett once had an apartment in this building, too, but they sold it. Garrett didn't like spending time here."

No. Garrett and Lawson were cut from the same cloth. Both cowboys to the core. Sophie had probably only been here so she could better run Granger Western, and now she could do that from Wrangler's Creek.

He went to the fridge, got a beer and offered her one by lifting a bottle. Eve shook her head. Alcohol, fatigue and Lawson weren't a good mix.

"I'll just grab a shower and go to bed. Which way?" she asked.

He motioned to the hall. "The second room on the left. That was Sophie's room, and there are still some clothes and toiletries in there that you're welcome to use. I'm also going to have some food delivered. You want anything?"

"No. I'm not hungry." She thanked him and was about to do the sensible thing and put some distance between them, but Eve found herself staying put and repeating that *thank you*.

He drank some of his beer and stared at her. "For what—not treating you like shit because I'm pissed at you, or for helping look for Tessie?"

"Both," she readily admitted. Eve could feel herself opening the can of worms that shouldn't be opened. Not tonight, anyway, when they were so blasted tired. "I know you probably don't want to hear this, but when I kept the pregnancy from you, I thought I was doing the right thing."

Lawson made a sarcastic-sounding grunt. Throughout the past two days, she'd seen a lot of different emotions on his face, but this one was more intense than the others.

"Let me guess why." He held up one finger. "It's because we'd had that nasty breakup." A second finger went up. "Or because I was still torn up about Brett." He lifted finger number three. "Or maybe you believed I was too young to be a father. Or," he quickly added when she was about to interrupt him. Finger number four. "You'd outgrown your small-town roots and the cowboy you used to fuck."

The fourth one gave Eve her own shot of anger. She went to him, took hold of his hand and pushed down the first three fingers he'd lifted. "Yes, to those. No, to this one." And she wasn't especially gentle when she shoved it back down. "Shortly after I found out I was pregnant, I did come back to Wrangler's Creek to tell you," she blurted out.

Well, that wasn't anger on his face now but rather

surprise, and she could almost see the wheels turning in his head. "When? And if you came all that way, why didn't you see me?"

"It was early that May, and I did see you. You just didn't see me," she quietly added.

He cursed. "I was with someone else." And he cursed some more as he came out from behind the white granite island that separated them. "That was the spring and summer of me screwing around."

Eve knew she was frowning now and feeling something she had no right to feel. Jealousy. But crap on a cracker, that May she'd still been crying buckets over him.

"How much screwing around?" she asked, walking closer to him. Now that they were out in the open and facing each other, it suddenly felt a little like an Old West showdown with each of them about to draw.

"Lots," he admitted, a frown on his face, too. "Who was I with? Because I'm sure as hell not going to remember who it was."

She considered letting him squirm awhile, but Eve had been trying to make a point, and she was getting way off track. "You were with Sugar, your favorite horse, and you were in the pasture out by your uncle Z.T.'s old place."

He opened his mouth. Then huffed. "What were you doing all the way back there? And why didn't you say anything to me?"

Since this was going to be a longish story, one not especially easy to relive, Eve took a deep breath. "When I was on a short break from the shooting schedule, I flew to San Antonio, and my grandfather picked me up and drove me to the Granger Ranch because he said that's where you were working. One of the hands told us where you were, so we used the old trail to drive there. Granddad had binoculars in his glove compartment, and I used those to spot you."

Lawson shook his head. "No ranch hand mentioned anything about you asking for me."

"It was some new guy who I didn't know, and even if I had, he probably wouldn't have recognized me. I was wearing a baseball cap and big sunglasses. The publicity was in full swing for *Demon High*, and I was already starting to hide out from the paparazzi. I hadn't wanted any of them following me out to see you."

"But you didn't *see* me," he quickly pointed out. "Why? What the heck was I doing that turned you off so much that you'd leave without saying a word?"

Here was more of that long painful story, but this part wasn't going to be nearly as easy to explain. "You were just riding, cutting through some cattle. I think you were checking on them, maybe even counting them." And it had most certainly not been a turnoff. Just the opposite. She'd wanted to go to him and pull him into her arms. "You looked…content."

That was the word that had come to mind then, and it came again. Normally, that was a good word, but it hadn't been eighteen and a half years ago.

"Content," he spit out. "Yeah, I could see why that would send you running." And yes, it was doused with plenty of sarcasm.

"It did send me running. Or rather, slinking away. Because in that moment I realized the ranch was the center of your universe. Your happy place. You definitely weren't crying buckets of tears over me." She could douse with some sarcasm, too, but it was short-lived because this particular old memory still carried a lot of pain.

"And you thought you'd…what? Map out my future for me? A future that didn't involve Tessie or you?"

"Something like that," Eve admitted, though it was going to earn her a huff. It did. "I knew you wouldn't be happy in California. And I also knew you hadn't forgiven me for Brett. Or for leaving. Plus, there was that little detail about you being a teenager and not wanting children. I was more or less locked into a future, but I didn't want to lock you in there with me."

He gave her one of those angry, flat looks, but Lawson must have remembered how things were then. Emotions had been high. Like now. The anger had been thick and hot. Also like now. But the old attraction would have been there, too.

Like now.

"You would have resented it," Eve added before he could argue. "Maybe not right then, but eventually you would have. If I'd told you that day in the pasture that I was pregnant, you would have been shocked. But you would have done the right thing. You would have asked me to marry you. I would have said yes because I was crying buckets and was lonely, and our marriage would have failed because we had too many strikes against us."

Of course, she'd just proved him right about her mapping out his future. Apparently, she'd *mapped out* a predicted outcome, too, which meant she'd said too much. She should have stopped after the first *thank you* and headed to bed. And that was what she turned to do. But Lawson stopped her in her tracks.

"You're right," he said.

At first, she thought this might be part of his continuing sarcasm, but there didn't appear to be any of it in his expression. Or his next grunt. In fact, his grunt seemed to be one of frustration. Not with her but with himself. Then again, that might be wishful thinking on her part.

"You cried *buckets* over me," he said. "I'm guessing that's a higher amount than usual for a teenage girl with a broken heart?"

She nodded. "I made everyone around me miserable."

He nodded, too, paused and blew out a heavy breath. "Yeah, I did the same. No tear-filled buckets, but there were lots of fights, skipping school and generally making a nuisance of myself. Roman threatened to drown me in the creek. My mom came home and made me see a counselor. That's when I started saying *fuck this* and *shit* on a daily basis."

The relief came, and it felt as if a heavy weight lifted off her shoulders. Not because she was glad that Lawson had gone through the same hell she had but because it finally felt as if they'd cleared some old, stenchy air between them.

"But it got better." Eve made sure that didn't sound like a question. Made sure she didn't mention Darby, either.

"Eventually. But during those dark days, my dad flew in just to tell me to suck it up and take it like a man. Dylan set me up with his girlfriends' and former girlfriends' sisters. And Lucian hired me a hooker."

That didn't stench up the air again. At least it probably didn't, but it was a surprise. "A hooker?"

He lifted his shoulder. "I'm pretty sure she was one,

anyway. Lucian's not very good at solving teenager angst. He just wanted me to shut up and quit causing problems since he was the one who was having to deal with the aftermath of most of those problems. I guess he figured if I kept busy having sex, I'd stay out of trouble."

And just like that, the air changed between them.

Eve was very familiar with that specific type of air change, especially when coupled with the mention of sex.

She fluttered her fingers toward the bedroom. "I should take that shower and get some sleep."

Eve got her feet working, and she even managed a few steps, but just as quickly, she found herself turning around to tell Lawson that they should keep their hands off each other. In the split second she did the turn around, she also came up with some reasons.

Fatigue, bad timing, spent adrenaline from worry. Oh, she couldn't forget the part about this complicating the heck out of their lives.

Eve might have actually managed to voice some of those reasons if she hadn't landed right in Lawson's arms. He didn't kiss her. Didn't really touch her except for the loose grip he had on her. She could have easily slipped away from him at any time.

She didn't.

She stayed put and made matters worse by looking up at him. They were too close and she took in his scent. She wasn't sure how he could smell both *cowboy* and *expensive* at the same time, but he managed it.

Eve's gaze went from his eyes. To his mouth. And that's when she realized he was doing the same thing. He was looking at her as if trying to decide just how

er eyes were also showing some heat. And she
ed dirty with the touching. She slid her fingers
entire length of him and then right back up, all the
ile her hot breath kept hitting against his mouth
d neck.

"I haven't had sex with you in nearly eighteen
ears," she reminded him. "Just how ready do you
ink I am?"

Plenty ready, he was sure of it, but that was the
brainless part of her talking. Unfortunately, it was making a lot of sense to his corresponding brainless part.
Despite that though, Lawson thought he was going to
get a reprieve so he could launch into that much-needed
discussion when Eve took her hand out of his jeans. But
he soon realized that she did that only so she could wet
her fingers with her mouth and go back in.

Hell.

He hadn't had much willpower left, and now his
brain cells were frying. Lawson knew he had to say
something with the pinch of breath that he managed
to gather, and he forced out one word.

"Lick," he said.

Okay, it was the right word, but it got Eve stopping
with the hand job, and there was now a little confusion
mixed with the heat. "You or me?" she asked.

"Me licking you." Because that might give him time
to get things under control. He still wasn't sure full-
blown sex was the way to go here.

She stared at him a moment, then smiled. "All right.
Then it'll be my turn."

And she started to get ready for her turn by unbut-
toning his shirt. She left it on but finished unzipping

much to mess this up. She went for the mess-up first
though by attempting to keep this light. Like a joke.

"Touch, lick or kiss?" she asked, and Eve made sure
she added a wink to it.

Lawson didn't wink.

"All of them," he drawled, and this time when he
pulled her to him, there was indeed some touching
going on.

APPARENTLY, AIR CLEARINGS could turn into some mighty
serious foreplay. Of course, breathing could be foreplay, too, when it came to Eve.

Touching took the foreplay up a whole bunch of
notches when their bodies landed against each other.
It wasn't really a surprise that his most prominent male
feature thought this was a stellar idea. His dick was
stupid. So was he. Because he immediately added yet
another component to this.

Kissing.

His mouth located hers. Not that he had to search
long for it. Eve was already moving in on him, and
their lips met a little harder than he'd planned. There
might have been some pain involved, but the pleasure
had a way of overriding that. Overriding any tiny shred
of common sense, too. That's because the kiss was
an ultimate pleasure generator. Third only to touching and sex.

"We keep doing this," she complained when they
broke for air.

Yes, they did, and despite the recent eighteen-year
break they'd had from each other, they just picked up
right where they'd left off. It was as if they were in the
baseball dugout again. Or the seat of his truck. And

then there'd been his mom's house, which Eve now owned. But this apartment had one huge advantage that the other places didn't.

Privacy.

Unlike every other single place where Eve and he had made out, there was no chance that someone could come walking in on them. Too bad. Because in those days and nights past, it had slowed them down so that he could keep watch. There was nothing to slow them down now, which meant it could lead to quick and dirty sex on the floor.

Emphasis on the quick.

He didn't mind being swept away on a tidal wave of lust, and he was willing to deal with regrets and consequences, but he wasn't sure Eve was ready for it. That's why he pulled back to give it one last shot at trying to talk to her.

She blinked as if puzzled by the halt. "Are we playing the game?" she asked before he could say anything, and she didn't wait for him to answer, either. "Because if so, I'd rather you just kiss me until I melt."

Those were not the right words to open up a logical discussion about this. However, it was effective in getting him to kiss her again. And Lawson thought she might indeed be melting. She was definitely soft and pliable in his arms, and while their tongues did some playing around, Eve played around by sliding her hands to his lower back and pulling him even closer against her.

Other than the millimeters of clothes, there was no more space between crucial parts of their bodies, and Lawson did something to rid them of that last obstacle.

He caught onto the hem of her loose ⟨...⟩ pulled it off over her head.

And he got a nice surprise.

A lacy red bra and panties. Not the p⟨...⟩ either. These were sheer and looked m⟨...⟩ than for covering anything vital. He could⟨...⟩ peeking out behind the lace.

She followed his gaze. "Now that I no lon⟨...⟩ nursing bra, my taste in underwear has gone⟨...⟩

"I like slutty," he assured her.

In fact, he liked it a lot because there wa⟨...⟩ peeking going on behind the lace in the panti⟨...⟩ But the nursing-bra comment was a reminder tha⟨...⟩ did need to do some talking as to whether or not ⟨...⟩ of this was emotionally a good idea. As oppose⟨...⟩ this just being a dumb thing physically. He would⟨...⟩ launched into that conversation, too.

If Eve hadn't unzipped him enough so she coul⟨...⟩ her hand in his pants.

She went right into the waist of his jeans and bo⟨...⟩ and found pay dirt. Of course, it wasn't difficult to f⟨...⟩ since he already had a raging hard-on.

"We used to do slutty quite well," she whisper⟨...⟩ her voice all breathy.

Yes, they had. They were doing a pretty damn go⟨...⟩ job of it now, as well. Because Lawson put his han⟨...⟩ in her panties.

"I just want to make sure you're ready for this,⟨...⟩ he said.

That didn't come out right, considering that at the exact moment those words left his mouth, his fingers slid through all that slick heat between her legs. At least she had the physically *ready* part down pat.

his jeans, making him wonder just where this licking was going to take them.

Apparently, it was going to take them to the floor.

That's because when he went to lick her lips, it turned into a full-fledged French kiss, complete with a new round of groping. Now, with even fewer millimeters of fabric between them, the heat skyrocketed right out of control.

Suddenly, he was starved for her. Also suddenly, time seemed to matter. The touches became more frantic. Ditto for the kisses. And that's why they started for the hardwood floor.

Lawson knew he had to make one last-ditch effort, and that's why he made sure they landed with him on top of Eve. He also pinned her hands so that she couldn't go underpants-exploring again.

"I really want to finish this the old-fashioned way," he assured her.

And that was a nice way of saying he wanted to be hard and deep inside her. Hard, deep and hitting her in just the right spot with his own much larger right spot. But he had just enough common sense to know that he didn't want to do something that could hurt her.

After all, it'd only been three months since she'd given birth to Aiden.

He gathered both of her wrists in one of his hands. Again, to cut down on the touching. She touched anyway, though, by lifting her hips to grind against his hard-on. It was possible his head exploded, but thankfully the rest of him didn't. With all her bucking and moving, he managed to get his right hand back in her panties.

One touch there, a couple of slippery slides of his fingers, and the urgency returned for Eve. She struggled to free her hands. No doubt so she could go after his dick. But Lawson held on. Kept on touching her, too. Thankfully, they'd had enough practice, and he hadn't forgotten all the ins and outs of her body.

Nope.

He didn't time it, but he got it right after what seemed like the flash of a few seconds. Much too short, considering that he was enjoying the feel of her, the look on her face. Still, he knew it couldn't last. And it didn't. He touched her, watched her and then kissed her as he took her right over the edge of the orgasm cliff.

Eve stopped struggling, stopped the body grinding and went limp. It gave Lawson some much-needed time to catch his breath and adjust himself. A needed adjustment since his hard-on was still on a mission to dive in and make this a double climaxing situation. That couldn't happen. Though Eve seemed to have a different notion about that.

After a few gulping postorgasmic breaths, she pushed aside his hand that was still making an adjustment and latched on to his jeans. Lawson hated to do this, but he stopped her.

"I don't want to hurt you," he said. "And I don't have a condom on me. I seriously doubt you want me to knock you up twice."

She stared at him, as if weighing options that didn't really exist. Or so he thought.

"There are other ways," she insisted, and she batted away his hand to go after his jeans again.

He batted back. She persisted. Until they were playing a very adult version of whack-a-mole. It probably would have gotten him off, too, but he heard something over the shuffling of their hands.

The doorbell.

Shit.

His first thought was that this was Sophie, coming there to check on them. He didn't want to face her, not with his erection about to bust out of his jeans, but he also knew if it was his cousin, then she could just use her key to get in.

But it wasn't Sophie.

"Mom?" someone called out from the other side of the door. "Are you in there? It's me—Tessie."

CHAPTER SEVENTEEN

TESSIE WASN'T SURE what she dreaded more—that her mother would come to the door or that she wouldn't. Her mom had to be just as angry as she was worried.

And Tessie couldn't blame her.

She was feeling that, too, but she thought her mom might believe that she was the winner of this round of worry and anger. She'd left her mom high and dry with no explanation as to the craziness going on in her heart, and now Tessie owed her some answers.

Too bad Tessie wasn't sure she had answers just yet.

Thankfully, she didn't have to wait long to find out whether or not her mom would come to the door. Within seconds after Tessie had called out to her, Eve did her own calling out.

"Tessie?" Her mother followed that with what sounded to be a string of *Oh, God*s. That was mixed with other sounds of footsteps and someone scrambling around in the apartment.

Tessie put her ear to the door to try to figure out what was going on, but just as she did that, the door flew open, and she came face-to-face with two very disheveled people. Her mom's dress was hiked up on one side because it was tucked into the waist of her red panties, and the cowboy had missed several buttons on his shirt. Adding in some seriously messed-up hair and her mom's flushed face, and Tessie was pretty sure she'd interrupted them having sex.

Great. Nothing like a side order of embarrassment to go with all the other emotions that were sloshing around.

Just as she'd done outside the bar in Wrangler's Creek, her mom hugged her, and she held on a lot longer than last time even though Tessie went stiff again. The cowboy just stayed back and watched. Tessie watched him, too.

And she saw the same resemblance she had before.

So, was he her father?

He'd been her mom's boyfriend back in high school, so the timing also fit. Tessie had done the math, and he could have gotten her mother pregnant shortly before she moved to LA. But Lawson wasn't the only guy she'd heard her mom talk about. There was Brett, who'd died, and whenever her mother had mentioned him, she'd gotten all teary. Maybe it had been some kind of love triangle that had ended in a bad way.

Her mom finally pulled back from the hug, and after a really short pause, the questions started. "Where were you? Why did you run away? And when and why did you start drinking? Have you lost your mind?"

They were all questions Tessie had expected, but before she could even try to answer them, her mother continued. "You scared me," she said, her voice quivering and tears threatening in her eyes. "I was terrified that you were hurt, or worse. Why would you do that?"

Tessie sighed, and since this conversation could go on for a while, she stepped inside. And also because she couldn't talk with her mom's panties showing, Tessie glanced at the messed-up clothes again.

"I see London, I see France…" Tessie muttered just loud enough for her mother to hear.

Her mom huffed when she saw that her "red flag" panties had been exposed. She fixed her dress and blushed again. However, even the embarrassment didn't stop the anger from creeping into her mom's eyes.

Tessie braced herself for yet another round of questions, but her mother only asked one.

"Why?" Her mom's voice wasn't exactly a friendly invitation, more like a demand. The cowboy was demanding, too, with his body language though he didn't say a word.

So, Tessie gave them an answer though it was one she doubted they'd like much. "I screwed up."

No, they didn't like it. Their frowns confirmed it.

They probably wanted her to start gushing out her feelings and swear to them that she'd changed and that none of this would ever happen again. They wanted everything wrapped up so they could feel happy. And part of Tessie wanted to give them that. Mainly so they would back off and quit worrying. But this wasn't something that could be fixed with an "I'm okay now."

"Why don't we sit down and talk," Tessie suggested. She looked at Lawson. "Maybe you can fix me a rum and Coke?" she joked.

Tessie had thought her mom could have angry eyes, but Lawson was clearly the champion of that particular skill.

"Obviously, I was just kidding," Tessie added when neither of them smiled. Also obviously, it was too soon for her to try to make light of this. Maybe four decades from now would still be too soon.

"How'd you know Eve and I were here?" Lawson asked her.

"Mom texted me the address. I didn't know you'd be here, too." Best not to mention that she'd expected to find her mom crying and worrying instead of looking as if she'd just had a couple of rounds of hot sex.

They went into the living room, where there were no signs of sex, thank goodness, and Tessie sat on the sofa. Her mom sat, too, next to her, but Lawson stayed standing with his arms folded over his chest. Evidently, he thought he had a right to be part of this. And maybe he did.

"Why?" Tessie repeated to give herself a moment to try to calm down her nerves. Clearly though, that wasn't going to happen. "Look, let me just say that I know I'm grounded. Maybe for life. Maybe even longer."

"You deserve to be grounded," her mom said. She had stopped being in a hugging, relief frame of mind.

Tessie nodded, and since she wasn't sure where to start with this, she looked up at Lawson. "I'm guessing you remember the day you saw me drunk at the sorority house?" She didn't wait for him to confirm it because, yeah, he remembered. "Well, that was the first time I'd ever had anything to drink. It was one drink, a margarita, and I think it's accurate to say that I don't handle my liquor well."

She couldn't tell if they believed her about that being her first time. Probably not. But it was the truth. Well, almost the truth. She hadn't even managed to finish the entire glass before she'd gotten shit-faced.

"Who were the two puking clowns with you?" Lawson snarled. Actually, his expression and body language were a snarl, as well.

"They're just some people I used to hang out with." Maybe he wouldn't ask for their names since she'd added the *used to*, as in she didn't hang out with them any longer. "The other girl was the one who fixed the drinks from stuff she got from someone she knew who lived up the street. The guy is…was her boyfriend."

"And where exactly were you going with these two puking clowns?" That didn't come from Lawson but rather her mom.

Tessie gave a weary sigh because no way were they going to believe this. "The other girl had thrown up in the room, and the smell was god-awful. We were going outside for some fresh air, but when we got on the elevator, the motion made us feel even sicker. Trust me, I've learned my lesson about tequila."

This was usually about the time when she would have added some humor—her go-to response when things got uncomfortable. Like now. But Tessie doubted there was any humor that was going to make this better.

"You went to rehab," her mom said. Apparently, they were moving on to the second part of "things that had gotten Tessie's butt in trouble."

Tessie nodded and knew this was going to hurt. "I went because I panicked when I figured Lawson had told you about seeing me drunk. But the panic isn't why I went to rehab. It's because my first reaction was to have another drink."

Her mom huffed. "I thought you said you'd learned your lesson."

"I did…about tequila. My panicking mind was leaning more toward a beer. Something to settle my nerves. Which obviously wasn't a good way to think, considering the other incident. So, I figured I could check myself into rehab to avoid seeing you and that I would also avoid being tempted to drink a beer. I didn't think there'd be many opportunities for getting drunk in rehab."

Oh, yes. Her go-to humor had not gone down well.

"You didn't stay in rehab though," Lawson pointed out. "Why not and where did you go?"

Tessie nodded again. "After my mental health exam and a boatload of personal questions, the worker was escorting me to my room, and I saw these other people. I think they were going through withdrawals or something. They looked *bad*. And I started to realize that I no longer had the least bit of desire for a beer or any other booze. So, I left and went to stay with a friend."

There it was—all the dumb she'd done, including but not limited to worrying the heck out of her mother. It made her sound like one of those privileged, wimpy kids in California that she'd hated. She had always sworn she wouldn't become one of them, but here she was talking about getting drunk, rehab and running away.

She wasn't just one of them now. She was the reigning princess of privileged, wimpy kids. And she saw what she believed to be disgust in Lawson's eyes. She didn't have to guess about the look in her mom's eyes though.

That was all hurt.

Tessie wanted to reach out to her and hug her, but there was still so much between them. Well, one thing, anyway. The lie that made her mom the reigning queen of liars in the Cooper household. As much as she wanted to forget that, Tessie just couldn't.

She wasn't the person she'd always thought she was. She wasn't Eve Cooper's adopted daughter. The child who was lucky enough to have been chosen by someone as beautiful and idolized as Eve.

Instead, she was the secret that her mom had tried to hide from her fans.

And now maybe she was trying to hide it from Lawson, too.

Tessie glanced at both of them, trying to figure how what she was about to say would go over with them. It'd be like the failed humor, but Tessie had to try to see if she could make some sense out of this. She didn't expect to get this new perspective from her mom, either.

But rather from a glaring cowboy who didn't seem to have a fatherly bone in his body.

Tessie slid her hand over her mom's, hoping it would soften the mood a bit. "I'd like to talk to Lawson alone for a few minutes. Is that okay?"

She might as well have asked if it was okay if she threw the cowboy out the window. "Why?" her mother pressed.

Oh, this was going to get touchy. If Tessie told her she was going on a paternity fishing expedition, no way would her mom agree. She might even blurt out everything. And if Lawson didn't know, this was not the way for him to find out.

Since there'd been enough lies, Tessie didn't want to go that route. "I just want to ask him some things. Please. It won't take long."

Tessie could practically hear the debate her mom was having with herself, but as usual, the *please* worked. Tessie could thank Cassidy for that. Her nanny–keeper of her mom's secrets had always told her *please* could open lots of doors. In this case, it closed one. Because her mom nodded—hesitantly though— and slowly walked to one of the rooms off the hall, went in and shut the door.

"She'll try to listen," Tessie and Lawson said at the same time.

Since they were right, Tessie took hold of his arm, leading him to the kitchen, where she turned on the exhaust fan over the stove, both faucets on the sink and the garbage disposal. From there, she led him to the fancy copper-framed mirror in the foyer.

While they stood side by side, their reflections said it all. Of course, Tessie couldn't help but add more.

"I learned in science that a kid inherits fifty percent of their DNA from their mom and fifty percent from their dad. What percentage of *your* DNA do you think it took to give me this face?"

His jaw tightened. "Enough of it."

When she'd tossed out that question, Tessie hadn't actually prepared herself for an answer. Or for the truth. But Lawson hadn't pulled any punches.

"At least now I know," she said. "How long have you known?" She didn't move. Neither did he. They just continued to stare at each other in the mirror.

"I found out two days ago," he snarled. "According to some people, I'm not very bright to have missed the family resemblance before then."

"And, of course, my mom wasn't jumping up and down to tell you. She lied to both of us."

He swiveled toward her so fast that Tessie heard joints snap. "Don't put this all on your mom."

Great. He was defending her. That meant everybody

who knew Eve was on her side when it came to this. Ironic, since it affected Tessie more than anyone else.

Tessie rolled her eyes at the same time he did, and she was reasonably sure the gesture was identical. It was creepy.

"You're going to give her a free pass for keeping you in the dark about being a father," Tessie said, tossing it out there.

"No. I'm not giving her a pass, but I'm sure as heck not giving you one, either. Yeah, she was wrong not to tell you the truth, but you'll run into liars and worse in your life. That's no excuse to act like a jackass."

Well, she'd just gotten her first fatherly lecture, and she didn't like it much. Of course, there wasn't much she liked about this situation.

"I should have known it was you," Tessie went on. "The only two guys she ever talked about were Brett and you."

Oh, no. Lawson didn't get teary-eyed, but he did go all gloom and doom on her. "What do you know about Brett?"

"More than Mom probably wants me to know. I read the newspaper articles about him on the internet. There was an inquest, and Mom, you and a whole bunch of other people were questioned." She paused, wondering just how far she should push this. Tessie went for broke. "Was Mom responsible somehow for Brett dying?"

He stayed quiet so long that Tessie thought he might not answer. "No," he finally said. "I was."

Lawson stepped away from her, heading back into the living room. She followed to ask him more. Not just about Brett but also about, well, them. Maybe he wanted nothing more to do with her, but if so, Tessie needed to know, and it seemed as if Lawson would tell her the truth. No matter how much it stung.

But before she could ask him anything else, her mom came out of the room. She went straight to the kitchen, turned off all the noise-making devices, and then she whirled around to face Tessie. For a moment, Tessie was going to ask her what Lawson and she talked about. She didn't.

"I've decided what's going to happen," her mom said, and it was definitely her mom tone, coupled with a mom look. "You're moving to Wrangler's Creek with me. You can commute to your classes, and I'll hire a driver to take you back and forth. You'll have no contact whatsoever with the girl who gave you that margarita. And you'll go to counseling."

Whoa.

Tessie had guessed that her mom would try to come down hard on her, but she hadn't seen this coming. She wanted to ask *and what if I don't?* In fact, the words nearly leaped right out of her mouth before Lawson shook his head. It seemed to be some kind of warning not to push this.

"Come on," her mom said, grabbing her purse. "We're leaving right now."

CHAPTER EIGHTEEN

EVE TRIED TO focus on the paperwork for her foundation for pregnant teens, but the spreadsheets were flurrying around like white noise in her head. The only thing that was mentally coming through with any urgency was Tessie.

Not a surprise because it'd been that way for the past two days since Eve had practically dragged Tessie to the house in Wrangler's Creek.

Tessie had spent most of that forty-eight hours either sleeping or giving Eve the silent treatment. That was mixed in with an occasional grunt that was meant to be some kind of acknowledgment to whatever Eve had just told her. Of course, the sleeping, silence, grunts and, yes, even the occasional stink eye were preferable to her teenage daughter drinking and acting out.

As Eve herself had done when she was that age.

That made her feel like a hypocrite, but she'd do whatever it took to keep Tessie from going through what Brett had. One death from underage drinking was enough, and while Tessie might not have learned that lesson yet, it was one that stayed with Eve every single day of her life. It had cost her a dear friend. Her peace of mind.

And Lawson.

Eve frowned. Of course, she'd added to that cost by

keeping Tessie a secret from him and keeping Lawson a secret from Tessie. While Lawson and she had nearly had sex in the Austin apartment, she doubted the near-sex came with a blanket forgiveness. No. Forgiveness couldn't be tempered with lust.

Forgiveness might not be tempered with genetics, either. When she was finally able to talk to Tessie about Lawson being her father, it was possible that it would launch Tessie into another round of dangerous behavior. And that's the justification Eve had used for waiting to tell her.

She picked up her phone to call Lawson so they could try to talk out what'd happened. Or talk about anything, for that matter. But as Eve had done for the past two days, she put the phone right back down. That's because she didn't know what to say to him. And it wasn't as if he'd called her.

He hadn't.

Thinking of that caused her to frown even more. Lawson hadn't driven from Austin to Wrangler's Creek with Tessie and her. Since his truck was there at the apartment building, he'd taken them to the sorority house where her car was parked, and then he'd come back on his own. He had texted, though, to make sure they arrived okay and had ended that text with Be in touch soon.

She wasn't sure if he'd meant for her to be in touch or that he would take the initiative when he was good and ready. If it was the latter, there was no telling when good and ready would happen. If ever.

That was the reason for picking up the phone, thinking-rethinking and putting it back down again. However, this time Eve still had hold of the phone when Cassidy walked into the office. She had a baby monitor in one hand and a Coke in the other.

Cassidy took one look at the cell and grumbled something disparaging under her breath. "Last I heard, a woman can call a man without fear of tar and feathering. Especially a man who's the father of her child." She paused. "Of course, that doesn't apply to Kellan. You'd risk tar and feathering by me if you took up with that asshat again."

"There's no chance of that," Eve assured her. "And speaking of the children, how are they?"

"Both sacked out."

Eve checked the time. Ten thirty in the morning. It was Aiden's usual nap time, but Tessie was obviously sleeping in again. "Any communication from Tessie that wasn't grunt-like? Shrugs don't count, either."

Cassidy had opened her mouth to answer until Eve added the last part. Then she lifted her shoulder. "No actual words, but last night her door was partially open, so I peeked in on her, and she was on the Wellsmore College website. It looked as if she was making arrangements to take some of her classes online for the rest of the semester."

Eve stared at her. "You got all of that from *peeking* in on her?"

"Well, maybe I looked at her laptop when she was in the bathroom. Okay, I snooped," Cassidy snapped after Eve just kept staring. "But I wanted to make sure she was all right."

Eve wasn't a proponent of snooping, but it was hard to scold Cassidy for doing it when it involved something this important. And when Cassidy cared so much about Tessie. Eve didn't want Tessie dropping out of college. Just the opposite. She thought staying in school would help her daughter regain her focus.

"I guess Tessie didn't want to take me up on the offer to have someone drive her to Austin for her classes." Though the driver was on call to do that.

"Nothing on the laptop about that, but she did have the note with the driver's phone number on her desk."

Good. Eve had been afraid Tessie would just put it in the trash and then demand to use her own car to get to Austin. But Eve wasn't handing over the car keys until Tessie had proved she could be trusted.

"What would you have done if Tessie hadn't come home with you?" Cassidy asked.

In the moment that Eve had made the demand, she'd been so angry that she hadn't thought out the consequences had Tessie refused. Eve probably would have ended up saying and doing something she would have regretted. Heck, she still might. But sometimes parenting just plain sucked, and you had to put your foot down.

"If Tessie hadn't come home, I would have cut her off financially. No car. No tuition. No credit card."

Cassidy made a sound of surprise. "You could have gone through with that?"

"To save her, yes."

Thankfully, though, it hadn't come down to that. Of course, they weren't out of the woods yet. Tessie could be upstairs seething and plotting to do something else stupid. If that happened, Eve would also have to make changes to the trust fund she'd set up for Tessie. She'd arranged it so Tessie would get it on her twenty-first birthday, a little over three years from now, but Tessie wouldn't see a dime of it unless she straightened up.

Eve heard the sound of a vehicle, and she nearly pulled a leg muscle hurrying to the window to see who it was. She hadn't realized just how much she was hoping it would be Lawson until the disappointment washed over her. But she couldn't wallow for long because she was apparently about to have some company.

Cassidy hurried to the window, choking on the gulp of Coke she'd just had. "Oh, God. That's Lucian Granger."

Yes, it was. He stepped from his truck, the movement and fall breeze causing his untucked shirt to whip a little like the cape of a superhero. Or more like a scary Swaron warrior. Unlike a Swaron warrior, though, Lucian was wearing jeans, cowboy boots and a black Stetson.

"Oh, God," Cassidy repeated. "I don't want to meet him when I look like this."

Apparently, *like this* was no makeup, puke stains on her shirt and peeling purple toenail polish. She ran off, spilling little blobs of Coke as she darted out of the office and up the stairs.

Lucian was on the phone, his expression as intense as ever, but he went to the passenger side of the truck, and he opened the door in a fluid stride that caused his shirt to flutter again.

Regina stepped out.

Eve groaned. She liked Regina well enough, and she wanted to find out how the woman was after her stay in the hospital, but since she'd had Lucian bring her, this could mean trouble. As in the kind of trouble that could happen if Lawson had told his mom about Tessie.

Eve definitely didn't need Regina showing up to see her granddaughter when the granddaughter was still in the dark about her Granger relatives.

Because Eve didn't want the doorbell to wake Aiden, she hurried to the door, holding her index finger to her mouth when she let Regina in.

"The baby's asleep," Eve whispered.

"Oh." Regina nodded, smiled.

Lucian did neither of those things, but he must have heard her because he stayed on the porch to continue his call.

"Would you like something to drink?" Eve asked, still whispering.

"No, thanks. I just got sprung from the hospital and wanted to come by and check on you."

Considering that Regina was glancing in the rooms off the foyer and the stairs, that might not be the truth. She could be looking for Tessie. Or maybe Lawson.

Eve gently took her by the arm so she could hopefully lead her into the family room. "How are you feeling?"

Regina didn't budge, but she did glance over her shoulder at Lucian. "I keep looking for vampire marks on my neck to make sure Dracula's not doing a little blood sucking when I'm asleep. I'm exhausted. But don't tell Lawson, Dylan or Lily Rose. You can tell Lucian. He won't hear you because he won't get off the phone."

Regina said that last part a lot louder, no doubt loud enough for Lucian to hear, and then she gave Eve a weak smile. Actually, the weak part applied to the rest of her, too, and Eve suddenly felt guilty for not wanting this visit. It had to be important for Regina to use what little energy she had to come here.

"Lucian's having a problem with a newspaper or something," Regina went on. "He's muttering bad words and fussing at people, so he might be out there awhile." She turned back to Eve. "I was wondering if your daughter was around. I wanted to meet her."

Bingo. Lawson had told his mom that she had a granddaughter. Eve wasn't exactly happy about that, but she couldn't fault him. He might have needed to talk to someone about it, and Regina had drawn that particular task.

Eve was about to tell Regina that it wasn't a good time to visit Tessie. Not a lie, either. But before Eve could say anything, she heard the footsteps on the stairs. She thought maybe it was Cassidy, but it was Tessie. Not in pj's and looking sleepy, either. She was wearing normal clothes—jeans, flip-flops and a top.

Tessie didn't smile, but then, she also didn't grunt, shrug or do anything else to communicate how sullen and filled with teenage angst she was.

"I heard someone drive up," Tessie said. She looked past them at Lucian. "I thought it was Lawson."

"No. That's his brother," Regina volunteered. With Eve trailing along right beside her, Regina went closer to Tessie. "But I'm Lawson's mother."

"It's nice to meet you." Tessie actually sounded, well, pleasant, but Eve knew that all was not well yet.

Regina was studying Tessie, and Tessie was studying her. The kind of studying someone might do if they were trying to recall how and when they'd met.

Or why the person looked familiar.

"I heard you're a student at Wellsmore," Regina went on. "I didn't go to college myself, but Lawson's father went. Lucian, too, for a short while." She tipped her head toward him, but Lucian was so engrossed in his phone call that he never even glanced their way.

Tessie nodded. Then paused. "Would you like some tea or something?"

Heck. Tessie sounded like her normal, often sweet self. Which meant there could be some trouble brewing.

"I'd love some tea," Regina said, gushing. Obviously, the woman had gotten thirsty in the past ninety seconds since Eve had asked her about that drink.

"Lucian, we'll be in the kitchen," she called out to her son.

Regina looped her arm around Tessie's waist, but before they could get to the kitchen, Cassidy came rushing down the first three or four steps on the stairs. She still had the Coke and baby monitor, but she'd changed out of her normal clothes.

Into a little black party dress.

It was probably the only dress that Cassidy owned, and it was as out of place as Regina's original rhinestone and red decor. Cassidy took the rest of the stair steps slowly as if posing. A pose no doubt meant for Lucian. Who wasn't even noticing her.

Regina noted the direction of Cassidy's *posing* attention. She looked at Lucian, too. "Go for it," Regina said, winking at Cassidy. "He needs a woman who can get that phone unglued from his ear."

Regina started walking but stopped again. This time, she looked at Eve. "And Lawson needs you."

With that total shell-shocker, Regina smiled and got moving again toward the kitchen. She nearly made it there, too, but this time the interruption came from Lucian. He came barreling into the house, definitely not doing any posing, and he seemed to take in the entire room with a sweeping glance.

However, his glance was slightly more than a glance when he noticed Tessie.

Lucian usually had a poker face. That wasn't the case now though. He had likely noticed the resemblance between Tessie and his brother, and he was piecing this all together.

"Shit," Lucian grumbled.

Okay, he hadn't liked what he'd pieced. But Eve hoped that he held on to his tongue until she could tell Tessie in private. And this time she would do it as soon as Regina and Lucian left. No more secrets.

"Don't curse around Tessie," Regina scolded Lucian, and she put her hands over Tessie's ears.

Cassidy quit trying to get Lucian's attention, probably because she could see the poop-storm that was about to come right at them. Eve shook her head at Lucian. So did Cassidy.

And his mother added a warning head shake, as well.

But Lucian might not have noticed them because he was staring at Tessie. "Have you seen it yet?" Lucian asked her. "Does your mother know?"

All right. Those weren't questions that Eve had expected. Judging from their openmouthed stares, neither had Regina or Cassidy. Tessie didn't seem nearly as surprised though.

"I found out a few minutes ago," Tessie answered, only adding to Eve, Cassidy and Regina's confusion.

"What's going on?" Eve demanded first of Tessie and then of Lucian.

It was Lucian who did something to give her an answer. He came closer, lifting his phone so she could see the screen. At first, Eve had no idea what she was seeing, and she took the phone from him for a closer look.

And she got one all right.

Despite her no-swearing rule, Eve didn't even try to silence the response that came out of her mouth. "Shit."

CHAPTER NINETEEN

LAWSON STARED AT the bottle of whiskey in his bottom-right desk drawer. Usually the only time he felt the overwhelming need for a shot was after a nightmare about Brett. But apparently fatherhood was having the same soul-sucking effect.

Well, the fears of fatherhood, anyway.

Tessie needed help, and he didn't know how to fix it. Hell, he didn't know how to fix himself or his tangled relationship with Eve. And now that tangle included their daughter.

Daughter.

At least the word wasn't sticking in his throat though there were still plenty of sticking points in his head. Not because he didn't love Tessie.

He did.

That had been a weird sort of realization that a DNA connection could produce such a strong feeling of love. Stronger than anything else he'd ever felt, and that's why he was scared spitless. If he screwed this up, there'd be no coming back from it.

But how did he *not* screw up? Lawson still didn't have a clue, which was the reason he was staring at a whiskey bottle in the middle of the day. Ditto for it being the reason he'd been avoiding Eve and Tessie.

He was hoping a fix would come to him before he had to see them again.

Cursing, he kicked the drawer shut and opened the bottom-left one. No whiskey here, but it was a torment of a different kind.

A manila envelope.

Unlike the bottle of whiskey, it wasn't in plain sight. Years ago, shortly after he'd gotten this office at the Granger Ranch, he'd made sure there were plenty of layers of paperwork and supplies on top of the envelope. Lawson hadn't wanted to risk seeing it when he was rummaging for a paper clip. That's why it was puzzling as to why he felt the need to see it now.

There was no label on the envelope, but over the past eighteen years, he'd given it a mental label. Usually with the word *shit* on it. *Shit to forget. Shit you should toss. Shit you should never open.* And the most often used one—*shit and more shit.*

Evidently, he had a somewhat limited vocabulary when it came to such things.

Despite the mental label-warning he'd once given the envelope, Lawson opened it now, and he dumped out the two small gift boxes on his desk. They were still tied up shut with the ribbon that'd once been white. It was now more the color of piss—which was probably some kind of metaphor for his life.

He didn't open the gifts. No need. His superpower was the unwanted ability to see what was in both. Gifts that he'd intended to give to Eve at the ill-fated Sadie Hawkins dance so that she would have, well, choices about where they were to go from there. She'd never gotten them, though, because where they'd gone from there was precisely nowhere. They'd broken up, and the gifts had gone in an envelope and eventually shoved into a bottom drawer.

According to what Cassidy had told him, Eve had hung on to an unused memento from that night, too. A dress that she'd intended to wear. And also according to Cassidy, Eve had been planning on telling him something.

Welcome to the club.

Lawson had rehearsed a thing or two he'd been going to say, as well. Things that he'd added to his shit-to-forget pile. Of course, he'd never forget them.

He was still staring at the two boxes when the sound of his phone ringing shot through the room. Lawson made a grunt of surprise that he hoped no one else in the house had heard, and he quickly raked the boxes back in the envelope. He shoved it in the drawer before he even looked at his phone screen.

Lucian.

Too bad he couldn't add his big brother to an actual shit-to-forget box, but since this call could be about their mother, Lawson answered it instead of doing what he usually did when he got a call from Lucian—let it go to voice mail.

"Have you heard?" Lucian asked right off.

"Is this a game of twenty questions?" The stab at sarcasm was a knee-jerk reaction, but Lawson quickly ditched it. "Did something happen to Mom?"

"Not Mom. She's at the house, resting. The trouble's with Tessie."

Lawson had already been steeling himself for Mom news, but there wasn't enough steeling in the world for Lucian saying Tessie's name in that tone. The same tone Lucian used with botched business deals and symptoms of stomach flu.

"What happened to Tessie?" Lawson couldn't get that out fast enough. But he reminded himself that Lucian could be calling because their mother had told him that Tessie was Lawson's daughter.

Lucian cursed. "You haven't heard." More cursing. "Someone at the rehab center in Austin sold info about Tessie's stay there to the tabloids. Then one of her so-called friends gave an interview about her getting drunk. It's about to be plastered all over those magazine covers where you don't want your picture plastered."

Hell. Now Lawson was cursing. And thinking of suing that half-assed clinic. "Tessie only stayed in rehab a couple of hours." But he knew that wouldn't matter. Eve was a celebrity, and Tessie was her daughter, so that made Tessie tabloid fodder, too.

"I tried several contacts but couldn't stop the pictures from being printed," Lucian added.

Well, crap. "There are pictures?"

"Yeah. Of Tessie in the hall of the clinic. Of Tessie coming out of the clinic. A third of Tessie drinking what appears to be margaritas with two friends. And a fourth photo of Tessie and Eve driving through the Heavenly Pastures gates at the ranch."

Ah, Lawson understood Lucian's concern then. It wasn't actually for Tessie. It was because the ranch and therefore the Grangers would get looped into this tabloid scandal. Dylan wouldn't care a rat about it since he was often at the center of local scandals. Lawson wouldn't have cared, either, but he didn't want Tessie's name dragged through the mud.

"There are LA reporters at the Longhorn," Lucian went on. "They're fishing for a story."

Lucian didn't demand that Lawson get over there now and put a stop to it, which meant his brother knew Lawson had a personal stake in this. "I'm on my way there," Lawson said, grabbing his keys and hat, but he was talking to the air because Lucian had already hung up.

Lawson headed out of the house, already trying to rein in his temper, but it riled him to the bone that someone had done this. Yes, Tessie had been wrong to get drunk and then run off the way she did, but news like this could cause her to go off the deep end. That meant after he took care of the reporters at the Longhorn, he needed to drive to Eve's and check on them.

However, Lawson hadn't even made it out of the driveway before he realized a trip to Eve's wouldn't be necessary. That's because he saw her car heading his way. The tires squealed when she braked to a too-fast stop, and she threw open her door while she was still turning off the engine.

She'd been crying.

Eve hurried to him and went straight into his arms. "Did you hear?"

He nodded, pulled her closer than necessary, considering this was supposed to be a hug of comfort. Since he didn't know what to say, Lawson just stayed quiet and let Eve continue.

"I just came from the Longhorn," she said. "No one from Wrangler's Creek is talking to the reporters, but they'll just make up the story they want to print, and it'll be far worse than the truth."

"They might not do that if I kick their asses," Lawson offered. He hadn't exactly meant it as a joke, but it caused Eve to pull back and give a brief, weary smile.

The smile vanished as quickly as it'd come, and she groaned. "Wellsmore is a private, conservative college. They have strict rules of conduct for their students, and this could get Tessie expelled. Or even arrested for underage drinking."

Lawson hated that because he didn't want her to have a juvie record. Or any kind of record, for that matter. Plus, school might be the anchor that Tessie needed to turn her life around. But he could definitely see where the dean would have grounds to kick her out.

"How's Tessie taking it?" he wanted to know.

"She's crying and locked herself in her room. I hid her car keys because I didn't want her driving off anywhere. Cassidy is there at the house, of course, and will call me if Tessie tries to leave. I would have stayed, but I was hoping I could talk the reporters into nixing the story. But they just started taking pictures of me." She motioned toward her tear-streaked face. "Now this will be in the tabloids, too."

Lawson had to fight that ass-kicking urge, but it was a sick SOB who made a living off someone else's misery.

"What can I do?" he asked. It wasn't lip service, but he figured there wasn't a whole lot that could be done by anyone right now.

Still, Eve pulled back and looked up at him. It had those sexual overtones that all their shared looks had, but the overtones were significantly diminished by her tears, bunched-up forehead and teeth clamped over her trembling bottom lip. She seemed on the verge of falling apart, and she probably didn't want to do that in front of the ranch hands who were milling around.

Lawson considered taking Eve to his office, but Nicky and the kids were home. Eve probably didn't want to face anyone right now. That's why Lawson got her into his truck and started driving.

"I can't go home right now," Eve said when she saw the direction he was going. "I don't want to be around Tessie or Aiden when I'm like this. This crying-mess is best for adult eyes only."

"I'm taking you to my place." It was risky. Eve and he usually had no willpower around each other, but Lawson figured they were safe from having sex, considering Eve's and his state of mind.

She didn't object to the destination, maybe because she'd be closer to Tessie but not right there with her. In fact, Eve could keep watch of her place with the binoculars that Lawson hadn't gotten around to throwing out.

Eve rummaged through his glove compartment and came up with a Kleenex so she could blot at the tears. "I was going to tell Tessie about you being her father, but I'll hold off. I don't want to add it to what she's already feeling."

"Uh." That's all Lawson managed to say because Eve snapped toward him.

Her teary eyes widened. "You told her?"

"She guessed when we were at the apartment in Austin, and I didn't lie to her. So, she knows."

He couldn't tell how Eve felt about that. She sure didn't look relieved. "How'd Tessie take it?"

That wasn't an easy question to answer. Tessie hadn't seemed upset. Not with him, anyway. But she had unleashed a little wrath about Eve. Lawson kept that to himself though. Eve was already beating herself up enough without dumping more on her.

"I think she's still trying to work out how she feels," Lawson said, settling for that. "That's why I haven't been by to see her. I wanted to give her some time."

Eve stared at him. "I thought you stayed away because you were avoiding me."

"I was but not for the reason you're probably thinking." It was the truth, but Lawson wished he'd thought about it before blurting it out.

She blinked. "Oh."

Yeah, *oh*. He'd wanted to give Eve and himself some thinking time, too. So they could come to terms with the fooling around they'd done in Austin.

He expected Eve to launch into a discussion as to what he was feeling, et cetera, but she sat in silence as they drove to Heavenly Pastures. The silence ended, though, when she saw what someone had left by the gate. The pile of curled horns looked as if a bear had taken a dump.

"Tessie's story will only make this sort of thing worse," she muttered.

Lawson knocked some horns from the top of the security box and entered the code to open the gate only after he checked around to make sure there were no hornies or paparazzi. He didn't see anyone, but with all the woods nearby, someone could be watching— that was likely how someone got that photo of Eve and Tessie. Just in case that someone tried to rush in and snap some more pictures, Lawson waited until the gate was fully closed behind them before he continued the drive to his house.

The first thing Lawson saw when he pulled into his

driveway was something he didn't want to see. Not a heap of horns or a Swaron trespasser. But rather Prissy Pants squawking and running around.

"Uh, what's a chicken doing here?" Eve asked.

Lawson had no idea how the hen had gotten there. Vita didn't have the security code for the gate unless the fates had revealed it to her. With the way his luck had been going, it was possible.

Lawson soon saw a clue as to the appearance of the chicken. A note was stuck in his door, and he immediately recognized the handwriting. It was Dylan's.

"'Saw Vita in town, and she insisted I bring this ugly chicken to you because she said you were in danger of being cursed again,'" Lawson read aloud. Dylan had triple underlined *insisted*. "'FYI, you're paying for the shit to be cleaned out of my truck. Dylan.'"

Lawson could only sigh. He wasn't in danger of being cursed. The curse seemed to already be there.

Since he rarely locked his door, Lawson was cautious when he opened it, and he looked around for any other curse paraphernalia from Vita. Or for Darby naked beneath a raincoat. Nothing, thank God. Maybe the fates felt they'd already given him enough for one day.

At least he didn't have ass stitches.

Not yet, anyway.

Eve took cautious steps when she walked in, too. She glanced at the binoculars by the front window and the bottle of whiskey on his coffee table.

"It's been a rough couple of days," he grumbled.

She went to the bottle and had a closer look. "It's not open."

"If it hadn't been a rough time, I would have opened

the bottle and had a shot or two." Lawson fully expected to have to give her some kind of explanation to go with that, but Eve only nodded and made a sound of understanding.

"It's like Ooey Gooey for me," she said.

Lawson was sure he gave her a blank stare because now he was the one who needed the explanation.

"It's ice cream," she added. "Or guaranteed cellulite in every bite, as Cassidy likes to call it. I only eat it if I want it, not because I'm trying to choke down my sorrows."

So, she did get it. More or less. He only hoped he didn't have to explain their coping mechanisms to anyone else.

Eve went to the window and used the binoculars to look at her house. "Tessie's car is still there, so no escape attempt yet." Her back was to him now, but he had no trouble seeing her shoulders drop. "God, Lawson. What are we going to do?"

It was another tough question, but at least Eve had made it a "we" instead of an "I." He'd been mulling over some possibilities in between tamping down the whole lust thing he had whenever Eve was around.

"Have you grounded her?" he asked.

She nodded. Sighed.

"Maybe we could arrange for her to see a counselor," Lawson suggested. "Roman's son, Tate, has been seeing one since he had some problems last year."

Another nod. "She has an appointment day after tomorrow. Not sure she'll go though. When I told her about it, she just grunted."

If Lawson thought it would do any good, he'd volunteer to take Tessie. Heck, he'd go to the appointment with her.

Lawson made a third suggestion. "I could try to talk to Tessie if you think it'll help."

Judging from Eve's even faster sigh, she'd already considered that, too. "She's just so angry, and it might stir her up even more than she already is."

He couldn't believe he was even thinking this, but he was going to take a page from Kellan's book on this. Right now, it could make things worse for him to be around his own child.

Even if that's where he wanted to be.

Well, hell. Sometime in the past couple of days, the daddy switch had flipped inside him, and suddenly none of his other problems could hold a candle to what was going on with Tessie. Ironic that the biggest issue in his life was one that he couldn't do anything to fix.

"I've even considered talking to Vita," Eve went on. Not a sigh this time but a groan, and she quickly waved it off.

Obviously, this was eating away at Eve for her to have thought of something that extreme. "I could lend you the chicken." It was a lousy joke, but Lawson was pleased when it earned him one of those half smiles from Eve.

With that half smile on her mouth and the weariness everywhere else on her face, Eve looked at him. Really looked. It was a connection that could only lead to trouble. Which was probably why she glanced away. She took her looks and glancing to his house, and it occurred to him this was the first time she'd been here.

"The place looks great," she said, putting her hands

on her hips. She probably didn't know that the gesture stretched her shirt buttons to the max. It created a gap that allowed him a peek at her bra.

He felt his body clench, then beg.

She walked past him and to the kitchen, and her face twisted up a little when she saw the green granite. "I'm guessing this wasn't your first choice," she said, running her hand along the smooth surface.

"It wasn't even my one-millionth choice."

That brought back some of the smile, and she kept walking, going through the kitchen and to the wall of windows that faced the creek. "Now, this was your first choice for a view."

Yeah, it was. And while he'd never actually imagined Eve standing there like that, she sure made a pretty picture with the light haloing all around her. Haloing through her thin top, too, since he could now see the outline of her body.

His body begged some more, but Lawson planted his feet and didn't move.

She sighed again and mumbled something he didn't catch. However, Lawson had no trouble hearing the rest of what she had to say. "This might be the only house in Wrangler's Creek where we haven't had sex." And with that comment, she looked over her shoulder at him. "Did you bring me here for sex?"

The right answer to that was no. And it was truthful. Well, truthul*ish*, anyway. He hadn't been thinking about sex when he'd brought Eve here, but he was thinking about it now.

"On a scale of one to ten, just how bad of an idea would it be?" she added. But Eve didn't wait for him to answer. She came charging toward him, hooking her arm around him and pulling him to her.

"Screw it," she grumbled. "Let's go for making it the worst idea we've ever had."

EVE KNEW THIS was wrong, but that was probably only adding an extra layer of heat to it. Forbidden fruit combined with bad timing and privacy was a recipe for unplanned sex. Of course, when it came to Lawson, breathing was its own recipe for what was happening.

And what was happening was full-blown foreplay. Right out of the gate.

There was kissing, groping and a level of urgency that made all of this seem as if sex was the cure for all their problems. Maybe the cure for world peace, too. Eve was pretty sure it would give her some peace, anyway. Well, it would after Lawson took care of this pressure-cooker need that was flash-firing inside her.

Thankfully, he had the cure for that.

Eve went after his clothes, aiming for the buttons on his shirt and the zipper of his jeans. She sucked at both, a reminder that as teenagers they'd often had sex while nearly fully clothed. That's what happened when lovemaking venues were truck seats and semipublic places. Panty removal, his zipper down, freeing him from his boxers, and a condom.

Easy peasy.

But now that escalating need gave her the fine motor skills of a toddler.

She gave up on the shirt though she did pop some of the buttons. Lawson, however, proved to her that he still had nimble fingers and an ample undressing skill set. He yanked off her top and tossed it somewhere

CHAPTER TWENTY

LAWSON WAS CONSIDERING two options. Finding a big rock so he could hit himself in the head. Or letting Prissy Pants peck out his eyes. Even though that might not be enough punishment for what he was feeling.

In all the years he'd been having sex, he'd never had a condom break. Maybe there was no good occasion for something like that to happen, but this sure as hell felt like crap timing. Aiden wasn't even four months old yet, and Eve was up to her eyeballs with Tessie. She didn't need a worry like this. Neither of them did.

Eve had assured him it was the wrong time of the month for her to get pregnant, but there'd been something in her eyes.

Fear.

Yeah, that was it.

Fear that there was no wrong time of the month when it came to her getting knocked up. After all, the condom hadn't broken all those years ago when he'd gotten her pregnant with Tessie, so they were perhaps the most fertile couple in Wrangler's Creek.

Still, despite their history, Eve had dismissed it, managed some goodbye kisses and a smile before she'd gotten dressed and walked home. Lawson had volunteered to drive her, but she'd insisted on walking. Prob-

before he scooped her up and went in the opposite direction of her shirt.

Wherever he was taking her, he kissed her along the way, which made the trip very pleasant indeed. He hadn't lost a step with that magic mouth because he managed to kiss her neck and the tops of her breasts before he maneuvered his way down a hall and to a bedroom. And he kept kissing when he laid her on the bed. At least he did until he pulled back.

Eve reached for him, hoping he hadn't changed his mind about this, but he was merely shimmying off her shoes and jeans. Panties, too. Leaving her stark naked except for her bra. But Lawson rid her of that as well, and while she very much wanted to be naked to hurry this along, she also wanted to be able to ogle him the way he was ogling her.

Oh, mercy. He was ogling her.

"I have stretch marks," she said, wishing that she'd done some extra time on the elliptical. And cut out that last carton of Ooey Gooey.

"I like stretch marks," he drawled, and he kissed a couple of them as if to prove that.

Eve had no idea if he was lying, but when he kept going, kissing her lower and lower, she didn't care about such trivial things as truth. When he gave her a kiss right between her legs, Eve no longer cared about ogling or oxygen. Yes, breathing was definitely overrated compared to this.

She let him continue with those special kisses until she was so close to an orgasm that she could feel it rippling through her. That's when she latched on to Lawson's hair and pulled him back up so they were aligned in just the right way for more than just special kisses. She also got serious about getting him out of his shirt, jeans and boxers, but she might have failed again if Lawson hadn't helped her with all three.

He fumbled around in the nightstand drawer and came up with a condom. Eve didn't even try to help with that because she was too busy getting in some of that ogling. It had definitely been worth the wait and the effort that it took to get him out of his clothes. This was no longer a boy's body but rather a man's. Lawson had filled out nicely.

In *all* areas.

She reaped the benefits when he finally got the condom on and pushed inside her. It was possible that fairies had strewn gold glitter behind her eyes and in her head. Possible, too, that she'd reached some level of pleasure that no woman had ever reached before.

Part of her didn't want to move for fear of scaring off the fairies and bringing on a too-quick climax, but Eve's body didn't give her a choice about that. She moved, lifting her hips to benefit from every one of those "filled out" thrusts. She hooked her legs around his waist and moved right into the rhythm with him.

The years just melted away. So did her troubles. So did the memory of her stretch marks. The only thing she could feel, see and taste was the amazing man who sent her and the fairy glitter soaring and flying. Lawson did his own soaring, too, and she felt the climax rack through him.

Well, it racked for a couple of seconds, anyway.

"Shit," he grumbled.

That wasn't the response Eve had been expecting. Lawson wasn't a talker when it came to climaxes. She'd

never even gotten an *Oh, God* fro word like that.

Nor had she gotten the words tha "Shit," he repeated. "The condom

ably so she could look for a big rock along the way to hit herself on the head.

Cursing himself and the condom company, Lawson showered, threw on his clothes and headed back to work. He'd frittered away a good chunk of the day thinking about Tessie and Eve. And thinking about having sex with Eve. Of course, a portion of that frittering had included actual sex.

Damn good sex.

In fact, he could have put it at the top of his best sex ever if it hadn't been for the condom malfunction.

He pulled his truck into the driveway of the Granger Ranch, and he immediately saw Roman. It wasn't unusual for Roman to be there since he lived just about fifty yards from the house. But it was Roman's expression that had Lawson's stomach knotting. Because that was Roman's troubled look. Lawson had already met his trouble quota for the year and definitely didn't want any more.

"This had better be about a cattle sale gone wrong and nothing personal," Lawson snarled when he stepped from his truck. "Because if it's anything but ranching business, I don't want to hear it."

"It's personal." Roman clearly hadn't heeded his warning. "I just saw Eve, and she had a hickey on her neck."

Lawson cursed. "If I left a hickey, it wasn't on her neck." Though one on her inner thigh was a possibility, but he seriously doubted that Roman had seen that part of her anatomy. Which meant this was a fishing expedition. One to reel in some personal information.

"So, you did have sex with her." Roman huffed.

"Now, normally I wouldn't care a rat's nuts about that, but she looked upset."

Hell. Lawson didn't doubt that. He was upset and likely looked it, too. "Did she say anything?"

"Only that she was out for a walk to clear her head. I'm pretty sure we already had a conversation about you not dicking around with her."

"I'm not dicking around with Eve!" Lawson said that a lot louder than he'd intended, and he got not only some ranch hands' attention but also the attention of Nicky and Belle, who were in the sunroom.

"Then what are you doing?" Roman asked.

Lawson didn't have a clue, and he didn't have to think of an answer that wouldn't have satisfied Roman anyway because the sound of a car engine gave him a reprieve. Or at least he thought it was a reprieve.

A confusing one.

It was Mila, but she wasn't alone. Her small car was jammed with people. Specifically, Tessie, Cassidy and Aiden, who was strapped into his infant seat between Cassidy and Tessie. No sign of Eve though.

Mila had a big smile on her face when she got out. A smile meant for Roman because she gave him a long kiss before she even acknowledged that Lawson was there.

"I brought some guests," Mila said, still beaming.

Cassidy and Tessie didn't share Mila's glee. Tessie was sullen. Cassidy was scowling. And Aiden was fussing and kicking. Cassidy took him from the seat and immediately handed him to Lawson.

"Aiden's gassy, cranky and teething," Cassidy informed Lawson. "Why don't you spend some time with the kids while Mila and I have a cup of coffee. I won't be long, and then Mila, Tessie and I are taking Aiden to the park to give Eve a break."

Cassidy didn't linger to make sure that was okay with Lawson or Tessie. It sure as heck wasn't okay with Aiden because he fussed, farted and kicked even harder.

Apparently, Roman was a fan of Cassidy's plan because he only gave Lawson a flat *you're on your own* look and went inside with the women.

Tessie gave him a flat look, too, but she did at least try to soothe her brother by patting his back. It didn't work. "Jiggle him a little," Tessie suggested. "And kind of rock him while you keep a good hold on the back of his neck. His head's not supposed to jiggle too much."

Lawson wasn't an expert at jiggling or rocking, but he gave it a try. "Since it appears you weren't hog-tied and dragged over here against your will, does that mean you came to talk to me?"

Judging from her suddenly sour expression, the answer to that was no. "I just wanted to get out of the house." She tipped her head to Roman, who was still in the doorway of the sunroom. "He's my cousin, right?"

Lawson nodded. "And you've got plenty more of them. Uncles and an aunt, too."

Her expression stayed sour. "I met Lucian." Well, that explained the sucking-lemons look. "I think he's a bit of an ass," she added.

There was nothing wrong with her instincts. Well, instincts about that, anyway. "I can be an ass, too, when it comes to the stunt you pulled."

Bringing up the subject was a risk. Tessie could just clam up or ask Mila to take her back home. But Lawson didn't intend to avoid the elephant in the room just because it could be risky. The biggest risk of all was having Tessie do something that stupid again.

"Are you going to lecture me about it, too?" she asked.

"Damn straight I am." He frowned though at the cursing. It was mild, but he was still doing it in front of two kids. "What you did was wrong, period. From here on out, no drinking at all until you're legal age. That should be about the same time your mom ungrounds you."

"If I'm lucky," Tessie grumbled.

Well, he certainly accomplished putting a damper on the mood. Not that it was a particularly good mood before the mini-lecture. But Tessie's expression immediately perked up when she spotted the new Appaloosas in the corral, and she hurried toward them. Lawson caught up with her, and while he continued to do some baby jostling, he recognized the look in Tessie's eyes.

Horse love.

Yeah, she was his kid all right.

For such a simple thing, it made him feel a whole heck of a lot. Like wanting to know more about her. And wanting to kick any guy's ass who ever laid a hand on her. That was an especially strong feeling. Ditto for wanting to repeat the whole drinking lecture until it sank into her teenage head.

"What are their names?" she asked. As if she'd done it her whole life, she climbed onto the wooden fence, straddling it. She held out her hand and made clicking noises to get the horses to come over.

"We don't tend to name the working horses," Lawson told her.

Aiden caught sight of the Appaloosas, too, and while he wasn't exactly starry-eyed, he quit fussing.

One of the horses moseyed toward Tessie, nudging her hand and causing her to smile. That smile washed away all the crappiness of the day. Lawson was afraid though that it wouldn't last when he had to ask her a question.

"Does your mom know you're here?"

Tessie nodded, kept her attention on the horses. All four of them were headed her way now. "Miss Mila came by and asked if she could bring me to the ranch, and Mom said yes—after she thought about it for a long time. It was Cassidy's idea to come with me."

Probably because Cassidy wanted to keep an eye on Tessie to make sure she didn't run off or anything. But she wasn't running anywhere right now. Instead, she looked ready to get in the corral with the horses.

"There should be a bag of treats just inside." Lawson tipped his head to the barn. "There's a tack room on the left."

Tessie got off the fence as easily as she'd gotten on, and she headed in that direction while Aiden volleyed some glances at Lawson, the horses and his sister. With the intensity of an artist analyzing a model, the kid stared at Lawson. Then he belched, farted and laughed all at the same time. Good. Maybe the belching and farting would put him in a better mood. It certainly put Lawson in a better one, and he brushed a kiss on the kid's head.

It wasn't long before Tessie came back, the bag of treats in hand, and she climbed on the fence again. Lawson was about to instruct her on how to give an

open palm treat to avoid a bite, but she'd already figured it out.

"You know how to ride?" he asked.

She nodded. "I've had lessons."

That made him want to cringe. Anyone with his
DNA should have been raised on horses. But Lawson decided it would be petty to hold that against Eve.

"I'm going to be a large-animal vet," Tessie went
on. But the glee vanished. "Or at least I was going to
be one." She looked at him. "You heard that I might
get kicked out of school?"

"Yeah. Can't say I blame the dean. Underage drinking is not only bad for your liver, brain cells and judg-
ment, it's also bad PR for a college."

Tessie didn't argue with that. In fact, she might have
made a teeny sound of agreement. "Now that everyone knows I'm a student there, Mom's crazy fans keep
leaving stuff outside my sorority house. Horns, capes
and those stupid fake weapons she used to carry on
the set. And the photographers keep trying to sneak
pictures of me."

"My advice—don't do anything else stupid to give
them a good picture. If you're boring enough, they'll
eventually find a new target." Lawson hoped so, anyway.

"Now I know how my mother feels about the press
always hounding her," Tessie added in a grumble.
"Don't tell her I said that. I'm not letting her off the
hook just yet. She still hasn't fessed up about you being
the dad."

Not *my* dad. *The* dad. At least she hadn't called
him a sperm donor or the a-hole who'd knocked up
her mother.

"Eve knows that you know about me," Lawson confessed. "I told her that you'd figured it out."

If Tessie had a reaction to that, she didn't show it. She gave another horse a treat. "Do you hate me?"

The question stunned him to the point that Lawson made a weird sound, part snort, part groan, part huff, and it was loud enough to spook the horses a little. It caused Aiden to jump, too.

"No," Lawson barked. "Of course not."

Tessie stared at him a moment as if waiting for more. And Lawson wanted to give her more, too, but he wasn't sure what he should say. He considered using the l-word. But it might scare her off. Still, he did have l-word feelings for this hardheaded teenager.

"What about him?" Tessie motioned toward Aiden. "Do you hate him because he's Kellan's son?"

This time, Lawson tried to keep his huff a little softer. "No, I don't hate him. I try to limit my hatred to people who actually deserve it. Your screwing up doesn't warrant any hatred. And neither does Aiden's gene pool." Though he was still hanging on to some hatred for Kellan.

"But you hate my mother for keeping me secret," she added. She didn't look at him but kept her attention on the horses.

"I don't hate Eve, either." Now he did add more. "Your mom was about the same age you are now when she had you. Think about that for a second. She maybe didn't make the smartest decision, but I think she did the best she could, all things considered."

Now Tessie's attention came back to him. She didn't address what he'd just said but instead tossed something else out there. "Apparently, my mom hasn't grasped the concept of safe sex."

Lawson immediately thought of the broken condom. The concept was there all right, but sometimes leaky latex could squash precautions.

"Is everything okay?" Cassidy called out to them. She was no longer in the sunroom but was making her way toward them.

"Fine," Tessie and Lawson said in unison.

Cassidy glanced at them as if trying to figure out if that was true, but then she shrugged. "Are you ready to go?" she asked Tessie as she took Aiden from Lawson.

Tessie hesitated, maybe wanting to stay. Probably not because of him, though, but because of the horses. She was giving them a longing look.

"Don't screw up for six months, and I'll buy you one," Lawson offered.

"You're bribing me?" Tessie asked.

"Yeah," he readily admitted.

Cassidy raised an eyebrow, maybe because bribes equaled bad parenting or something, but it had always worked on him. Well, for matters that didn't concern Eve it had, anyway.

"Thanks, but I've got my own money," Tessie grumbled, walking away.

That had a distinctive *don't let the door hit you in the ass on the way out* tone to it, but Lawson tried not to take it personally. He remembered the whole teenage-angst thing and had a daily reminder of it with Tate. Still, it stung, especially considering they had an actual conversation prior to the snark.

Lawson stayed by the corral and watched Mila drive

off with them. Roman left, too, heading in the direction of his own house on the other side of the driveway.

It was strange, but Lawson suddenly felt a little, well, empty. No belching, laughing baby in his arms. No horse-loving teenager who might be grounded until infinity. Everything was…normal again. And yet it didn't feel normal at all.

It felt shitty.

And it only got worse when he saw the car approaching. Not Mila doubling back for an extended visit. It was Darby.

Lawson tried to buck himself up, and he hoped like the devil that his ex was wearing more than a raincoat and a twinkle in her eye. She was. When she stepped from the car, he could see that she was wearing scrubs.

They walked toward each other, meeting halfway between the house and the barn. "Don't worry," Darby said right off. "I'm not here for *that*."

Good—they were on the same page. About that, anyway.

"I heard about Eve's daughter," Darby went on.

Hell. He hadn't expected it to stay a secret about Tessie being his, but he really didn't want to have this conversation with Darby.

"I might be able to help," Darby added.

He raised an eyebrow and was about to ask her if she'd created a time machine to go back and undo the pregnancy. Something he definitely didn't want undone.

"Thanks for the offer…" he started, but he didn't get to finish because Darby interrupted him.

"My dad's college roommate is the head of a department at Wellsmore College. He can talk to the dean and maybe stop Tessie from being expelled. I wanted to make sure it was okay with Eve before I had him do anything like that, but I figured Eve would rather hear it from you than me."

Darby was right about that, but Lawson wasn't sure Eve would want to hear it from anyone. Having strings like that pulled might make Tessie believe she was going to get bailed out if she messed up. Lawson didn't want that notion planted in her head. Still, this wasn't his call to make. *The dad* wasn't the same as *Dad*.

"I'll mention it to Eve. Thanks," he said and then started for the house.

But Darby went right along with him. "How's Eve doing? I suspect she's having a lot of mixed emotions right now."

Lawson kept walking, but he glanced at her, trying to figure out what the heck that meant. Was there some kind of rumor about Eve and him having sex? Or was this Tessie related?

"Eve's okay," Lawson answered, hoping that would suffice and send Darby on her way.

It didn't.

"So, you think Eve will stay here in Wrangler's Creek?" Darby asked.

That got him stopping on the porch step. He didn't like the sound of that. "Why wouldn't she?"

Darby lifted her shoulder. "I just figured Kellan Carver wouldn't want to live here. This doesn't seem like the kind of place that would suit him."

Lawson huffed, put his hands on his hips. "Is there something you're trying to tell me? Because I'm not getting it."

"Oh." Darby blinked. "I thought you knew."

"Knew what?" Lawson growled.

Darby shook her head, mumbled another "Oh," and she took out her phone. She hit the play button on a video and showed it to him. It was a video of Kellan giving an interview to reporters. Not in California, either. It appeared to be in front of the Longhorn Bar.

"Yeah, you heard me right," Kellan said, sounding like the cocky ass that he was. He swiped his hand through his hair and flashed that Hollywood smile. "Eve Cooper's daughter, Tessie, is my child. *Our* child," Kellan corrected himself.

For shit's sake. What was this about?

The bombshell lie caused a flurry of questions, and the photographers were clicking off a boatload of pictures. Pictures of Kellan's lying, smiling face.

"Don't worry," Kellan went on. "I'll be sharing lots of details and pics of me, Eve and our kiddos when we start our new life together." He outstretched his arms. "Baby-Cakes, I'm on my way home to you."

CHAPTER TWENTY-ONE

EVE SQUEALED AND did a happy dance around her bathroom. She'd never been so glad to get her period. Finally, something was going her way. And she didn't even mind the cramps and bloating she was going to have for the next three days.

Nope.

Because this meant the condom malfunction wasn't an issue. She'd been right about it being the wrong time of the month. Of course, at the time she hadn't known if she was right or not, but that also wasn't an issue since the period proved she had nothing to worry about. Well, nothing related to an unplanned pregnancy, anyway. She'd already had two of those, so it was best not to add another.

She finished her shower, hit her playlist on her phone and continued dancing around her bedroom while wearing only her bra and panties. Since Cassidy, Tessie and Aiden were still with Mila, it meant there'd be no one in the house to hear her celebrate, so she cranked up the volume and did something she hadn't done in years. She jumped on her bed and used it as a trampoline.

The jumping lasted a couple of seconds until she landed wrong, perhaps pulling a groin muscle. The pain put somewhat of a damper on her celebration, but it didn't completely kill the natural buzz. She was going to pour herself a big glass of wine and dig out the pint of Ooey Gooey she'd stashed in the freezer. Not exactly a gourmet pairing, but she didn't care.

She tugged on a pair of shorts, which normally would have been a reminder for her to lose weight—and to skip the Ooey Gooey—but she squeezed into them anyway. She threw on a top, yanked open the door.

And nearly had a heart attack.

Because there was a wall of people in front of her. Tessie, Cassidy and Lawson. Mila was standing behind them, and she had Aiden on her hip. All of them, including Aiden, had very concerned looks on their faces.

"Oh, God. What happened?" Eve blurted out.

No one jumped to answer that, but Lawson, Tessie and Cassidy all took out their phones. They hit the play buttons, seconds apart, and the same video started playing at staggered intervals. It was a video of Kellan, that much she could see, but because the three audios were competing with each other, it was next to impossible to hear what he was saying. However, Eve did catch a word here and there.

Tessie. Child. Baby-Cakes.

She scowled because she didn't want any of those words coming out of Kellan's mouth. Eve poked the buttons on each of the phones to stop the videos and the garbled dialogue.

"Give me the condensed version," Eve insisted. "What did he say?"

Tessie's eyes narrowed. Cassidy rolled her eyes. And it was Lawson who eventually answered her. "Kellan's in Wrangler's Creek, and he just told reporters that Tessie was his daughter and that all four of you were ready to start your new life together." A muscle flickered in his jaw. "He promised photos."

Lots of really bad curse words went through her head, but they thankfully didn't make it out of her mouth because her throat muscles clamped up. The clamping was from the shock followed by the jolt of really bad anger.

"He did what?" Eve howled. She figured her out-rage should have been enough to confirm to everyone in the room that Kellan was lying.

It apparently wasn't though.

"You told me Kellan wasn't my father," Tessie said, and she was back to using the tone that was a mix of angst, anger and defiance.

"He's not." And Eve repeated that to Lawson. There was no need to verify it to Cassidy because she knew the truth.

"His *fans* will believe Kellan," Tessie insisted, "and it'll only cause more of those creeps and photographers to hound us. He must have believed this is what you wanted him to do."

Eve sighed. "No. Kellan is an idiot. He did it because it was what *he* wanted to do." Another sigh. "He might have thought he was helping, that this would be enough of a distraction to overshadow the rehab stories."

It wouldn't overshadow anything though. The rehab would just get folded into this, and Tessie was right. It would create a firestorm of publicity that no one under this roof wanted.

But Kellan would. He lived for firestorms of pub-licity.

That gave Eve a new wallop of anger, and she

snatched up her phone to call the doofus. No answer. It went to voice mail, and she had to listen to his recorded gag-worthy greeting—"Hey, it's Kell. Say something sweet to me, and I'll get back to you with something sweeter."—before she could leave him a message that definitely didn't fall into the sweet category.

"Call me, you asshole." Eve instantly regretted using the crude term. Even though it was accurate. Still, she'd said it in front of Tessie and Aiden.

"You know why Kellan did this," Cassidy said. It wasn't a question.

Yes, Eve did know. "This will get Kellan's name in the tabloids. It could spur some new interest in a re-union show for *Demon High*."

Tessie's mouth dropped open. "You're not doing *Demon High* again, are you?"

"No," Eve quickly reassured her. She repeated that *no* to Lawson. "Not a chance, but Kellan's been pres-suring me for years."

"Yes, because he can't get another acting job where women drool over him and fondle his horns," Cassidy interjected.

That was true, as well. "You said Kellan was here in town?" Eve asked Lawson.

He nodded. "He was at the Longhorn when he did that lying sack of crap interview. According to the time it was uploaded on the internet, he talked to those re-porters only an hour ago. You want me to kick his butt for doing this?"

"Yes!" Cassidy and Tessie answered in unison.

It was tempting, but that would only make matters worse. "The press would get pictures and then do big blow-up articles about you punching out Kellan's lights because you're jealous of him and me. That could lead to speculations about the jealousy, and some nosy reporter could even make the connection that you're Tessie's father."

Cassidy groaned. "And then the Granger Ranch would get sucked into this cesspool of news. Tessie would, too. She doesn't need any more publicity right now with her expulsion under review."

Until Cassidy had added that last part, both Tessie and Lawson both looked as if they might still lobby for Kellan to get a good butt-kicking. Thankfully, that seemed to make them grasp just how ugly this could get if not handled properly.

Eve grabbed her purse. "I'll go find Kellan and quietly talk this out with him—away from reporters and the press. I'll keep it all very low-key."

That sounded civilized enough, and Kellan was going to agree to it—even if she had to threaten him with the butt-whipping. Of course, a low-key chat was just the beginning. Eventually, they'd have to work out what Kellan would say to the press about Tessie. Maybe the best way to go was to say nothing about Kellan's lie. Then Lawson and the Grangers wouldn't get dragged into this.

"I'll go with you," Lawson offered.

Eve didn't even have to think about it. She shook her head. "Low-key," she repeated. "I'll call you after I've talked to him."

She brushed a quick kiss on Tessie's and Aiden's cheeks and wanted to do the same to Lawson, but the timing was bad for that. Later though, maybe she could work in some kisses or at least a good hug when she told him they'd dodged a bullet with the defective condom.

As she got into her car, Eve tried to call Kellan again, but when it went to voice mail, she hung up rather than waiting for his greeting or leaving another message. She drove out of the ranch, frustrated when she saw a fresh pile of horns, a Swaron and a photographer.

Good grief.

Since they weren't actually on the ranch, they weren't trespassing, but they had no right to be there. She opened the gate and got out to demand that they leave. However, the moment she opened her car door, three more Swarons came rushing out from behind the bushes. And they didn't just rush. They yodeled that Swaron battle cry just as the actors had done on *Demon High*.

Even though she knew these were hornies, her body geared up for an attack. "Get back!" she yelled in the best Ulyana voice she could manage. But it didn't work. The three of them latched on to her, one on each arm and the third one catching onto her waist.

Eve kicked the center one in the nuts. He cursed, howled, caught onto his family jewels and dropped to his knees. "My nuts!" he yelled.

She was about to pivot and do the same to the other two when she heard something else she didn't want to hear.

Applause.

Then laughter, followed by more clapping.

"I told you she hadn't lost any of her form," someone said.

Kellan.

And he was the clapping fool who stepped out of the bushes along with two photographers who were snapping pictures of her. A third guy was making a video of this debacle. The guy on the ground was gasping for air, holding his groin and yelling "My nuts."

"Well, maybe she lost a little step," Kellan went on—clearly oblivious to the scalpel-sharp glare she was giving him. And the yelling Swaron. "But that'll all come back with some training."

He went to her, still oblivious, and he hooked his arm around her. "Stavros and Ulyana back together again," he announced to more applause and pictures.

"No. We're. Not," Eve managed to say through clenched teeth, which Kellan didn't seem to notice, either.

"Play along, Baby-Cakes," he whispered when he brushed a kiss next to her ear. "This is the start of something big. When the studio sees this, they'll jump to get us back."

Eve untangled herself from him so he could see her angry face when she spoke. "I don't want the studio to jump at us because I'm not doing another episode of *Demon High*."

The standing Swarons gasped. The one on the ground started another round of yelling about his nuts. The photographers kept clicking and filming.

"Play along," Kellan warned her again. "This is a good deal for both of us."

In that moment, Kellan had never been a bigger ass. "No, it's not a good deal for me."

He ignored her, gave a fake Hollywood laugh and kissed her scowling, tight lips. "Don't screw this up for me, Baby-Cakes. I didn't put up a fuss when you were knocked up with Tessie on the set and when you had Aiden. So, you more or less owe me."

Eve had thought the old saying "seeing red" was just a cliché. Not something literal. But she saw red. Bright, angry, mean, bad-tempered red. That's why it wasn't a good idea when Kellan took hold of her shoulders to keep her from getting back in her car.

Kellan held on. Eve brought up her hands to shove him away. He turned. She turned. And somehow her hip ended up ramming him in the groin. It was apparently just as effective as a kneeing because Kellan howled, grabbed his crotch and went down like the Swaron.

Eve reached for Kellan, not that he deserved to be helped to his feet, but she hadn't intended to hurt him. Ditto for the Swaron. But as she was reaching for Kellan, the photographers started running. They were heading back to their vehicles, which were parked just up the road.

Getting away.

And Eve knew exactly where they were going. Within an hour, maybe less, the picture of her hitting Stavros in his privates would be front-page news on the tabloids.

LAWSON KNEW THAT people had different definitions of what *low-key* meant, but he seriously doubted this picture was on any part of anyone's low-key scale. Especially Eve's.

It was the latest photo of the encounter she'd had with Kellan two days earlier, and it was making the rounds on the internet and TV gossip shows. Making the rounds on his phone, too, since people kept sending it to him. In this case, Lucian was the messenger. He'd texted Lawson a copy at 2:00 a.m. Not that Lawson had been asleep. No. A nightmare about Brett had seen to that, and he'd been pacing in his living room in his boxers, glancing at the whiskey bottle, when his phone had dinged. Because of the hour, he had known it wouldn't be good news.

And it wasn't.

This photo was not only a different angle of the actual balls-bump that had sent Kellan to his knees. It also included the Heavenly Pastures name on the gate. Lucian hadn't included a message with the photo, but Lawson knew there was only one thing his brother would want to say.

Fix this.

Of course, there was no putting that particular cat back in the bag, but Lawson figured the tabloids would soon latch on to something else, and it would die down. It might not die down for Tessie though until she found out if she was going to be kicked out of college. And then her expulsion could only stir up the paparazzi again.

That was on Lawson's mind, too, as he kept pacing. So was Eve. And even Kellan since the man was still rankled at Eve and vice versa. But the thing that was weighing heaviest right now were the pieces of the nightmare that were still with him.

Especially the different pieces.

Normally, the nightmares were all the same. Various fragments of the party. Eve. Always Eve. And then assorted versions of them discovering Brett unconscious. Not so much of an actual nightmare but the real memories that ate away at him.

This one had been different though.

This time, Lawson had gone down the stairs, alone,

and he'd seen Brett on the sofa. Not unconscious—yet. But still drinking. Still alive. The dream was still a dream in that things weren't as they'd been. Furniture in odd places. The blurred edges of the images.

It had felt real.

Was it?

Had he actually gone down those stairs in time to stop what was about to go wrong? Until tonight, Lawson would have said no, that he had no memories in between sacking out with Eve and finding Brett the following morning. That's why most folks had blamed Eve. She had seen Brett. She had gone down those stairs. But maybe Eve had gotten a bad rap. Maybe he was the person solely to blame for this.

Lawson groaned, pressing his hands to the sides of his head, wishing for some peace that wouldn't come. Well, it could come with the whiskey, but it would be only temporary. Still, temporary seemed pretty damn good right now, and Lawson was losing his battle with his willpower.

Until someone knocked on his door.

His gut tightened even more than it had with the photo that Lucian had sent. Because a wee-hours-of-the-morning knock was almost certainly going to be worse than a text arriving at that same time.

Or not.

He opened his door to find Eve on his porch. She was wearing a robe over a nightgown, both short, and she had a pint of Ooey Gooey ice cream and a spoon in her hand. A pint and spoon that she thrust at him.

"I was up and pacing and looked through the binoculars to see you doing the same thing." She walked in, her body brushing against his. "Maybe you should invest in curtains because I clearly have no willpower when it comes to spying on you. Sorry about that."

Lawson wasn't sorry—though he should consider curtains. He'd needed something but wasn't sure what until he saw Eve. And no, this wasn't about sex. It just eased the nightmare to have her there. A first. Because usually coupling her with the memories of Brett only made things worse.

"How did you get here?" he asked. "I didn't hear your car."

"I walked, using the flashlight on my phone." She put the ice cream and spoon in his hand and tipped her head to the whiskey. "I saw that, too," she added. "Saw how you were eyeing it. And I came up with an idea. You eat my vice, and I'll drink yours. That way, neither one of us will be giving in to the demons."

Leave it to Eve to come up with something like that, but Lawson couldn't help but smile. He shut the door, following her into the living room, but she made a detour into the kitchen to come up with a shot glass.

She did indeed pour herself a drink, took a sip, grimaced. Then gagged. "My coping mechanism tastes better than yours."

He had a bite of the ice cream and agreed. But unless he ate enough to put him in a sugar coma, the whiskey was going to work better at shoving aside those memories. Shoving aside common sense though, too. But at least the Ooey Gooey wouldn't leave him with a hangover.

"So, why were you pacing?" Lawson asked, sitting on the sofa next to her. "This isn't about the condom, is it?"

She shook her head, had another sip of the whiskey.

Another grimace followed. "No. That all worked out. I was right about it being the wrong time of the month. Hortense came."

He was going to assume that Hortense was what she called her period and that some other person hadn't come into this crazy episode that was their lives. But at least now they wouldn't have to add an unplanned pregnancy on top of everything else.

"I was pacing because of bad dreams," she said. "You?"

Lawson nodded. "A nightmare about Brett. I thought I came down the stairs and saw him. I thought I could have saved him."

She looked at him, lowering the shot glass that she'd had right against her mouth. "You didn't come downstairs."

He looked at her, too. "Are you saying that to try to make me feel better?"

"No. Nothing will make us feel better about what happened to Brett that night. This is always going to suck, and it's never going to heal."

There it was, all in an ugly little nutshell. Whiskey and ice cream wouldn't fix that. Apparently, neither could time.

"I said you didn't go downstairs because you didn't," she went on. "You sleep like a rock, especially after sex, and I don't. If you'd gotten out of bed, I would have known it." She turned away, staring down into the glass. "I was the only one who could have saved Brett, and I didn't."

That wasn't completely true. And maybe it was the sugar rush or the exhaustion from lack of sleep, but Lawson suddenly had a light-bulb moment. "Brett could have saved himself by not drinking. No way though could we blame him because we feel so guilty about losing him."

Suddenly, there were tears in Eve's eyes, and while he could be clueless sometimes about emotions, he knew these weren't of the happy variety. On a heavy sigh, he slipped his arm around her and pulled her to him.

"Maybe we're not supposed to forget," he went on, wishing he knew the right thing to say. "Maybe that's the price of loving and losing someone. It's always with us. Always there. Always bittersweet."

She lifted her head from his shoulder, their gazes connecting. "Like us?"

"Like us," he agreed.

Lawson didn't kiss her though their mouths were only inches apart. He held back not because he didn't want to kiss her—he did—but because the timing was definitely wrong. She hadn't come here for kissing and sex but rather to soothe some of their raw edges from grief.

The silence crawled on for a few long moments before she had another sip of the whiskey. While she grimaced, she motioned toward the ice cream. "If you eat a big spoonful, the brain freeze will help chase away the images. Of course, you'll get a bad headache, too."

Pain. Something Lawson hadn't considered for coping. He tried it. It worked. But now he was the one grimacing.

"How's Tessie?" he asked, hoping it didn't cause her eyes to tear up again.

"Moody and moping. A lot like what I've been

doing. I suppose you've seen the pictures of Kellan and his injured nuts?"

He settled for a nod. "I'm sure he deserved it. And more. He didn't fess up to the lie he told about being Tessie's father."

She tossed back the rest of the shot before she answered. "No, and I haven't pushed it because anything that any of us says right now will only fan the tabloid flames."

Lawson agreed. Maybe Kellan would work with that same theory and stay out of sight while nursing his bruised balls.

"Does Lucian want me to move off the ranch?" she asked.

Because both Eve and he knew Lucian well, Lawson had figured the question was coming. "Probably. But that's no reason for you to go. It's nice to see Lucian irritated about something not going his way."

She made a sound of agreement, took the spoon from him and had a bite of the ice cream.

"I heard about Darby's offer to contact the dean." Eve handed him back the spoon. "Or rather Cassidy heard about it when she went into town to get some groceries."

So, that was on the gossips' agenda. Surprising, since there were so many other tidbits to spread around.

"It was nice of Darby to offer," Eve went on, "but I'm worried it'll come with strings attached. Strings for you."

He would have loved to deny that, but as a general rule Lawson didn't like to fudge the truth to himself. Darby might indeed see this as a way back into his life especially since she thought that Kellan was Tessie's father. That might cause Darby to believe that Lawson would be free to take up with her again.

"I'll text Darby and tell her thanks but no thanks," Lawson assured her. It was something he'd strongly considered doing, but he hadn't wanted to get rid of a possible lifeline if Eve felt it was a good one.

She stood, recapped the whiskey. "I should be leaving so we can both get some rest." He stood, too, but she didn't move, and there seemed to be a whole lot of hesitation in her eyes. Maybe because she was going to launch into the kissing and sex that Lawson had already ruled out.

Or not.

"I decided not to sell my California house," she said, throwing that out there. "In fact, I'm thinking if Tessie does get expelled, then Aiden, Cassidy, her and me will move back there for a while."

And with that bombshell, she turned to leave. Hell. Was this goodbye? But she stopped and looked at him over her shoulder. Maybe now she would say she was just kidding or that it was the whiskey talking.

Or not.

"Lawson, I really am sorry for screwing up your life," Eve added before she hurried down the steps and disappeared into the night.

CHAPTER TWENTY-TWO

TESSIE FIGURED THIS visit was going to get her into even more trouble—especially since she hadn't been completely honest with her mom about where she was going. Tessie had told her that she was going for a ride on the chestnut mare named Nelly, which she'd borrowed from Dylan. And it was a ride.

All the way to the Granger Ranch.

It'd been a while since she'd been on a horse and never for the five miles or so it would take to reach the ranch. By the time she reined in at the Granger barn, she was sweaty, sore and rethinking this idea of seeing Lawson. Especially when she didn't even know if he was there. He could be on a business trip.

Or avoiding her.

She couldn't blame him if he did that because she hadn't exactly been a ray of sunshine in his life. And then there was the shit-storm with Kellan and her mom. Lawson might be trying to avoid her mom, too.

She got off the horse and glanced around. No sign of Lawson, so she went looking for him. She didn't see him, but she sure heard him.

"Shit on a son of a bitching stick," he growled.

Lawson came limping in through the back opening of the barn, and he kept belting out some really bad words. There was a cut just over his right eyebrow and what appeared to be the start of a bruise on his jaw. When he saw her though, he immediately straightened, quit cussing and used his hat to knock off some of the dirt that was on his jeans.

"Are you okay?" she asked.

"Horse threw me." He said it like someone who was super embarrassed. And super mad. But if so, it was measly compared to the embarrassing crap she'd done.

His attention went from her to the mare. "Dylan's," he grumbled.

She nodded. "He said I could borrow her."

He kept knocking off the dirt, wincing with some of the movements as he walked closer to her. "Two questions. Are you still grounded, and does your mom know you're here?"

Like the day in Austin, he sounded a little like a cop again. Or a dad. "Yes to the first. No to the second. But she won't mind me coming over." At least Tessie didn't think she would. "You might want to do something about that cut above your eye. You're bleeding."

He touched it, cursed under his breath when he did indeed see blood and headed to the tack room. "Did you hear back about school?" he asked, taking out a first-aid kit.

"Yeah." Since his hands were dirty, Tessie nudged him aside and took over. She poured some hydrogen peroxide on a gauze pad and dabbed at the cut. It gave her something to do other than looking him in the eye when she told him the rest. "I got kicked out of school. I can reapply but not until next semester."

She braced herself for his reaction, figuring it'd be similar to her mom's. Her mom had gone very silent and had said something about her maybe going to another college in California. Her mom hadn't yelled, cried or gotten pissed off. It was as if hearing it had broken something inside her. Her mom had managed a smile, a hug and had added that it would be all right.

But Tessie knew that was a lie because she certainly wasn't feeling all right, not by a long shot.

By drinking and then running off, she had made it so that it would never be the same between her mom and her. And now she was going to put a big wedge between Lawson and her when it sank in that she'd been expelled. Not that Lawson had ever cared about her the way her mom had, but Tessie didn't want him seeing her with that same broken look that she'd gotten from her mother.

"Is Eve moving you back to California?" he asked.

She lifted her shoulder. "She's talking about it." A lot.

He dragged in a breath that was a little uneven maybe because the antiseptic cream that she smeared on the cut was stinging. "All right. Until then, I'm grounding you. This is separate from your mom's grounding. You might say it's an additional sentence to the one you already had."

She stared at him. He did sound a little pissed off, but he wasn't all sad and drowning in doom and gloom.

"That doesn't mean sitting around in your room feeling sorry for yourself," he went on. "Until your mom makes up her mind about moving, you've got to tend the horses. That includes mucking out the crap in the stalls."

Yes, he was pissed off all right, but for some stupid reason it didn't make her feel bad. She hadn't broken him, maybe because he'd had to put up with less of her mess than her mom had. Or maybe because he thought there might be some hope for her after all.

"Can I ride the horses if I take care of them?" Tessie bargained as she put the bandage on Lawson's head.

He thought about that for a couple of moments before he nodded. "Yeah, but not that Appaloosa bi...*witch* that just threw me. Oh, you can name her, too, as long as it's something mean like..." He sputtered out some syllables, probably because he couldn't think of anything that didn't involve cuss words.

"I'll keep the name PG-rated," Tessie grumbled. But she did like the idea of naming a horse. Even a mean one.

She put away the first-aid kit and followed Lawson out of the tack room. He was still hobbling a bit, making her wonder if he needed to go to the hospital.

"You rode that mare all the way over here?" he asked.

Tessie nodded.

"How sore are you?" he added.

"Sore." Though she hated to admit it. It sounded prissy, and she doubted Lawson would want his kid to be prissy. If he ever thought of her as his kid, that is. She wasn't sure either one of them actually wanted that.

"If you want, I can drive you home, and one of the hands can take the mare back," Lawson offered.

"It's okay. I'll do it." And then she'd be hobbling as bad as he was. But it felt like the right thing to do, and she needed to do something right. Not for Lawson or her mom but for herself.

"I wasn't always a screwup," she said. "I got all As in school and never busted curfew. Not until the blowup with my mom about her lying to me."

"I figured as much." When they made it back out of the barn, he stopped and turned to her. "This is one of those life-lesson stories. I don't tell them very often, so listen up. I was the middle child of five kids and was nothing special. I definitely didn't stand out in a sea of Grangers who were smarter, nicer and better looking than me, so I tried to be as good as I could be. The perfect kid." He lifted his shoulder. "That all went down the drain when my folks got divorced. I was angry and blamed both of them for messing up, and that's why I messed up, too."

She waited for him to add more to the life lesson, but he just kept staring at her. "So, you understand why I did what I did?"

He made a face. "Hell, no." Then he made another face. "I mean, *heck*, no. I didn't understand why I was doing it then or why you did it now. It's like we put these big targets on our feet so we can shoot ourselves there, and it doesn't help squat. It only hurts and pisses people off, and in my case, it hurt someone a lot."

Tessie didn't think he was talking about her mom. This was about the friend who'd died. The one her mom still cried about.

"So, you're telling me not to make the same mistakes you did?" she asked.

"Yeah, that's what life lessons are all about." He started walking again, and Tessie fell in step beside him. "Don't expect a lot of them from me though, because I meant what I said about not giving them very often."

Tessie didn't get a chance to say anything about that because they suddenly realized they weren't alone. Tessie went stiff when she saw the dark figure step out from the side of the barn. Lawson reacted, too. He hooked his arm around her, pushing her behind him.

"Who the hell are you?" Lawson growled, and he sounded very mean.

The guy came out, his hands in the air, and when Lawson and she got a better look at him, they both groaned. Because it was one of her mom's fans dressed like a stupid Swaron warrior.

"I'm Todd," the guy said. His voice sounded shaky, probably because Lawson was scowling at him as if he might tear his leg off.

"You're trespassing," Lawson warned him.

Todd's nod was shaky, as well. "I just wanted a picture of Stavros and Ulyana's daughter."

The twerp had his phone aimed and ready to take a photo that Tessie was pretty sure Lawson wasn't going to let him take.

"She's not Stavros's daughter," Lawson said. Tessie wasn't sure how he managed to do it, but he sounded even scarier than he looked. "She's mine."

Todd swallowed hard, nodded, but he didn't look as if he was buying that. Not until Lawson maneuvered her out from behind him. Once Lawson and she were side by side, Todd nodded again. This time, for real.

"Take your damn picture," Lawson ordered. "Put it on every social network site you can find with the caption 'Tessie Cooper with her father, Lawson Granger.'"

Todd gave another nod. An eager one, this time.

"You're sure you want to do this?" Tessie whispered to Lawson.

He looked her straight in the eyes. "Yeah. You're my daughter, and I want everyone to know it."

That felt a lot better than Tessie had thought it

would. "Even with all the trouble I've gotten into?" she pressed.

"Even then." Lawson brushed a kiss on her cheek and put his arm around her for the photo that Todd snapped.

"So, you're not an ass after all?" she muttered to Lawson.

"Only on occasion. By the way, you're still grounded."

EVE FIGURED SHE looked like a crazy person. She was crying and smiling at the same time—and both were genuine emotions. That's what she got for taking Aiden with her to visit Brett's grave.

Aiden was in a great mood, cooing and smiling, and it was impossible for her not to smile back and make goofy sounds that only another parent would understand. He was her precious little man, and she loved every ounce of him.

What she didn't love was the grief that bubbled up inside her when she saw Brett's shiny gray marble tombstone. Of course, she'd known what it would say. His name along with the dates of his birth and death. She hadn't known about the quote on it though.

In our hearts forever.

Eve was certain his parents had chosen those handful of words, and they were true. Brett would indeed always be in her heart. Too bad she couldn't keep him out of her nightmares, but she had to hope that one day those nightmares would turn to dreams. Dreams of the good times they'd had with Brett and not just the miserable mistake of that night.

Aiden made an especially loud coo and started kicking and flailing his arms. When Eve followed his gaze, she spotted Lawson making his way toward them. Her son was certainly overjoyed to see him, but Eve was feeling a little less enthusiastic. That's because she needed to give him the bad news about Tessie.

"I saw your car parked out by the cemetery gate," he said.

When he got closer, Aiden immediately reached for him, and with all the ease of a veteran parent, Lawson took him. The kiss he brushed on top of Aiden's head looked plenty natural, too.

"No farting on me today," Lawson told Aiden, and the boy laughed the way someone would at a fine man-joke that he completely understood.

There was no trace of the joke though when Lawson looked at her. "Are you okay?"

Eve hadn't forgotten about the fresh tears in her eyes, but she quickly wiped them away. "It's my first time here."

He nodded as if no other explanation was necessary. "It gets easier after a while. The visit, I mean."

Yes, the rest would never fall into the easier category. "What about you?" She tipped her head to the bandage above his eye. "Are you all right?"

"I lost a battle of wills with an Appaloosa."

She figured that had to sting—not just his ego but literally. At least it didn't look serious.

Eve took a deep breath, prepared to tell him about Tessie, but Lawson spoke before she could say anything.

"Tessie came by the ranch a couple of hours ago. She rode Dylan's horse there."

Her first response was to groan. "She was grounded. She shouldn't have gone there without permission."

He acknowledged that with a nod. "I grounded her again. She'll be tending the horses for me."

Again, she wanted to groan. "You know that's not much of a punishment for someone who's horse crazy like she is?"

"No, but mucking out the stalls will be." He paused. "I'll lift the punishment if you want. Or if you're leaving anytime soon." Lawson hadn't changed his tone with that last bit, but Eve knew it was a question.

A question she didn't know how to answer. She wasn't even sure where to start, but she went with the most obvious one. "If Tessie came to see you, then you must know she got kicked out of school."

"She told me. I think she's sorry it happened. Sorry for what she did."

Yes, Eve thought that as well, but it didn't mend things. And Tessie wasn't the only issue here. "It's all over the tabloids that I'm a liar. 'Slut' has been mentioned, too. It's cost a lot of donations for my foundation for teen mothers."

A muscle tightened in Lawson's jaw. "How much has it cost you?"

She sighed. "You're not going to try to fix this with Granger money."

"I've got a trust fund I'm not using."

"You're not going to try to fix this with Granger money," she repeated and hoped it got through. "But you can see the problem I'm having. I don't especially want to go back to my old life, but I'm ruining things here. I'm creating a big distraction for you, your family and everybody else in town."

She wasn't sure how he was going to respond to that, but she wasn't expecting him to do what he did.

Lawson hooked his hand around her neck, dragged her to him and French-kissed her. It was scalding hot but caused Aiden to laugh and bop at them with his fist.

Even with the bopping, she could feel all the right things. The slight stubble on Lawson's jaw. The gentle but firm grip on her neck. The way the left half of his body landed against hers. And that scent. Ah. Saddle leather and cowboy.

When Lawson had left her breathless, confused and giddy, he pulled back, met her eye to eye. "You've always been a distraction to me. As for everybody else, screw them. And notice, I didn't use the f-word because of little ears."

Eve had definitely noticed, and she smiled before she remembered there wasn't anything to smile about. Well, other than that tingly feeling the kiss had given her.

"Things might not get better before they get worse," she reminded him.

"Yeah. About that." His forehead bunched up. "A Swaron named Todd trespassed onto the ranch and took a picture of Tessie and me together. I told him that Tessie was my daughter. By now, it's probably been uploaded pretty much everywhere."

She had no trouble getting rid of the smile when she heard that, but Eve did have some trouble talking. "Was Tessie okay with that? Were you okay with that?" And was *she* okay with it?

"Tessie's fine. So am I. We knew that sooner or later the press would learn the truth. This way, the latest crap-storm should have blown over by the time Tessie starts back to school in January."

He had a point, and it was a point that made Eve

see she was okay with it. For this moment, anyway, but she really did need to sit down and work out what was best for everyone.

"I've got to go," he said, passing Aiden back to her. "I need to sign for an order at the feed store."

"I should get back home, too." So that she could have a long talk with Tessie.

He kissed Aiden's cheek, dropped a kiss on her mouth and got moving. He didn't say anything else though until Eve and he started walking. "Will you go on a date with me Friday night? I can pick you up at eight at your house."

Again, he'd surprised her, but that didn't leave her nearly as tingly as the kiss. "A date?" she questioned.

"Not sex," he clarified. "Though that's always an option. I'm asking you out on a…dance date."

Eve repeated that last part to herself to make sure she hadn't misunderstood. "You don't dance," she reminded him. "Or at least you didn't when we were teenagers."

"I still don't. That doesn't mean we can't go on a dance date."

She wanted to point out that was exactly what it meant, but he just continued.

"I want you to wear the dress you bought eighteen years ago for the Sadie Hawkins dance," he added when they made it to his truck. It was parked right next to her car, and she put Aiden in his seat in the back. "The dance we didn't get to go to because you left town."

There was no need for him to clarify that last part. "How'd you know I had a dress?" But then she huffed. "Cassidy blabbed. What else did she tell you?"

"That the dance meant a lot to you."

It had. Oh, the hours she'd spent planning for that one night. There was no way the actual dance could have lived up to the hype she'd given it.

Lawson leaned down, forcing eye contact with her when she looked away. "Did Cassidy have it right? Did the dance mean a lot to you?"

She nodded. He was clearly waiting for her to add more. And she did. But she waited until she was behind the wheel of her car and ready to drive off. Because what she had to say was best said as an exit line.

"The dance was important," she said, "because I was going to tell you that I loved you and that I wanted to spend the rest of my life with you."

The exit line would have been a lot more effective if her car hadn't stalled when she hit the accelerator. The engine bucked and died, which meant she couldn't escape now that she'd said a word that would never set well with him.

Love.

Thankfully, Lawson didn't say anything. Probably because she had stunned him into silence. He was almost certainly rethinking that dance date now. And with the confusion widening his eyes, Eve finally got her car started and drove away.

CHAPTER TWENTY-THREE

"Suck in your breath," Cassidy instructed.

Eve was already doing that. She was also sucking in her stomach, her butt and anything else in or on her body that she could suck or clench.

It wasn't helping.

The dress that she'd bought eighteen years ago for the Sadie Hawkins dance was meant for a teenager's body, not the mother of two. In hindsight, she should have tried it on after Cassidy had had it dry-cleaned, but Eve had been so tied up in knots over Tessie and Lawson that it had slipped her mind. Plus, she had assumed that the corset bodice would be more accommodating to her "womanly" figure.

"You could try one of those full-body girdles on top of the control-top panties," Tessie suggested, eyeing the two-inch gap where the corseted back didn't meet.

Eve was eyeing it, too, because Cassidy had set up three mirrors at various angles so that she wouldn't miss a single moment of this frustrating, humiliating experience. Even Aiden was getting a good look because he was in his carrier seat on the floor just a few yards away. He was watching them the way a kid would feast on a cartoon playing out in front of him.

"I don't own a full-body girdle," Eve said, and she prayed that Tessie and Cassidy didn't, either. She could barely breathe as it was, and she didn't want to vise her stomach and lungs any more than they already were.

Cassidy and Tessie kept tugging, pulling, eyeing and adjusting the corset laces until Eve had had enough. "I knew this was a stupid idea."

Cassidy made a *yeah right* sound. "You can't make me believe you don't want to go on a date with Lawson. You've fixed your hair. Put on some makeup. And you've been giddy all day. You even laid out those silver hooker stilettos that I made you buy but you've never worn."

Yes to all those things, but answering this was tricky territory because Tessie was right there, and since Lawson was her father, Eve had to watch what she said. Definitely no mention of sex. Or love. Or the fact that Lawson was the only man Eve had ever really wanted. Tessie was already on an emotional roller coaster, and it was best for Eve not to crash into it with her own carnival ride of feelings.

She'd told Lawson she loved him. That was no big deal. She'd mumbled that a time or two during the afterglow of orgasms.

But the "living the rest of my life with you" was huge.

It wasn't just a hint of the c-word, it was the very definition of it. In fact, she was surprised that Lawson hadn't run and then canceled this dance date. But he hadn't. When Eve had texted him earlier in the day to ask if they were still on for eight o'clock, he'd answered back with a thumbs-up emoji.

That didn't mean he wasn't *mentally* running for the hills though. And Eve figured she should steel herself in case he wanted to break things off with her. He could be using this date as the big finale to the dance they'd never had.

The goodbye they'd never gotten to say.

Of course, he might not have any breaking-off opportunities if she didn't show up, and while that was somewhat tempting, she did want to see him. Then she could take back her c-word, and they could continue to, well, do whatever the heck they were doing. She had to be careful, though, so that she didn't spoil the relationship that seemed to be budding between Tessie and him.

Eve let go of everything she was clinching and sucking in, making the laces on the dress pull even tighter. "I need to find something else to wear."

Cassidy huffed. "You've hung on to this dress for nearly two decades. You're wearing it. Maybe you can turn it around so the gaps will be in the front. It'll be sexy, showing some cleavage."

"It won't be sexy because my boobs will be smashed together and my stomach will be showing. The pudge will poke through the tight laces."

Tessie and Cassidy looked at the gap again and made sounds and gestures of agreement. "How about wearing your Ulyana costume underneath it?" Tessie suggested. "You know, the one that fits like a scuba suit."

Eve shook her head, but she knew exactly which one Tessie meant. Even if she had been able to find the outfit, she'd have to oil her body just to get into it. Plus, it had a high neck, which meant the dark red leather would show big-time beneath the strapless dress.

"Maybe we can cut off the top of a camisole and use it like a lining underneath the dress to cover up the gap," Cassidy tried again.

Tessie nodded. "And then Mom can wear a shawl over it."

They were both bad ideas, but Tessie and Cassidy ran with it as if it were a genius plan. It'd been a while since Eve had seen Tessie move with such enthusiasm, so she didn't stop her as she raced off. Cassidy barreled up the stairs, no doubt on her own clothing scavenger hunt.

Eve pulled off the vising control-top panties and tossed them in the trash. She was about to head to her closet to find anything else, but her phone rang, and the moment she saw Kellan's name on the screen, Eve knew she had to answer it.

"You worthless piece of worm s-h-i-t!" Eve greeted him. It wasn't nearly as satisfying to spell *shit* as it was to say it, but she didn't want to curse in front of Aiden. "And if you call me Baby-Cakes, I'm going to reach through this phone and rip out your effing tonsils."

Silence. Which meant Kellan had indeed been about to call her that.

"I'm hearing a lot of anger in your voice," Kellan finally said.

"Then listen harder because it's more than just a lot. It's a massive amount. Even bigger than your ego. You had no right, none, to say that Tessie was your daughter."

"I thought it would help. I thought it would get Lawson off the hook. But I can see now I was wrong. Lawson seems to want to stay on that hook."

Eve wasn't sure of any of that, but she was especially suspicious of Kellan's motives. "You lied because you wanted the publicity. Well, listen here, Baby-Cakes. If you screw with my life and my daughter again, I'll rip out the rest of your internal organs and shove them up your a-s-s. Have you got that?"

"Uh. Yes. I think you painted a very clear picture for me." He paused. "Hey, gotta go, Baby...uh, Eve. I'm about to do an interview with a reporter about the rumors of the remake of *Demon High*. Say, I don't guess I could talk you into reconsidering doing some reunion episodes?"

She had to get her teeth unclenched before she could speak. "Remember that clear picture I just painted for you? Ask me that question again, and the picture will become your reality."

"Oh. Okay." He was already in his slick PR mode, which meant the reporter was probably right there and listening. "I'll remember that." And then he added something that sounded surprisingly sincere. "I am really sorry, and it won't happen again."

Eve jabbed the end-call button with enough force to break the screen just as Tessie came back into the room. Not rushing the way she'd made her exit. And she glanced at Eve's phone.

"Kellan?" Tessie concluded.

"Yes. We were talking about, uh, art, among other things."

Tessie stayed quiet a moment. "You chewed him out for lying?"

Eve nodded.

If Tessie had given her any hint that she wanted to know more about the conversation, Eve would have filled her in, minus the spelled-out profanity. But Tessie only held up the two items she was holding.

A gold bolero sweater that wasn't large enough to

cover anything but her shoulders and a sparkly silver shawl with a bead fringe.

"I had the shawl on my lampshade to diffuse the light," Tessie explained. "It's chic boho."

She draped it around Eve's shoulders, and while it wasn't her style, at least it covered up the gap. Well, it would if she didn't move around too much.

"I'll never be able to dance in this," Eve mumbled.

Though dancing was iffy anyway. And if Lawson and she did miraculously make it onto a dance floor, he would probably be concentrating on his recently learned moves rather than her semibare back.

"Thanks," Eve told Tessie, and she kissed her daughter's cheek.

Tessie didn't recoil, didn't huff and didn't look at her with that awful *you're a liar* expression. That alone was worth the discomfort of wearing an ill-fitting dress. Plus, Eve had the added benefit of knowing that no one but Lawson would see her in this garb. There was no way he would want a dance date to happen in a public place. Eve was thinking he might take her to the barn or a pasture at the Granger Ranch. Which was fine by her. It'd be hard for him to see the back of the dress in the dark.

"I'm really sorry that I didn't tell you about Lawson sooner," Eve said.

Tessie shrugged, the way a person did when it wasn't important. But it was, so Eve took her by the shoulders and looked her straight in the eyes.

"I'm sorry," Eve repeated.

Tessie gave her another shrug, followed by a slight huff. Then a sigh. "Lawson made me see your side of things." Her chin came up. "You know, if I'd gotten pregnant at seventeen, you would have had a cow."

"Yes, I would have. But I would have still loved you as much as I always have."

Tessie stared at her, and while she didn't actually make a sound of agreement, Eve could see it in her eyes. Tessie knew she was, and always would be, loved.

"How are things between Lawson and you?" Eve risked asking.

"Okay. He's okay," Tessie added. "And I'm a little okay with him being my father."

That put a huge lump in her throat. It wasn't a gush of affection, but it was a start, and for now, that was, well, okay. Eve would take it.

Breathing hard from the running, Cassidy came back in with a pink camisole and a pair of scissors. Eve wanted to tell her not to ruin the camisole, but Cassidy immediately started cutting until it was a chopped-off silk tube top. Of course, once she was done, it meant undoing the corset laces so Eve could slip it on, and both Tessie and Cassidy tugged and pulled until everything was back in place.

Mostly, anyway.

Her bare back was no longer showing, but the pink colors weren't even close to being an identical match. Again though, it wouldn't matter in the dark, and she doubted Lawson was going to be studying her back.

The doorbell rang, giving Eve a jolt that was akin to terror. It was barely seven thirty, which meant it was still a half hour until Lawson was due to pick her up. She'd counted on having that extra time in case she decided to come up with an excuse as to why she couldn't go.

Cassidy scooped up Aiden in the carrier and went ahead of Eve and Tessie to answer the door. It was a false alarm though, but it was still a reason for concern.

Because it was Darby.

The woman wasn't wearing her usual scrubs today but rather a black cocktail dress that hugged her tiny, perfect body in all the right places. Definitely no pudge. Or shawl to cover up pudge.

Darby immediately looked past Cassidy, her attention landing on Eve. The woman's eyes widened a little, the kind of reaction a person might have if they'd interrupted something. That might have been why Darby glanced around the foyer and the living room. Maybe she was looking for Lawson.

"Uh, I'm sorry," Darby said. "I won't take long, but could we talk?"

Eve silently groaned and then debated it. It would be so easy to lie and say she was pressed for time, but instead she heard herself offer a friendly-sounding "Sure."

Cassidy and Tessie obviously weren't sold on the idea because they lingered in the foyer while Eve ushered Darby into the living room.

"I wondered if Lawson mentioned anything about my father talking to the head of the department at Tessie's college?" Darby asked, her voice practically a whisper.

Eve nodded. "The decision's already been made, but thanks for the offer."

She thought she knew where Darby had hoped to go with this. It was perhaps about those strings that Darby wanted on Lawson.

"Look, Darby." Eve was just going to put it all out there and tell Darby that she wasn't certain where Lawson and she were heading, but that she didn't intend to end things with him. And even if things didn't work out that it might not give Darby a clear path to getting Lawson back.

"You're in love with Lawson," Darby said before Eve could finish. "I think he might feel the same way about you. That's why I'm moving on with my life. I have a date tonight."

Eve certainly hadn't been expecting that, but the relief she felt wasn't a surprise. Despite the clinging and hanging on that Darby had done—and yes, that included the raincoat incident—Eve didn't want to see the woman hurt any more than she already had been.

"I want more than just a commitment for weekly dates and moral support," Darby went on. "I want marriage. Kids. And we both know I never could have gotten that from Lawson. Well, not the marriage and commitment parts, anyway." Her gaze drifted toward Tessie.

"Yes, she's his daughter," Eve told her.

"I can see that. I could see it in the picture that got posted on the internet, too. I suppose Lawson's forgiven you for not telling him?"

No. But Eve didn't have to answer because Darby waved off the question. "I should be going," the woman said, but she gave Eve one last look. "Does your dress have something to do with the party that's being set up at the high school gym?"

Eve pulled back her shoulders in surprise. The original Sadie Hawkins dance had indeed been held at the gym, but she hadn't imagined that Lawson would take her there for a date.

"I'm not sure," Eve admitted.

Darby smiled. "Well, we'll soon find out."

With that cryptic remark, Darby would have just walked out if Eve hadn't stepped in front of her. "Are you going to the dance, too?" Eve asked.

But it was such a ridiculous question. At least Eve hoped it was.

It wasn't.

Darby nodded. "I'm not sure who planned the party, but whoever it was sent out invitations. Everyone who's ever attended Wrangler's Creek High School was invited. I suspect most of the town will go. See you there."

Darby obviously didn't notice the gobsmacked look on Eve's face because she gave a perky wave as she headed out the door.

CHAPTER TWENTY-FOUR

"THERE'S A CURSE on you, Lawson Granger."

Lawson groaned when he heard those words. And again when he spotted the curse-bearer by his truck as he came out of his office in the Granger house.

He definitely didn't have time for Vita or the fates who'd cursed him—again. He was running late and had to pick up Eve for their date. A date he didn't want her canceling, and that's why when she'd called, he'd let it go to voice mail. If she was going to bail on him, she was going to have to do it to his face.

"I don't have time to talk," Lawson told Vita. He mumbled some profanity under his breath when he heard the rumble of thunder in the distance. Maybe the rain would at least hold off until he'd picked up Eve.

"Yeah, I know. You got a date at the high school gym. But this is serious. You want stitches in your heinie again?" Vita asked.

"Not especially." But he'd take the stitches over being late for Eve. And lateness wouldn't have been an issue if he hadn't realized he had forgotten the envelope with the boxes in his desk. So much for all his careful planning.

Lawson threw open his truck door and tossed the envelope on the dash before he turned to Vita. "Mix up a potion to nix the curse. Then do whatever it is you need to do with it."

The old woman eyed him with plenty of suspicion. Even though it was already dark, the backyard was well lit, so Lawson had no trouble seeing her face. The suspicion was likely because he'd never shown any faith whatsoever in her *craft*, and he didn't have faith in it now, either.

"A potion like that could be expensive," Vita said. "Maybe twenty or thirty bucks."

"Good. Then make five or six of them to be sure it rids me of the curse and then send me a bill."

Vita beamed with a smile. Hell, if he'd known it was this easy to get rid of her, he would have ordered potions earlier. A thousand of them.

"Don't ride your bike home in the dark," Lawson added. "It's about to rain. Have one of the hands drive you back."

That caused her to smile even more, and she patted his arm. "You've got a good heart, Lawson Granger. But I'm going to see Mila and Roman for a while. They can give me a ride." She tipped her head to the envelope. "Is that for Eve?"

Since he doubted she had actual ESP, it meant she was guessing. Not even a good guess, either, since she must have known his date was with Eve. But yes, the envelope with the two boxes was for her.

Lawson nodded. Now he had to hope she'd choose the right box.

He was about to drive off when his phone rang, and Kellan's name popped up. The only reason the idiot was in his contacts was because Lawson had called him multiple times when Tessie had gone missing. They hadn't exactly been on friendly terms then, and it was a whole lot worse now.

"You dickhead," Lawson said the moment he answered. He didn't start driving because he didn't think it was a good idea to be on the road while he gave this turd a piece of his mind.

"You know, you and Eve should really work on your greeting skills," Kellan said. "She called me 'worm shit.'"

"Good for her. I'm going to call you a lot worse, but hear this—you don't dick around with my daughter, with Eve or with me. Have I made myself clear?"

"As clear as a picture." And that was a little sarcastic. "I called to apologize and to ask you a favor."

"Dickheads don't deserve favors, and your apology isn't accepted. I'll beat you over the head with a shit-covered shovel if you tell another lie about Tessie."

"Again, a very clear picture, but the favor isn't for me. It's for Aiden."

That got Lawson's attention. "You don't dick with him, either," Lawson warned him. "In fact, Aiden goes to the top of the list of things you can't dick with, or I'll beat you with two shovels."

"Agreed, and even though I wish I could think of another word other than *dick*, it works here." Kellan paused. "I'll mess things up if I'm his dad. You know that. So does Eve. Hell, Aiden probably knows it, too."

"I'm not disagreeing with you," Lawson said when Kellan paused again.

"That's why I'm passing the whole dad thing to you. I could say something cocky that'd make me sound like more of an ass than I am, but you seem like a solid guy. So, do Aiden a favor and make sure he doesn't turn out like me."

"Aiden could never turn out like you," Lawson growled.

"And there we have the reason why you'd be a lot better at daddy-hood than I ever would be. Aiden is yours, you know. I mean, in every way that counts. You were with him right from the start, and you'd never let anyone, including me, dick around with him."

"Damn straight," Lawson snapped just as Kellan hung up.

Lawson sat there, replaying his own words and the words of the dickhead. Shit. He'd just agreed to help raise Aiden. Eve might have something to say about that, but he almost hoped she wouldn't nix the idea. Because it felt...right.

With that confusing thought going through his head, he finally got his truck moving. But he'd barely made it to the end of the driveway when he saw the headlights of an approaching vehicle. A vehicle he instantly recognized.

Eve.

He doubted this was a good sign. Maybe since he hadn't answered her call, she'd come over to cancel.

She pulled off the side of the driveway, turned off the engine and hurried to his truck. At least she was wearing the dress. Well, maybe she was. It was a dress, anyway, but she was clutching a wrap thingy around it, so it was hard to tell if it was the dress that Cassidy had described to him.

Cassidy certainly hadn't described those heels though. They were a mile high, and Eve teetered on them as she made her way to his truck. She threw open the passenger door and got in. Not easily. Apparently, it wasn't easy to maneuver in the dress, which made him feel guilty since he'd been the one to ask her to wear it. But Lawson had thought it was what she wanted since she'd kept it all this time.

"Did you really invite the whole town to our date?" she asked before he could bring up his conversation with Kellan.

"I did invite the whole town," he confirmed. "Or rather my sister did. She's the one who handled sending out the invites. According to the RSVPs, there'll be about two hundred people. Not bad, considering it was short notice. I guess the lure of free food and a DJ had folks saying yes."

Eve shook her head and stared at him. "Why?"

"You'll see." Lawson smiled and kissed her. Though the kiss was a mistake since it was a reminder that with Eve one kiss was never enough. Still, he forced himself to start driving.

"I don't want to face a bunch of people," she went on.

Good. They were on the same page. He wanted Eve alone. Preferably out of that dress. But that could wait because he really needed to do something he'd had on hold for the past eighteen years.

"You look really nice, by the way," he told her.

She made a sound as if she didn't agree with that. "Thanks, but I'm squeezed into this dress in a bad way. The seams might blow."

He should be so lucky. But maybe those seams would hold a little longer.

"You look really nice, too," she added.

"Thanks." Lawson had tried. His best jeans, a white

shirt, a jacket, and he'd cleaned his boots. It was formal wear compared to the working clothes he usually wore.

The concern returned to Eve's face when he pulled into the high school parking lot. It was packed, and there were people scurrying from their vehicles into the building. He drove past all of them and headed to the side entrance. Since it was clear on the other side of the building from the gym, there was no one else parked there.

Lawson stuffed the envelope in his jacket pocket and got Eve moving as fast as he could. Fast wasn't fast enough though, because the sky opened up. It didn't help, either, that the rainfall was sheeting off the roof and falling right in front of the door. It felt as if they'd stood under a waterfall before they got inside. Worse, the A/C was on, and the cool air suddenly felt a whole lot cooler now that they were soaking wet.

Hell.

Eve was shivering, and that little silver wrap wasn't going to do much to keep her warm. Neither was her being in his arms because he was as wet as she was.

Even over her teeth chattering, he could still hear the music coming from the gym. It would have been loud enough to go through with his plan of a private dance in the empty hall between the rows of metal lockers, but he doubted Eve wanted to risk pneumonia. If he didn't find something or someplace warmer fast, he was going to have to nix this plan and get her back in the truck so he could turn on the heater.

It'd been years since Lawson had actually stepped foot inside the high school, so he headed toward the nurse's office, where maybe there'd be a blanket or some other items of clothing. But it was locked.

"Let's go to the girls' dressing room," he suggested. He also took off his wet jacket, making sure the envelope didn't fall out, and then he peeled off his shirt. It was a lot drier than Eve's dress, so he slipped it over her shoulders.

The dressing room was right behind the gym, so there wouldn't be any trouble hearing the music. Eve and he might just be able to go through with that dance after all.

Or not.

This door was locked, too.

He huffed, ready to go back to the truck, but Eve stopped him. She opened the little purse she was carrying, pulled out a nail file and went after the lock. "It's something I learned on the set. Ulyana had to pick a lot of locks."

And she'd obviously honed that particular skill because Eve had it open in just a couple of seconds. But when she threw open the door, Lawson immediately saw another problem.

It wasn't the girls' dressing room.

There were lights outside the windows that made it easy enough for Lawson to see the *Demon High* posters that were all over the walls.

"It's the new drama department," Eve muttered. "Mrs. Hattersfield told me about it."

Mrs. Hattersfield had been the drama teacher for as long as he could remember, but Lawson definitely hadn't heard anyone mention that she'd set up what appeared to be a shrine for her star pupil—Eve.

She hugged his shirt tighter around her shoulders as she made her way past one poster right after another.

Of course, Kellan was in some of the pictures, too, causing Lawson to automatically scowl.

"My name," Eve said, sounding a little in awe as she pointed at something.

Yep, there was a banner stretched across the stage, and it did indeed have her name on it. The Eve Cooper Center for Dramatic Studies.

It was a mouthful all right, and a pretty grandiose title for what'd once been a locker room.

It didn't take long though for the surprise of seeing all of this to wear off, and Eve started shivering again. Lawson wasn't exactly warm, especially now that he was shirtless and carrying a wet jacket, so that was his cue to get the dance started. Since the song the DJ was playing was already halfway done, Eve wouldn't have to risk him stepping on her feet for more than a minute or so. Then he could get her back to the truck to finish out this evening.

Lawson reached out to pull her into his arms, but Eve was already heading to the front of the room. At first he thought it was so she could have a closer look at the banner, but she went to the room on the side of the stage. She opened the door, flicked on a light switch.

And gasped.

That sent Lawson running to her because he thought maybe she'd seen a snake or a serial killer. It was neither, but it was a long narrow room filled with costumes. The ones right up front and facing them were all familiar, too. Because they were costumes from *Demon High*.

"Holy crap. Did you give these to Mrs. Hattersfield?" he asked.

Eve shook her head and examined one of the sleeves

of a red leather bodysuit costume. It looked exactly like
the one that Ulyana had worn while fighting demons.
"Mrs. Hattersfield must have made them. Or had someone do it for her." Eve glanced through the rest of the
rack. "All of these are handmade."

She plucked a red cape from one of the costumes
and put it on over his shirt and her dress. Obviously,
the total outfit wasn't the same as what she'd worn on
set, but seeing it on her brought back some memories.

"What?" she asked when she caught him looking
at her.

"There were tons of pictures of you in that cape,"
he said. "I used to see them everywhere."

She nodded. "Must have brought back some bad
memories for you." Eve sounded very sorry about that.

"Sometimes. Other times it gave me a hard-on." He
shrugged when her mouth dropped open. "Hey, I had a
very clear picture of what was beneath all that leather,
and it had an effect on me."

Eve smiled and went to him, putting her hands on
his chest and leaning in to kiss him. She'd already
pursed her lips and closed her eyes, but she stopped.
"God, you're freezing."

Yeah, he was, but he didn't care as long as he got
that kiss. But Eve obviously cared because she riffled
through the clothes rack and came up with another
cape. One that didn't produce a hard-on. It was long
and black, the garb worn by those Swaron idiots.

She lifted an eyebrow when she saw his scowl. "At
least it's not Stavros's coat."

There was that.

"And I did have a make-out scene with a Swaron
once," she went on. "A redeemed one." She put the

cape on him, catching onto the high collar and using the grip to pull him to her.

Now he finally got that kiss.

And it was everything he'd thought it would be. Minus the fact they were dressed like a superhero and a villain. Still, he was warm, and the kiss was making that heat go up a couple of notches.

It would have been so easy just to fall right into the kissing, touching…and other things, but he had promised Eve a dance. So, Lawson dropped his wet coat on the floor, took hold of her and snapped her to him.

"Do you like this song?" he asked.

"I don't know. I can't hear it. That kiss caused my pulse to throb in my ears."

Pulse throbbing was a good sign, but it didn't deter him from the dance. Such that it was. Lily Rose had given up teaching him after only an hour because she said her feet couldn't take any more bruises, but Lawson thought maybe he'd learned enough to make this less painful while fulfilling Eve's high school wish.

She moved against him, swaying to the couple of steps he managed to make. "Thank you for this," she whispered against his mouth. She moved into another kiss, too, but when her body bumped against his, she pulled back and looked up at him. "Did this cape really have *that* effect on you?"

His eyes crossed when Eve slid her hand over the front of his jeans.

"Not the cape," he assured her. "You."

But yeah, the cape had helped a little. It was more like an involuntary reflex that hurled him back to his teenage years when it wasn't so easy to control getting a hard-on.

Lawson tried not to let his physical condition affect his plan. He still wanted to give Eve what was in the envelope, but the next kiss she gave him killed not only the plan but probably some brain cells, as well. Along with shooting the heck out of most of his common sense.

"I brought a condom," Eve said, and she reached behind her and shut the door.

There went the rest of common sense, and it started a kissing battle that he figured they would both win. Though they might have a bruise or two. That's because Eve dragged him to the floor in the same motion that she was attempting to get him unzipped. It wasn't pretty. Plus, she was tackling the lesser of the two problems since she had on a heck of a lot more clothes than he did.

Lawson slid his hand beneath the cape, under his shirt and then to the back of the dress. There were laces, all tied up tight, and even with some fumbling, he couldn't find a way to start loosening them.

"Hold on," Eve said. "It took two people to get me into this, and you'll need some help."

She twisted the dress around, and the fabric and the pink thing beneath it both shifted so that he got a peek of her right breast. He couldn't resist that, so he gave her a nipple kiss. Then used his tongue.

"Leave the dress on." Her voice was breathy now, and she'd fisted her hand in his hair.

Good idea. It was much easier just to lift the layers though not nearly as much fun as stripping her naked. Once they'd burned through this first condom and sated some of the heat, maybe then he could get her out of the dress for a much slower second round.

Round one got much better when he finally got her dress shoved up and discovered she had gone commando.

"The panty line would have shown under the tight dress," she muttered.

Then hooray for avoiding panty lines. It gave him easy access to touch her. Kiss her and fool around with his tongue until she grabbed him by the hair again. She fumbled through her purse, came up with not one condom but three.

Lawson really liked her way of thinking. He'd done some thinking, too, since he'd brought four with him.

For now though, he put a dent in their combined stash by putting on one of them so he could experience first-hand what it was like to have sex with a superhero. It didn't hold a candle to having sex with Eve, but since she was one and the same, it was like getting two desserts.

He pushed into her and watched that dreamy look of pleasure glide right over Eve's face. But she was also watching him, and she turned, flipping him onto his back so she could ride him hard.

That was like getting six desserts.

She planted her hands on his chest and shoved herself over his erection. She got the speed right. The rhythm. Everything.

With each thrust, the cape moved, sort of like it was billowing back, and it made her look like a fierce warrior who'd just stepped away from the battle. Her rain-smudged makeup and askew clothes only added to that, and Lawson took a moment to admire the whole package.

But only a moment.

Because that hard ride was doing exactly what it was

supposed to be doing. It was slinging him right toward a climax. Which he had no trouble having. Thanks to Eve. She had her own climax, too. She pushed against him one last time, groaned a delicious sound of pleasure and collapsed against him.

EVE STAYED ON the floor of the dressing room while Lawson went in search of a bathroom. She stretched out on the floor—as much as the dress would allow her to stretch, that is. The corset laces were still hanging on for dear life.

Her body felt great despite the fact that her hair was wet and part of her boob was poking out of the dress from where she'd twisted it around. She did fix that and cocooned herself in the cape, waiting for Lawson to return.

And then he'd want to talk.

She knew it was coming, and while it probably wasn't the main reason for this past-fulfilling dance date, it had to be part of it. After all, she'd put the "I love you" out there. Now she had to decide if she wanted to take it back. Or if she wanted to put her heart on the line and hope that it didn't get crushed.

Eve turned on her side, searching for a more comfortable spot, when her head landed on something wet. His jacket. She picked it up, intending to put it aside, but something fell out.

A folded manila envelope. It was open, and she had no trouble seeing the two small gift boxes inside. At least she didn't have trouble seeing them when they spilled out in her hand.

And that's how Lawson found her when he came back in the dressing room.

Since she still had his shirt, he was wearing the black cape, and his bare chest distracted her for a moment, but Eve sat up and quickly shoved the boxes back in the envelope. "You brought me gifts? I didn't bring you anything."

Lawson smiled in that lazy but hot way that only he and a Greek god could have managed, and he sat down on the floor beside her. "You brought me a condom."

"Three of them," she reminded him, and with the way he was looking, they might need them all.

He kissed her and flashed that dreamy smile again. "I got those gifts for you eighteen years ago. I was going to give them to you at the Sadie Hawkins dance."

So, she hadn't been the only one who'd made big plans for that night. Plans for this night, too, since he'd brought them with him.

"I thought you would run for the hills when I told you I loved you," Eve said.

"I'm a super villain," he joked. "The l-word doesn't scare me." He paused, kissed her until she was breathless and then asked, "Is it true? Do you love me?"

Of course, he'd asked her that after rendering her incapable of human speech, so Eve had to take a couple of moments. "Yes. You were my first love, and you still are."

Maybe the realization would finally hit him, and she would see the panic she was expecting, but instead he looked at her. "Kellan called me," he said.

Her jaw automatically tightened. "Me, too. He's worm shit, and I'm not even going to spell it."

Lawson smiled. Then it faded. "He wanted to pass this whole dad thing over to me."

Eve felt the flare of temper, but Lawson quickly

cooled it with a kiss. "I agree with him. On this," he added. "He shouldn't be Aiden's father, and if you're okay with it, maybe I should take the daddy thing… when Aiden or you need a daddy thing, that is."

This certainly wasn't the conversation she'd expected, but it was a good one. "I'd like that," she said around the lump in her throat. "Aiden would like it, too."

From the way Lawson swallowed hard, he might have also had a lump. "That would work out better if you were here in Wrangler's Creek so I could see both Tessie and him."

That lump just kept on growing, and with the afterglow of great sex, she would have agreed to anything.

Except…

This wasn't about afterglows. Heck, this wasn't even about sex. This was about Lawson. And coming home.

Being home.

"I'm staying," she assured him, and it earned her a breath of relief and a kiss from Lawson. In that order.

After the breath and kiss, he put the boxes on her lap. "I was going to give you both. It's sort of a choice," he added.

A choice about what? But rather than ask that, Eve opened the first box and had a look for herself. It was a rodeo buckle. A shiny silver one. And while it was nice, it did have her raising an eyebrow.

"I'd given you a rodeo buckle before," he explained. "Remember?"

Oh, yes. She remembered. "It was the first time I told you I loved you."

He nodded. "Well, I thought the buckle could be a way of you choosing love. Just love."

She wanted to point out that there was no such thing as *just love* when it came to kids and Lawson, but then he opened the second box, and she saw the ring. It was gold and had a little bitty diamond in the center.

"It's a promise ring," he explained. "It was a promise to love you and to be with you forever."

As each word sank in, Eve felt the tears, but she blinked them back. This was the choice. She could have the "just love" rodeo buckle or she could have the whole shebang.

Eve wanted shebang. But she also wanted to make sure Lawson knew what he was getting into.

"I'm a package deal these days," she reminded him. "Aiden and Tessie. You'd definitely have to do the daddy thing and do it full-time."

"Wouldn't have it any other way." Lawson slipped the ring on her finger. "You need a microscope to see the diamond," he added. "But the promise part of this ring was that I'd buy you something much better when we were adults."

It was hard to blink back those tears now, but again a kiss helped. "There's nothing better than this ring," she assured him. It was the shebang plus. She looked at the ring again. "But isn't this like a...commitment?"

Lawson smiled, gave her that look that would almost certainly lead to sex, and he hauled her onto his lap. "It damn well better be."

* * * * *

Texas rancher Dylan Granger has always had
a way with women, but when life-altering news
brings the one who got away back home to Texas,
Dylan isn't sure if his heart will ever recover...

Don't miss
LONE STAR BLUES,
the next book in the
A WRANGLER'S CREEK NOVEL *series,*
by USA TODAY
bestselling author Delores Fossen,
on sale in May 2018!

COWBOY DREAMING

CHAPTER ONE

"Uh...is that, uh, our boss walking this way?" Josh Whitlock heard the new ranch hand ask.

While Josh dragged the saddle off the gelding he'd just ridden, he wondered why the heck the new hand, Tommie "Termite" Tompkins, had added those "uh"s to the question. After all, there was only one woman on the Applewood Ranch, and that one woman, Hope Applewood, was indeed the boss. So, seeing a female heading toward the barn shouldn't have caused much confusion even from a hand who seemed proud of the nickname Termite.

However, when Josh threw a quick look over his shoulder, he saw the reason for Termite's puzzlement.

Holy crap. It was Hope all right. But she didn't look much like the boss of a successful ranch. Nope. For one thing, he could see some of her legs and thighs since she wasn't wearing her usual crud-crusted jeans. She had on a dress that was red enough, and short enough, to stop speeding interstate traffic. It certainly stopped Josh and made him take a long look.

Oh, man.

Josh groaned. He was thinking thoughts that he darn sure shouldn't be thinking about his boss. Like how it would feel to slide his hand under that little red dress and discover if she preferred cotton or lace when it came to her panties.

Actually, Josh wondered what it would be like to get her out of those panties, too. But then, that was a thought he was always fighting when it came to Hope. She was a looker all right with that honey-blond hair, fresh face and thunderstorm-gray eyes.

The rest of Hope's "outfit" thankfully didn't fuel the fantasies going on behind the zipper of Josh's jeans. She'd paired that smoking-hot dress with what appeared to be a tablecloth that she was using for a shawl, and she had on cowboy boots. Not the fashion-statement kind of boots that city girls wore, either. These were the same ones she'd worn for the entire three years that Josh had worked for her.

"Uh," Hope said as she stepped into the barn.

Apparently, "uh" was the preferred word of communication today, but Josh didn't think it was aimed at him but rather Termite. "This is our new hand," Josh told her. "Tommie Tompkins."

"Termite," Tommie corrected him, extending his hand for her to shake. "I used to chew on number-two pencils when I was a kid, and that's how I got the name."

She shook his hand, nodded, smiled, but shaking, nodding and smiling seemed to be the last things that Hope wanted to do right now. She seemed nervous or something.

Josh checked his watch. "You're not out here to work, are you? Because you're supposed to be getting ready for the party right about now."

No need to clarify what party because it was indeed *the* party. An annual one put on by Wrangler's Creek royalty, the Grangers. To the best of Josh's knowledge, it was the only party that Hope ever attended, mainly because she saw it as a business obligation, but for the past three years, she'd worn the same black pants outfit.

"That's what I've been trying to do—get ready," Hope answered, and she volleyed a few glances between Termite and him. "Uh, I need some help," she added to Josh. "Could you come to the tack room with me?"

Hope didn't wait for him to answer. She took hold of his arm and started leading Josh in that direction.

"My date canceled," she grumbled. "And Karlee, who was supposed to help me get ready, had to cancel, too, because she's running late. Personally, I think that's an excuse, and she just doesn't want to face me. She tossed my pantsuit so I'd have to wear this dress she bought instead."

Josh didn't know who Hope's date had been. Probably one of the people they did business with. But Karlee was Karlee O'Malley, Hope's good friend. However, at the moment Hope didn't sound very friendly about the woman. Tossing the pantsuit would have done it, though, and it explained the red dress. It was more Karlee's style than Hope's.

"I'm surprised you didn't go through the trash looking for the pantsuit," Josh said.

"I did!" She didn't let go of him until they were in the tack room—and she closed the door. "I think Karlee took it with her. That, and most of the other clothes in my closet. It was this dress or nothing."

The "nothing" gave Josh another wave of those scalding thoughts until Hope added the next part. "Please, Josh, I need you to come to the party with me. My folks will be there, and if I show up without a date, they'll spend the evening trying to fix me up with assorted sons of their assorted friends."

She'd started the request with that *please*, but that didn't help. Josh shook his head. "Trust me, even if I'm with you, they'll spend the evening trying to fix you up with the *right* assorted guy. I'm not the man they want to see on the arm of their princess daughter. My collar's much too blue for their liking."

"So is mine," she said under her breath. "Well, it normally is when I'm not wearing this blasted red dress." Hope looked up at him. "Please go with me. *Please*."

He looked down at her. "No." Though that second and especially the third "please" had given him a couple of moments of hesitation, Hope's red dress hadn't given him amnesia, so he knew what would be in store for him. Lusting over her while having a miserable time.

"Remember, my folks will be at the party, too," he said.

Of course, his parental dilemma was a little different from Hope's. His dad, Elgin, was a hand at the Granger Ranch, and the Grangers always invited all their employees and spouses to this shindig. If Josh went, too, he would have to listen to his mom and dad go on about how disappointed they were that he hadn't made something more of himself, what with all the sacrifices they'd made. Specifically, the scrimping and saving they'd done since his birth so he could go to college and be a doctor.

And they would use the actual word, *sacrifices*, too. No matter how many times Josh had told them he didn't want college or medical school, they just badgered on. A party setting wouldn't cause them to ease up on that, either. They'd just badger in front of an audience.

Hope huffed. Stared at him, probably trying to think of some way to change his mind. Her next huff let him know that she hadn't come up with such a miracle. "All right, then at least help me get ready."

She might as well have announced that she needed him to perform brain surgery. "Uh, you look fine to me." And yep, he'd added that "uh." It was catching.

"Then look again," she complained. "So help me, you'd better not tell anyone about this." Hope threw off the tablecloth/shawl and whirled around with her back to him.

And all the air was suddenly sucked off the entire planet.

That was because the back of the dress was open— *wide* open—and Josh could see her naked back. He could also see the top of her naked butt. Holy moly. Either she was wearing the tiniest panties in the known world or...

"I had to ditch the bra because the straps were showing," she added. "The panties, too, because they gave me a muffin top."

That was better than the hard-on he was getting from being aware that she had gone commando. Best to minimize the time he had of this view by fixing the zipper. Fast. Josh immediately started to tug at it.

"I know the boots don't go with the outfit," Hope went on. "Karlee took me shopping, and I bought some sparkly sandals, but I didn't have time to get a pedi, and my feet look awful. I've got some scabby bits of toenail polish still there from the pedi I had done about six months ago. People notice things like that."

Since he'd never paid attention to a person's toes, he wasn't buying it. "They're more likely to notice the horse shit on those boots," he mumbled, but obviously he needed to work on his mumbling skills because she heard it just fine. She made a sound of agreement and looked down at the boots.

"Just wear the sandals," he advised her though he had no idea why he suddenly considered himself a fashion guru.

It probably had to do with his fried brain.

The zipper wasn't budging, and the dress was as slick as saddle oil. It kept riding up with each tug, and in order to hold it in place, he had to place his hand on Hope's left butt cheek. Hence, the fried brain.

"I'm guessing you don't have a lot of experience getting a woman *into* a dress," she said, with a chuckle.

None. But thankfully he hadn't needed any help with getting a woman out of one. Best, though, to keep that remark to himself—especially when Hope decided she should help. She reached back between them, her fingers knocking into his. Also knocking against the front of his jeans.

And she went stiff.

Josh didn't have to guess why. She'd felt his erection.

She turned, looking up at him. Causing Josh to curse. "I'm a man," he reminded her. "That dress is hot. And I've seen parts of you that your ranch hand shouldn't see."

The corner of her mouth lifted though there sure as hell wasn't anything to smile about, and she slid her gaze down the front of him. From his shirt all the way to the part of him that'd caused her to turn toward him in the first place.

"You can look at the dress all night long if you come to the party with me," she said with a wink and a sly smile.

Josh laughed before he could stop himself—though there wasn't anything to laugh about, either. But leave it to Hope to say the right thing to make this situation a little less embarrassing.

Of course, the embarrassment gave way to a new problem. That was because she kept staring up at him. So close. Just a few inches away. He'd seen that look in her eyes before. The day they'd let a prize stallion cover some of the mares.

Horse sex.

Lots of it.

And while it wasn't especially romantic to watch, maybe it had reminded her of human sex. Because in one unguarded moment when Hope had glanced at him, Josh had seen the itch inside her.

An itch she was considering, and one that he could scratch just fine.

He could have, too. Josh could have peeled off her jeans, got between her legs and taken her then and there against the corral fence, but those minutes of *scratching* could mess up things for years. Maybe forever. After all, when the sex had finished, she would still be his boss, and he loved this job too much to screw it up by screwing Hope.

"Well?" she prompted. "You'll go with me to the party?"

"No," he repeated, getting his mind off sex and such,

and he caught just a glimpse of her scowl before he whirled her around to have another go at the zipper.

Josh tugged and pulled. Unfortunately, he pulled hard enough that this time Hope's butt bumped against the front of his jeans. Despite the logical argument that he'd just given himself about loving his job/not screwing it up, he got the other reminder.

The *I'm a man* one.

Just when Josh thought he was going to have to excuse himself to take a cold shower, the zipper from hell finally gave up the fight, and it slithered closed from butt to nape. No more peep show or booty bumps, so maybe now his erection could soften. He got a jump start on that softening, though, when the tack room door opened.

Hope and he scampered away from each other as if they'd been caught doing something wrong. However, the jumpy movement got the attention of the people in the doorway.

His mom and dad, Mattie and Elgin.

They were clearly on their way to the party and had on their Sunday best. His dad was wearing a suit, looking about as uncomfortable as Josh would be if he had to wear a tie. His mom was in a blue dress that she had probably saved for months to buy. Her grandmother's rhinestone necklace glimmered around her neck.

Both of them looked at Hope and him before looking at each other. Their eyebrows were raised as if trying to figure out what was going on, but then they shook their heads and shrugged. Obviously they thought there was no chance in hell that Hope Applewood would have anything to do with the likes of him.

"Beaver told us you were in here, talking to Miss Applewood," his mother commented.

"Termite," the hand called out to correct her.

"Mr. and Mrs. Whitlock," Hope said, going to them. She shook their hands. "It's good to see you. And please call me Hope."

His parents both gave her polite smiles and greetings—which didn't extend in any way to Josh. "You're not dressed for the party," his mother pointed out, her voice crisp and weary at the same time. "I told you he wouldn't be dressed," she added to her husband.

"I'm not going." And Josh hoped he didn't have to keep saying that.

Tears sprang to his mother's eyes. Yes, actual tears. Mattie was a crier, complete with a trembling bottom lip, and while he wasn't completely unaffected by it— she was his mother, after all—Josh had grown tired of it. Better yet, he'd learned not to give in to it as he had for the first thirty years of his life.

Hope fluttered her fingers toward the door. "I'll just go and give you some time with your folks."

Josh didn't want time with them when he knew what was coming—a browbeating attempt to get him to that party. Apparently, though, his parents did want that time because they stayed put. They didn't intentionally block Hope's exit, but that's what they were doing. Probably because they had their attention nailed on Josh and no longer noticed she was there.

"Your mom told you that she'd arranged for you to meet someone at the party," his dad piped up.

"Yes, the new doctor at the hospital," Josh verified. Dr. Marie Stapleton was the daughter of one of the former maids at the Granger Ranch. Marie had apparently done what Josh's folks had wanted him to do, so maybe they thought he needed a visual to clarify their dreams for him. "I told Mom I didn't want to meet her." Josh braced himself because the crap-storm was about to hit.

His mom's eyes got even more teary. His dad huffed. For such a simple sound, it carried a lot of emotion and old baggage. "We just want something better for you than you have."

"Something better than *we* have," his mother amended. "Give us one good reason why you won't go to the party and meet Dr. Stapleton. Just one good reason," she emphasized.

Hope turned to him, and it wasn't the itch look she gave him this time. There was sympathy in her eyes. And maybe a little anger, too, because this was the kind of stuff she got from her own parents. She had an advantage, though, because her parents didn't live in Wrangler's Creek, so they weren't always right underfoot, but they did make trips back to see their daughter and to attend parties thrown by their old friends, the Grangers.

"One good reason?" Hope repeated. "Well, I did ask Josh to go to the party with me."

And she'd just thrown the ball into his court.

"I was just trying to convince him to go when you came in," Hope tacked onto her thrown ball.

That silenced his parents. Not a good silence, though. Their quiet, condemning stares were riddled with suspicion, and they likely thought he'd put Hope up to saying that. They also likely thought that he didn't stand a snowflake's chance in an El Paso summer of being with an Applewood. And they wouldn't believe that it had been his choice not to pursue her because they hadn't been around for the "itch" look she'd given him.

A slow storm moved through him, and no, it didn't have anything to do with the activity that Hope and her dress had caused behind the zipper of his jeans. This had to do with throwing back some of that suspicious condemnation. It had to do with, well, some *I'll show you.*

"I'm going to the party with Hope," Josh heard himself say. And he sealed the deal by catching that ball and doing something stupid with it.

Josh hooked his arm around Hope's waist, yanked her to him and kissed her.

CHAPTER TWO

MY, OH, MY. Hope hadn't seen the kiss coming, but it turned out that seeing it wasn't really necessary anyway. She felt it—mercy, did she—and that was much, much better than getting any advance warning that Josh was going to do it.

Actually, she figured he hadn't known he was going to do it, either. This was no doubt a knee-jerk reaction to his parents' jerk remarks. But Hope would take it, and for these few scalding moments, she would pretend that it was the real deal.

Finally!

She'd wanted this to happen for so long that it certainly felt real. Deep-immersion fantasizing could do that, and she'd been fantasizing about Josh since he'd first walked into her office three years ago and applied for a job. Like now, he'd been wearing those Wranglers that were snug and worn in all the right places. With his rumpled black hair, and chiseled body, he'd looked ready for a photo shoot for one of those magazines that put tough cowboys on the covers.

He'd looked ready for her to take him to bed, too.

She hadn't, but Hope had thought a lot about it. Because of his experience training horses and references, she'd hired him on the spot and had put him in charge of the other hands, but she'd done that know-

ing that the notion of kissing him and having sex with
him was always simmering just beneath the surface.
Right now, the simmer was a full boil, and there was
nothing beneath about it.

It was a nice touch that he'd made the kiss French.
And that he'd smashed her against him. A good kind
of smashing where all their parts lined up just right to
make her remember that she wasn't wearing panties.

And that his parents were right there watching them.

Josh must have remembered that, too, or maybe like
her he was just in critical need of oxygen because he
finally broke the kiss.

He pulled back, their eyes meeting, and a single
word left his mouth. "Shit."

Well, it wasn't exactly what a woman wanted to hear
after getting the kiss of her dreams, but if he was feeling all the things she was feeling, then every part of his
body was tingling and reacting. Again, not necessarily
a good thing to happen in front of parents.

"So, it's settled, then," Hope said just to fill the awk-
ward silence. She didn't even aim the comment at anyone in particular.

Josh's mother huffed and lifted her nose in the air
as if she'd gotten a whiff of the crap on Hope's boots.

"Think long and hard about this," his father warned
him. "This could be the biggest mistake of your life."
He huffed, too, took his wife by the arm and marched
her out of there.

Whoa, that was pretty deep gloom and doom for
just a kiss. And it told Hope loads as to how they felt
about her. In their way of thinking, she was the wrong
woman for their son. They probably thought she was a
pampered rich girl who only wore the stinky cowboy

boots to try to fit into this ranch world. They didn't know that this place owned every bit of her heart and that she'd spent nearly every penny of her trust fund to buy it when her parents had sold it.

Hope had wanted the place to be hers, and it had cost her plenty, including some of her parents' ire—they had outright refused to sell it to her because they wanted bigger things for her. The ranch was as *bigger of a thing* as she'd ever wanted, so she'd made the man they'd sold the place to an offer he couldn't refuse. Basically, Hope had paid nearly double what the ranch was worth on paper, and all these years later, she knew it was the best investment she'd ever made.

Josh stood there a moment, staring at the empty doorway and repeating that one word of profanity again. "I guess I need to change for the party," he finally grumbled, and he headed out the back of the barn and in the direction of his log cabin.

The cabin had once been a guesthouse, but he'd moved there when they'd expanded the ranch a year ago and brought in the palominos. Good thing, too, since he worked as many hours as she did and never took a day off.

"Everything okay?" Termite called out to them.

"Fine," Josh snapped. "Just take care of the gelding and do the other chores I told you about before you quit for the day."

"Will do. Have fun at that party."

There was zero chance of that, and Hope suddenly felt guilty that she'd roped him into doing this. Of course, if she hadn't, she might not have gotten that kiss.

"I've had some experience with parents' disapproval," Hope said, catching up with him. "My folks had rather me be at their corporate office in Austin so they can groom me to take over the world."

He glanced back at her as if to see if that was an exaggeration. It was only a slight one, but then, he'd almost certainly heard about her parents' quest to gobble up as much money and stuff as they could—only to get bored with the stuff they'd gobbled and go after something else to conquer. Their latest venture was the buyout of a cookie company, and they were on the track to world domination of snickerdoodles, her father's favorite sweet treat.

Once, the ranch had been their quest, one they'd bought her senior year of high school. Once they'd grown tired of it, they'd moved on. They'd probably thought she would have the same mind-set as them and move on, too, but it'd been ten years now, and Hope had never felt more grounded. That was saying something since Josh's kiss had practically lifted her feet off the ground.

Josh threw open the front door of the cabin as if it'd been the object that had riled him, and he went straight into the bedroom. Hope stayed put in the living room, figuring the time had come to go ahead and offer him an out.

"You don't have to do this," she said.

No answer, and a split second later she heard him turn on the shower. She went closer, peering into the bedroom, and saw the trail of clothes he'd dropped along the way to the adjoining bathroom.

She didn't mean to snoop, but it was hard to miss the homey way he'd decorated the room. The deep blue Lone Star quilt on the bed and framed photos of the back pasture that rimmed the creek. She knew the spot, also knew it was one of his favorite places to ride. Apparently, he had a knack for photography.

And reading.

There was a foot-high stack of books on the nightstand. Books about horse management and pedigree studies mixed in with horror paperbacks and one simply titled *Sex*.

Hope found herself moving toward it. A moth-to-a-flame kind of reaction. All she wanted was a peek, and she blamed it on the kiss. She suddenly had sex on the mind—and in her hands. She plucked the book from the stack and got an eyeful on the very first page. A couple engaged in…something. She turned the book to get a different angle of the page, to see if she could make sense of it, but then she got another eyeful.

Of Josh.

He came out of the shower, his back to her, while he dried off with a towel. His body was about the only thing getting dry right now because Hope responded. To his naked butt. To all those muscles pulling and tightening as he moved. And speaking of moving, he did. He looked over his shoulder at her and then said something very confusing.

"You found my trap." Then he tipped his head to the book she was holding.

Hope slapped it shut and put it back on the nightstand. "Trap?"

He nodded, and with the towel covering the most interesting parts of him, Josh walked out of her line of sight and into the closet on the other side of the bathroom. "Yeah, a couple of the books are actually props with hollowed-out centers where I keep spare cash. I never lock my doors, so I figure if someone with sticky fingers comes up looking for something to steal, then *Sex* will distract them."

Well, it had certainly distracted her, but it was nothing like the distraction that happened when Josh came back into the room. No more towel. He was dressed, for the most part, and was tucking in a crisp white shirt.

God, had his jeans always fit like that, framing his...? Great balls of fire, she was looking at his crotch! And Josh was looking at her looking at his crotch.

The corner of his mouth lifted. "I think we just opened Pandora's box," he drawled.

JOSH PAUSED. THEN he cursed. There were a lot of smart things he could have said to Hope, but that Pandora's-box comment sure wasn't one of them.

"We should probably close that box, though," he quickly amended. "Especially after that kiss. Sorry about that, by the way. I was trying to make a point to my folks."

Exactly what point, he wasn't sure. Again, not a smart thing.

"I'm not sorry it happened," Hope blurted out.

Apparently, he wasn't the only one putting his foot in his mouth tonight. Of course, a foot was better than her tongue, something that'd happened during the kiss that a) he had already decided was a mistake and b) every blasted inch of his body would remember for the rest of his life.

Josh just stared at her, his right eyebrow sliding up. He was reminding her that employee-employer sex complicated the devil out of things. Especially things framed in his jeans that she'd been staring at.

She nodded, mumbled something he didn't catch and nodded again. "So, we'll put in an appearance at the party, silence our parents, and tomorrow we'll pretend that I never saw you naked."

"Ditto," he agreed.

Of course, they were lying to each other. Like the kiss in the barn, there was no chance of them forgetting something like nakedness when the air was suddenly scalding hot between them. Scalding hot and next to a bed and a book filled with X-rated sex poses. If she looked at page sixteen, then the "ditto" facade would evaporate as fast as the wrapper on the condom he carried in his wallet. That "threat" was definitely his cue to get them moving.

"And no more kissing," she added as they left the cabin. It sounded like a question, but Josh decided it was best if he treated it like an iron-clad contract that they'd both signed in blood.

Hope made a stop by her house to change into the sparkly sandals, but thankfully she hurried—saying something about the sooner they got there, the sooner they could leave. Josh agreed. As it was, the party was going to be packed enough, and that would mean having to gab with more people as they trickled in. He wasn't antisocial—by his own standards, anyway—but he preferred being at the ranch...and avoiding their parents. He wouldn't be able to do either tonight, but at least he could try to minimize their interactions if they made a quick exit.

They used Josh's truck to drive to the Granger Ranch. It wasn't far, less than five miles, but then, it didn't take long to get anywhere in Wrangler's Creek. The town itself was primarily a Main Street dotted with mom-and-pop businesses, and it had ranches surrounding it on all sides. The Granger Ranch and the one owned by their cousins—yet more Grangers—claimed a good chunk of the acreage. Considering their ancestors had founded the town, that only seemed right.

"I need to talk to Karlee," Hope complained as Josh drove. "To chew her butt out for throwing away my pants. And then once we find Roger Hawley and put in some face time with him, we should be able to leave. We haven't shaken hands on the deal with Roger, and I won't breathe easier until we do."

Josh nodded, not to the chewing-out-Karlee part but to the other. He'd yet to meet Roger Hawley, but Josh certainly knew who the man was. He was one of the largest horse brokers in the state and was critical to Hope's plans to bring in a new champion line of palominos.

Actually, it was Josh's plan, too.

It would improve the stock and give the Applewood Ranch even more respect than it already had. More important, it would help Hope fulfill that dream she'd always had for the ranch to be the place where everyone went when they were looking for quality, well-trained horses. Her parents might even be impressed by that and get off her back.

Might.

Josh would definitely be impressed, and he was glad to be part of it. Because the ranch felt like it was his, too.

He'd been right about the party being packed, but the Grangers had taken down one of the fences to turn a pasture into a huge makeshift parking lot. There was a sea of trucks and Cadillacs with longhorns on the grilles. The sea continued inside with dozens of people threading in and out of the multiple rooms that fed off the giant foyer.

The word *giant* applied to the rest of the house, too. Once Josh had asked one of the owners, Dylan Granger, how many rooms were in the place, and Dylan had said they'd narrowed it down to somewhere between thirty and thirty-three. Josh didn't think that was a joke. The place was so big that it would have been easy to lose count.

With all those people, there should have been plenty of food, beer and conversation to keep everyone occupied, but when Hope and he walked in, the immediate areas went silent. All eyes landed on them. Not smiling, approving eyes, either.

Gossip eyes.

It wouldn't be long before the rumor mill embellished their arrival together as a full-fledged affair, complete with reenactments from page sixteen of the sex book. From there, it would morph into talk that Josh was a man-whore/gold digger and Hope an airhead for falling in bed with the hired help.

"I told you people would notice my flaky toenail polish," Hope mumbled.

Josh laughed before he could rein it in. God, it was hard not to like her. Even harder not to lust after her, but he reined that in, too, and forced himself to walk into the crowd. He wasn't going toward anyone per se, but he did see a gleaming silver tray of longneck beers on the back side of the foyer. He snagged one for himself and a glass of wine for Hope, but when he turned around to hand it to her, she was bringing him something.

Or rather *someone*.

"This is Roger Hawley," Hope said. She bit her bottom lip, her nerves showing, a reminder of just how important this meeting was.

"I'm Josh Whitlock." Josh gave Hope the wine so he could shake the man's hand. First impression wasn't good. The guy had a wimpy grip, and he didn't make eye contact. That was because Roger was looking down the front of Hope's dress.

Since it was best not to punch the very man who was critical to the ranch's future, Josh slid his arm around Hope's waist and eased her next to him to rob Roger of his peep-show angle. Roger noticed the maneuver, too. And frowned. Maybe because he was no longer able to see Hope's boobs or it could be that Roger was filling in the blanks along with the rest of the gossips. In this case, the filling in might lead Roger to believe that Hope and he were lovers.

"I promise I won't stay up too late tonight," Hope told Roger. "I'll get plenty of sleep before our meeting tomorrow."

Roger slid glances at both of them. "You'll be there at the meeting, of course." His glance settled on Josh for that.

Josh nodded. "We've worked up some breeding charts so that Hope and I can show you what she'd like for you to supply the ranch."

"What *she'd* like," Roger repeated. He did more of those glances, even one aimed at Hope's breasts.

Crap. The guy was one of those assholes who didn't respect women. Josh had run into them from time to time. It could happen in a business like theirs, but it riled him to the core that this turd had dismissed Hope because she had breasts.

Maybe Roger saw the bad fire in Josh's eyes or perhaps he picked up on the fact that Josh was about to shatter his beer bottle with his grip. Either way, Roger mumbled something about seeing them tomorrow, and he wandered off. However, before Josh could get Hope's take on what had just happened, or vent about it, he spotted someone else who wasn't going to loosen his grip on the beer.

Alister and Beverly Applewood. Hope's parents.

Her father went straight to Hope, pulling her into a hug before he shook Josh's hand. Definitely not wimpy, nor had it been the one other time Josh had met him. And Alister made good eye contact. Not Beverly, though. Her attention went straight to Hope's feet.

"My God, don't they have a nail salon in Wrangler's Creek?" Beverly asked her daughter.

"They do, but I've been too busy running the ranch and opening Pandora's box," Hope grumbled, causing her mom to frown even though there was probably little chance that Beverly got the reference. Josh hoped the woman hadn't, anyway. "How's the cookie business these days?"

"We're baking along," her dad answered, causing Hope to smile over the groan-worthy joke.

No smile from Hope's mom. Beverly turned her frosty, toenail-disapproving gaze on Josh. "I suppose you're here because of business obligations." She didn't give Josh even a second to respond to that. "It's the same for us. We just sealed the deal to supply Oscar Pendleton baked goods for all six of his dude ranches.

Applewood snickerdoodles will be in every one of his guesthouses and restaurants."

It was hard to keep a serious face when discussing cookies, especially those with a funny name, but somehow Josh managed it.

"But we're mixing some pleasure with it, too," Beverly continued a moment later, "and we were hoping our daughter would do the same."

Well, the earlier kiss had been plenty pleasurable, but it was best for Josh not to mention that.

"Mark came with us," Beverly went on. "Mark Wainwright," she added to Josh. "He's a real-estate mogul in Austin. Hope, you should spend some time tonight getting to know Mark." She turned toward her daughter. "And maybe he won't look at your feet."

Or her breasts. But that particular wish from Josh might have been motivated by a tad of jealousy. Roger was just a horn-ball ogler, but this Mark was obviously meant to be Beverly's version of Mr. Right Son-in-Law.

"Actually, I don't plan to spend time with Mark," Hope said, "because I'm here with Josh."

Josh had been on the receiving end of plenty of stink eye, but the one Beverly gave him qualified for the Stink Eye of the Century award. She did a quick follow-up with a huff.

"I know what you're doing," Beverly declared. "You're pretending to be with your ranch hand so that you won't have to talk to Mark. But that's nonsense. Mark is perfect for you, and you can't pass up this opportunity."

Hope started repeating some of those words under her breath. *Pretending. Nonsense. Ranch hand.* And

Josh cursed because he knew what was coming next. Hope latched on to a handful of his hair, then yanked him down to her.

And she kissed him.

CHAPTER THREE

HOPE HADN'T MEANT to copy Josh's earlier "I'll show you" kiss, but it was the first thing that popped into her head. And it worked. It shut her mother up, anyway.

Along with shutting everyone else up.

The area around them went silent again except for the thudding, and she soon realized that was the sound of her heartbeat in her ears. A shut-up kiss certainly packed a punch.

Hope didn't let the lip-lock go on for too long. A few seconds was enough to make her point, along with making Josh look about as comfortable as a bull calf facing a castration knife. Obviously, he had a different view on a pretend kiss in front of two people versus one in front of dozens.

Those dozens included his own parents.

Hope spotted them in the adjacent family room, and like everybody else, they were staring.

"Uh, I'll just have a word with my folks," Josh said when his mom and dad started toward him.

Josh wisely thought it wouldn't be a good idea for this foursome conversation to turn into a six-some. Or rather a seven-some because the Whitlocks were with Dr. Marie Stapleton, the woman they wanted for their son. Hope could see why, too. Marie was beautiful, and it appeared that she'd had a recent pedi for the occasion. Her toes glimmered with a flirty shade of pink.

"I'll grab us another drink," her father insisted. "Remember to keep your voice down," he added to his wife.

"Really?" her mother said the moment Hope's father had stepped away. Beverly's voice was an angry whisper. "Was that fake kiss necessary?" As usual, she didn't give Hope a chance to answer. "You're twenty-eight, not twelve, and acting out like this is embarrassing—"

"Who said it was a fake?" Hope countered. "I've kissed Josh before." And she could say it with a straight face since it wasn't a flat-out lie.

Her mother huffed, though, as if it were a whopper. "I knew it was a mistake to let you stay here and try to run the ranch."

There were so many things wrong with that comment that Hope needed a couple of gulps of wine before she could return fire without including a fit of temper. "You didn't let me run the ranch. I used my trust fund to buy it. And I don't *try*, I *do* run it. Me and Josh. No matter what you think of him, the ranch wouldn't be as successful as it is without him."

Her mother's scowl intensified when her gaze drifted toward Josh, the doctor and his parents. Actually, Hope was pretty sure she scowled a bit, too, because Marie was flashing Josh a smile, then a laugh before leaning in and whispering something to him. If the doctor got any closer, she'd tongue his earlobe.

"I don't like to talk about this," Beverly went on, "but I married down. Beneath my station in life. And it had a huge effect on my family."

For someone who didn't like to talk about it, Beverly

certainly talked about it a lot. Beverly's multimillion-aire father owned the company where Hope's dad had been the CFO. When Beverly and he had fallen in love, it had apparently fueled the gossips for a while and cost Beverly's father some business deals from old farts who thought less of him because he hadn't been able to keep the socialite reins on his daughter.

Still, her mom and dad had stayed together despite the gossip and lost revenue, so in Hope's way of thinking, it had all worked out. Especially since she likely wouldn't have been conceived if Beverly hadn't hooked up with the hired help. With a different half of a gene pool, she could have turned out like the doctor who was flirting with Josh.

Sheez Louise, the woman had bumped her boob against Josh's arm.

"You probably haven't thought about how this is affecting Josh," her mom continued.

That snagged Hope's full attention. At least it did until she realized her mother wasn't talking about the doctor's boob swipe because she wasn't even looking at Josh. Beverly had her "I'm about to dole out advice" look nailed to Hope.

"How many other hands do you have working for you?" Beverly asked.

"Four full-time and another two part-time. Don't worry. I'm not kissing any of them."

Her mother was the queen of flat looks, squinty eyes and other facial dressing-downs. "They report directly to Josh, and Josh reports to you." Again, no waiting for a response. "Well, think how those other hands will feel about him if they believe he's sleeping with the boss. They might question Josh's authority, and that could hurt the whole operation. A smooth-running chain of command is critical to managing a business."

Hope didn't have a comeback for that, and it put a balled-up knot in her stomach to think it might be true. It didn't help that living proof was standing right in front of her. Well, it was proof if she was to believe her mother's marriage had indeed hurt her family business.

While Hope was mulling that over and silently cursing the boob-swiping, ear-tonguing doctor, her father returned. He didn't have wine or beer but rather two shot glasses filled with strong booze that he probably figured Hope could use after the conversation she'd just had with her mother. He handed one of them to her.

"I was just telling Hope why she has to nip this thing with Josh in the bud," Beverly explained to her husband. "That's best for—"

"There's Mark," her father interrupted. He made a vague motion toward the living room that was jammed with guests. "Beverly, why don't you bring him over here to meet Hope?"

That got her mom's gaze firing all around the crowd. "Of course. I'll be right back."

"Did you really see Mark?" Hope asked the moment Beverly was out of earshot.

"No, but I thought you could use a break." He sipped his drink. "Did your mom tell you all about her marrying down?"

Hope winced, hating how that must make her father feel. Of course, he'd likely heard it so many times he was probably numb to it. "I think she got the better deal in this marriage."

He smiled and brushed a kiss on her forehead. "It's not so bad. I enjoy reinventing myself every couple of years. Never did want to put down roots, and your mom's completely on board with that."

"Yes, I figured that out around the time I realized my roots were growing deep into the proverbial soil of the Applewood Ranch."

Her father made a sound of agreement. "For whatever reason, though, your mother has decided that our lifestyle should be yours. And that you shouldn't make your own mistakes, that you should have the perfect life."

"I already have that," Hope pointed out. Well, almost perfect. "The ranch is a success and will be an even bigger one when I close the deal with the horse broker I just chatted with." A sleazy, pervy one, but she'd done business before with men like that and could handle it.

"And Josh?" her father asked.

It was the million-dollar question, maybe literally. Because if she messed things up with Josh, it could lead to not only a broken heart but a whole bunch of lost revenue, as well.

Hope finally caught sight of Karlee, but before she could wave down her friend and yell at her, her dad continued.

"Josh is a good man, on and off paper," he said. "And yes, I vetted him. Don't look at me like that. You're my daughter, and when you told me he was going to be living in the cabin just steps from your back door, I had him checked out. You might be relieved to know that there were no red flags."

Oh, yes, there was. Josh was hot, a good kisser and had an incredible butt. All red flags to her body.

"You're lucky to have him," her father added.

Hope could add another yes to that. The only reason he'd come to her for a job was because of the death of the owner of the ranch where Josh had worked for ten years, and the rancher's kids had decided to sell—for a whopping ten million dollars. That high price tag had put it well out of Josh's financial reach, so he'd started over. At her place.

Her father had another sip of his drink and looked at her from over the top of his glass. "So, are you going to take the risk and go after Josh? And before you re-peat all the reasons your mom just gave you for why that wouldn't be a good idea, let me add my two cents' worth. Life's short. Be with someone who's the doodle to your snicker."

Hope stared at him. "Wh-what?"

"There'd be no snicker without a doodle," he added as if that explained everything, and she hoped that wasn't some kind of sexual reference. No way did she want to talk sex with her dad. But someone came her way who might fill the sex-talk bill.

Josh.

But he definitely didn't seem to be in a sex mood. Or even a good one. "I need to go," he said, though she wasn't sure how he could talk with his teeth clenched like that. "Stay as long as you want. I'll wait for you in the truck unless you want to get another ride."

Hope didn't hesitate even a blink before she went after him, saying goodbye to her father as she got mov-ing. "What happened?" she asked when she caught up with him on the porch.

"My mom. She called you a name."

She frowned and had to keep catching up with him because Josh was walking so fast. This trek would

have been a whole lot easier in her broken-in cowboy
boots. "What name?"

"Blonde," he spit out.

Despite the fact her breath was getting a little short
from the jaunt across the pasture, Hope felt some relief. "Uh, I am blonde."

Josh threw a glance at her, and even in the darkness
she could see there was still some teeth clenching and
face tightening going on. "She didn't mean it as an ob-
servation or a compliment."

"Oh." That stung for a second or two, though not
as much as her lungs were stinging by the time they
reached his truck. "I don't think Roger meant it as a
compliment when he was eyeballing my breasts. What
about the doctor?" she tacked onto that.

Josh frowned when he opened the door for her, and
she got inside. "Did she eyeball your breasts, too?"
he asked.

"No. She…" But Hope waved that off. There was
nothing she could say that wouldn't make her sound
jealous. Which she had been. Her mouth had never
been that close to Josh's ear, and she'd known him a
lot longer than Dr. Flirt-a-Lot had.

Josh stared at her a moment as if trying to suss out
what she'd been about to spill, but he finally gave up
and got in the truck. He started the engine but then
turned to her.

"I don't want to fake a relationship to get our folks
off our backs," he said. "Because it could cause problems elsewhere."

Now she was the one trying to suss out what he
meant. "You're talking about the other hands losing
respect for you."

His forehead bunched up. Obviously, she'd sussed in the wrong direction, though she was certain that possibility had been on his radar. Her mom couldn't have been the only one who'd come up with that pitfall in the making. But if Josh hadn't meant that at this exact moment, then that left the other possible snag.

"Us," she amended. "This attraction could ruin what we have." Hope paused. "Of course, it could maybe add to it. Sorry," she quickly tacked onto that. "That's the lust talking."

He looked at her, and now the angle of the moonlight was right for her to see the slight change in his expression. The muscles in his jaw relaxed a bit. No relaxation, though, for his eyes.

"I was managing the lust just fine until I saw you in that dress," he grumbled.

So, that had been the trigger, but she suspected the stuck zipper had helped some, too. "Well, I was managing it just fine until the Pandora's-box thing," she grumbled right back. "And also seeing you get out of the shower. No way am I forgetting that."

This would have been a good time for one of them to smile just to chill the air between them. But no smiles. Their eyes locked, and she found herself staring at that scrumptious face. She also found herself moving, but Hope soon realized it was because Josh had hold of her waist and was pulling her toward him.

It happened so fast, more like a swish of motion, and she was in his arms with his mouth on hers. Mouth and tongue. She'd thought the other kisses were scorchers, but Hope immediately figured out the difference between a kiss for show with Josh and a real kiss from Josh.

This was a real kiss.

Heck, she'd had third-base foreplay that hadn't generated this much heat. That probably had something to do with Josh putting his whole body into it. Literally. It wasn't just his mouth on hers or his chest against her breasts. It was the fact that he hauled her onto his lap. With nothing between them but their clothes, the kiss became more like a head-to-toe experience.

She heard herself moan. Pure pleasure. And she especially liked the way his hand slid over her dress to grip her right butt cheek. He was using the grip to nudge and adjust her so that their zipper areas were aligned. But that's also when Hope remembered that she didn't have a zipper.

Or panties.

Josh remembered it, too, because he went stiff when his hand landed on her bare skin.

He stopped the kiss, pulled back and looked at her. "Hell."

Again, not the romantic thing to say, but along with being on his lap, she was also on the same page with him, and Hope knew those missing panties could be the difference between foreplay and full-blown sex. She'd never actually been thankful for a muffin top, but she was starting to see the advantages of it.

"We're in a truck," he said, but he seemed to be talking to himself. Forcing himself to remember that he was just one zipper-lowering away from being inside her.

He groaned, slid his hand from her butt to the front of her. Between her legs. And then Hope was the one moaning. He wasn't actually touching her *there*—not yet, anyway—but his fingers were dallying on her inner thigh.

"We're in a truck," he repeated, sounding a little crazy now.

Hope felt that, too. She was crazy. And hot. And so ready for him to touch her that she moved things along. She shifted herself enough so that his fingers brushed against the most sensitive part of her body, and it wasn't her thigh.

Her next moan of pleasure was considerably louder and was tinged with an eager urgency.

"We're in a truck." Josh, again. But thankfully his reminder-mantra wasn't working because he moved his fingers. It was a slippery little slide in just the right spot.

"We're in a truck," Hope gutted out. She didn't know why the words came out of her mouth, but perhaps it had something to do with Josh's fingers making her mindless.

With their gazes still locked, he added a flick to the slippery slide, and Hope knew she was just one index finger away from an orgasm.

In a truck.

Where someone could come walking up at any minute. That reminder should have stopped her long enough to demand that Josh take her back to the ranch and to his bed. Or to her bed. That part was optional. But before she could get her mouth working to demand anything, there were two dinging sounds.

Their phones.

Hope was surprised that sounds so soft could make it through her lust-crazed mind, but they did, and it seemed odd that both Josh and she had gotten texts at the same exact moment. Even with that oddity, Hope could have ignored them, if there hadn't been a second pair of dings.

Josh cursed and stopped to take out his phone, which caused Hope to curse because he'd stopped. Since her phone would just keep dinging if she didn't clear the messages, she took out her cell, too, but she was still close enough to Josh that she saw the message on his screen.

Keep your zipper up and don't give in to your hankerings and have sex in your truck, his dad had texted.

Obviously, Josh's dad had had a hunch about his son's feelings if he knew about hankerings.

Josh scowled and moved on to the cause of his second ding. A text from his mother. Bi bwws dir tiy ri fi.

"My mom can't text without her reading glasses," Josh added when Hope stared at him. He tipped his head to her phone. "Who messaged you?"

She showed him the screen with the first text from her mom. Get back here and meet Mark. So help me, you'd better not be having sex with Josh in yours or his truck.

Maybe his dad and her mom had binoculars and could see them from the house. Of course, it was just as likely that her mom had noticed Hope's own hankerings, too.

While Josh was still watching, she scrolled down the screen to the next one she'd gotten. Remember to find the doodle, her dad had texted.

"My dad can't text without his reading glasses," Hope told Josh when he raised an eyebrow.

No way did she want to get into an explanation about what her dad was referring to. But it turned out that she wouldn't have had a chance to do that anyway because their phones dinged again.

Both Josh and she groaned, and they looked at their screens to see what words or gibberish of reason their parents had to add, but it wasn't from either set of them. It was a message that Roger Hawley had sent to both of them. And unlike the others, this one wasn't a meddling annoyance and there was no mention of a truck. However, there was a mention of something that got their attention along with cooling down their lust.

Disappointed with our meeting tonight, Roger had texted. I never did cotton to the notion that it was wise for a man to diddle his boss. Have rethought things and I won't be doing business with you after all.

CHAPTER FOUR

OVER THE PAST WEEK, two words kept going through Josh's head. *Doodle* and *diddle*. He still wasn't sure what a doodle was, perhaps an ingredient in those cookies the Applewoods made. But the diddle had come across loud and clear in Roger's text.

It didn't matter that Josh hadn't actually diddled Hope—though he had come close to doing just that in the truck. All that mattered was Roger had believed that sex was going on, and it'd been enough for him to pull out of the deal. Which, in turn, had sent Hope and Josh into moping mode.

Losing the horses was a low blow, and that, along with his concerns about losing the ranch hands' respect, had been enough for Josh to rethink everything. He'd kept his zipper up and his hands off Hope. Not easy, but it was easier to do when he didn't have to see her. Josh had managed that by fastening his butt in his office chair and working on plan B, which was trying to get the palomino stock from another seller. That had failed. So had the next ones.

He was now mulling over plan G.

Hope must have been in the rethink and mull mode as well because she hadn't sent him any of those smoldering looks, and he was pretty sure she hadn't skipped wearing panties. Of course, it was best if he didn't think of Hope's underwear choices. Or the dream he'd had about the two of them acting out page sixteen of the sex book.

"You gonna go in there, boss man?" Josh heard Termite ask. "Or are you figuring the boss lady's still sleeping?"

Josh had been so deep in thought that he hadn't heard the hand come up behind him. Termite came to stand beside Josh, put his hands on his bony hips and stared at Hope's house—the very thing Josh had been staring at for a couple of minutes while he mulled over their situation.

"She'll be awake," Josh assured Termite. Like him, Hope was an early riser, and since it was already eight, she would have been up for a couple of hours. "I'm just trying to figure out how to word this proposal I'm working on," Josh said. But when he heard his own words, he quickly added, "*Business* proposal." He even lifted the printout he was holding in case Termite doubted that.

"Ah." Over the past week Josh had learned it was one of Termite's favorite "words." Along with *uh* and *huh*. "This is about buying those blondie horses y'all both like so much."

Josh nodded and wondered how Hope was going to take the news that plan G was going to cost her double or more than buying them from Roger. Maybe she would take it better than Josh had because he was plenty pissed off at himself for ruining this deal for her.

"There's a lot of talk about you and the boss lady," Termite went on. "Talk of y'all kissing and such."

The *such*—what had gone on in his truck—would have caused a lot more talk if folks had actually known about it. "It won't affect how Hope and I do the job here," Josh assured him.

Termite made a face, the kind of expression a man might make if someone had just stated the obvious. Termite shook his head. "Never figured kissing would mess up ranch work. I mean, you probably wouldn't want to kiss at the same time we're worming the livestock or maybe on stall mucking day, but those are my chores, not yours or the boss lady's."

Those were wise words. *Surprisingly* wise words. "The other hands might not feel the same way," Josh pointed out.

Termite snickered as if that was a fine joke, and he hitched his thumb to Shane Ellery, who was training a mare in the corral just off the barn. Then to Davy Martin, who was riding in from the pasture where he would have been repairing fences. "We talk about you and the boss lady a lot, and they don't care if you kiss her, either. Davy thinks she looks kinda sad and mopey when you and her don't spend so much time together."

Apparently, Termite and the others had too much time on their hands, and Josh needed to add more work to their schedules. Still, it eased his mind a little to know that he hadn't screwed that up for Hope, too.

"Well, if you run out of ideas about where to get those horses," Termite went on, "just come see me. I know a guy who might know a guy."

Josh wouldn't hold his breath on that, but he mentally chalked up Termite as plan H. He thanked the hand and got moving to the house. The back door was open as it usually was in the mornings, but Josh couldn't see inside because of the dark screen slider

that kept the bugs out. When he reached the porch, he
was about to knock, but then he heard Karlee's voice.

"So, does this mean you forgive me?" Karlee asked.

He hadn't seen Hope's friend arrive, which meant
she must have gotten there before he'd started his backyard staring session/chat with Termite, and Karlee had
likely parked in front of the house.

"No, I'm not forgiving you for throwing away my
pants," Hope answered. From the sound of it, they were
at the kitchen table, which was just to the right of the
door. Also from the sound of it, she was eating something. "But if it hadn't been for the red dress, Josh
might have never noticed me."

Actually, he'd noticed her plenty of times before
that, but the dress had just allowed him to notice *more*
of her. The noticing had been hard enough, but now
that he'd kissed her, it was impossible to push Hope
out of his mind.

Since he didn't want to stand out there and eaves-
drop, Josh was about to leave, but then Karlee said
something that stopped him in his tracks. "You're falling in love with Josh."

He figured Hope would laugh and say it was just
a lust thing.

She didn't.

"I think I've been falling in love with him for years,"
Hope said.

His heart stopped, too. Flat-out stopped. No beats
whatsoever. What the hell? Hope was falling in love
with him? That couldn't be.

"Yes," Hope continued a moment later, "I take
things slow with him and me. Well, except when I

don't go slow like at the party last week. Don't ask for details because I'm not kissing and telling."

Karlee chuckled. "Whether you take things slow or fast, or whether you kiss and tell, just know that I approve. Josh is a good guy, and I'm pretty sure he's been falling in love with you for years, too."

"Say what?" he blurted out, but he wished he'd stapled his mouth together to stay quiet. Or unglued his feet from the porch so he hadn't heard a word of this.

Judging from the horrified expression on Hope's face when she opened the screen door, she had the same wish.

"I should be getting to work," Karlee said, checking the time that he was certain she didn't need to check. She gave Josh a silent apology and hurried out, heading toward the front.

"How much did you hear?" Hope asked him, but she waved that off, sighed and motioned for him to come in.

Josh wasn't certain he wanted to go in, but Hope took hold of his arm and pulled him inside anyway. That's when he caught her scent. Cinnamon and sugar. And that's when he saw the source. There were huge stacks of boxes of Applewood cookies on the table.

"Mom sent them," she said when she followed his gaze. "It's her way of saying she's sorry for pressuring me to be with Mark. By the way, Mark asked out your flirty doctor friend, and according to gossip, they seem to be hitting it off."

That was good. It would stop the pressure from his mom. At least until she found someone else that she thought was suitable for him.

Because he was just standing there as if incapable of speech, Hope sighed again and took the proposal from him. She glanced through it, handed it back and then handed him a paper she took from the table.

"I was going to bring this over to you after Karlee left," Hope explained.

It was a nearly identical version of his for a deal with a livestock broker, Lucky McCord, over in Spring Hill. "It's not ideal. Lucky can only get us a fraction of what we need. And it'll cost more than we want to spend because he'll have to get them from out of state."

She nodded as if she'd already suspected that, sank down at the table and bit into a cookie. Considering the amount of crumbs on the table and plate, it wasn't her first of the day, and it wouldn't be her last. If Josh had thought they would help, he'd eat the contents of all the boxes.

"Let's think on this deal with McCord for a day or two," she finally said. "Maybe in the meantime, something else will come up."

It'd been the very advice he'd been about to give her, proof once again that when it came to business, they were on the same page. Their operation was fine just as it was, and there was no urgency.

Well, not with the horses, anyway.

Looking at her caused some urgency to start building in his body. No red dress today. She was in her usual jeans and a blue top and was barefooted. There was nothing particularly glamorous about how she looked, but because this was Hope, the hotness was automatic.

She bit into the cookie, licking a crumb off her bottom lip, but she missed another one. She looked up at him as if waiting for him to do something. Maybe for him to talk about what he'd heard while eavesdropping at the door.

That wasn't going to happen.

If the subject came up, it would come from her, and then she could laugh and dismiss it as girl talk. She could assure him that she didn't have feelings for him that would complicate the hell out of everything. Then he could assure her he felt the same and then they could have sex on those cookie crumbs.

He frowned, pushed away that last thought.

Hope didn't help with that thought pushing, though. She kept up the cookie nibbling, kept staring at him. Kept looking good enough that he wanted her mouth to nibble at him like that. His heartbeat decided to return in full force. That was a big-ass warning for him to get out of there.

"I've got a few more calls to make," he told her. They were past the long-shot stage when it came to horse deals and into the realm of astronomical probability, but he kept that to himself, and he walked out, heading back to the office in his cabin. He made it all the way, too. Even managed to get inside when he heard the hurried footsteps.

"That's it?" Hope asked, coming through the door. "You hear me admit that I'm falling in love with you and you don't say anything?"

Josh weighed his answers. He could admit he didn't know what to say. He could ask her if she was sure. He could prattle on with reminders about how this wasn't a good thing for the ranch. Or he could do something, well, stupid.

He took the stupid option.

Josh leaned in and licked that cookie crumb right off her bottom lip.

SPOILING FOR A FIGHT, Hope had stomped her way over to Josh's cabin to have it out with him, but that lip lick caused her anger to vanish. Some confusion came in its place. She hadn't even known that she was walking around with a cookie bit until she saw it disappear into Josh's mouth.

"Cinnamon," he commented.

It wasn't the right comment, but then, anything he said that wasn't related to the overheard conversation would fall into the wrong category. That's why she stood there scowling at him.

Josh stood there and stared. And stared. "I think it's this that's messing with our heads." He motioned at their zipper areas. "It's like those beepers that go off on the fryers at fast-food places when you're waiting in line to order."

While she wasn't totally sure she agreed with him, she'd followed him on the first part. Not the last, though. "Fryers?"

He nodded. "They just keep beeping and beeping when the fries are ready and no one's taken them out yet. *Beep, beep, beep.*" Josh made the noise, though an audio cue hadn't been necessary. "And after a while, the racket is so distracting that you forget about the hot delicious fries and think only about the blasted beeps."

Okay, she understood that. The sound was annoying, but she couldn't see how that fit their situation…

Oh.

"This is like the beeper." Hope motioned to their

zipper areas. "And until we stop the noise, we can't deal with the fries."

Fries equaled feelings. Specifically, all that falling she'd been doing for him. And maybe it also included getting back to being fully focused on the ranch.

Which brought her to the bottom line of the point he was almost certainly trying to make. He was saying they should just have sex and try to stop that beeper.

That was it, right?

She hoped this wasn't some kind of life lesson that would lead to him not getting in her pants.

Thankfully, it wasn't.

Josh went to her, sliding his hand around the back of her neck and pulling her to him as he kicked the front door shut. He did all of that in the blink of an eye, and Hope might have seen what he was doing if he hadn't rendered her blind with that molten-lava kiss. Judging from the rattling sound, though, he'd locked the door. Good. She had just enough sense left to know that she didn't want anyone walking in on them.

Her shred of common sense vanished, however, when he put her back against the door and pressed his body to hers. Not quite zipper to zipper because he was taller than she was, but she stood on her tiptoes to try to get a better feel of what was in store for her.

Oh, my.

There was a *lot* in store for her.

She wouldn't have minded having that then and there, but Josh obviously had some more licking to do. On her mouth, then her neck, and then he shoved up her top and did his mouth trick on her nipples. Hope hadn't thought it could get any better or that he could build the heat any hotter.

But she was wrong.

He stopped kissing her and, while looking her straight in the eyes and with his warm breath gusting against her mouth, he got in her pants. Part of him did, anyway. She was so thankful she was wearing her loose jeans because he slipped his hand right past the waist and into her panties.

"Pay dirt," he drawled.

She'd never heard that part of her body called that before, and she didn't care. *Pay dirt* worked, and so did his fingers. He touched and watched her face while his breath felt as if he were kissing her all over. Just when Hope thought he was going to finish her off with his hand, he didn't.

Josh dragged her into his arms, his hands moving to her butt, and they started walking. Well, he walked, and he sort of dragged her along since Hope could no longer feel her feet. Thankfully, she could feel the rest of herself just fine.

He took her into the bedroom and eased her onto the mattress. She reached for him, ready to pull him down with her, but now she was the one stopping when Josh peeled off his shirt. Then his boots and jeans. Even though she was burning for him, she watched.

And lusted.

She lusted a lot.

Oh, he was perfect. She'd seen the backside of him the day after his shower, but the front side was even better. He had a six-pack. Of course he did. And he had a really interesting chest, complete with enough tight, tanned muscles…

He dropped his boxers, and she forgot how to breathe.

Forgot how to move, too, but Josh had that worked

out, as well. With all those inches right there so close
to her face, he started shimmying her out of her clothes.
Hope was too spellbound to help, but she slowed him
down when she managed to get in a lick of her own.

Josh cursed her and then he set a speed record getting her out of the rest of her clothes. Somehow, he'd
managed to hold on to some of his common sense because he put on a condom that he took from the nightstand drawer.

"We're not doing page sixteen," he mumbled.

Color her clueless as to what that meant. Nor did
she care. That's because he got on the bed with her, his
body against hers again. But this time, they were butt
naked. Front naked, too. She got more kisses. More
touches, and she finally got those inches.

All of them.

He pushed into her and just kept pushing. The man
was a pro at finding the right angle. The right spot.
The right pace.

Of course, Hope figured that was because he was
the right man.

And with that thought flashing through her head,
she let those inches work their magic, and they silenced
the *beep, beep, beep.*

CHAPTER FIVE

JOSH HEARD THE *bang, bang, bang*, and he cursed because someone was knocking on his flippin' door. Hell's bells. He'd intended on spending the next hour or two with Hope, and he didn't want any interruptions. Apparently, neither did Hope because she latched on to him when he sat up.

"Who is it?" Josh yelled to the idiot banging.

"It's me—Termite. Uh, boss, you got a visitor. He says it's important."

"Is he gushing blood?" Josh growled. "Or does he have the solution to world peace?"

"Uh, no," Termite answered. "He didn't say anything about peace, and he appears to be okay."

"It's me," someone else said, and even though Josh had only heard the man's voice at the party, he recognized it.

Roger.

"Great," Hope grumbled. "Maybe he's here to give us another lecture about diddling. Not what I had in mind for a post-orgasmic orgasm."

Despite the interruption that had pissed him off, Josh smiled, but then, Hope could usually make him smile when things went south. But this was going to be a temporary, short venture in the southerly direction because Josh would send Roger and Termite on their way.

Josh dragged on his clothes. "Stay naked," he told her when she, too, started to get dressed. He looked at her then, naked and reaching for her panties. "In fact, get back in bed. It'll speed things along when I finish with our *guests*."

He didn't bother putting on his boots or buttoning his shirt. Josh just went to the door, unlocked it and threw it open, and he hoped his ornery expression conveyed that he wanted this to be a very brief visit.

"Whoa," Termite said, obviously noticing Josh's disheveled appearance and expression but not being bright enough to figure out what might have been going on. Of course, Termite might not have seen Hope come into the cabin.

"You can go now," Roger told Termite, and when the hand walked off, Roger would have walked right in if Josh hadn't stayed put, blocking the doorway.

"I thought we'd said all there was to say," Josh reminded him. He wouldn't remind Roger that he'd been a jerk not just to Josh but especially to Hope.

Roger glanced around and shuffled his feet. "I've heard some talk," he said. "Talk that Hope and you aren't really lovers after all."

Obviously, Roger hadn't listened to the same gossips as Termite had. Or taken a whiff of Josh because he had Hope's scent all over him.

"I heard you and Hope put on that show at the party because you were trying to get your parents off your backs," Roger added. "Trust me, I understand that. I'm forty-six, and my mom keeps trying to fix me up. I hate it, probably just as much as you do. So, that's why I'm here, to tell you that I understand and that our deal is still on. I haven't found another buyer for the horses, so I can sell you all you need."

Josh couldn't have been more surprised if Roger had slugged him. Or so he thought. His surprise went up a notch when Hope came out of his bedroom. Obviously, she'd heard every word of their conversation because there was only about ten feet of space between the front door and the bedroom.

Roger's surprise-notch went up even more, causing Josh to groan. He wouldn't have lied to Roger by telling him that nothing was going on between Hope and him, that the version of the gossip the man had heard was true. But Josh wouldn't have admitted the truth, either, because that would have ultimately cost Hope those horses. Apparently, though, Hope intended to set things straight no matter what it cost her.

"You really shouldn't listen to gossip," Hope told the man. She was dressed for the most part, but she'd obviously done that in a hurry because her bra was dangling from her shirt. One of the back hooks had caught onto the fabric.

Roger volleyed a few glances at both of them. Then more glances at her breasts. "So, you two are—"

"Diddling, yes," Hope verified. "And despite the fact this is none of your business, you should know that it doesn't affect the ranch one bit. That's because Josh isn't just a ranch hand. He's my partner. We run this place together."

Josh wanted to give her a high five. And a kiss. As soon as they got rid of Roger, he'd do both, along with thank her for what she'd just said. He'd known she felt that way, of course, but it was nice to hear it.

"Together," Roger repeated, and he didn't make it sound like a curse word. "So, it's not just a fling."

Josh frowned and was about to tell this clown that wasn't any of his business, either, but Roger just kept on.

"Well, good," the man concluded. "My mom wouldn't have liked it had she heard about me doing business with someone when there was just diddling going on. She can be old-fashioned about things like that. But if it's not diddling or a fling, if it's something more serious, then she would approve. So, I'm here to finalize the deal on those horses."

Hope looked at him, but Josh knew they were on the same page—again. She motioned for Josh to deliver their verdict.

"The deal will go through with a new condition," Josh told him. "You drop the price by ten percent. And before you start howling about that being unfair..." But Roger had already started howling out a protest, one that Josh and Hope ignored. "You need to make this deal as much as we do, and your piddling around has cost us time and money. That ten percent will compensate us for that."

Josh had no idea if Roger would accept that, or if his pride would cause him to storm off the porch. So, Josh just stood there, waiting.

Hope didn't wait, though. She filled in the time with conversation—with Josh. "What we have isn't about the beeps. In fact, I think your idea about that was wrong."

"Beeps?" Roger asked.

"Yes, beeps!" Hope verified, but she thankfully didn't try to explain it. "And quit ogling my breasts," she added in a much louder voice than she had probably intended. "Do you accept the deal with the ten-percent cut in price?" This time her voice was both loud and mean.

Muscles flickered all over Roger's face, but he finally nodded. "I'll have the papers sent over later today."

"Good." Hope still sounded plenty riled, but they all shook hands on it. In these parts, that was the sign of a done deal, but Josh would make sure everything got signed as soon as he had the contract.

Roger was looking a little relieved and shell-shocked when he turned and walked away. Thankfully, what he didn't do was spare a glance at Hope's breasts. Or even the bra that was still dangling from her shirt. Just in case Roger did get a case of wandering eyeballs, Josh shut the door and locked it. If he'd had a Do Not Disturb sign, he would have put that up, too, because it was obvious that Hope had some personal things to say to him.

And do to him.

She kissed him. It had none of the meanness that'd been in her voice just seconds earlier. This kiss was long and sweet, just the way he liked his kisses from Hope.

"This is not an annoyance," Hope said when she finally broke for air. She motioned toward him, then her. "It's a need, one that I have for you, and no matter how many times we're together, that need isn't going to go away. I can already tell. I meant it when I said I've been falling in love with you for years."

Yeah, he could see that now. He could see a lot of things, and they were all right there in Hope's face.

"I want to do pages one through one hundred and eighty-four with you," he said. He saw the confusion in her eyes until he added the next part. "That's how many pages are in the book on my nightstand."

She smiled.

"And when we're done with those," he went on, "we can start over from the beginning or get another book with a lot of pages."

Hope smiled even more and gave him a naughty wink. "That sounds as if it'll take a long time, considering there'll be days and nights off for business and such."

"It'll take a very long time," Josh assured her. He pulled her to him and kissed that smile. "Years. Maybe years and years. And during that time, we can keep falling in love with each other."

The next kiss wasn't to taste that smile. It was a hungry one that let her know they could start on page one right now. Hope had the same notion because she jumped up into his arms, hooking her hands around his neck and her legs around his waist.

"My dad was right," she whispered against his mouth. And then she said something that was just plain confusing. Something that he would ask her about later after a post-orgasmic orgasm. "There'd be no snicker without a doodle. Josh Whitlock, you're definitely my doodle."

Josh had never been called that before, but he'd take it. And to let her know that he was just fine with it, he kissed Hope all the way to the bedroom.

* * * * *

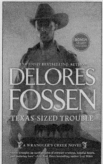
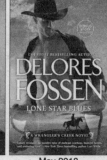

"I can't go to them." Her voice was raw and strained.

"Because you broke off ties with them," Cameron
commented. "Don't worry about that. You're still their sister,
and they'll help you. They love you," he added, hoping that
would ease the tension he could practically feel radiating
off her.

Lauren blinked, shook her head. "No. Because their
houses are on the main road and someone might see me."
She turned, glanced around again, and that was when
Cameron spotted the gun tucked in the back waistband of
her jeans.

He cursed again. "What's wrong?"

A weary sigh left her mouth. The kind of reaction a
person had when there was so much wrong that she didn't
know where to start. But Cameron figured he knew what
this was about.

"We've all been getting threatening letters and emails,"
he volunteered. "I'm guessing you got one, too?"

She nodded, dismissed it with a shake of her head.
"You're raising your sister's child?"

Again, she'd managed to stun him. First with her arrival
and now with the question. It didn't seem the right thing to

ask since this wasn't a "catching up" kind of conversation.

"Gilly's son, Isaac," Cameron clarified. It had been a year since his kid sister's death, and he still couldn't say her name without feeling as if someone had put a meaty fist around his heart. "What about him?"

Lauren didn't jump to answer that. With her forehead bunched up, she glanced behind her again. "Is he…okay?"

Isaac was fine. Better than fine, actually. His nephew was healthy and happy. That wasn't what he said to Lauren, though. "Why are you asking?"

"I need to see him. I need to see Gilly's son."

That definitely wasn't an answer.

Cameron didn't bother cursing again, but he did give her a flat look. "I'll want to know a lot more about what's going on. Start talking. Why are you here, and if you're in some kind of trouble, why didn't you call your brothers? Because I think you and I both know I'm the last person on earth you'd come to for help."

She didn't disagree with that, but another sound left her mouth. A hoarse sob. And that was when tears sprang to her eyes. "Please let me see him."

He wasn't immune to those tears, and it gave him a tug of a different kind, one he didn't want. "Tell me what's going on," Cameron repeated.

Lauren frantically shook her head. "There isn't time."

Cameron huffed in frustration. "Then, make time. Is someone after you? And what does that have to do with Gilly's son?"

She stared at him, her mouth trembling now, and those tears still watering her eyes. "Someone tried to kill me."

Don't miss LAWMAN FROM HER PAST,
available February 2018 wherever
Harlequin Intrigue® books and ebooks are sold.

www.Harlequin.com

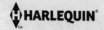

INTRIGUE
EDGE-OF-YOUR-SEAT INTRIGUE, FEARLESS ROMANCE.

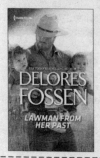

Save **$1.00**

on the purchase of ANY
Harlequin® Intrigue book.

Available wherever books are sold,
including most bookstores, supermarkets,
drugstores and discount stores.

- ✂

Save $1.00

on the purchase of any Harlequin® Intrigue book.

Coupon valid until May 31, 2018.
Redeemable at participating outlets in the U.S. and Canada only.
Not redeemable at Barnes & Noble stores. Limit one coupon per customer.

52615304

Canadian Retailers: Harlequin Enterprises Limited will pay the face value of this coupon plus 10.25¢ if submitted by customer for this product only. Any other use constitutes fraud. Coupon is nonassignable. Void if taxed, prohibited or restricted by law. Consumer must pay any government taxes. Void if copied. Inmar Promotional Services ("IPS") customers submit coupons and proof of sales to Harlequin Enterprises Limited, P.O. Box 31000, Scarborough, ON M1R 0E7, Canada. Non-IPS retailer—for reimbursement submit coupons and proof of sales directly to Harlequin Enterprises Limited, Retail Marketing Department, 225 Duncan Mill Rd., Don Mills, ON M3B 3K9, Canada.

U.S. Retailers: Harlequin Enterprises Limited will pay the face value of this coupon plus 8¢ if submitted by customer for this product only. Any other use constitutes fraud. Coupon is nonassignable. Void if taxed, prohibited or restricted by law. Consumer must pay any government taxes. Void if copied. For reimbursement submit coupons and proof of sales directly to Harlequin Enterprises, Ltd 482, NCH Marketing Services, P.O. Box 880001, El Paso, TX 88588-0001, U.S.A. Cash value 1/100 cents.

5 65373 00076 2   (8100)0 12323

® and ™ are trademarks owned and used by the trademark owner and/or its licensee.

© 2018 Harlequin Enterprises Limited

HIDFCCOUPBPA0218

Get 2 Free Books,
<u>Plus</u> 2 Free Gifts –
just for trying the *Reader Service!*

Get 2 Free Books,
Plus 2 Free Gifts—
just for trying the Reader Service!

Get 2 Free Books,
Plus 2 Free Gifts—
just for trying the Reader Service!

HARLEQUIN *Desire*